The Hunt for The Red Cardinal

OTHER TITLES BY ERIC FLINT'S RING OF FIRE PRESS

Bartley's Man
Blood in Erfurt
Essen Defiant
Essen Steel
Gloom Despair and Agony on You
Incident in Alaska Prefecture
Joseph Hanauer
Letters from Gronow
Letters Home
Love and Chemistry
Medicine and Disease after the Ring of Fire
Muse of Music
No ship for Tranquebar
Pandora's Crew
Second Chance Bird
Storm Signals
The Battle for Newfoundland
The Danish Scheme
The Demons of Paris
The Evening of the Day
The Heirloom
The Masks of Mirada
The Play's the Thing
The Persistence of Dreams
The Society of Saint Philip of the Screwdriver
Turn Your Radio On

The Hunt for The Red Cardinal

by

Bradley H. Sinor
Susan P. Sinor

The Hunt for The Red Cardinal Copyright © 2018 by Bradley H. Sinor and Susan P. Sinor, All Rights Reserved.

All rights reserved. No part of this book may be reproduced in any form or by any electronic or mechanical means including information storage and retrieval systems, without permission in writing from the author. The only exception is by a reviewer, who may quote short excerpts in a review.

Eric Flint's Ring of Fire Press handles DRM, Digital Rights Management, simply: We trust in the *Honor* of our readers.

Cover art by: Laura Givens

This book is a work of fiction. Names, characters, places, and incidents either are products of the author's imagination or are used fictitiously. Any resemblance to actual persons, living or dead, events, or locales is entirely coincidental.

Bradley H. Sinor and Susan P. Sinor

Printed in the United States of America

First Printing: Aug 2018

Published by Eric Flint's Ring of Fire Press

ISBN-13 978-1-948818-05-6

Contents

On The Matter of D'Artagnan 1
To End The Evening...19
All For One 35
The Hunt for The Red Cardinal 54
Chapter One..55
Chapter Two..65
Chapter Three...73
Chapter Four...81
Chapter Five..93
Chapter Six 105
Chapter Seven..113
Chapter Eight..119
Chapter Nine...135
Chapter Ten...147
Chapter Eleven 159
Chapter Twelve...169
Chapter Thirteen 183
Chapter Fourteen 195
Chapter Fifteen 205
Chapter Sixteen..217
Chapter Seventeen...225
Chapter Eighteen 241

Chapter Nineteen 253
Chapter Twenty 265
Chapter Twenty-One 285
Chapter Twenty-Two 295
Chapter Twenty-Three 307
Chapter Twenty-Four 321
Chapter Twenty-Five 337
Dramatis Personae 347

On The Matter of D'Artagnan

By Bradley H. Sinor

"Charlton Heston or Tim Curry?" mused Cardinal Richelieu.

Since there was no one else in the room, the chief minister to His Majesty Louis XIII of France was speaking for his own benefit.

Richelieu sat in a large chair behind the huge desk that dominated the room serving as his office. Two candelabra provided more than enough light for him to work. He brought out a pair of small boxes from one of the desk drawers and put them next to a glass of wine he had poured earlier.

He found himself having to squint slightly to study the boxes. His eyes were good for a man his age, but not as good as they had been more than a decade before, when Jean du Plessis had first been created a cardinal-prince of the Roman Catholic Church.

The printing on the boxes was in English, a language he had only a smattering of, but it was the pictures on them that really interested him. They were not paintings, but rather what were called photographs, just another in a seemingly unending stream of new terms he had learned since the Americans and the town of Grantville had appeared on the scene.

Richelieu had long been an admirer of art; photographs, however, were far different from any paintings that he had ever seen. They showed what really was, not an artist's interpretation.

The photographs were scenes from "movies." As best he understood them, movies were like plays, only they could be watched over and over again—not repeat performances, but the same one, with no differences.

These two movies were of special interest to Richelieu. They were the same basic story, entitled "The Three Musketeers," but they used different performers and had been made several decades apart. Viewing them was an impossibility since he had neither the machine to do it nor the power to run the machine if he had it. So, his agents in Grantville had also supplied very detailed summaries of the plots.

True, the movies did exaggerate events—not to mention playing rather fast and loose with actual facts, as had the book, by someone named Dumas. They even included a supposed relationship between Queen Anne and the English duke of Buckingham.

Richelieu, himself, was a character in the story. It certainly didn't hurt his ego to know that he would be remembered nearly four hundred years in the future, not just in the history books but apparently as part of popular culture.

That he found himself portrayed as a villain and schemer didn't bother him one bit. A fact of life he had learned a long time ago was that whether or not someone came off as a villain or a hero depended on who was telling the story.

Something about the picture of Curry reminded Richelieu of himself, back when he had first come to the church. It was, perhaps, the gleam in the man's eye, which gave an almost predatory, animal look to the man's face. On the other hand, the older man, Heston, with his hands steepled in front of him, projected the quiet dignified look that Richelieu fancied for himself.

"Yes, I think Heston is more me."

"Excuse me, Your Eminence." Richelieu looked toward the door where one of his secretaries, Monsignor Henri Ryan, had appeared. The young man held several thick folios under one arm.

"Yes, Henri?"

"I have just received word that the Italian delegation will be here within the hour." Henri placed the documents he carried in front of Richelieu. "These are the reports on the things they want to discuss with you."

The younger priest stared for a moment at the two movie boxes lying on the desk. His distaste for them was rather obvious. Richelieu made a mental note to have a long talk with Henri about learning to conceal his feelings on some subjects, whether it was the Americans or the Spanish or whatever. That was one of a wide variety of skills Henri needed to develop.

"Very well, let me refresh my memories of these matters, and then bring them in when they arrive."

"Of course, sir." Henri started to leave, but stopped a few steps from the door and turned back toward the desk. "Also, that man, Montaigne, arrived a short time ago, saying he needed to see you."

Richelieu cocked his head slightly. Montaigne was not due to report for at least a week. His unexpected appearance suggested that he came bearing news.

Of course, the Italian matter was also pressing.

"Very well. Have him wait in the smaller library. If he is hungry, have the kitchen prepare something. I shouldn't be more than an hour or two at the most. Did he say what he needed to speak to me about?"

"Yes, Your Eminence. He said it was on the matter of D'Artagnan."

∞ ∞ ∞

Charles D'Artagnan stared out the window. It was an hour after sunrise and the narrow street below was already filled with people: there were food vendors, merchants, barbers, craftsman, and their customers. A woman screaming at a man in a greasy apron, who was selling meat pies of some kind, caught his attention.

The exchange continued for a few minutes, with invectives flying between the two. The verbal combat only stopped when the woman handed several coins across and the vendor passed her back several of the meat pies. The two parted with smiles and wishes for the best of the day.

D'Artagnan felt something small and furry rub against the side of his hand. He looked down to the window ledge and found himself confronting a tiger-striped kitten who was very vehemently demanding attention.

He reached down and gently picked up the animal. The kitten was not happy with this idea, preferring to be petted rather than held, and struggled to escape his grip even as he began to stroke the animal's temples and then under its chin. The response came quickly, and the kitten stretched out, offering its neck for more attention, showing its approval with some very loud purring.

"Like that, do you, little one?"

"I must say, you certainly have a way with animals, my dear Charles." A dark-haired woman, clothed only in a sheet, stretched out on the bed that filled much of the room. She had raised herself up on one elbow and leaned across the impression in the mattress that, until several minutes before, D'Artagnan had filled.

"I have had a bit of experience with the wilder creatures of the world." He smiled.

"Do you think you can bring out the animal in me?" Charlotte Blackson laughed.

"I'll do what I can," he said, walking back to the bed.

He set the kitten down on a side table, much to the chagrin of the animal. The cat reached out to try to drag his hand back, but D'Artagnan ignored the protests, intent on a different goal now.

He reached over and gently ran his finger along the edge of Charlotte's chin. The gesture brought a purr to her lips and a very inviting smile.

Charlotte Blackson was a beautiful woman. Her husband, a Musketeer, had been killed in the war. While not rich, he had left her well off. Charlotte had, in turn, taken her inheritance and shrewdly parleyed it into much, much more. Now, six years later, she was the proprietor of a dozen businesses and a partner in several more. She had even begun to move into some of the minor social circles of Paris. D'Artagnan had met her a few months earlier when he had stopped a thief intent on making off with her purse. In spite of the fact that she was more than a decade older than he, D'Artagnan soon found himself enamored of her.

"Yes, you do have a way with animals." Charlotte reached up and wrapped her arms around him. The sheet fell away, its edge dropping over the end table and trapping the kitten for a few moments.

"I try," he said as she plastered her lips against his.

∞ ∞ ∞

"So what do you have for me, Montaigne?" asked Richelieu.

Montaigne was a small man, dressed in shades of brown, with a face that, other than having an immaculate pencil thin moustache, was not unique in any way whatsoever. Two minutes after they had seen him, few people could describe the man; most failed to even notice his presence, which had often proved a major advantage.

He stopped a half dozen steps in front of the cardinal's desk. Montaigne never approached any closer than that; it was as if there was a line on the floor that he could not, or perhaps would not, cross.

Richelieu had employed Montaigne for nearly four years but actually knew very little about the man, other than the fact that he was loyal to France, i.e. Richelieu and that he had been remarkably effective in the various tasks that were set for him.

"I have located the man you are seeking. His name is actually Charles de Gatz-Casthenese. His mother's family was named D'Artagnan. He is from Lupiac, but he was raised in Gascony and came to Paris just over a year ago. He has been calling himself simply Charles D'Artagnan. He has not made a secret of who he is, but neither has he gone out of the way to make it known."

"Indeed," Richelieu prompted.

Montaigne nodded. "He attempted to get into the Musketeers but was turned down, I believe because of his lack of military experience. However, he was able to secure an appointment with the Royal Guard."

"Continue."

"From the reports I have seen, he has proven to be quite the gifted swordsman. He also turns out to not only be good with his sword but also knows when to fight and when to walk away. I suspect his superiors have an eye on him for eventual promotion."

"What of the other three men I asked you to find?"

"Oh, yes. I'm afraid I have bad news in that area. I could find no trace of anyone by the name of Athos, Porthos or Aramis currently serving in the Musketeers. From the way they were described in that book you gave me, I should have been able to find them or at least someone who had heard of them. It's really a pity; the story makes them seem the sort of fellows I would have liked. However, I have found some very young men, barely in their teens. Issac de Porteau, Henri d'Aramirz, and Armund de Sillegue d'Athos d'A'Autevielle. I suspect they may have been the ones that this Dumas fellow modeled his characters on. They are all relatives, to one degree or another, of the commander of the Musketeers, Monsieur de Tourvelle. So I did not inquire too extensively. I can, should you require more information on them."

"Unnecessary." De Tourvelle was a man that Richelieu knew of quite well. He bore watching and could be either friend or foe to the cardinal, depending on the needs of the moment.

Perhaps it was true that the Athos, Porthos, and Aramis of the movies and the book might not exist. It was entirely possible that those three were indeed simply characters who had been invented for the purposes of these entertainments. However, that did not mean they might not eventually still be of use to him.

"Have you actually met this D'Artagnan?"

"No, Your Eminence. I didn't feel that wise at this time. I have learned enough about him to know that this young Gascon is someone that you might do well to be wary of. He would not be easy to control and could end up being very much of a loose cannon."

Richelieu had come to trust Montaigne's opinions. But he had also learned that there were times when you wanted someone who was not easily controlled, so this young man might suit him quite well. "Very well. Bring him to me, but do it quietly. I do not want the world to know of my interest in this man. Not quite yet."

"That might prove difficult. If it were a formal summons he would come, of that I have no doubt. However, D'Artagnan seems to have an agenda of his own, and I do not see it allying with others, even you, sir," said Montaigne.

Richelieu meditated on the man's words for a few moments and then took a single sheet of paper and began writing on it. He added a large daub of hot sealing wax to the bottom of the page, into which he placed not only his official church seal but that of the chief minister of France.

"You must wait until the chance offers itself and bring him to me. If he is indeed as stubborn as you suggest you may have to *persuade* him." Richelieu passed the paper to Montaigne. "This may be of assistance. I will trust in your discretion about when and how to use it."

∞ ∞ ∞

D'Artagnan stood quietly in the doorway of an abandoned storefront. This was not the best part of town. From the look of the grime on the windows and the rust on the shutters, this place could have been shut up for decades. *That* suited D'Artagnan's needs perfectly.

From here he had a clear view of the Flying Pig, a tavern just down the block, and few would be able to see him even if they were standing directly in front of him. A covered lantern sat at his feet. To add to his camouflage, D'Artagnan had left his uniform in the wardrobe at Charlotte's home. Tonight was not a night to be known as a Royal Guardsman.

No, tonight was a night for personal matters.

The Flying Pig was a low dive at its best. At its worst, it was a dump. The clientele asked no questions and only demanded to be left alone to muddle their dark thoughts in cheap wine and nearly tasteless ale.

D'Artagnan had gone into the Flying Pig twice, two times more than he would have wished. The smell inside the building reminded him of a charnel house or a battlefield when the crows held forth, long after the fighting was over. It was not a place that, even in the darkest of moods, he would willingly seek out.

Yet the Flying Pig fit the man he was seeking like a glove.

D'Artagnan had watched his quarry enter, small forms that seemed to be fleeing from the moonlight that filled the street. At just past ten o'clock the tavern door opened and two men emerged. Both were short and round, their clothes the color of sand stained dark after a rainstorm. Neither man was steady on his feet. It seemed a miracle that they both didn't end up face down in the mud.

They stopped for a moment, almost directly in front of his hiding place, then moved on. One of them began to sing, very badly.

D'Artagnan came up behind them in a few steps, grabbed both, and slammed them hard against each other. Then he dragged them backwards, kicking open the door of the abandoned shop and pulling them inside. By the time the door had swung shut he had both of his prisoners on the floor.

The whole incident had taken less than thirty seconds.

Hand on the hilt of his sword, D'Artagnan waited to see if the attack had caught anyone's attention. One minute, then a second, passed and there were no cries of alarm.

He recovered his lantern and opened it to look down at them. One was barely breathing and would not be waking up anytime soon. But the other, the one that D'Artagnan wanted, surprised him. The man had actually begun to snore. This wasn't what he had expected, though the man fairly reeked of cheap wine and ale, which explained it.

D'Artagnan grabbed him by the lapels of his threadbare coat and shook him hard. "Wake up, you scum-sucking piece of filth."

There was no response at first. "If it's money you're wanting," the man finally said, "then you're too late. What few coins I had have been sent to keep company with their cousins in the tavern keeper's cashbox."

D'Artagnan snorted. "I sincerely doubt that you have ever had enough money to interest me."

"What do you want from me, then?"

"I want your memory." D'Artagnan shook him again, then, while the man was still rattled, dropped him and held the lantern up close to his face. "I know who you are, André Marro. I know that you were once seneschal to the family LeVlanc, as your father and grandfather had been before you. It is for that reason that I've come looking for you, that I want your memory."

At the mention of his name Marro's eye's shot open. If it were possible, his face went paler than it had been.

"I . . . I . . . I . . ."

"Don't deny it. That will only make things worse. I know all about what happened to the LeVlancs and why it happened. You do as well, since you were there. I've tracked down the other servants who survived the purge. They didn't know the name of the man that the LeVlancs trusted to organize the whole thing, but they all agreed on one point. *You* knew who it was."

Marro groaned. D'Artagnan slapped him twice. Finally he muttered a name, a name that D'Artagnan recognized.

"If you have lied to me, I will find you, no matter where you run or hide."

Marro curled into a ball and tried to shrink into the floor. D'Artagnan walked away and slammed the door.

∞ ∞ ∞

D'Artagnan came awake with a start and pulled himself up almost completely out of bed before he was fully aware. He struggled for each breath, every one coming as a hard won victory, while cold, clammy, beads of sweat rolled down his face.

Images cascaded though his mind: blood, the edges of swords, screams, the smell of burnt gunpowder, all rolling over and over and over. Intermixed with them was a single face, one that brought him a feeling of warmth, yet cut into the very fiber of his being.

"Charles, what is the matter?" Charlotte's voice was a distant sound for him.

"I'll be all right," he gasped. "Everything is all right."

"Right. You have nightmares like this all the time." Charlotte pulled the covers up around his shoulders to warm him, her arms wrapped tightly to hold it in place.

"This will pass." He knew the reason for the dream--the reason had followed him for more than twenty years. "It is not the first time I have had to face demons in my dreams."

"I don't understand."

D'Artagnan drew the blanket tighter around himself but let his arm slide out to put around Charlotte. "It's complicated," he said, finally. "I must face someone, someone I have been searching for a long time. I know where he is, but I have never been able to find him alone."

"Who is this person?"

When he told her, Charlotte's reaction was not what D'Artagnan expected.

"I think I might be able to help, my dearest," she said with the hint of a smile.

∞ ∞ ∞

"Please, Monsieur, is this the act of a gentleman?" Charlotte giggled.

"I hardly think a gentleman is what you want right now." The man who had been nuzzling her neck for the last few minutes laughed.

They were standing in a garden to one side of the Hotel Transylvania, where a ball had been going on for many hours. Charlotte wasn't even certain who was throwing this ball; she had the feeling that a great many of the guests felt the same way though most would sooner die than admit it.

Manuel Zarubin had been standing near one of the windows when Charlotte spotted him. He was not openly circulating among the guests but remained in one place, letting others come to him. It had taken nearly an hour for Charlotte to gain his attention and finally lead him into the darkness of the garden.

"It would all depend on what the gentleman in question might be offering. So what are you offering, my good sir?" Charlotte drew her words out so each one was a breathy echo.

Zarubin was fully twenty years her senior but still muscled like a soldier. His neatly trimmed beard was streaked with grey, but in a manner that made him seem exotic rather than ancient. A few streaks of graying hair had snaked out from beneath the perfectly coiffed wig he wore.

"Perhaps I can show you." He pushed her back into the shadowed area between two large trees. His hands moved quickly into the opening presented by her cleavage; the staves of her corset screamed as they were pushed out of shape.

"Sir, I beg you, do not do that. I am, after all, a lady." Charlotte tried to pull back. Her action threw her up against the fork in a tree just behind them, lodging her where she could not move.

"You are no lady, tart," Zarubin said, pushing his hand further down.

"My good sir, I believe that lady said she was not interested in what you had in mind." D'Artagnan moved toward the couple from behind a gazebo, where he had been waiting.

Zarubin twisted his head, his face showing surprise and anger at being interrupted. "Begone, sir! This is none of your affair."

"On that matter—" D'Artagnan laughed. "—I would say that you are definitely wrong. This is mostly definitely my affair."

He grabbed Zarubin and yanked him away from Charlotte. That the man managed to stay on his feet was a surprise, though his wig did go flying off onto the ground.

"You are a dead man, assassin." The Spaniard's voice was quiet and cold.

"We all die, sometime. Perhaps it is my time, perhaps not. Personally, I would put money on my walking away from here alive."

Zarubin pulled a rather fancily decorated sword from the sheath at his side. "Then you would lose your money, just as you are going to lose your life. I suggest, instead of boasting, that you put steel into your hand."

"My name is D'Artagnan," he said, and brought his own weapon free. "Prepare to die."

Zarubin made the first blow with a driving lunge meant to end the fight immediately. D'Artagnan parried the thrust and responded with several of his own.

"Enjoy this, dear Charlotte." Zarubin didn't take his eyes off his opponent. "You obviously know this young upstart. I hope you had a chance to say goodbye to him. Once I am finished with him, we can resume our little tête-à-tête."

D'Artagnan said nothing. He struck for Zarubin's chest with three quick jabs, which the man parried with ease, his battle hardened reflexes obvious with every move. As he parried Zarubin's counter strikes, D'Artagnan stepped to one side, his foot hit an uneven patch of ground and he went down, his sword slipping out of his grasp and out of reach.

"Now you are mine." Zarubin closed the distance, looming over his foe, intent on finishing the fight as quickly as possible.

D'Artagnan's dagger came into his hand as he rolled to one side. Striking blindly, D'Artagnan drove the blade hard into Zarubin's heart. The man trembled for a heartbeat and then fell, the light fading from his eyes.

"Fight, don't talk," D'Artagnan muttered.

"Monsieur, do not move or we will be forced to shoot!"

The command came from two men in Musketeer's uniforms with pistols in their hands. They had come from the direction of the hotel. Others were coming behind them to find the source of the disturbance.

"Charles, would you please settle this whole matter," said someone from behind D'Artagnan.

Startled, he turned to see a small man, dressed in brown, who was stroking his thin moustache as he spoke, walking forward from behind a statue of the Greek god Prometheus.

"I must say, it is rather cold out here, and I think that Mademoiselle Blackson would definitely like us to escort her home," said the stranger.

The small man stood looming over D'Artagnan for a moment, just staring at him, before he offered him his hand. Once D'Artagnan was back on his feet, the newcomer's small fingers slid into the pocket on the right side of D'Artagnan's vest, producing a small folded sheet of paper, one that D'Artagnan knew for certain had not been there earlier.

"There are times, my old friend, when you get so centered on your task I suspect that you would lose your way in your own home." The little man turned to the Musketeers and offered the paper. "I believe that you will find that my friend had a full and proper warrant for what he did this evening."

∞ ∞ ∞

"The bearer has done what he has done by my order and for the good of the state," intoned D'Artagnan as he stared at Cardinal Richelieu.

The cleric said nothing, just cocked his head slightly and waited. D'Artagnan wasn't sure just what he had expected to happen. From the moment his blade had plunged into Manuel Zarubin he had expected to wind up in the Bastille, not standing in front of the king's chief minister.

"I know what is on that warrant, young man, since I wrote it," Richelieu said finally.

Once the Musketeers had read the warrant, D'Artagnan and his companions had been released. After escorting Charlotte home, the small man, who refused to even give his name, led him to Richelieu.

That the cardinal had been awake and working in his office fit his reputation for having a hand in everything that happened in Paris and all of France every minute of the day and night.

"Then I suppose I have you to thank for my freedom, Your Eminence?"

"Indeed, you do," Richelieu agreed. "And how do you propose to repay me for that favor?"

"What would you call fair payment? You seem to have some interest in me. This fellow," he gestured toward Montaigne, "obviously works for you, and I would guess has been following me for some time."

"That he does, Charles de Gatz-Casthenese." Richelieu smiled. "Don't look so surprised, I know who you are. The question is, what I do with you? You have obviously been planning the death of Señor Zarubin for some time. So let me ask you the next question. Why?"

D'Artagnan didn't know whether to smile or be worried at this latest turn of events. "Justice, Your Eminence, justice."

"I thought the king and I were the dispensers of justice in the realm."

"You are, but sometimes that task falls into the hands of others. In the case of Zarubin, it fell to me. I had no choice in the matter. If you will recall, the year before he was murdered our current king's father, Henry IV, was the victim of another assassination attempt.

"Most of the conspirators were captured and executed, as they should have been, but not the man who organized it. My father was killed while still searching for him, although it took a long time. My mother was convinced that he must have gotten too close to the ring leader and was murdered for it. I have searched for most of my life to find out who that was. Three weeks ago I found out that it was Zarubin."

"You were duty bound to avenge the attack on his late majesty?" Richelieu steepled his fingers.

"Duty bound, yes, but not for that reason. If you will recall, the king was unhurt. My father, however . . . I have known all my life that for my father's soul to rest there must be justice. It was a matter of the honor of my family."

Richelieu was silent for some time. "There will be consequences for his death, political problems that I really did not need at this time."

"I regret nothing that I have done. I am prepared to accept whatever penalty I have earned for my action."

Richelieu pulled a folded sheet of paper out of his desk. It bore both his personal seal and the seal of his office. It had obviously been prepared some time ago. He passed it to D'Artagnan.

He could feel his jaw hanging open as he read the document. "I do not understand, Your Eminence."

"What is there to understand? That is a commission as a lieutenant in my personal guard. If you accept this, know that while your loyalty must always be to myself—and that means to France—I will, from time to time, call on you, for shall we say, special duties."

The man in brown chuckled. "Do you think Dumas would approve, Your Eminence?"

"Dumas?" asked D'Artagnan, but Richelieu waved the question away. "What of the consequences for the death of Zarubin?" he continued. "If I recall your statement not minutes ago, you said that you didn't need the political problems that might come from it."

"True, but there are ways to turn them to the advantage of France." Richelieu's smile was cold. "That is where a statesman can be as deadly as a swordsman. As for you, Charles D'Artagnan, I feel that *your* skills can be of use to me, and in turn to France, in these most unsettled times."

"How did you know of me?" asked D'Artagnan.

Richelieu hesitated for a moment and then smiled. "Let us say that you came to my attention because of a man named Charlton Heston."

D'Artagnan shook his head. "I have never heard of this person."

"It is highly unlikely and completely unnecessary that you have. Perhaps one day I may explain who he is." Richelieu took a bag of coins and tossed them toward D'Artagnan. "Consider this an enlistment bonus."

"Why do I have a feeling that my life has just become quite interesting?"

"Because it has," said Montaigne. "Personally, I think that a celebration is in order." D'Artagnan had almost forgotten the little man's presence.

"It is late, gentlemen, and I am tired. I will leave the celebrations to you young men." Richelieu turned and left the room.

"I, for one, could use a drink," said the small man to D'Artagnan. "I also know an excellent tavern not a stone's throw from here."

"Lead on. I think I am going to need several drinks," said D'Artagnan. "By the way, it occurs to me that you still have not told me your name. I have no idea who you are."

He grinned and flamboyantly traced the line of his moustache. "I have many names. Why don't you call me Aramis?"

To End The Evening

By
Bradley H. Sinor

Barnabas Marcoli gingerly ran his fingers up along the side if his head. Dried blood had already matted his hair into clumps around a lump half the size of a small goose egg.

This was definitely not the way he planned to end his first evening free in nearly two weeks.

Barnabas sagged back against the wall of the tavern and closed his eyes. From the far end of the room he could hear voices speaking a variety of languages—Italian, mixed in with a flurry of German and something that sounded vaguely Eastern European – the sort of mixture that could be found in most places like this in Venice.

Someone pressed a mug into Barnabas's left hand; his fingers closed around the pewter surface automatically. He hesitated for a moment and then downed the contents in two quick swallows. The wine was sharp and bitter, not the kind that he normally preferred to drink, but at that moment he didn't care.

"Easy, lad, take a few deep breaths and see if you can get your wits about you before you tear into any more of this miserable excuse for wine."

Barnabas found himself looking at a tall, lanky man, several years his elder, dressed in plain, slightly worn clothing, with a sword hanging at his waist. The stranger had a had a neatly trimmed mustache and dark hair. From his accent there was no doubt that he was French: his Italian was good, but not quite good enough to hide his origins.

"Can I ask a stupid question?" said Barnabas. "What in the hell happened to me?"

"Oh, that." His companion chuckled. "Seems a pair of ruffians wanted to relieve you of your purse and weren't too picky in the way they did it. I'm glad I happened along at the right time."

Barnabas nodded. He remembered how he had been cutting through a narrow alley just east of the American Embassy when a man had appeared in front of him and demanded money. Before Barnabas could react, someone else struck him from behind. Everything after that, until this stranger had guided him into the tavern, remained something of a blur.

"Damn," Barnabas muttered as he reached inside of his shirt but found nothing there.

"Would this be what you might be looking for?" A small burgundy coin bag slid across the table.

Barnabas left out long sigh. It was true that there wasn't much money in it; apprentice metal workers weren't rich, but it was his money. Not to mention the fact that Barnabas knew full well that his cousins would not let him forget it if they discovered that he had been robbed.

"I thank you, sir. My name is Marcoli, Barnabas Marcoli. I owe you not only my life, but my dignity. I will pray for you at mass," he said. "And who might I name as my Good Samaritan?"

"D'Artagnan, Charles D'Artagnan."

Barnabas stared at the man for a time.

"I have the feeling that I know of you, sir." Something about that name was familiar, but the throbbing in Barnabas's head didn't help his concentration. He repeated it over and over in his mind. The memory was there, and close, infuriatingly close, but he could not bring it to the surface.

"I think not. I am new come to Venice. Before the little altercation with those ruffians, had you dined?" When Barnabas shook his head, D'Artagnan smiled and motioned for the tavern girl. "Good. Neither have I."

A few minutes later they had plates of chicken, cheese and bread set in front of them.

"I hope you ordered enough for three."

Barnabas turned with a start and found a small man dressed in brown sitting next to him. The newcomer looked like he could be only five foot one or two. He had an ordinary-looking face with nothing on it that would have distinguished him from anyone else on the streets of Venice.

"I wondered when you were going to show up," said D'Artagnan.

The small man shrugged, motioning for the serving girl to bring him something to drink. "I was working. After all, we do have a reason for being here besides wenching and drinking."

"Pity," laughed D'Artagnan. "Barnabas, let me introduce you to my traveling companion, Aramis."

"Aramis? D'Artagnan?" Barnabas cocked his head at both men, suddenly feeling very pleased with himself. "So where are the other two?"

"Other two?" said D'Artagnan.

"Obviously, he's read the book," said the small man called Aramis, switching from Italian to English.

"Indeed I have," Barnabas responded, somewhat unsure of his English but wanting to use it now, nonetheless. "The Three Musketeers was only one of several novels that Frank Stone, that young man my cousin Giovanna has been making eyes at, lent me. He said they would help me learn American faster. So, are you really the one in the book?"

"I suppose I really should go get a copy of the book some time," muttered D'Artagnan. "Yes, I am the one that book was about."

It occurred to Barnabas that there were several things that might be interesting to ask the Frenchman about concerning the events in that book, but the look on the man's face suggested that this might be a good time to let those questions lie.

"I obviously owe you my life, Monsieur D'Artagnan. If there is any way in which I can repay you, do not hesitate to say so. Had you not come along I suspect I would have ended up face down in the canal," Barnabas said.

"Thing nothing of it," said D'Artagnan.

"Actually," said Aramis, a thin smile on his face, "I think that you can help us."

∞ ∞ ∞

"I take it you have a plan?" D'Artagnan said in a whisper to Aramis.

In the time that D'Artagnan had known Aramis, he had learned that the small man had a sharp sense of strategy and planning, not to mention the ability to think on his feet. That skill alone had saved both of their lives on more than one occasion.

They spoke quietly because while their newly acquired Italian companion was most probably Catholic, they definitely did not know his political bent. So the fact that the two Frenchmen were in the service of Armand Jean du Plessis de Richelieu, Cardinal Richelieu, the first minister of France, was a piece of information best kept to themselves.

"It isn't a plan, exactly, just a way that young Marcoli can be of assistance," he said. "Most of it we will have to make up as we go along."

The two Frenchmen had been in Venice for just over a week. In that time D'Artagnan had begun to feel somewhat frustrated. He preferred direct action; give him a sword in his hand and an enemy to face, and that was the best of all possible worlds. Aramis, on the other hand, preferred to wait in the shadows, unseen until he was ready to act.

Three months before, late one evening, D'Artagnan had been summoned to the Louvre by the cardinal. Once there he found himself waiting near the door, while at the far end of the gallery that served Richelieu as an office, the churchman spoke at length with a woman in dark colors who had a Spanish look about her. D'Artagnan presumed that, given the circumstances, she was another one of Richelieu's agents rather than a supplicant come to beg some favor from the most powerful man in France.

When she departed, the woman had smiled briefly at D'Artagnan but had not spoken. As she passed him, D'Artagnan had inclined his head toward her and said simply, "Good evening, milady."

"When necessary, that woman can be quite as dangerous as you, my young friend," said Richelieu.

"I shouldn't doubt it," D'Artagnan said. "If there is one thing besides the use of the blade that my uncle taught me, it was to be wary of certain women, and I think her to be one of them."

"Indeed. He sounds like a most wise and practical man. I think you may take after him in some ways," said the cardinal. Richelieu had made use of the young swordsman several times since, on impulse, taking him into his personal guard. While the results had not always been what he would have preferred, D'Artagnan's performance had been enough to keep him keenly aware of the young swordsman.

"That is why I am going to trust you with a most delicate mission, one that I think will fit your skills quite well."

From a drawer in his desk, the cardinal pulled out several sheets of paper and passed them to D'Artagnan. One of them was a travel warrant, giving the bearer priority access to transport anywhere within the boundaries of France. The other bore a highly detailed sketch of a face. This was followed by two small bags of gold. Expense money, no doubt, speculated D'Artagnan. There was one thing that came with working for Richelieu: he was definitely not ungenerous with the state's money.

"You are to go to Italy. Venice, to be exact. I need you to locate the man whose face is on that paper. His name is Ramsey Culhane. He is the nephew and principal heir of one Jameson Culhane, an Irish Catholic gentleman whom I would appreciate having in my debt," said Richelieu.

"I take it he is not in Venice of his own accord."

"Indeed not. There is a matter of a rather large sum of money owed to one of the trading houses in the form of a gambling debtI don't have the specifics as of yet. They've demanded payment from his uncle or they will kill the wastrel. Under other circumstances, I would just pay the ransom myself. However, there are certain alliances that might be put in jeopardy if that were discovered. So we must resort to your unique skills, Lieutenant."

"It shall be done, Your Eminence. If you have no objections, I will take Aramis with me."

"Take him. He is useful, but at times gives me a headache," said Richelieu. As D'Artagnan left, he saw the churchman spreading several maps of the French-Spanish border areas across his desk.

∞ ∞ ∞

A goodly portion of the far western districts in Venice were devoted to docks and warehouses. In the time since he had come to the city to apprentice as a metal worker with his uncle, Antonio Marcoli, Barnabas had become quite familiar with the area.

From the shadowed corner where the three men had stopped, Barnabas could see lights from a few torches and lanterns that marked where some people worked, even now.

The streets were never completely empty, even at nearly midnight. It was just quieter as businesses awaited the coming of the tide to bring in more cargo, and daylight to guide transports that would carry the contents of the warehouses away.

The farther they traveled from the center of the city, the more Barnabas' urge to repay his guardian angel had faded. Not a small portion of his mind wondered if the two Frenchmen would turn around and help themselves to his purse and pick up a few extra coins selling his body to a medical school.

"I have a feeling that my uncle may not be all that pleased at my involvement with whatever you have in mind," Barnabas said. "Tell me truthfully, is this thing you want me to do legal?"

"Truthfully, no," said D'Artagnan. "It is also more than likely going to be dangerous. But I say this without a doubt: should we succeed, it will not cause any harm to the reputation of the Marcoli family."

From under his jacket, the tall Frenchman produced a single-shot pistol that he passed to Barnabas. The weapon weighed no more than a few ounces. Barnabas had fired muskets while hunting, but never at another person. He was more at home with the long knife that hung on his belt, although he preferred not to use it unless there was no choice in the matter.

"I hope that I won't find a need for this," he told the Frenchman.

"True, but isn't it better to have something and not need it that to . . ."

". . . need it and not have it. You sound like my cousin, Giovanna."

"The one whose friend gave you the book about me? A wise woman," said D'Artagnan.

"Barnabas, do you know this place?" Aramis asked, pointing at a small two-story building just down the way. Barnabas stared for a few minutes. Just past it were the burnt remnants of another warehouse. According to some of his cousins, the place had been set afire four years ago under rather odd circumstances. And, just as oddly, no one had taken over the property, even though it was quite valuable because of its location.

"Yes, I do. As far as anyone knows, it is supposed to belong to Roberto Salvatore. But, according to my uncle, old Salvatore sold the place a few months back to the Kurtz brothers. They're Austrian, I think, and may even have some Russian connections," said Barnabas. "What are we here for?"

"Nothing too difficult," Aramis said. The small man had a slight smile on his face as he spoke that gave Barnabas a chill. It occurred to him that this was the sort of fellow who could as cheerfully slit your throat as share the latest gossip with you. "I just want you to get us inside by telling the men behind that door exactly who you are. The Marcoli name carries weight, even at this ungodly late hour. With any kind of luck, that should get us inside the place without things getting too messy."

As outrageous as it sounded, Barnabas could actually imagine that sort of bluff working with some people. He'd more than once seen his uncle push his way through situations by doing just exactly that.

"You did say," he repeated, "that this whole matter would not reflect badly on my family."

"It shouldn't, if things work out, but you never know," Aramis said. "Besides, if things go wrong, there is a chance that none of us will have to worry about who gets blamed, since we might all be dead."

Barnabas was overcome with an urge to run, but he blocked that by reminding himself that he did owe his life to the tall Frenchman. Instead, he drew a deep breath and headed toward the warehouse, moving quickly in order to not give himself time to think of reasons why he shouldn't be involved in this whole matter.

Things had already gone wrong when Barnabas reached the warehouse's main door. It was open and there was no sign of any watchmen or other sort of guard. From the look on his two companions' faces, Barnabas was certain this was a discovery that neither of them had expected.

Once they were inside, a short narrow hallway led into the main part of the warehouse. The smell of the canals and the sound of splashing around the warehouse pilings mixed into the darkness.

There were several dozen bales of cloth blocking off one corner of the room where a table with bottles of wine and mugs sat, along with a bowl filled with cheese and a half loaf of bread.

A movement to one side of the room caught Barnabas' attention. A moment later a man emerged through a door and came charging forward with a large, rather nasty-looking ax in his hand. Barnabas attempted to step backward, but found his feet tangled among a couple of chairs, and it was only a miracle that kept him on his feet.

D'Artagnan came from behind one of the bales of cloth and threw himself hard against the stranger. That was enough to make the man drop his weapon and give the Frenchman a chance to fire two quick blows to his opponent's stomach and chin, putting an end to the fight and the man on the floor.

"Do you always attack a man with an ax with only your fists?" asked Barnabas, not even sure that he had seen what he had seen.

"It worked, didn't it? Do you know this fellow?" D'Artagnan held his lantern close to the unconscious man's face.

Barnabas stared at the prostrate form for a moment. "Yes, I believe I do know him. I think his name is Brouila, Mordaunt Brouila. He works for the Quinniaros; they are rivals of the Kurtzes."

"I wonder if they discovered that the Kurtzes were holding Culhane and decided to cut themselves in on the matter. The ransom that the Kurtzes were demanding was going to be a tidy sum," said D'Artagnan.

"Possibly. There are two bodies over at the other end of the warehouse, and given the circumstances, I suspect they worked for the Kurtzes," said Aramis. "I'm guessing that the Quinniaros got what they came for, meaning Culhane. This leaves us at a loss as to where they have taken him, unless our friend there would be willing to give us the information we need. It is possible that if we can wake him up he can be persuaded to tell us where they went."

"I would presume," said Barnabas, "that we are not going to be informing the authorities of what has happened to him."

"Indeed not," said D'Artagnan.

"Wait, we might not need Brouila. Wouldn't they want to get off the streets as quickly as possible?" Barnabas asked. The Quinniaros had interest in several ships, but that was all that Barnabas knew for certain. But he had heard that they had an interest in a nearby business.

"That would be what I would do," said Aramis.

"Then I may have an idea on where to find them," said Barnabas.

∞ ∞ ∞

Barnabas and his companions found their way through the streets of Venice quickly. Their goal was a building only a few streets from the docks. Sandwiched between two warehouses, it looked like nothing more than offices for the various businesses that operated in the area. Were it not for the single lantern hanging in front of the heavy oak door, it would have been easy to miss the dark green door.

"Welcome," said a woman dressed in emerald and crimson velvet, her long hair hanging in ornate curls, after the three men were admitted.

That she was mistress of the house there was no doubt. She was not young, and according to the tales that Barnabas had heard, Madam Paulette and her establishment had been a fixture in Venice for many years. Her careful makeup and the room's lighting took at least a decade off her age. The serious look in the woman's eyes showed that she was no common street whore, but rather a woman who had learned to make her way in the world and indulge in a taste for finer things.

D'Artagnan rubbed his chin and studied the place. That it was a brothel was obvious, but Barnabas had already told them that. The windows were masked with heavy curtains. In spite of the hour, there seemed to be a brisk business going on, some sailors and a mixed lot of workmen. There were perhaps a half dozen men there, some with drinks in their hands, others talking to women in revealing gowns.

"You would be Madam Paulette?" asked Barnabas.

"Indeed I am. What can I do for some fine gentlemen like yourselves?" she said. On Madam Paulette's shoulder was a highly intricate butterfly brooch, the stones on it reflecting different colors each way that she turned. D'Artagnan suspected that while it looked valuable, it might be nothing more than paste. On more than one occasion, he had seen that skill and craftsmanship could make paste look like the most valuable jewels in the world.

"I suppose it is your years of experience that tells you we aren't just sailors out moving from one tavern to another, seeking various entertainments," said D'Artagnan.

"I've learned to recognize those who are in need of the services that we offer here. I do have customers from the lower decks of many of the ships that make port here, but also the ranks and officers have been known to hang their hats in my parlor. From the look of you, your manner and attitude, in spite of the plainness of your dress, you are gentlemen," she said. "So how may I help you? I presume you are interested in some female company this evening?"

"Were the evening ours, I am certain that passing it in the company of one of the young ladies you employ would be quite enjoyable," said Aramis. "However, the night is not ours to do with as we would please. Instead, we are seeking some . . . acquaintances we think might have arrived here in the last several hours."

Madam Paulette smiled, suppressing a slight laugh. "You would have to be a good deal more exact about who it might be that you are looking for. Business has been good this evening; a number of gentleman callers have come through the door. Besides, why should I tell you anything about who has come and gone? My customers, even the lower ranking ones, expect a good deal of privacy. They certainly don't expect to have their names shouted by the crier in the town square."

"And they will not be, Madam Paulette," said Barnabas. "I know that there are members of my family who might be grateful for any aid you might render us."

"And your name would be?"

"Marcoli. Barnabas Marcoli."

The woman arched her head slightly to one side as she weighed the possibilities.

She turned and headed toward a door at the side of the room. From the smells that were coming from that direction, Barnabas suspected that there might be kitchens somewhere close. Once they were away from the parlor, she turned to face the three men, staring at them, and then looking upwards toward the ceiling for a moment before she spoke.

"Gentlemen, I'm sorry to say this, but there is nothing that I can do to assist you in this matter. I run a quiet house; my girls and I try to stay out of anyone else's business. I can think of seven reasons that should remain true. I trust that you can find your own way out. Please convey my respects to your uncle, Signor Marcoli."

With a turn, she vanished through the door into the back part of the house.

It bothered Barnabas that Madam Paulette seemed to be more familiar with his family than he had expected. He sincerely hoped that in the months to come he would not regret telling her his name.

"This is no time to linger," said D'Artagnan as he motioned for the others to follow him up a stairway at the end of the hall.

Two lanterns lit the narrow hallway, and from behind several doors D'Artagnan caught the sounds of moans and other noises that proved the rooms were being well put to use.

"I should think . . . this one," said D'Artagnan, as he came to a door at the far end of the hallway. Barnabas noticed that it was the seventh door.

That was when they heard the sound of something crashing onto the floor from inside the room.

D'Artagnan's sword slid into one hand, a dagger in the other. Then he kicked the door open. The wood cracked under his heel with a sharp sound, but it was almost masked by the sounds within.

"Stay here," the tall Frenchman said over his shoulder to Barnabas, who was only a few steps behind him. "Let no one pass."

Barnabas let out a sigh; with his heart pounding wildly in his chest, Barnabas was more than happy to obey the Frenchman's instructions.

In the dim light, D'Artagnan could see two large apparitions, one wearing a cape and the other a long jacket. A smoking pistol was in the hand of the first man, the other had his arms around a smaller struggling man with sandy hair, who was presumably Culhane. An overturned chair with ropes twisted around it suggested that he had managed to free himself, to the surprise of his captors.

The Frenchman let fly with his dagger. It creased the head of the man holding Culhane, gouging his ear and sending blood flying. The man responded with a yelp and a string of curses equal to those of some sailors.

The other man threw himself at D'Artagnan, using his empty pistol as a club. The Frenchman twisted, hit his opponent in the stomach, and then drove his knee into the fellow's crotch. Before the first man had gone to the floor, D'Artagnan whirled about and sent the pommel of his sword slamming squarely into the other man's face, the sound of a nose breaking confirming its effectiveness. Two more blows with the same part of this sword put the man on the floor at D'Artagnan's feet.

Like most fights, this one was over quickly, almost before Barnabas could be certain of what was happening. He quickly looked back and forth in the hallway, expecting intruders seeking to discover the source of the disturbance.

The first man rose from the floor with a start, grabbing one of the broken pieces of a chair and diving for D'Artagnan. The blade at Barnabas' belt came into his hand and went flying, burying itself into the man's left eye.

"I'm not sure if Madam Paulette is going to be pleased with the condition you have left her room in," said Aramis, who had several of the house's bouncers standing behind him. D'Artagnan couldn't help but notice that the little man also had a pistol in one hand and a bottle of wine in the other.

"No doubt she will vehemently vent her vexation about the matter. She can bill the Quinniaro family. However, I'm sure they paid her well enough to let them keep him here. Besides, I'll lay you even money that she has more damage than this on any given Saturday night," said D'Artagnan.

"More than likely," agreed Aramis.

"You stupid bastards," yelled the man with the sandy hair as he struggled up from the floor, his Irish accent heavy in his voice. "You almost got me killed! Do you have any idea of how easy it would have been for him to snap my neck? You call this rescuing me?"

D'Artagnan covered the distance between himself and the man in three steps, then grabbed him by the collar of his dirty and stained shirt and slammed him hard against the wall. Then he lifted him up several inches above the floor.

"Is your name Culhane? Ramsey Culhane?"

"Y-y-yesss!" the man stuttered.

"Well, listen well, Monsieur Ramsey Culhane, and know this. You live because of me and my friends. It would have been very easy to leave you in the hands of these men who would as soon slit your throat and dump you into the canals as listen to your so-called righteous anger.

"Quite honestly, I suspect it is your own fault that these men were threatening your life. Of course, it may not have been, but then again, I really don't care. When you see your uncle again, just remind him that he is now in the debt of Cardinal Richelieu for having you alive. Do you think you can remember that?"

"Yes, I do." Culhane managed to push the words out of his throat between gasps for air.

"I'll remember it."

D'Artagnan released Culhane to the floor, holding the man's arm to keep him steady. They had taken a couple of steps before he pushed the man up close to the unconscious form of the man in the long leather jacket.

"Remember something else, my ungrateful friend. Your uncle owes the cardinal a favor for the saving of your sorry hide. But it is you who owe me your life. Someday I may come to you and demand that you pay back that favor, and you will," he growled.

"I understand," Culhane stuttered before passing out.

∞ ∞ ∞

D'Artagnan dropped a leather pouch on the table in front of Barnabas as the two men sat at a small table in Madam Paulette's parlor. The thud when the bag hit the table showed that it was full. The younger man picked it up and spilled out the contents into his hand; mixed in with the silver were a number of gold coins.

"It seems that our adversaries had been paid in advance, and they didn't spread the wealth around all that much," said D'Artagnan. "But far be it from me to criticize the house of Quinniaro over their financial dealings, especially when it works out to our advantage."

"Our advantage?" asked Barnabas.

"I gave Madam Paulette a portion of it to pay for damages and her silence. Half of what is left is yours. Call it payment for your services this evening and also your silence--the spoils of war, so to speak."

Barnabas stared at the money for a moment; this would more than double the amount of money in his own purse.

"I did not do this for money but because you saved my life. It was a matter of honor."

"Quite true, and you've more than repaid that debt, not only by helping Aramis and myself. But when you stepped in and saved my life, the scales were balanced. There is no reason you should not get a reward," said the Frenchman. "Personally, I would suggest you use some of those coins to make some arrangements with one of Madam Paulette's ladies."

"Then you are planning on staying?" asked Barnabas.

"Indeed; the soonest we can get passage will be another day or so. The Quinniaros are tied up in Madam Paulette's cellar, and Aramis will stay with Culhane to prevent him from wandering away. Since it is doubtful that the Quinniaros will send others, this is an excellent place to hole up. I suspect I may make an arrangement or two with one of Madam Paulette's employees myself."

Two young women, one in green velvet and the other yellow, had entered the room, taking seats on a chaise longue near the door.

Yes, it seemed to him that D'Artagnan had the right idea. Remaining here might definitely be an excellent way to end the evening.

All For One

By
Bradley H. Sinor & Susan P. Sinor

"Let me tell you, my friend; women are nothing but trouble! They will do nothing but bat their eyelashes and get you into trouble! And when you think they are gone, then they come back to haunt you."

Charles D'Artagnan took a sip of his wine and rolled his eyes as he looked over toward where the voice seemed to come from. The speaker was a young man, perhaps twenty-one or -two, yet he had a world-weary look about him that D'Artagnan could empathize with.

"Can I get you some more, Monsieur?" said the innkeeper. A gray-haired man in his fifties, he moved in and out among the tables with practiced ease.

"Just let me know when your supper is ready. I have spent far too long at sea and am famished," D'Artagnan said.

In truth, it was good to be back on solid ground. After concluding their business in Venice, he and his companion, Réne Montaigne, had taken a ship out of Venice, intent on reaching the southern French coast. However, storms had delayed their arrival by nearly a week, a very long week for him. Not that D'Artagnan was prone to seasickness; it was more the fact that there had been nothing to do onboard, and, with the weather, they had been confined below decks for several days.

"Not to worry, sir. I call my wife the best cook in the province. You will find her meals the next best thing to a banquet at the palace of the King himself," said the innkeeper, patting a rather large belly. "I have been the beneficiary of them for more than two decades, ever since I left the king's army."

"In that case, Innkeeper, I look forward to it," said D'Artagnan as he reached into his coat pocket and produced a clay pipe and bag of shag tobacco.

"Porthos, you of all people can understand this," said the young man that D'Artagnan had been listening to. "I've seen your heart be broken by a woman."

The mention of the name Porthos caught D'Artagnan's attention.

"Athos, Athos," the other man sighed. "I do the heart breaking, not the other way around."

Athos, Porthos? Those two names pulled D'Artagnan out of his relaxed stupor. In the time since he had been in the service of Cardinal Richelieu, he had come to know those names very well. Apparently, in the up-time, those two and their cousin, Aramis, as well as D'Artagnan himself, were quite well known in certain circles because of a book and those things called movies. Montaigne himself had been known to use the name Aramis, but that was just one among many names that the man who could fade into any crowd preferred to use.

"I tell you I saw her, Porthos; she was here not an hour ago walking down the street. The same blonde hair, in a green dress, the same walk," he said, with a hint of anger in his voice, or perhaps it was despair. D'Artagnan couldn't quite be certain.

"And by the time you got there she was nowhere to be found. You do tend to get in melancholy moods, my friend, so I suspect you saw some other woman who had a slight resemblance to this woman and your mind added the details," said Porthos.

"Your pardon, gentlemen," said a voice from just behind D'Artagnan. He looked up to see the familiar face of his partner, Montaigne. That the small man had been able to come so silently, so unnoticed into the inn did not surprise him in the least. Montaigne had been on shipboard with D'Artagnan but had disappeared shortly after they had come ashore, saying that he would see the young man back in Paris after dealing with a few necessary matters. D'Artagnan hadn't bothered to ask for any details; he had learned from experience that the little man was not forthcoming with details except when it suited him.

The matters might have been another assignment from the Cardinal or, possibly, something else. D'Artagnan had met people who didn't let their left hands know what their right hands were doing. He sometimes suspected that Montaigne didn't let his fingers know what his thumbs were doing.

"This is a private conversation," said the man called Athos, his stare a dark thing, especially for one so young.

"I am aware and do apologize for intruding, but I had to ask you. This woman you mentioned, the one in the green dress. I am also seeking her, so I think we have common cause in this matter." Montaigne turned to order a drink from the innkeeper. "Plus, I believe it might settle your companion's mind to know if this woman is who he thinks she is."

"And you are seeking her, why?" asked Porthos.

"For reasons that will bear no harm to her or to you gentlemen," said Montaigne.

Athos muttered something, but the sound was lost as he drained the mug in front of him. Porthos looked at the newcomer for a few moments before speaking. "My cousin is subject to the woes of too much drink, but perhaps it would not be a bad thing to go in search of this woman and let him see that it is not this phantom of his heart," he said. "Very well, shall we meet you by the fountain in front of the convent in, say, a half hour?"

D'Artagnan considered the possibility of entering into the conversation himself but it seemed the wiser thing, for the moment, to hold back and see what Montaigne had in mind.

Montaigne left a moment after the two men, passing by D'Artagnan's table with a particular twitch of his fingers. D'Artagnan let himself sit for a few minutes, casually finishing his drink and the last of the dinner that the innkeeper had brought him. He stood, taking his time to straighten his clothing, and moved toward the door.

The stable was just behind the tavern, and the young Gascon casually walked up to the stall where the dark horse he had purchased at the port the day before was standing. The animal was quietly munching on hay and hardly seemed to be aware of D'Artagnan.

"So, you have some interest in this 'lady in green'," D'Artagnan asked. "Anything you can tell me about? Is this why you wanted to come here? After all, it's not the most direct route back to Paris."

Montaigne climbed down from the hayloft, brushing a few strands off his clothing. "Quite true," the smaller man replied. "I suppose, as the Americans would say, it's a matter of 'national security'."

"What isn't, these days? I would like to get back to Paris and see Charlotte," D'Artagnan said.

"Your lady friend can wait. I'm sure a businesswoman like her has numerous matters to occupy her time. I need you to see if you can find this other woman.

"The woman in the green dress?"

"Indeed, although I suppose the dress color doesn't matter; it can be changed. And if she is who I think she is, she will have more than one change of clothing." He peered around the side of the stables toward the inn. "I have to go now. Do what you can to aid them. If I need to reach you I'll leave a message with the innkeeper addressed to Monsieur de Largo."

"One thing," said D'Artagnan, "I have to know. Those two men, Athos and Porthos, are they who I think they are?"

Montaigne smiled. "They are Issac de Porteau and Armund de Sillegue d'Athos d'A'Autevielle, who you may have heard of under the names of Athos and Porthos. They are cousins and members of the King's Musketeers. I would suspect they are on leave, since I think they may have relatives who live in this province."

That Montaigne knew the men did not surprise D'Artagnan in the slightest. After Cardinal Richelieu had become aware of the up-time novel "The Three Musketeers," and that it was based on some bits of actual history, he had dispatched Montaigne to find D'Artagnan and the others. The results had ended with the young Gascon enlisted in the churchman's service.

"And the third . . . Aramis?"

"I'm not sure where he is."

Before D'Artagnan could ask for more details, Montaigne slipped around the corner and disappeared.

∞ ∞ ∞

When one is looking for a person or an object, it helps to have some idea of where to look. It wasn't that the town was that large; it was the sort where a man at one end of the town could hear when a mouse farted at the other end. So since there was one man who knew where this 'woman in the green dress' had been seen, it seemed the logical thing to seek him out.

The fight had just ended when D'Artagnan walked through the convent entranceway into the main hall. Athos stood at the far end of the room, methodically wiping blood off of his sword with the tunic of the freshly dead body. Porthos was a dozen steps away, his sword in one hand and a chicken leg in the other. He took several bites out of it as he poked at another corpse with the toe of his boot.

D'Artagnan stopped to pick up an un-broken bottle of wine from the floor. "Did I miss the entertainment?"

The two Musketeers eyed him warily, but when he pulled the cork from the bottle, took a swallow and then passed it to Athos, they seemed to relax.

"Friends of yours?" D'Artagnan gestured at the bodies on the floor.

"They were screaming at a couple of the Sisters and seemed to take umbrage when we politely asked them to stop," said Athos.

"It was strictly self-defense," said Porthos.

"Of course," said D'Artagnan.

One of the nuns emerged from a far room, shaking her head as she looked at the damage. From her manner, D'Artagnan couldn't help but wonder if she was the Mother Superior. If she wasn't, he suspected it might not be too many years until she ascended to that office. "I should make you ruffians clean this up, though I know that you were defending yourselves. I hope that the men these bullies were looking for appreciate what you have done."

Moments later several other nuns appeared and in swift order carried off the two bodies. The chances were that both men were dead and would soon be making their explanations to the good Lord rather than the local magistrates, which suited D'Artagnan. Even before he had gone to work for the Cardinal, he had preferred not to cross paths with the local magistrates any more than necessary. D'Artagnan thought it best not to ask what was going to happen to the bodies.

"Who were they looking for?" he asked the nun.

"I didn't recognize the names - Athos and Porthos," said the nun.

D'Artagnan's two new acquaintances looked at each other. He wasn't sure if it was a look of surprise, amusement or relief on their faces.

Athos turned to D'Artagnan. "My good sir, if memory does not fail me, were you not just at the inn up the hill? What brings you here?"

"The same thing as you, gentleman, and the same person. I work with the man you spoke to concerning the woman in the green dress. He suggested that I accompany you in her pursuit. He was needed elsewhere."

Athos eyed D'Artagnan for a moment, looked at Porthos, and then nodded.

"Very well," said Porthos. "I am Porthos, this is my cousin Athos. And your name, my good sir?"

"Charles D'…..de Largo," said D'Artagnan. Why he had not given these two his real name, he couldn't say; it just seemed the right thing to do for now.

"Very well; so now we are three," said Porthos.

"Where do we go to look for a ghost? A memory come to life; that is what this woman in the green dress appears to be," said D'Artagnan.

"Your pardon, gentleman," said the nun who had spoken to D'Artagnan earlier. "I know of whom you speak. I believe I have seen her on several occasions, at a distance. She is not someone I know personally. I know she is not staying with us at the convent. I think I saw her yesterday, going into a dress shop some two streets over."

"We have yet to actually begin our search, except for asking here," replied Porthos. "I believe I know the establishment you speak of; we will certainly ask after her there. Thank you, Sister, and good day." The three men doffed their hats and bowed, then filed out of the convent and headed toward the street indicated.

"What happened?" asked D'Artagnan. "Were those men rifling the poor box?"

"That's what we assumed when we heard the commotion. But from what the nun said they apparently had other motives."

"Pity you couldn't have asked them who they were working for."

"Indeed," said Porthos. "Who do we owe money to around here?"

"No one that I know of," said Athos. "Unless you got into a dice game last night and haven't mentioned it."

"Me? Not that I recall?" Are you sure you don't owe anyone any money?" asked Porthos.

"None that I recall, save for a few sous to Aramis," said Athos.

"Hardly a motive to dispatch leg-breaking assassins to track you down," said Porthos. "Besides, he would want to do that himself. "

"Indeed," Athos said. "

The village was small but its streets were winding, so it took a quarter hour to locate the dressmaker's shop that the nun had spoken of. The woman running it had red hair and a provocative smile when she saw the three men walk through the door.

"Good morn, my good woman," D'Artagnan said. "How are you this fine day?"

"Very well, good sirs. And yourselves? Are you looking for some finery for your ladies? I have a very good selection." She pointed out some odds and ends of frippery along with several bolts of bright colored cloth.

"Alas, no. But we are looking for the – cousin – of my friend here." D'Artagnan pointed to Athos. "She is of medium height and of good figure, with light hair. One of the sisters at the convent said she saw her come in here yesterday. I wonder if she might have said where she was going after she left. We haven't seen her in several hours and are somewhat concerned."

The woman stared at the three men for a few seconds and then smiled. "I remember the woman. She was in here yesterday, dressed in green with a silver swan necklace. I think I saw her heading east when she left, going toward the warehouse district." That was near the other end of town.

"I thank you, dear woman, for your assistance. May your custom be profitable," said Porthos, though he did take time for a long lingering look into the woman's eyes. The smile she responded with suggested, at least to D'Artagnan's mind, that she would not object to the young man making a return visit to her establishment.

∞ ∞ ∞

"Wasn't this where you thought you saw her?" asked D'Artagnan.

Athos made a sound deep in his chest and nodded, pointing toward the street corner a half block away. "Yes, friend De Largo. I was standing there and saw a movement out of the corner of my eye. Something about it made me turn, and <u>then </u>I saw her, for just a moment"

"She saw you?"

"I suspect so. She turned toward me, as if looking to see if I or someone were following her, then vanished into the alleyway. By the time I got there I could find no sign that she or anyone else had been there for some time. It was late; I presumed I had imagined the whole thing."

"Yet, cousin, you could not stop brooding on it," chuckled Porthos.

The alley that Athos led them to was a dead end, running up against a wall that was a good ten feet high. Climbing it would have been possible, as far as D'Artagnan could see, even by a woman in a dress; although, he admitted, he doubted the dress would be in any presentable shape afterwards.

"If she didn't come out where you could have seen her, then we have to presume that she went into one of the buildings," said Porthos.

There were four doors opening into the alley. Two were securely locked and one of them looked like it had not been opened in years. The third, however, had been freshly painted and bore a sign with the single word: **Deliveries**.

"When you have one choice," said Athos, gesturing at the door, "You take it."

"I suspect that if your blonde lady came here, she was just passing through and is long gone. I don't think there will be anyone here but us and a few rats," said D'Artagnan.

"You might be right," said a man dressed in a dark brown doublet with no insignia, a cocked pistol in one hand. He had moved quietly, and none of the three had heard his approach. "But then, again, you might just be totally wrong," he added.

"One man, one pistol. Really, unless you are very good with that sword I see at your side, you should take into account the fact that there are three of us." D'Artagnan looked at the stranger and sighed.

That was when a half-dozen others appeared at the entrance to the alley, all armed like the first. They were all dressed in plain clothes with no sigils or any other sign of allegiance, although each of their weapons looked well cared for and extremely functional.

"We could take them," said Porthos softly. He had locked eyes with two of the men and seemed ready to charge into the fray without a moment's hesitation.

"True," said Athos. "But I suspect that they know where the lady in question is. So why should we waste our time searching for her? Let them lead us to her instead."

"A sound plan."

"Now, we can do this quite easily. If you gentleman will divest yourselves of your weapons we can get on with things," said the first man. "Please understand that all of my men are excellent shots, plus they are armed with more than one pistol each."

D'Artagnan looked at his two new friends. They each nodded and then removed their swords, laying them on the ground, as well as each placing several daggers next to them. D'Artagnan had two other smaller blades on his person. While he didn't know it for a fact, he felt that Athos and Porthos were no doubt similarly armed.

"There are those in Paris who would be shocked to see this," muttered Porthos.

The Musketeers and D'Artagnan found themselves being taken to a house two streets away from the alley. It was the sort of place that could have been found anywhere on any street in any country. Their captors had gathered up the discarded weapons and were looking at them with much interest.

Inside, the party moved to a stairway and down into the basement. There were several small lamps set up, casting an odd glow to the whole scene. In the center of the room a man was sitting in a chair, facing them. It was fairly obvious that he was securely bound to the chair. Standing next to him was a blond woman dressed in green, a silver swan necklace around her throat. It was a fairly safe guess for D'Artagnan to presume that this was the woman they had been looking for.

"I believe you gentlemen belong on the groom's side," said a thin, grey-haired man who held an eagle-headed cane in one hand, looking like he could brandish it as a weapon at a moment's notice.

D'Artagnan angled his head slightly, taking in the scene: there were the half-dozen thugs who had escorted them here, the man in the chair, and the girl. It all seemed rather surreal. The girl rested her hand on the chair; she was definitely not happy to be there. She looked as if she could either burst into tears or scream out in anger. It was a little hard to tell which to expect.

"You know this fellow?" the thin man with the cane asked, gesturing toward the chair.

"Our cousin, Aramis," said Athos. "Although I suspect you already knew that."

This was not the face that D'Artagnan was accustomed to associating with the name Aramis. This man was taller, with sharp features. He had known all along that Montaigne's real name was not Aramis, any more than

René Montaigne was. For some, names were things that suited a given situation.

"Good," he said. "My name is Maximilian André Castellans Moreau. The young lady over there is my daughter, Celine. She is my pride and joy and that bastard, your cousin, dishonored her and insulted my family honor."

"Father! It's not true! You burst in on us and started screaming at the top of your lungs before you knew what was happening," said the girl called Celine.

"I am not a fool! You were lying in your bed and this insult to humanity was standing over you. When I entered, he leaped from the balcony of our house in Paris! He did not have the honor to stand still so I could shoot him!" The older man's face went red with anger.

"I wonder if that was the night Aramis showed up at the barracks with blood all over his buttocks," mused Porthos. "Actually, Monsieur, I don't think you missed. He had trouble sitting down for a week."

"Then he had the effrontery to follow us here! He pollutes the very air that we breathe. I will have my daughter's honor vindicated. I will see her married this night and her honor restored. Then she will become a widow and take holy orders with the sisters of San Carlo," snorted Moreau, stamping his cane down to emphasize his words.

"My lord, I understand why you are fiercely angry with my cousin," said Athos. "And you should be. But realize he did not know that your family had come to this village and follow you here. The three of us stopped here to rest and resupply ourselves before returning to Paris."

D'Artagnan could see Aramis's eyes get as large as grapefruits. He tried squirming in the chair, but whoever had tied him had done yeoman's work, and he could barely move. He looked at Athos and Porthos. Both men nodded almost imperceptibly. They knew that if they did not do something, and quickly, this wasn't going to end well.

"Bring in the monk. Let us get this wedding on the way. I grow tired of being in the same room with this scum." He slapped Aramis hard and stepped away.

Two of the men who had brought D'Artagnan and the other two into the room came in from a side door, escorting a little man in a homespun monk's cassock. The monk walked with slumped shoulders, the hood of his robe up and a Bible clutched in his arms.

"This is Brother Cornelius; the other monk is sick and could not come," said one of the men.

"I don't care if he's His Holiness the Pope, let's get this done," growled Moreau.

The monk, his head still bowed, moved in front of Aramis and Celine. As he opened his Bible, everyone turned to watch the ceremony. That was the moment that D'Artagnan had been waiting for. He kicked the leg of the man standing in front of him. The dagger he had up his sleeve came sliding down into his hand as he turned to slash at the guardsman at one side of him.

Athos and Porthos were not wasting any time, either. They grabbed Moreau's men standing next to them. Porthos slammed two of them into each other, making a most satisfying sound in the process. Meanwhile, Athos, fists flying, hit several of the men and sent them down. The three men grabbed dropped swords and pistols from the floor. There were still three of Moreau's men standing, their jaws hanging, seemingly not at all sure of whether to run or attack.

"Kill them!" screamed Moreau.

"I do not think so, Monsieur," said Aramis. He was on his feet, the chair empty, a sword in his hand. Celine stared at the whole scene, confused. "I give you my word that in spite of the compromising situation you found your daughter and myself in, I had not dishonored her. Also, I pledge to you that I did not come seeking you or your daughter, that we came to the town you live in purely by chance.

"Now that my cousins and this other gentleman have matters well in hand, remember that there are now four of us. I would not want to see Celine, who is truly a treasure, lose her father. We are going to leave now and will be gone from this town in a few hours and never trouble you again." He turned to D'Artagnan and the other two and said, "Come, gentlemen."

∞ ∞ ∞

"I thought you said we were going to leave within a few hours," D'Artagnan said as the four of them sat at a table in the inn where he had first encountered Athos and Porthos.

Porthos took a large bite out of the chicken that the tavern maid had just deposited in front of him. "You cannot expect a man to travel on an empty stomach. Eating is always a good reason for changing your plans, almost as good a one as drinking.

"True, sir," said D'Artagnan. "But don't you think that Monsieur Moreau will be watching? He does seem to wield a wee bit of power in this town. Am I not correct, innkeeper?"

The owner of the inn looked at the four men and shook his head. He had not been happy when they had come through his door in such a hurry--it suggested problems that he may not have wanted to be involved with. But the coins that had made their way into his till seemed to have allayed his dissatisfaction.

"The Moreau family has been prominent in this area for a long time. If you are making enemies of them, I would really prefer you to find some other place for your revelries."

"Worry not, my good man," said Athos. "We will be long gone before they are even aware that we were here. You have my word on that."

"Very well." The innkeeper shook his head as he started toward the kitchen. "Oh, Monsieur, did you find that lady you thought you had seen?"

"Indeed," nodded Athos, without looking up from his tankard. "And I thank God that she was not the person I thought she was."

"When they brought you in that door I wasn't sure," said Aramis, "if you were relieved to see the girl or to see me tied to that chair."

"Perhaps he thought being tied up would keep you from getting yourself and us further into trouble, if that were possible," said Porthos. "Speaking of being tied to that chair: how the dickens did you get loose? Was it the girl?"

"Hardly," said his cousin. "She seemed so angry and confused I think if someone had put a knife in her hand she would have used it on her father, or me, or both of us. When you three started that little diversion someone cut my ropes from behind. I didn't bother looking, just stepped in to help my relatives."

His cousins smiled in agreement at this statement. "It was Monsieur D'Largo who struck the first blow," Porthos acknowledged. "Although I'm sure we would have outnumbered them even without him."

The three cousins looked at each other and then at D'Artagnan. Just then a small robed figure came walking toward them from the direction of the kitchen. It was the monk, Brother Cornelius, only this time instead of a Bible he had a leather drinking mug in his hand.

"Actually, gentlemen," he said, "it was I who took care of the ropes."

This time D'Artagnan recognized the voice, just as he realized that the monk was actually somewhat larger than he had thought he was earlier in the evening, although not by much.

"Well, Brother Cornelius, or should I be calling you Montaigne?"

"Friend of yours, de Largo?" asked Porthos.

"You could say that," D'Artagnan nodded. "And I have a gut feeling he has been in the middle of all the events of the evening. Am I not right, old friend?"

Montaigne didn't speak until he had divested himself of the monk's robe, which he tossed into a corner of the room. Two cats, a yellow tabby and a gray one, began to sniff at the garment, but they soon found other smells from the kitchen demanding their attention.

"Well, perhaps I had planned to come to this charming little village, perhaps I was even looking for the family Moreau," he said. "Let us simply say that I had business with the head of the family and would prefer to be gone before he knows it was transacted."

"What sort of business?" asked Aramis.

Montaigne said nothing.

"Don't bother asking, my friend," said D'Artagnan. "Montaigne is good at keeping secrets."

"I have a feeling it involves politics," said Porthos. "I hate politics, don't you, de Largo?"

"I'm not fond of them, and, by the way, I should let you know that my name is not de Largo, it's D'Artagnan."

The three cousins sat staring at him for fully half a minute, the only sound being that of the crackling of the fire. Porthos took another swallow from his glass.

"Really," he said, then turned to Athos. "You owe me ten sous."

The oldest of the three Musketeers took out his purse and dropped several coins from it on the table in front of his cousin.

"I don't understand. How do you know who I am?" asked D'Artagnan, glancing toward Montaigne, who was smiling.

"It's quite simple, my friend," laughed Porthos. "I have been seeing a lady in Paris who is well acquainted with one Charlotte Blackson, a close friend of yours, I believe. You were even pointed out to me departing

Madam Blackson's residence before sunrise. My friend, you really need to be more careful about your comings and goings from a lady's boudoir."

"It is what I have said all along: women will be the death of us all," muttered Athos. "Besides, I have read *that* book. I had been wondering when we were going to cross paths with you."

"And we have, thus earning me some money." Porthos turned toward Athos. "Cousin Aramis, you owe us a little explanation about this evening."

Aramis fidgeted a moment, then took up the tale.

"Well," he began, looking everywhere but at his companions. "When we were in Paris, I met a young lady--I use the term loosely--and struck up an acquaintance. She was lovely, blonde with a slender figure. She was quite flirtatious. We arranged an assignation for later that evening. She pointed out her house and showed me an easy way of climbing into her window, out of view of passers-by. She warned me to be quiet as there were others who resided there." He paused for a moment before continuing. "I arrived at the right time and climbed through the window. There she lay on the bed. The covers were pulled up, almost covering her face, but I could see her sun-colored hair. I called her name and began to divest myself of encumbrances.

"Then things began to go wrong. When she opened her eyes she took one look at me and gasped. At that very moment I could tell that the young lady in the bed was not the one I had talked to earlier. I backed toward the window, apologizing for the mistake, when her father burst into the room and began screaming at me. I leaped for the window but the balls from his firearm creased my backside. I fell through before I could be injured further and escaped. The first "lady" must have had something against me or the other young woman to have done that, may she rot in Hell. There, you have it, and I swear that it is the truth. I owe my freedom and very life to you." Aramis took a long draught from his tankard and sat back in relief.

"Quite a story, cousin," Porthos said. "I think I will believe you. It's easier that way. But you left out how you came to be in the hands of said young lady's father."

Aramis shook his head and smiled. "Quite literally I came walking around the corner and found myself facing her, her father, and several of those rather doltish-looking fellows in his employ. Before I had a chance to unsheathe my sword, one of them got behind me and applied what felt like an iron bar to the back of my head. When I woke up I found out I was to be the guest of honor at a wedding and, I suspect, a funeral to follow immediately afterwards. It definitely made taking holy vows look quite appealing, which is what I intend to do, eventually."

"You've been saying that since you were ten years old, cousin, and I don't see you any closer now than you were then," said Athos.

"It will come," intoned Aramis.

"By the way," said D'Artagnan. "If you don't mind my asking, what are you three doing here? This hardly seems like an outpost for the king's Musketeers."

"It isn't," said Aramis. "We're here under orders. Several weeks ago Monsieur de Treville, commander of the Musketeer Corp, ordered us out of Paris; a little matter of too much dueling with the cardinal's guard. He stuck his finger on a map and found this delightful town, suggesting that we not return to Paris for some months."

"And yet, here you sit drinking with a lieutenant in the cardinal's guard," said Montaigne. D'Artagnan noticed that he did not mention his own connection to the Prime Minister of France.

"I will drink with any man who fights at my side," said Athos. "I care little what tabard he does or does not wear. Besides, who knows but we can convince you to transfer to the Musketeers."

"Me, a Musketeer? Hardly," laughed D'Artagnan.

The Hunt for The Red Cardinal

By
Bradley H. Sinor and
Susan P. Sinor

Chapter One

May 1636 Paris

One morning, Luc Boyea was passing by the radio room on the top floor of the Paris townhouse of Louis, Count de Soissons. His brother, André, who was responsible for receiving, transcribing, and delivering radio messages, worked there. André had just completed a transcription and was heading out to deliver it when he ran into Luc, nearly knocking him to the floor.

"Important message?" Luc asked, after steadying himself against the doorway.

"Very," his brother, who seemed hurried, replied almost in a whisper. "Don't ask what it is. I can't tell you that the queen is about to give birth." He realized what he had done, clapped his hands to his face and said, pleadingly, "Don't even mention what I said to yourself. I could get in a lot of trouble."

"The queen is . . .?" Luc looked around to see if anyone else was there, listening. "Don't worry. I won't even breathe it." But, he thought, I will remember it and listen at doors for anything I can hear. He had done that many times before, learning things he probably shouldn't know, but no one ever found him out. He was very reticent about telling anyone the secrets he kept.

His position at the townhouse was to do whatever he was told. That included taking messages to various people around the city, fetching anything his master requested, and staying up until all hours waiting for the count to dismiss him. His family had all worked for the count for generations. His father was the stable master, and his mother was the head housekeeper. Two of his sisters were housemaids, and his other brother, the eldest, oversaw the count's armory. They were at the historical home of the count's family in the village of Soissons. Only he and his brother, André, had gone to the Paris townhouse.

Luc somehow meant to advance his position in the household. He was old enough, he thought, to be responsible for something other than fetching and carrying.

Right then he arranged to find himself at any door which had conversations going on behind it. He had very good hearing and a very good memory of what he heard.

He followed his brother at a distance as he rushed down the sumptuously carpeted stairs and hallway to deliver the message. When he saw André leave the room where he had presented the message to the count, Luc calmly made his way in that direction, busying himself with the large bowl of flowers on the ornate gold-covered table beside the door. Presently, he heard the voices he hoped to hear.

"Somewhere to the west, not terribly far from Paris. I'm not sure just where. It is unknown if the child has been born yet, but I know that Richelieu," the name sounded as though it was a nasty taste in the speaker's mouth, "is going there." It was the voice of the count, and he was talking to his friend, Claude de Bourdeille, Comte de Montrésor, who was visiting. Luc knew just what to do to accomplish his goal.

∞ ∞ ∞

Charlotte Blackson, a wealthy divorcée of middle age, but hardly looking it, stretched and looked out the second-story window of her Paris townhouse. The open were blowing in the breeze, and the sun shone through the window on her golden hair, warming her creamy skin and highlighting her blue eyes. She realized that it was some time after dawn since she could hear the sounds of commerce in the street: venders hawked their wares, whether they were selling food, household goods, or themselves.

Wrapped only in a sheet, she was enjoying herself immensely. That was not unusual when she was in the presence of Charles. He made her happy, and she liked being happy. Much of her past had not been happy, so she took it whenever she could get it.

Charles, lying on the large bed, rose up on one elbow in order to see her face. "Charlotte, what are you thinking about? You're certainly quiet right now."

She smiled up at him, turning her head to admire his bare chest and his handsome, chiseled face, and brown eyes.

"Oh, nothing, really. I'm just trying to avoid doing anything constructive for a while. I know I have many things that I must accomplish, but I just don't want to right now." She turned the rest of the way to face him, stretching again, the sheet slipping from around her. "And what are you thinking of, my young guardsman?"

"Ah. The past several minutes, for one. And the view just now is most delightful, m'lady." He made as much of a bow as he could from his position. "But my leisure brings to mind that I am not with my fellow guardsman, wherever they went with the cardinal yesterday morning. As much as I like being with you, I don't like not being with them on whatever it is they are doing. It is my duty, after all," he said with a flourish of his hand, which came close to meeting with Charlotte's head.

"Of course, my darling, but you do get a day off now and then," she said as she leaned away to keep his hand from knocking against her. "Besides, I'd rather you were here with me."

He had leaned farther toward her and bent his head for another kiss when there was a knock at the door. "Madame. Madame?"

"Yes, Sophie?"

"A letter has come for Monsieur D'Artagnan. It was sent to him at his barracks, but the messenger was told he might be here."

Charlotte looked at D'Artagnan, rose, wrapped herself in a dressing gown, and went to the bedroom door. Opening it just wide enough for the paper to pass through it, she replied, "Thank you, Sophie. I'll give it to him."

"Yes, Madame." Sophie, as Charlotte knew, was aware that the gentleman was with her, but neither would ever let on what they knew. It would certainly not be proper form for a servant to have any opinion about what the master or mistress did. However, Charlotte knew that servants always knew what was going on in the house.

"A letter has come for you, Charles," she said, waving it at him. "I wonder from whom it could be. Are you expecting a letter, my love?" She waved it around some more, trying to keep it from him, her robe loosening as she spun. He rose, not bothering with a robe, and joined the game, chasing her around the room. When he was able to grab it from her hand, he looked at the stamp. "The seal is blank, but it does have my name on it, so . . ." He broke the seal and unfolded it. He started reading it to her. "To Monsieur Charles D'Artagnan, from His Eminence, Cardinal . . ." He read the rest quickly, reread the letter, and folded the page.

"My dear Charlotte, I must leave. The cardinal wants to see me at once." He headed for the door, taking his hat and placing it on his head.

"Darling, perhaps you should put your trousers on first."

"Oh, yes." He turned toward her, flourishing his hat and bowing. "If I must."

"But it is still early, my dear. Must you leave now?" she whispered, reclining enticingly on the bed.

He gazed at her for a moment, then sighing, replied, "I must leave regardless of the hour whenever the cardinal summons me." He quickly dressed himself and left the room before she could ask any of the many questions he was sure she had.

She sighed. Well, she thought, I have things to do myself. Best get on with it.

∞ ∞ ∞

It was noon when Charles D'Artagnan entered the parish church, Saint-Étienne-du-Grès, as instructed by the message sent him by François Leclerc, Cardinal Tremblay, and found the statue of Notre Dame de Bonne Délivrance, The Black Madonna, indicated in the note. D'Artagnan was of average height and build, which belied his strength and skill with weapons. His demeanor led his betters to believe him of average intelligence, which was a mistake. His friends knew this, as did his master, Armand Jean du Plessis, Cardinal Richelieu. His countenance, however, immediately caught the attention of all around him, especially of women of any age.

As directed by the letter, he was not wearing his usual uniform but clothing a laborer might wear, something he might be overlooked wearing. He was wearing plain breeches and stockings and a simple shirt and sleeved cloak. His boots were the ones he always wore. He would not wear footwear other than his own comfortable and sturdy boots. He waited patiently. Patience was a virtue he had cultivated in his career as one of Cardinal Richelieu's guards. Sometimes he thought the motto of the Guard should be, as the up-timers said, "Hurry up and wait."

He didn't have to wait very long, though. Before he knew someone was near, he heard a low voice saying, "Thank you for being prompt." He recognized Cardinal Tremblay's distinctive voice.

Out of the corner of his eye, D'Artagnan glimpsed a tall man in a monk's robe with the hood covering his head.

"Don't look at me, just look around as if you were admiring the art. But be attentive. I have grave news and a task for you."

D'Artagnan nodded slowly and gazed at a painting hanging nearby. "What is the news?" he asked in a low voice. "And the task you have for me?"

"I will explain when you attend me this afternoon at my residence. You will be admitted at the servants' entrance. Come at four o'clock and be ready to travel."

Without another word, the tall monk turned and walked farther into the church. D'Artagnan waited a moment, then turned the other way and walked slowly toward the door.

∞ ∞ ∞

Back in his room at the barracks, D'Artagnan mused on what might have happened to cause a respected man such as Cardinal Tremblay to be so secretive. He knew that her majesty, the queen, was in confinement awaiting the birth of the royal heir, but that should be another month away. He also knew that Cardinal Richelieu had taken a small contingent of guards and left for an undisclosed location the day before. His not being with them was a result of his attending to other matters. And where, he wondered, was he to go? And why was it at Cardinal Tremblay's direction instead of his master, Cardinal Richelieu's?

D'Artagnan did as instructed, packing a saddlebag and arriving on horseback at the cardinal's home at the appointed hour.

"My name is Charles D'Artagnan," he told the maid who opened the back door when he knocked. "I have an appointment with His Eminence."

After looking him up and down appreciatively, she said, "Yes, monsieur, come with me. You are expected. My name is Audrey." The maid led him down a plain but clean hallway and handed him off to a man D'Artagnan assumed was the butler. He was led up the back staircase to a room on the second floor. The man knocked on the door, opened it for D'Artagnan to enter, and then closed the door again.

It was a small room, as the rooms of a cardinal's residence went, with two chairs, placed on either side of a massive, ornate fireplace. Farther from the fireplace was a beautifully carved mahogany table which would seat six, with heavily brocaded chairs to match. The room was at the back of the house, looking out over the kitchen garden, with a tall stone wall at the back of the property. Heavy red velvet drapes were pulled back from the windows to admit sunlight.

"Ah, you've arrived. Good," the cardinal said as D'Artagnan kneeled, and kissed the cardinal's ring. "Would you have some wine?"

Cardinal Tremblay, known for his austerity, was a bearded man in his late fifties. He kept the residence and servants he was accorded due to his office, but refused extravagance and preferred the cloak and persona of Pere' Joseph.

D'Artagnan replied, "Yes, thank you, Your Eminence."

Cardinal Tremblay poured for both of them and gestured for D'Artagnan to sit, indicating one of the chairs by the fireplace, where a small fire had been lit.

"Your Eminence, you hinted that something has happened."

"Yes, it has. I'll tell you the whole story, but it must be kept between us." The cardinal took a deep breath, exhaled, and then took a sip of his wine. "Two days ago, Cardinal Richelieu received a radio message that the queen would give birth very soon. He told the king, who insisted on going along, but dressed as one of the cardinal's guards. In the group were a dozen guards, the king, the cardinal, and his secretary, Servien. Along the way they were set upon by what was thought at first to be a group of highwaymen." He paused, took another breath, another sip, and continued. "His Majesty was killed and the cardinal was injured on his side by a gunshot. Servien and one guard got away unscathed. They escaped with the cardinal to a nearby church, leaving the rest behind. If they had stayed, they would have probably all been killed, and no one would have known who the killers were."

D'Artagnan reacted with a gasp and a cry. "Not the king! What terrible news. And the cardinal? If only I had been with him, perhaps this horrible thing would not have happened. What of his circumstance?"

Cardinal Tremblay went on, dryly. "I doubt that one more guard would have changed the outcome of the attack, regardless of your prowess with the sword or the musket. It is by God's grace that you still live to carry out what needs now to be done. Cardinal Richelieu's situation is unknown, except that when the young guard who informed me of this left the church to return to Paris, he was alive."

"And the queen? Has she been told?"

Tremblay nodded. "The secretary, Servien, went on to the destination and gave them the news."

"And the heir? Has the child been born? Is it a boy?"

The cardinal replied, "I don't have that information yet. Regardless, your orders are to go to the small monastery at Clairefontaine, where the cardinal was taken. If the cardinal is alive and improving, he must be removed from the monastery as soon as he can travel."

"Yes, Your Eminence," he said. "But if he has succumbed, God forbid, to his injuries, what should be done?"

"If he is alive, time will be of the essence. If he is able to travel, he should be moved to a more secure location. Otherwise, a . . . replacement . . . must be found and persuaded to go in his stead."

"A replacement? What do you mean?"

"I mean that Gaston should believe that the cardinal is alive but not know where he is."

"If he is alive and able to travel, I would request that trusted friends of mine be included in the party. They would be invaluable in keeping the cardinal protected."

"Who are these friends of yours?" Cardinal Tremblay asked.

"They are in the king's Musketeers, Athos de la Fere, Porthos du Vallon, and Aramis, also known as René d'Herblay. They will be loyal to the throne and to the Queen and the heir. They excel at shooting and are excellent swordsmen, as well," D'Artagnan explained. "Also, they are all cousins."

"And you vouch for them?"

"On my life," D'Artagnan replied.

The cardinal thought a moment. "And if a . . .substitute . . . is needed?"

"I should like them to accompany me regardless. Since the king was murdered, his Musketeers will likely disband, and my friends might be in danger. It could be safer for them to leave Paris."

"I will send for them while you are away. I will provide food and drink for your journey so you won't have to stop for it on the way." Tremblay handed him a sealed letter. "Give this to the abbot when you arrive," he said, and called for a servant to go to the kitchen and procure the provisions.

"Might I ask the name of the guard who survived?"

"Of course. He is Jean D'Aubisson."

"Thank the good Lord," D'Artagnan exclaimed in relief. "He is the youngest of the guards, and I have a fondness for him, as he reminds me of myself. Do you know where he is now?"

"Yes. I myself sent him on a journey. He should be in no danger, so don't be concerned about him," the cardinal said.

"Where is the place that I am going?" he asked.

"Oh, yes. The place is southwest of here, near Rambouillet: the village of Clairefontaine. I will draw you a rough map." He took quill and parchment and drew on it, adding directions, then handed it to D'Artagnan.

"And where should I ultimately take his enimence? Or his replacement?" The words sounded very wrong to D'Artagnan.

"I have a place in mind which should be safe for my friend, but is a far distance from here, so it may take you many weeks or months to arrive. I will give you directions when you return."

"If the cardinal cannot ride, how should he be moved?"

"The monastery is not wealthy and would not be able to help monetarily with this journey, but I believe they have a small cart they can provide. I can provide a horse for the cart." He handed the guard a small leather bag. "This is in case you need funds for this first trip. I will give you more to fund your journey when you return. Now, go at once," Cardinal Tremblay said. "By the way, I think it best if you use another name."

"Other than my own. Certainly. What name should I use?"

"Allais, I think, would be suitable. Allais Dubois. Report to me when you return. God go with you."

D'Artagnan stood, bowed to the Cardinal, and took his leave.

Chapter Two

Luc Boyea had intended to set out from the Count's townhouse immediately upon hearing the conversation regarding Queen Anne. He had borrowed a horse from the Count's stable to ride as fast as he could through the streets of Paris, then west and a little south from there. However, it took a short while for Boyea to actually leave the Count's townhouse, since he had to procure money as well as the horse. He put a few items in the horse's saddlebag with all the cash he had squirreled away from his pay. Not knowing how long he'd be gone, he also tucked in a change of clothing, something non-descript if he needed to be anonymous, and a bit of food from the kitchens where a cousin worked.

He had no map, so he wasn't quite sure where his destination on the west side of Paris was. He rode to the edge of the city and turned slightly south on a road that seemed likely. The road happened to be the road the cardinal's party had taken just hours before. He was far enough behind the cardinal's party that he did not catch up to them but followed from a distance. When he arrived at the scene where the attack had taken place, somewhat past midnight, he was stunned. There were bodies lying everywhere, most of them dead. He could tell they were the Red Cardinal's men by their uniforms.

He searched for anyone who might still be alive and found a man who seemed near death but was still conscious.

"You," he said to the man. "Were you with the cardinal? Who attacked you? Where were you going?"

The man breathed heavily and pointed, as if to say, that way. Boyea checked to see if anyone else was still living. The only face he recognized was the face of the king, who was certainly dead. He saw no one who looked like Cardinal Richelieu.

There was no road leading the way indicated, but Boyea went anyway, leaving the man to complete his death.

After riding over land for some way, he found himself at a small village. It was some time until dawn, so he decided to find a place in the nearby woods to rest until it was late enough to inquire at the village inn for information.

While looking for a likely place to camp, he passed a church with another large building behind it.

A monastery? he thought. I could request shelter there later. Then he thought, I have nowhere to leave the horse and my belongings. I'll tell the brothers that I've been robbed and have nothing. I can take the horse to the stable in the village in the morning and request shelter for tomorrow night from the monks.

He rode on and found a grassy patch next to a river with a gentle bank. He tied the horse to a tree limb, settled on the ground with his back to the tree, and dozed until the morning sun woke him.

∞ ∞ ∞

D'Artagnan arrived at his destination, the church at Clairefontaine, the next afternoon after a hard ride. He had left Paris immediately after speaking with Cardinal Tremblay and had ridden all night, only stopping briefly to rest, feed, and water the horse. The trip had been long and not as smooth as he would have liked. The way was hilly and rocky, and the ground was muddy in places, as it had rained the day before. There was always the possibility of his horse tripping and falling.

The church compound was a short way outside the village and was comprised of the church itself, the chapter house, and a few outbuildings. Entering and looking through the foyer, he saw monks at prayer. He stood in the doorway to the sanctuary and waited for one of them to conclude his prayers. He examined the interior of the country church, finding it plain compared to the cathedrals of Paris, but it was beautiful, never-the-less. There were several paintings of the Madonna and other historical scenes, statues, and stained-glass windows. The altar had been supurbly painted and was a sight to behold, with a stark crucifix above it. The monks sat on benches that reached from one side to the other. At that time of day, the benches had only the monks and a few of the townspeople on them. On regular days and times of worship, they were filled with pious adults trying to control active children and crying infants.

Presently one of the monks rose and noticed the visitor.

"Good day, monsieur. I am Brother Paulo. Have you come to worship or make your confession?" the monk asked D'Artagnan.

"In other circumstances, it would be my desire. But I am on official business for the Church and must speak to your abbot."

"Then please follow me to our chapter house. Our abbot will see you." The monk led him along a covered walkway to an adjacent building, which housed a monastery small enough that everyone knew everyone else.

When they entered, the monk called to another, "Brother Julius, is Abbe' Michel available to see this traveler. He says he's here on church business."

D'Artagnan saw another monk pass by and stared at him for a moment. He looked very like Cardinal Richelieu, although he seemed younger and more robust. The Cardinal had been gaunt as long as D'Artagnan had known him. If, God forbid, the cardinal should not survive, this man could very well take his place on the journey.

"Abbe' Michel has just entered his office." Brother Julius said, looking at D'Artagnan. "Please follow me."

Brother Julius led him along a hallway with several doors on each side, then knocked on one of them. After being bidden to enter, the monk opened the door and motioned D'Artagnan through it.

D'Artagnan bowed to the abbot, a thin, middle-aged man with a well-manicured tonsure, and said "Abbe', forgive me for coming unannounced. My name is Charles D'Artagnan of Cardinal Richeliou's guard. I come at the behest of Cardinal Tremblay. Here is a letter he bade me present to you. I believe it will explain the reason for my presence." He handed the letter to the abbot, who opened and read it immediately.

"I see," the abbot said, folding it and sliding it into a drawer in his desk. Then he rose and walked around it. "But I'm afraid he is not up to seeing visitors right now."

"But he is still alive? What is his condition?"

"He is very weak. It is hard to tell if he will live or not. One of the monks is with him, praying for his recovery, but only God knows what will happen."

"I know he is probably asleep, but may I, at least, look in at him? I promise I will not try to wake him; I just want to reassure myself that he still lives."

"Of course," the abbot replied, and led him to a remote room in a mostly-unused wing of the chapterhouse where the cardinal had been taken.

When they entered, the cardinal was asleep, another monk keeping watch over him. The abbot motioned the monk to leave the room, then closed the door behind himself as he followed.

D'Artagnan stood, looking at his master, assessing his condition. Presently Richelieu opened his eyes and saw his visitor standing there.

He said in a soft, breathy voice, slowly, "My dear D'Artagnan, have you come to see me?"

D'Artagnan bowed and knelt by the bed to kiss the ring, but the ring wasn't on his finger. "Eminence, I have come to see you, but has your ring been stolen or lost?"

"I gave it to Servien to take with him."

"Cardinal Tremblay sent me to see you. He told me of the recent events. I grieve for his Majesty and my brother guards, and am grateful that you still live."

"I, as well," the cardinal replied. He made an effort to say more, but could not, and seemed to go back to sleep. However, after only a moment he roused and said, "I must leave this place. I am a danger to it."

D'Artagnan had to lean close to hear what the cardinal said, but understood perfectly what he meant. Seeing his master like that seemed impossible to D'Artagnan. Cardinal Richelieu had always been commanding, intelligent and sometimes abrupt and unpleasant, but always strong. D'Artagnan had been a faithful and loyal guard since he had joined the guard and would remain so until he had successfully delivered the cardinal to wherever he was going.

The abbot opened the door and motioned for D'Artagnan to leave the room as the monk guarding the cardinal returned. "We have a guest room you may rest in. I know you must have ridden all night from Paris to get here. Attend Vespers and eat our evening meal with us and then sleep."

"Thank you, Abbe', but I have plans to make. His Eminence must be moved to a safer place as soon as he is able to travel," D'Artagnan said.

"Yes, but right now he is too ill. However, you are correct that he must go. His presence also potentially places this monastery in danger. But Vespers will begin soon. Then we will eat. We all think better with food and rest."

"Yes, Abbe'. Oh, if you speak of me to anyone else, Cardinal Tremblay has suggested that I use the nom de plume of Allais Dubois."

"To keep your true identity a secret?" the abbot said. "I will use that name for you in the future."

D'Artagnan did as told, joining the others at Vespers and the evening meal. Then he went to the guest room and slept through the night, awaking at the call to Vigils. It was later than he had planned to wake, so he quickly rose, dressed and joined the monks on their way to the chapel. Sine he hadn't attended any of the rituals in a very long time, he felt the need for the peace he thought he needed, if only for a short time. While the other monks were praying the prescribed prayers, he prayed fervently for the cardinal's recovery. Afterward, he kept his thoughts to himself as he ate.

D'Artagnan looked in on the cardinal, who was asleep, and he decided not to disturb him. Instead, he went to look for the Abbot.

"Abbe', I know that the cardinal is not able to travel yet, but I believe, and I think Cardinal Tremblay would agree, that we must make the arrangements now," D'Artagnan said.

"I agree. What will you need? We are a poor monastery, not materially wealthy as some are, but wealthy in spirit," the abbot said, "but we can provide food and drink and, I would think, a horse and small cart for him to ride in."

"That is much appreciated, but Cardinal Tremblay has already provided a horse and is financing the journey. I do have need of the cart, though. I have friends who should be able to go along to assure safety. But I need to ask you another question. How many of the brothers here know the identity of your patient?"

"Well, when he was brought in to us it was very late and not many of us were awake. There was some disturbance, of course. The Night Watcher let them in and roused me. Two or three other brothers were awake and helped carry him to the table where he was examined by our resident healer, Brother André. Our 'patient' was badly wounded and needed immediate care, so those present did what needed to be done. Some of them went to the chapel to pray. But the rest of the residents were left sleeping and were not told of his identity."

"So only those five or six of you that were present know who he is? Are you sure of their loyalty?" D'Artagnan asked.

"Their loyalty?" the abbot replied. "Of course they are loyal. They are men of God."

"I mean their loyalty to the Crown. Were you told of what happened to cause the Cardinal's injuries, and what happened to the others in his party?"

"We were told that there had been an attack and that everyone, except the three that came here, were killed," the abbot said.

"Do you know any details of that attack?"

"No, just what I told you. Can you say what the details are? Who was killed? What can you tell me?"

D'Artagnan thought for a moment, and made a decision. "The news will come out, and probably soon. It might be best if you, yourself, know what happened, but please, no one else must know until it is made public to everyone." He took a breath. Cardinal Tremblay hadn't authorized him to reveal the details, even to the abbot, but he continued anyway. "The party was going to visit the Queen in her confinement. The cardinal had received news that the birth would be soon. He advised the King that he was going, and His Majesty insisted on going along, disguised as one of the guards. The instigators of the attack had gotten word somehow of what was going on and staged the attack, killing the king along with all the guards except the one that guided the cardinal and his secretary to you."

The abbot gasped, "But how could someone know. Did the cardinal tell anyone in the court? Anyone who had reason to want the king dead? Or the cardinal, even? How did they know where to go?"

"I'm afraid I don't know. I do know that Monsieur Gaston, when he receives the news, is certain to claim the crown for himself. That is where the danger to this abbey lies. Gaston and his brother, César Vendôme, hate Cardinal Richelieu. If the attack was orchestrated by them, then the cardinal was probably their target. That the king was also killed would be a welcome bonus to them. That is why the cardinal must be moved as soon as possible."

"Of course. I will see that your provisions are ready when you need them."

"Thank you, but, as I said, Cardinal Tremblay has provided what we will need. I must go back to Paris to collect my friends, the horse and instructions on where we are to go."

"Go with God, my son. Be safe. I think the future of France may lie with you."

Chapter Three

A tall, young, beardless man, dressed in the clothing of a country peasant, approached the door to the country church and knocked. It was late, he was tired and hungry and on foot. When the door opened, he said, "Can you help a poor man with lodgings for the night? And maybe a little food?"

"Of course," the monk at the door said. "Please come in. All are welcome in God's house. I don't recognize you. Are you from the village?"

"No. I'm traveling to Paris to stay with my sister and her husband. I was riding with only my meager belongings until I was beset by robbers. They took my horse and all I had. I barely got away. I was fortunate they didn't take my clothing, as well. But, with a little help, I'll be able to get to Paris, where I can work for my sister's husband."

"You poor man. Please come eat with us. What is your name?" the monk asked "I am Brother Jacques."

"My name is Luc. Luc Boyea." He had decided that it was easier to use his own name than have to remember a different one. No one there would have heard of him; he was only a lowly servant, after all. "I'm traveling from Ablis. I don't even know exactly where I am, now." He followed Brother Jacques through the church and into the dining hall of the chapter house. It was a medium-sized room with several rows of long tables and benches. On the far side was a door to another room.

He inhaled the aromas coming from the kitchen appreciatively. They smelled delicious. He hadn't had anything to eat since he had left Paris the day before, and was very hungry.

"We have rooms for travelers in need. You may stay one night or two before you go on your way. Sit here," he was told. "Someone will bring you some dinner in a moment."

The monk walked away toward the door which must have been to the kitchen. Monsieur Boyea could hear the noise of pots and utensils from that direction. He looked around the room; some of the tables and benches were occupied. This was obviously not a silent order; there was much talking and some laughter. They seemed a happy lot, and welcoming. That was good. Monsieur Boyea was on a mission.

Another monk set a plate on the table. "I hope you will enjoy your meal. I am Brother Maurice. It is simple food, but we are simple folks here. We do serve good wine, though." He filled a glass from a pitcher of wine and handed it to Monsieur Boyea.

After Boyea finished his meal of, he assumed, homegrown vegetables, fresh bread and cheese, both probably made there in the monastery, Brother Jacques returned to guide him to a small room with a narrow bed, a small table and a chair. "I think this should serve you for the brief time you will be with us," he said.

"Thank you. I am very grateful for your generosity."

"You are quite welcome," Brother Jacques said, and walked away.

Monsieur Boyea took off his boots and lay down on the bed, meaning to stay awake, but instead fell asleep.

∞ ∞ ∞

D'Artagnan arrived in Paris just after dark the next day. After sending a message to Cardinal Tremblay that he had returned, he planned to retire for a meal and few hours' sleep at Charlotte's townhouse.

Charlotte Blackson was at home when he arrived.

"Charles, where have you been? I was worried sick that you had come to harm." She rushed at him and embraced him.

"I was sent somewhere by the cardinal. I regret that I had no time to send you a message first," he told her.

"Naughty boy. I will forgive you, but you must earn my forgiveness first. Come with me." She headed for the stairs, beckoning him to follow. "This way, Charles."

"My dear Charlotte, nothing would make me happier than attempting to earn your forgiveness, but duty is not finished with me. I have to leave again, and have time, most likely, for only a few hours of sleep. This time I may not be back for a very long time," he told her.

"What? But why? Tell me what you must do."

"I'm so sorry, but I've been sworn to secrecy and may tell no one."

"No one? Then you must make it up to me now. Then I will let you sleep."

Resigned and excited, he followed her up the stairs.

He was awakened by a messenger with a note from the cardinal at seven o'clock the next morning

"Please attend me at eight o'clock this morning, as before.
Only one of your friends was found. He will be in
attendance."

He dressed and packed his saddlebag, then ate a quick meal and left. Charlotte was still asleep, and he didn't want to wake her, so he left a note for her.

My dear Charlotte, I have been summoned by the cardinal to go on an important journey. I believe that in time you will understand the circumstances that have caused my absence from you. Pray forgive me for not revealing all to you, as I have been forbidden to speak of this. I will miss you every day that I am gone, and hope to rejoin you without excessive delay. All regards, Charles.

As it was near to eight o'clock, D'Artagnan left immediately for the meeting, taking his horse as he was sure to be leaving for Clairefontaine immediately. It was a lovely morning. The trees had begun to produce leaves and flowers were popping up with buds almost ready to burst. He arrived at his destination a few minutes early, and knocked at the servant's entrance.

"Good evening, Audrey," he said to the kitchen maid who opened the door. "His Eminence has summoned me, but I am a little early. Might I enter anyway?"

"But of course, monsieur. Would you like a bite to eat? Breakfast is just over and there is some left." She smiled at him as she held open the door.

Since he hadn't eaten before he left, and thought it might be awhile before he could eat again, he said, "That would be welcome, Audrey. Thank you." He entered into the hallway that led to the kitchen, into which they went. Audrey had him sit at the large kitchen table and brought him a plate of bread and cheese, with a small glass of small beer.

Just as D'Artagnan swallowed the last bite of cheese, the butler arrived to take him to the cardinal. He quickly finished the drink, and with a nod of thanks to the kitchen maid, he left.

"Ah, D'Artagnan, how was your journey?" the cardinal said as D'Artagnan knelt to kiss his ring. "But more importantly, how fares the cardinal?" Cardinal Tremblay asked, indicating a chair at the table. "I'm afraid that the only Musketeer I could find on such short notice was Athos. He should be here shortly." Tremblay poured two cups of tea as D'Artagnan sat.

"Your Eminence, the journey was tiring, but no matter. I found Cardinal Richelieu alive, but very weak and unable to travel yet. He insists he will be well enough to travel before long, and reiterates the necessity of doing so. I have set the plan in motion."

"Good, good. Let us pray that when you return there he will be stronger and able to travel."

There was a rap at the door, which opened to admit Athos.

"D'Artagnan! How do you fare? It has been awhile since we have met," the young musketeer cried. He was shorter than D'Artagnan by some two inches, and slim, with dark hair and beard. He wore a costume similar to D'Artagnan's. After the two embraced, D'Artagnan indicated Cardinal Tremblay.

"Athos, have you met His Eminence, Cardinal Tremblay?"

Athos turned and knelt to the cardinal, kissing his ring. "Eminence, please accept my sincere apology for greeting my friend first."

"I understand, but please seat yourself. We have much to discuss." The cardinal poured another cup of tea and put it in front of Athos.

"Your message gave no information on the reason for your summons." Athos sat and took a sip of the tea, smiling appreciatively.

"The reason is this in a nutshell: Cardinal Richelieu left a few days ago to visit the queen after receiving notice that she was about to give birth. Yes, I know this was early. He informed the king, who insisted on going along disguised as one of his guards. Somewhere along the way they were attacked. All the guards but one were killed. Cardinal Richelieu was injured. His servant and one uninjured guard escaped with him to a monastery."

"Were you the uninjured guard?" Athos turned toward D'Artagnan.

"I was not with them," was the reply.

"Thank God for that, my friend," Athos said. "But what of the king? Was he the uninjured guard?"

"No. I'm afraid that the His Majesty was killed, as well."

Athos gasped. "What terrible news. We must search for the villains!" He began to stand.

"An admirable thought," Cardinal Tremblay said, waving Athos back to his seat. "But misguided. We do know who the villains are, but they are inaccessible, for now. There is a more pressing task at the moment." Cardinal Tremblay looked at Athos, then at D'Artagnan. "Back to the business at hand."

"But why have you summoned me?" Athos asked, looking at the cardinal. "Are you asking me to assist with this task?"

"I am," the cardinal replied.

"I will give whatever assistance I can; I am at your service, Your Eminence" Athos assured the two men.

"The task," Cardinal Tremblay said, "is to remove the cardinal from the monastery where he is being cared for and take him to a safer place to recover from his wounds. I also ask that you use another name on the journey."

Athos thought a moment, not wanting to refuse a cardinal or a friend, but reluctant to agree to protecting a man for whom he had no fondness. Finally, he realized that it was something he had to do. "A false name?"

"Yes. Gerard Le Roi would be a good name to use."

D'Artagnan took up the story. "Sir, I spotted a monk at Clairefontaine who looks very much like the cardinal. In the remote chance that the cardinal, er, dies before the journey begins, I could ask the abbot if this monk could go in his place."

Cardinal Tremblay thought a moment. "Very good. Let us pray it will not be necessary. If it is not, perhaps you should call the cardinal by this monk's name."

"His name is Brother Etienne. We will use that name when needed," D'Artagnan assured him.

Cardinal Tremblay paused a moment before continuing. "I would like you to leave at once for the monastery, and then to leave as soon as possible with the cardinal. I know of a place which should be safe, but it's some weeks' ride from here, at least, and I know the cardinal is weak. I have an itinerary that could help you find your destination. The two of you must return to him and prepare him for the journey. If you leave now, you should arrive by late evening. Sleep when you arrive; your journey will be long and possibly fraught with danger. You must be at your best."

"Your Eminence, I have an uncomfortable question." At the cardinal's nod, D'Artagnan continued. "What should we do if, God forbid, the cardinal should die during the journey? And what if it should happen when other people are around, such as at an inn."

The cardinal thought a moment. "If such a thing should happen, this is what I think should be done. If it is at an inn, since you all are traveling incognito and, if asked, your story is that you are taking him to his family's home in the west, you will transport his body out of the town. When you are well away from there, or if he should die in an uninhabited area, bury him in the woods, taking care to remember where."

D'Artagnan took a deep breath. "I understand, but regret, the need to do so. Is the grave to be marked so that others can find it to bury him properly?"

"That is correct. Then go on your way, and at every town and city spread the rumor that he has been seen in a different one."

He handed D'Artagnan a letter and a package. "This is another letter for the abbot, and this package contains funds for the trip. It should be sufficient, but be careful with it. There won't be more." Another pause.

"Of course, Eminence. You said you have an itinerary?"

"Yes." He handed D'Artagnan a sealed document. "It is the most direct route, but I know that sometimes the most direct is not the best. You will be the best judge. I have included a list of several safe people, who will be sympathetic to our cause. Use them if you need to. I have provisions ready for you, packed on a horse you may take. Yes, I know that the Abbot said he would give you a horse, but his is not a wealthy abbey, as, I'm sure, he already told you. Now he may keep his horse and give you just the cart. I know it's early, but time is of the essence. Be sure to be at your first stop within two days. Now go."

Athos and D'Artagnan were dismissed.

"I can't believe what I have learned tonight," Athos said as they left Cardinal Tremblay's residence after being given the extra horse and provisions. "The king, dead; Cardinal Richelieu gravely injured. What will happen to our beloved France now?"

"This is something we must not talk about when near others. No one must know but those of us who already know." They talked in low voices as they walked their horses through the streets.

"But what about Porthos and Aramis? Are they to be left out?"

"Cardinal Tremblay failed to find them. Are they away on their own business?" D'Artagnan asked.

"Not that I know of."

"They may still show up and get the message from the cardinal. Perhaps they will join us after all. The future may be unknowable, but we must do our best to guess correctly."

They mounted their horses and rode quickly toward Clairefontaine and the monastery.

Chapter Four

"Eminence, a message for you," Cardinal Tremblay's secretary, Pascal, said.

"A message? Do you know who brought it?" the cardinal asked him.

"No, sir. The housemaid received it. She didn't recognize the messenger," he replied as he handed the sealed missive over. "And, as you can see, the stamp is blank."

"Hm. I have been hoping for a return message. I wonder if this is it." He picked up his letter knife and slit it open. "Thank you, Pascal."

He unfolded it and read, then got out a sheet of his own blank stationary and began to write. Finishing, he folded and sealed it with his own blank stamp he kept for anonymous correspondence. On the front he penned two names.

"Pascal, please have this sent to one or both of these two men at the King's Musketeers' barracks. I think there won't be a reply."

∞ ∞ ∞

Since it was late when he arrived, it was morning bells that woke Monsieur Boyea. The monastery was busy with the monks going to morning prayers. He quickly rose and pulled his boots on. He then joined them, moving smoothly from the chapter house to the chapel. During the prayers, instead of bowing his head, he looked around surreptitiously. He was looking for a particular face, one he was familiar with by having seen the person during his stay in Paris.

"There! That looks much like him," he thought. "But younger. It could be, though. I must keep an eye on him."

After the morning service, he followed the others to the dining hall. It was a meager breakfast of thin porridge and bread, but it was filling. He hadn't had much time to eat as he searched the countryside to find the famed cardinal for his master. As he ate, he looked around for the man he had seen that looked like Richelieu. The man wasn't in the dining hall, but a plump young monk sat down beside him and began to talk to him.

"What a lovely day our Lord has given us, monsieur. I am Brother Xavier, new to this monastery. I understand that you are just stopping on your way to Paris. I've never been to Paris. I hear it has very grand cathedrals, and, of course, Their Majesties live there." He finally paused to take a mouthful.

"Good morning, Brother Xavier," he said. "My name is Luc, and, yes, I am on my way to Paris." He lowered his voice. "I understand I am not the only visitor here. I thought I overheard someone say that a man came here, and that he may be Cardinal Richelieu. Now that would be a man of God to talk to. He must be a great teacher, as well."

"Yes, I think I heard that, also. I don't remember where. How I would like to learn from him," Brother Xavier said.

"But if he's here, why could you not talk to him?"

"I also heard a rumor that he is gravely injured, and was to leave soon for somewhere else," the young monk said. "I fear I won't have the opportunity."

Boyea thought quickly. "But if you were to go along with him, you would have vast opportunity. With his tutoring, perhaps you could be a cardinal someday."

The monk's eyes grew large. "Yes. I perhaps could, couldn't I?" he replied. "But how would I manage to get permission? I haven't been here but only a few days."

"Maybe if you were to talk to the abbot. If he knew how much you want to learn from the great cardinal, maybe he would let you go? Perhaps you could help care for him on the way."

"I could. I have had some medical training. I will go to the abbot and make my request. He'll probably say no, but I will have tried. Thank you, Monsieur Luc. Thank you."

"If you are allowed to go, I would very much like to hear what you learn from the cardinal. Would it be possible for you to send letters to me in Paris, telling me what he has taught you? I can give you my sister's address."

"I suppose I could do that. If I am allowed to go, of course. And if I have the means to write and post letters."

Boyea searched amongst his clothing for a bit of paper and writing implement, which he knew he didn't have. "I'm afraid I have nothing to write the address on. Could you, perhaps, find a scrap to write it on? Then find me and I will tell you the address."

"I'll see what I can do, Monsieur Luc."

"Thank you, Brother Xavier. It is my dream to become a priest, but I fear I will never be able to realize it. But learning anything from such a great man of God would be a blessing to me," Boyea told him.

With that, Brother Xavier took his plate and bowl to the kitchen, then headed toward the abbot's office.

Monsieur Boyea followed the monks to their next prayer services, looking for the man he thought might be Richelieu, again. He caught glimpses of him, but never got close enough to confirm his identity. The monk did look a little too healthy to have been wounded, though. Regardless, Boyea decided to wait until night and search the building.

After the monks' noon repast, during an afternoon prayer service, Boyea left the monastery and walked to the village. He had stabled his horse there, with his belongings stored with it.

"Good afternoon, monsieur," he said to the stable master. "I need to send a message. Could you tell me if there is anyone who could take my letter to its recipient?"

"Of course, Monsieur Boyea. My son works as a messenger when needed. Do you have paper and ink, or do you need it provided?"

"Excellent. I have what I need in a saddlebag, if you will bring it to me. The letter will not take long to write, but I need it delivered as soon as possible, and will pay extra for it."

"Very well. I will get your saddlebag for you. Will you be staying another night?"

"No, I will be leaving now. If you could have my horse saddled, as well?"

"Certainly, monsieur. I will be only a moment." The stable master went to the stall the horse was kept in and returned with the saddlebag. By the time the letter was addressed and sealed, the horse was ready.

"Thank you, monsieur. Here is your fee, and some extra for your son."

"Merci, Monsieur."

Monsieur Boyea mounted his horse and rode toward the monastery, veering off the road when he was out of sight of the village. He went back to the spot where he had slept before. It was next to a sunny patch of soft grass where his horse could graze as-well-as drink until he returned. He tied the end of the reins to a tree close to both the creek and the patch of grass, and returned to the monastery.

Evening finally came, and with it another prayer service. Boyea tried to get near to the monk who looked like the cardinal, but as hard as he tried, he could not manage to squeeze between the other monks in the way. He could see the monk across the room, and studied him closely, trying to determine if the man was who he sought.

Afterwards came dinner, which was much like the midday meal, but with wine or ale. He couldn't spot the tall monk in the room, but Brother Xavier sat next to him again.

"Monsieur Boyea, I talked to the abbot and got permission to go on the journey with the 'patient,' as he is called. I will endeavor to send messages back to you of the lessons I will be learning. I have a bit of paper and a quill, if you will tell me the address," the young monk told him, excitedly. "I don't know when he will be leaving, though. He is still ill and it may be several days before he is well enough for the trip. I must ask for more paper and ink in order to take notes of what I am taught."

Brother Xavier rose and quickly walked away.

Later, when the two encountered each other again, Boyea gave the Count's address to the monk, who wrote it on the scrap of paper. Then he went back to his room and lay down again. It was a long wait for the monastery to become silent, but he was able to stay awake until then.

When he was sure everyone had gone to bed, he rose and, leaving his boots in the room and lighting the candle on the table, began his search.

There were several other doors along the hallway where his room was located. He assumed they were also rooms for visitors. Silently, he went to the nearest door and opened it a bit. Peeking in, he could see it was empty. Then he went to the next and repeated what he had done. Empty again. And the next.

Through the fourth door, which he was able to open only a little way, he saw someone sitting in the chair. The man looked up and said, "Monsieur? This room is occupied. May I help you with something?" he whispered.

"Apologies, Brother. I have been to the privy and didn't remember which room is mine." Then he closed the door and walked on.

The monk in the room peeked out, but the man was already out of sight, so he closed the door, checked on his patient, and sat back down. It occurred to him that he hadn't heard footsteps in the corridor, but decided that his mind must have been wandering.

Monsieur Boyea kept looking in rooms. He began to open another door when he heard someone walking toward him in the corridor.

"May I help you find something?" a monk asked him.

"I was just looking for the privy," he answered.

"Well, it's not inside, so you needn't look in here," the monk replied. "I am going there, myself. Come with me and I'll show you, myself."

Boyea followed the monk outside and to the rear of the building.

"I don't recognize you. Are you a visitor to our church?" the monk said.

"I'm just here for one night; then I'll be on my way."

"Are you just traveling through?"

"Uh, yes. I am going to Paris and was robbed of everything a couple of days ago," he said. *Better, he thought, to continue the story I already told than to make something else up.* "I'll be leaving in the morning."

"Ah, here we are," the monk said as they arrived at the small building. "Please, you go first."

"Thank you," Boyea said, and entered.

As he exited, the monk said, "I will look for you in the morning at breakfast."

Boyea returned to his room until he heard the monk enter the building and go back to his room. Then he continued to search.

Most of the rooms were occupied by monks asleep in bed. Then he entered a room without a bed. There was a table, though, and the table had what looked like a garment laying on it. He inspected it carefully by the light of the lamp. It was hard to tell in the dim light, but it looked as though it might be red. There were rents in the fabric and what might have been blood staining it. Could that be the robe that the cardinal had been wearing when his party was attacked? He searched through the robe for pockets, which were empty, the ones he could find. Ah well; the chance of finding anything else that belonged to the cardinal was slight, at best. He folded the robe into a small bundle and laid the biretta, which he found under the robe, on top. He took off his vest and wrapped it around the bundle. Then he carefully and silently returned to his room. He snuffed out the candle, put his boots back on and crawled through the small window, just barely fitting through.

The window was not far above the ground, so his fall wasn't far. He lay there a moment, listening for any sound from inside. There was none.

Getting up, he picked up the bundle he had dropped to the ground and slowly crept toward the place he had tethered his horse.

"This will make a good prize for his lordship the count," Monsieur Boyea thought to himself. "Perhaps I will be rewarded. Perhaps when Monsieur Gaston is crowned king of France he will give me some reward, as well. Perhaps instead of taking this back to Paris, I should take it to the Duke?" He had once been to Turin with the count's household, so, of course, he thought he knew the way.

He pulled a length of heavy string and a spare shirt from a saddlebag, replacing the vest around the bundle with the shirt and tying it to the back of his saddle. Then he rode toward the southeast, carefully, since it was very dark with only a sliver of moon to light his way.

∞ ∞ ∞

Two somewhat bedraggled young men knocked at the servants' entrance to the home of Cardinal Tremblay. One was tall and thin, and the other was a bit shorter and bulkier. They looked as though they had been wearing the same threadbare clothes for days.

The kitchen maid, Audrey, opened the door and looked at the two beggars who stood there. She had been instructed long before that if beggars came to the door, she should give them a bit of bread and cheese, a drink from the well, and send them on their way.

"Wait a moment and I will fetch you something," she told them, and started to shut the door.

"A moment, please, mademoiselle. We are instructed to ask for Pere' Joseph," Porthos replied.

She looked more closely at him and at his friend, peering at them from their dark and neatly trimmed hair down to their surprisingly well-kept boots, seeing clean faces and passably good teeth, then let them in.

"Wait here and I will ask about you. Your names?" She then went in search of Pascal, who confirmed Porthos' story.

"I guess that's what we get for looking so disreputable. He did say to dress this way, though, didn't he?" said Porthos, a muscular, cheerful young man.

The slim, more ascetic Aramis nodded. "That's what it looked like to me. Ah, here comes the secretary, I suspect."

"Monsieurs, please come this way." Pascal let them to the room in which their friend, D'Artagnan had met the cardinal two days earlier.

"Monsieur Aramis? Monsieur Porthos? I thank you for coming," Cardinal Tremblay said.

Each nodded when his name was spoken, then they both knelt to kiss the cardinal's ring. "Your Eminence," they said together.

"Please sit," the cardinal said, indicating the pitcher of wine and glasses on a tray on the table. At their nods, he poured three glasses. "I asked you to come to receive grave news and because your aid has been requested."

"Our aid? Who has requested it?" Porthos asked. "But, Eminence, what is the grave news you spoke of?"

"This is not public knowledge yet, but it will be soon. Recently, Cardinal Richelieu received word that the birth of the heir would be soon. He left for the location of the Queen's confinement, along with his secretary, a number of his own guards, and His Majesty, disguised as one of the guards. Along the way they were attacked. None survived except for Cardinal Richelieu, his secretary, Servien, and one guard. That guard was not the king."

It took the two musketeers a moment to absorb the news that the king of France was dead. "Who are the villains who did this deed?" Aramis asked. "Do you know? We must find them and bring them to justice!"

"Just like a good Musketeer. Yes, we know. No, I will not tell you. Do not concern yourselves; the culprits will be brought to justice. Your aid is needed elsewhere," Cardinal Tremblay admonished. "Cardinal Richelieu was injured. His servant and the young guard got him to safety. The young guard was sent to tell me the news, and I sent him on to another location."

"Has the cardinal survived, then? Is his servant with him?" asked Aramis.

"He sent his servant to tell the Queen and then go elsewhere, himself. Two days ago I asked the Cardinal's Guard, D'Artagnan, to meet with me. I told him what had happened and bade him go to see how the cardinal fared. He asked if I would inform you two and your friend, Athos, of these events. I told D'Artagnan to return with news of the cardinal. When he returned, Athos joined us and promised to go with D'Artagnan to remove the cardinal from the monastery to a safer place. They have the use of a cart for the cardinal to ride in. Now that you two have reappeared and come to see me, I would like to ask you to join them on their journey."

"Thank the good Lord that D'Artagnan is safe," Aramis exclaimed. "But, as you may know, the cardinal has not always, er, approved of the musketeers. There has been some animosity between his guards and our company. We will, of course, do as you ask, especially because our friend, D'Artagnan, has requested our help. But where are we to go? Are we going as musketeers to guard the cardinal? Do you think the cardinal will be well enough to travel?"

"So many questions, and I can answer only one. You will go as itinerant mercenaries, the same as D'Artagnan and Athos. You will follow the itinerary I provided as best you can. I don't expect that you will make good time; a cart is a slow vehicle, especially with an injured man riding in it, so take as much time as you need. But be wary. Many people may be after the cardinal, looking everywhere in France.

"But…"

"Enough questions. I know very little more than you do. This is the place you will go first, to wait for the others to arrive if they haven't already. If they have arrived but left, try to catch up to them." Cardinal Tremblay handed Aramis a sealed document. "But first, I have a question: do many people outside of Paris know who you are? Yes, I've heard about the up-time novel that makes the four of you famous, to 'up-timers', as they call themselves. But I doubt that very many down-timers, such as we, especially in the countryside, have read it." Cardinal Tremblay looked at each of them expectantly."

"Uh, no. I don't think so." Porthos looked at Aramis questioningly.

"I think not, as well," Aramis said. "We have done no more than the other musketeers. I think the up-timers say, 'we have kept our heads down.' Are you asking if we should use other names?"

"I am. Perhaps it would be safer if you did. Perhaps you should call yourselves – Emile Gillette and Georges Moreau."

"I think you look more like an Emile," Porthos said, looking at Aramis.

"Oh? Do you think you look like a Georges?" he replied.

"Do you think you look more like a Georges than I?"

"Gentlemen! I really don't think it makes any difference who uses which name. You can decide on your way." Cardinal Tremblay handed over a small drawstring bag, shaking it slightly so that it jingled. "Here are funds for your trip. I have given D'Artagnan the bulk of the funding, so this should be sufficient for you until you join the rest. And here is a map to your first stop."

The pair rose and bowed. "Your Eminence, we shall do our best to protect the cardinal on his journey. Thank you for your trust in us," Porthos said formally.

"It is D'Artagnan who trusts you. See that you are worthy of it."

Aramis and Porthos bowed again and took their leave.

They paused in the kitchen garden. "It is very late now. Do you think we should wait until tomorrow to start our quest?" Aramis asked Porthos.

"Quest? Is this the twelfth century now? But yes, I think a good night's sleep and a good meal would be preferable to riding the rest of the night on an empty stomach. But we must be up and ready to leave at daybreak."

"Agreed."

Bradley H. Sinor, Susan P. Sinor

Chapter Five

D'Artagnan and Athos arrived at the monastery at Clairefontaine late that night. After waking the stable master to tend to their horses, they entered the chapterhouse.

The night watcher let them in, recognizing D'Artagnan.

"I'm sure the abbot is asleep," D'Artagnan said to the monk.

"I believe he may still be awake," the monk replied. "He often stays up late to pray. Come with me."

"Thank you, Brother, Julius, isn't it?"

"Yes, monsieur," the monk said and led them into the sanctuary. He stood beside the kneeling abbot until he was noticed, then indicated the two visitors.

"Ah, Monsieur D'Artagnan. You have brought one of your friends with you."

"Yes, Abbe'. This is Athos, one of the friends I mentioned to you. He will be using the name Gerard Le Roi. How is the patient?"

Athos bowed to the abbot. "Abbe'."

"Much the same, I'm afraid. But I know you must be on your way. I have a horse and cart ready for you."

"Thank you, but Cardinal Tremblay provided us with an extra horse, so we won't need to deprive the monastery of one. We will need the cart, though."

The Abbot rose and beckoned them to follow him. "The cart is in the stable, with as many blankets as we could spare to keep the patient warm. But it is much too late to leave now. You must sleep before you leave. Would you like to see the patient now?"

They arrived at the cardinal's room after only a moment's walk. The abbot knocked lightly and opened the door.

The cardinal woke at their entrance and smiled at D'Artagnan. In the same slow and breathy voice, he said, "I see you are back. And who is this fellow you have with you? I don't recognize him."

"This is my friend and, now, former king's Musketeer, Athos. He will be going with us."

The cardinal nodded once and went back to sleep.

The abbot said. "I suggest you leave during the morning prayers. It will still be dark at that time, so you won't be seen."

D'Artagnan and Athos stepped away to discuss the offer. After deciding that an early morning departure might be better than leaving immediately, even though they would get little sleep, they turned back to the abbot.

"Thank you, Abbe'. Early morning would be a good time," D'Artagnan told him. "We will arise with everyone else and, once the rest have gone to the chapel, we will slip out."

They left the cardinal to continue sleeping and went to find rooms for themselves. As the night progressed, the cardinal grew weaker, and the monk guarding him sent for the monk who had treated the cardinal when he had first been brought to the monastery.

"He is still breathing, but it is slow," the monk said to D'Artagnan and the abbot, who had also been sent for.

By that time the cardinal was asleep. His breath was still slow and somewhat labored, but his heartbeat had become stronger and he looked as though he was not in pain.

"Should we wait longer to leave?" D'Artagnan asked the abbot, who looked at the monk first, then said, "No, I think you should leave at the time we agreed on."

The monk spoke up. "He should be all right as long as you keep to the smoother roads and he isn't jostled too much. You must drive slowly, as well."

The abbot went on. "I know you want to get as far away from here as soon as you can, but his life is at stake. Perhaps a different direction at first?"

"Yes, that is the plan," D'Artagnan told him.

"I will come to assist you when you're leaving. You will need help carrying him to the cart," said the monk—a large, strong-looking man-- who had guarded the cardinal.

"We thank you for your help, and I'm sure that – our patient – would say the same," said D'Artagnan. "Please pray for our journey, that we get him to our destination safely."

"Of course, my son. God will be with you."

∞ ∞ ∞

It was just past dawn and chilly but dry when the group set out from the monastery at Clairefontaine. The cardinal had been dressed in a clean but simple monk's habit and was asleep, huddled under blankets in the cart, with the young monk, Brother Xavier, driving. The remaining space in the cart, such as it was, was filled with their supplies.

"It's good we got an early start," D'Artagnan said to Athos when they were about half a mile from the monastery.

"And that we got a good breakfast. How far are we to go today?" Athos asked. D'Artagnan pulled the letter from Cardinal Tremblay from inside his vest. "Rambouillet. I think it's about five miles from here. Fortunately, I have a fairly accurate map."

"Is there an inn there, or do we have to camp under the trees?"

"An inn. I believe it's called The Surly Pig."

"Sounds charming. At least we can sleep inside. It would be much too cold, especially for the cardinal, to have to sleep outside." Athos looked back at the cart a few yards behind them. "I'm still not sure about bringing Brother Xavier along with us."

"Well, he seemed to really want to come. Said something about a pilgrimage. But he doesn't know where we're going. Besides, he's helping by driving the cart. And he seems to know how to take care of our patient."

Late the previous evening, after D'Artagnan and Athos had gone to bed, the young monk had gone to the abbot, begging to be allowed to travel with the 'pilgrims' that were leaving the next morning. Brother Xavier had been questioned by the abbot and explained, "I saw the man who will be leaving here. He seems wounded. I have had training in medical care. I can care for Cardinal Richelieu."

"Why do you think he is the cardinal?" the abbot asked him. "His name is Brother Etienne."

"Because I saw the good cardinal in Paris once. This man looks exactly like him. Abbe', please let me go. I so desire to learn from such a great man of God as His Eminence."

The abbot sighed. "He is Brother Etienne."

"Please."

I will have to talk with his guard, Allais."

The abbot sent for D'Artagnan. "Brother Xavier is quite intent on going with you. I know that might cause a problem, but another problem might be caused by refusing him. Or, he could be of help to you."

"What problem could be caused by refusing his request?" D'Artagnan asked.

"His disappointment in being refused might lead him to complain to others, who do not know the true identity of our patient. We want to keep the secret that the cardinal has been cared for here."

D'Artagnan agreed. "We will accept his help, but if he causes any problems, we will leave him at the next church or monastery we come to."

"That will have to do, then. Thank you," said the abbot. "One thing more I should tell you about. After the cardinal's robes were removed, they were laid on a table in one of the smaller rooms. Frankly, we forgot about them for a short time. The day after he was brought to us, a stranger stopped, seeking shelter for the night. We, of course, welcomed him, but kept him away from where the cardinal was. Two days later, the stranger was gone. No one thought much about it until Brother Alfred remembered the robes and went to get them. They were gone. After questioning everyone who might have come across them, it was decided that the stranger must have stolen them. I didn't send anyone after him since we had no idea which way he might have gone. I will send a letter to Cardinal Tremblay about the incident and pray that they weren't stolen for a nefarious reason."

"Thank you for telling me," said D'Artagnan. "I can imagine why they were stolen. I think it must be to have proof where Cardinal Richelieu was taken, although it won't prove that he's alive, or dead. Or still here."

"At least if anyone comes looking for him, he won't find any proof that the cardinal was here," the abbot added. "Because there won't be."

∞ ∞ ∞

The small group finally arrived at their first destination, The Surly Pig in Rambouillet, in time for a late supper.

The village was barely large enough to have an inn. There were no more than five shops and two dozen homes. The church was not imposing like the cathedrals in Paris but was all that was needed for the villagers.

"Brother Xavier, would you please drive the cart around back while I secure a room or two for us?" D'Artagnan said. "Remember, he is to be called Brother Etienne. Athos, please go with him and see what the stable is like."

D'Artagnan entered the inn. It looked much like any other inn that he had stayed at during previous travels. Since the weather was warming, the fire in the fireplace was banked and the windows were uncovered to let light in. The room wasn't overlarge, with dark paneled walls and a polished dark wood counter. There were only five long board tables, one of which was occupied by several men. The innkeeper approached him, wiping his hands on a towel.

"Two rooms, please, if you have them. Or one with two large beds, if not. Do you have any rooms on the ground floor?" D'Artagnan asked the innkeeper.

"I'm afraid not," was the man's response. "I do have one large room upstairs, with two large beds."

"That will do nicely. And supper for three."

"It will be ready shortly. Would you like to be shown the room first?"

"Yes, please. One of our company is ill, or rather, injured, so we will take supper in the room."

"You are sure he is not ill?" asked the innkeeper, who seemed on the edge of panic.

At D'Artagnan's assurance, the innkeeper said, "Very good, sir. Rachael," he called to a young woman. "Show this man to the larger room."

After seeing the room and finding it suitable, D'Artagnan paid for one night and went back out to the cart.

"We can take Brother Etienne up to the room now," he told Brother Xavier.

Athos, who had been looking at the interior of the stable, had just rejoined them. "The stable is clean and adequate for our needs."

"I will carry Brother Etienne up the back staircase to our room. Brother Xavier, would you join me and bring some of our possessions with you?"

D'Artagnan asked. "Gerard, please see to the horse and cart. Our room is the third on the left upstairs."

D'Artagnan carried the cardinal up the stairs and into the room, placing him on the bed farther away from the door, while Brother Xavier brought up their belongings and supplies.

"Brother Xavier, would you go back down and wait for supper to be ready?" D'Artagnan said. "When it is, please bring two plates up with you. I'll go down to get the third."

`"What about the car – Brother Etienne? Shouldn't he have something to eat?"

"If he wakes enough, we can give him some of the food from our plates."

With that, Brother Xavier returned to the first floor to wait on their meals as Athos was going up the stairs to join D'Artagnan in the room.

Moments later there was a knock at the door.

The two men looked at each other. "Are we expecting anyone other than Xavier returning with the food? Seems too soon for that, though," said Athos.

D'Artagnan opened the door a sliver; outside stood the innkeeper. "Sir, might you be coming from Paris? And are you called Allais Dubois?"

"I am. What is this about?"

"A letter just arrived here for you. The seal is blank, but it was addressed to 'Allais Dubois from Paris'. It must be important, for the messenger who brought it in was out of breath."

D'Artagnan held out his hand for the letter, which the innkeeper placed in it, then closed the door behind him.

D'Artagnan stood behind the door and broke the seal. As he thought, it was from Cardinal Tremblay.

"I have sent your friends, Emile Gillette and Georges Moreau, after you. They will meet you at your next stop and ride with you thereafter. Take care," he read to Athos. It was signed Pere' Joseph.

"Emile and Georges, huh? I wonder which is which," he said. "I guess we'll find out when we see them." He noticed that the cardinal's eyes were open. "How are you feeling, Your Eminence?"

The cardinal breathed shallowly for a few moments, then said slowly, "I am very tired and my wound pains me, but I will not give in to it." He breathed a few more moments, then went on. "Where am I?"

"Your Eminence, we are at an inn. We are taking you to someplace safe where your enemies will not be able to find you, where you will be able to recover your health."

Then the cardinal nodded and closed his eyes again.

Soon they heard a sound like the door being kicked. "That must be Brother Xavier now." D'Artagnan said, opening the door.

"Our suppers," Brother Xavier said as he entered.

"Thank you, Brother. Please set the plates on the table by the window," D'Artagnan said.

The noise of kicking the door, followed by the voices, woke the cardinal again. He looked at the young monk who was setting two plates of food on the table.

"Who is this?" the cardinal said, motioning to Brother Xavier.

D'Artagnan answered. "He is the young monk who will be driving the cart you ride in. His name is Brother Xavier."

The cardinal looked at him more closely. "Do you trust him?" he said in a loud, if slow, whisper.

"We have questioned him and believe he is trustworthy," D'Artagnan said, moving closer to the cardinal's bed. "But we will keep a close eye on him, as well. Now why don't you two go ahead and eat. I'll go down and get the other plates and bring them up."

D'Artagnan descended the stairs slowly, scanning the room for anything or anyone who might cause a danger to the cardinal or their mission. Then he collected the meals and returned to the room.

∞ ∞ ∞

Luc Boyea hadn't gotten any sleep that night at the monastery, but he was able to ride several hours into the next day. He stopped midmorning for a quick meal at an inn before continuing his journey. He took his precious bundle into the inn with him. He didn't dare leave it tied to his saddle.

"Just passing through, monsieur, or do you want a room for the night? It is a little early for that, though," the innkeeper said, chuckling. He saw the brown, cloth-wrapped bundle that his customer kept on his lap. "A present for someone, eh?" he said, pointing to it. "I'm sure she will be pleased, eh." He winked.

"Yes, uh, I hope so," Monsieur Boyea said. "I'm just passing through, but could I buy some bread and cheese and a bottle of small beer for the road?"

"Of course, of course. I'll see to that immediately." The innkeeper returned within a few minutes with a small package. "Here you are, monsieur. Have a safe trip."

Monsieur Boyea paid for his food and went on his way, this time tying the bundle in front of him, around his waist.

He made good time during the afternoon, stopping only a half our at a time, at some distance off the road, to rest his horse and himself. Several days later, as he was mounting his horse after a short rest, he saw two men on horseback approaching. He looked closely at them to see if he recognized them. No, they didn't look familiar. He started along the road, hoping to just pass them, but kept one hand on the pistol he had stolen from the count's arsenal and the other on the reins and the bundle.

As he came abreast of the two men, he nodded, politely. "Bonjour," he said, and rode on. A moment later the two riders wheeled around and caught up to him.

"Bonjour to you, monsieur," one said, pointing a pistol at him. "Do please give us all your possessions."

Monsieur Boyea looked as if he was about to comply, then spurred his horse and galloped on toward the bridge over a river. He heard shots from behind, which startled him and his horse, but none hit them as he rode. As he got close to the bridge, he spotted more men on the other side.

He assumed they were associates of the two men he was fleeing and turned off the road and toward the river, hoping to cross there.

The river bank was steep, but not dangerously so. Boyea turned his horse away from the bridge, going downstream, hoping to put more distance between himself and anyone who might shoot at him from the middle of the bridge. He hoped the current would wash him farther away from his pursuers.

Unfortunately, the water was deeper than he expected and the current swifter. His horse was less of a swimmer than he had thought, and foundered. As he was washed off, he grabbed for the saddle. His hand, however, missed and he was swept away. Although he tried to keep hold of the bundle, the string was not as strong as he had hoped, and the bundle broke free, floating out of reach, even though he tried to swim toward it.

He heard another shot and felt an impact near his shoulder. Looking back, he saw one of the highwaymen in the river on his own horse. That horse was able to swim, and its rider was able to get off the shot that hit him, then catch up to the foundering horse and grab its reins, pulling it toward the far shore.

Monsieur Boyea floated down the river, trailing a stream of blood behind him. Presently he fetched up against a dead tree that had fallen into the river and was caught. One of the robbers saw what happened.

"François, I will get him. He may have silver on him, or something else valuable," the robber said. "Wait for me."

When the robber had reunited with his fellows, Boyea's body draped across his horse, they went through his clothing, first confirming that he was dead.

"Aha!" he exclaimed, pulling a small drawstring bag out of the man's vest and shaking it. They heard jingling. "Do you think we could salvage his clothing?"

"Why bother? There isn't much, but we can buy something new with his money," another said. "Should we bury him?"

"No. just throw him back in the river. He'll be long gone from here before anyone comes looking for him."

Bradley H. Sinor, Susan P. Sinor

Chapter Six

The next day the small group of Brother Xavier and the two guards were up early. The cardinal still slept, and they all were loath to try to wake him.

"I'll secure food for our breakfasts," D'Artagnan told the others. "Gerard, if you will carry our patient down to the cart, and Brother Xavier, if you will gather all our belongings and follow Gerard, I will meet you there. First I will ask the stable master to bring the cart around to the front door."

The innkeeper, seeing D'Artagnan standing by the bar, approached and asked, "How was your room, monsieur? Did you all sleep well?"

"Well enough, monsieur, well enough. Brother Etienne had some pain, due to his injury, but all-in-all, a pleasant night," D'Artagnan told him. "We must leave now. Would you have our cart brought around to the front door so our patient doesn't have to be carried as far? Then could you wrap the food for our breakfasts so we can take it with us? Thank you."

"Of course. Enjoy your breakfast and have a pleasant journey."

The innkeeper returned to the kitchen and pulled his wife aside. "The older man being carried had the hood of his robe almost pulled entirely over his head, but I'd swear, from what I could see of him, he looks remarkably like the Red Cardinal, Richelieu, whom I saw not long ago when I travelled to Paris. Go find your cousin, Jean, and have him follow the group, then report back to me. I know Monsieur and his brother,

Vendôme, would reward anyone who could give them information on the whereabouts of the man. If we can secure him, or at least send word where he has been seen, we may be rewarded for it." He rubbed his hands together. "Go." Then he went out to the stable to fetch the cart and horses.

His wife rushed out of the inn to find her cousin with thoughts of silver running through her head.and her husband's and her families had ties to Monsieur and would be glad to see him on the throne of France, instead of the childless Louis. No one knew whether the child of the queen was a male, or Louis', or even if it lived.

∞ ∞ ∞

The small company had been on the road for several hours, and D'Artagnan and Athos had been riding behind to have a conversation, when D'Artagnan spotted a person riding some distance away but parallel to them. He had been scouting, watching for others on the road who might be agents of Monsieur Gaston looking for evidence of Cardinal Richelieu.

"I saw someone riding some yards over that way," he said to Athos. "I'm going to try to find him. I should be back soon."

He left, riding carefully and trying to not make noise. It had rained the night before and the trees were still dripping. The remaining clouds cast an eerie effect to the forest to either side of the road.

First D'Artagnan went to the opposite side of the road, circling around to the rear and then back across the road until he was a little farther into the woods and farther back than the rider was. After that, he rode forward again, intending to catch up with and challenge him.

The weather in early May was pleasant and the grass had begun to spring up, cushioning the ground. Dead leaves from the previous autumn had fallen apart and dead tree limbs had been broken by passing wildlife. The rain had added another layer to the silence of the forest, so his ride was fairly quiet.

Before long, he saw the rider in the near distance. He seemed to be trying to watch the group but not make contact. D'Artagnan spurred his horse, catching up to the rider within a few minutes.

"Hello, monsieur," he called to the man. "Lovely morning, isn't it? The sunlight, the fresh air, the smell of spring. You seem to be tracking my little group of travelers. I was just wondering why."

The man looked around to see if anyone else was there to confront him. "Why would I be tracking you? You are of no consequence."

D'Artagnan observed a frightened look in the man's eyes and a quaver in his voice, despite his seeming bravado.

"Eh, then why are you not riding on the road instead of through the countryside? It's a much easier ride than having to dodge trees and bushes."

"I ride where I wish. Leave me be or I will make you wish you had," the man said.

"Indeed? Is that a challenge?" The rider said nothing. "Then I accept." D'Artagnan drew his sword and rode closer, sitting easily on his horse.

The man drew his own sword and rushed at D'Artagnan, but he seemed an uneasy horseman and almost lost his seat. When he recovered it he had to move quickly away from D'Artagnan's blade to avoid it. He then turned to face D'Artagnan and moved to strike him, but the guard's arm was quick enough to parry the other man's thrust. His sword connected with the attacker's arm, leaving a slit in his sleeve and a nick in his arm and almost unseating him again. That caused the other man to try to regain control of his horse and switch hands.

He was not skilled with that hand either, and after a few moments he found himself wounded a second time and on his back on the ground.

He got to his feet, raising his sword in salute to D'Artagnan, then sheathed it, mounted his horse and spurred it back the way he had come.

D'Artagnan rode after him for a short while, then gave up the chase and rode back to the others. They had not stopped when D'Artagnan engaged the rider, but had traveled on.

"The man rode back with a good cut on each arm. I don't think he will come after us again, but someone else might, so keep watch to the sides," he said to Athos, quietly. "I will ride at a distance again to keep watch behind."

"Do you think Monsieur knows where we are, or where Cardinal Richelieu is, in particular?" Athos asked in a soft voice.

"I don't know how he could, but anything is possible. I think he's sent agents to all parts of France, searching for the cardinal. His concern is to discover if the cardinal is dead or alive. If he is told that the cardinal is alive, he will move Heaven and Earth to change that. Our concern, besides getting Brother Etienne to safety, is to spread rumors that the cardinal is alive and has been seen everywhere in the country. Everywhere but with us."

"I see. That way Monsieur will have many sleepless nights and headaches during the days," Athos said.

"Exactly!"

∞ ∞ ∞

"Did you get a good look in the cart?" the innkeeper asked his wife's cousin, Jean. "Was the one they're looking for in it?"

They were standing in the inn's kitchen after Jean had returned to the village.

"There was someone in the cart, I think. The back was piled with blankets, but I thought I saw a head wearing the hood of a monk's habit. Also, the monk driving the cart kept looking back at whatever was in the bed. I couldn't get close enough. One of his guards spotted me and confronted me. That's how I got these gashes on my arms," the young man replied. "Of course I fought back, but another guard joined him. They were both more skilled than I at swordplay, and it was all I could do to get away. The two guards are keeping close watch of their surroundings."

"But you know what way they are headed?" The innkeeper seemed excited for the news.

"They were going in a somewhat westerly direction, but there are many ways they could go. I must return with more men."

"I can send two more with you, but you must find them. You said that they have another monk with them? Did you see him?" the older man said.

"Yes, I saw a younger man driving the cart. I don't know if he will be a problem or not."

"Then take your two men and find out. When you know who is in the cart, send one back with the message. If they are not who we seek, keep looking." With that, the innkeeper dismissed the young man and left to see if there were any new customers.

"Here, let me see to your cuts," the innkeeper's wife told her cousin, Jean. "They must be bandaged before you do anything else."

Jean sat down while his cousin took care of him. Then she gave him some lunch. By the time the two other men arrived to accompany him, it was well after noon. Even riding at a moderately fast pace, the three men didn't catch up that day with the party they were seeking.

∞ ∞ ∞

D'Artagnan and his small party arrived without further trouble at their next stop, Epernon. It was a small village, too small to have an inn. But the church's rectory had room for visitors who needed lodging.

The rectory had two stories, and was, of course, not far from the church. The front door opened into a small wood-paneled foyer, with several straight-backed chairs along the walls for visitors. Behind it was a sitting room with sofas and chairs. Other rooms were on either side.

"We are very grateful, Father, for taking us in," said D'Artagnan as he and Athos entered. "My name is Allais Dubois and this is Gerard Le Roi.

A young monk, Brother Xavier, is still in the cart watching over Brother Etienne, who has been injured and is not always conscious."

"Not at all, my son. All travelers are welcome here. If you can bring your Brother Etienne inside, we can lay him on the settee in my study," said Father Andreas.

Athos went back out to help carry Brother Etienne inside.

"Have you eaten?" Father Andreas said. "Dinner will be ready shortly. I hope you don't mind simple food."

"Thank you, Father. We are quite accustomed to simple food and are grateful for it," D'Artagnan said.

"I will gladly stay by his side," Brother Xavier said, looking at Brother Etienne, "while you eat, and take my meal later."

"I can have a plate sent to you in the study. You need not wait," the young priest said.

"Thank you, Father," Brother Xavier replied.

"We have rooms available for your party. You two guards may share one and the monks, the other. My housekeeper will show you to them. I'm afraid that they are both on the second floor. Will you be able to carry Brother Etienne up the stairs?"

While D'Artagnan and Father Andreas were talking, Athos and Brother Xavier were bringing in their belongings. Athos overheard Father Andreas' question, and said, "Brother Xavier and I can carry him up the stairs."

"I have had some medical training, if you would like me to look at his wound," Father Andreas said.

"We would be in your debt, Father. Brother Xavier has been tending Brother Etienne, but a fresh pair of eyes would be welcome," D'Artagnan told him.

"I can examine him now, before dinner, and then again later, after he has been taken to his room.

About that time, the rectory's housekeeper entered the study. "I can show you to your rooms, if you'd like, Monsieurs. Right this way." She started up the stairs, with D'Artagnan and Athos following, carrying their belongings.

The rooms were not overlarge, with two narrow beds, a chest of drawers, and two chairs in each. The rooms were across from each other, overlooking the front and back of the house.

"Thank you, madam," D'Artagnan told the housekeeper.

"Dinner will be in a few minutes, if you would like to refresh yourselves." She pointed to the basins and pitchers of water in each room. "There is a privy out the back, and a chamber pot under each bed."

Then she turned and went back downstairs, leaving the men standing in the hall. They each went into a room to wash the road dust off of their hands and faces, then returned downstairs, ready for dinner.

The two guards met Father Andreas in the dining room.

"I am afraid that Brother Etienne's wound is not healing well, at all. The journey is very hard on him and his stamina must be low," Father Andreas told them. "He seemed to be muttering something while he slept. Would it be possible for you to stay another day so he can rest?"

"I'm sorry, Father, but we have been urged to not tarry on this journey, but if it would be too dangerous for him to continue on the journey tomorrow, we would have to wait. Is it?" D'Artagnan was afraid that word would get out if they stayed too long, but he didn't want to endanger the cardinal's health.

"Well, no, it shouldn't be overly dangerous for him, if the way isn't too rough, but it could be debilitating."

"In that case, Father, I'm afraid that we must be on our way," D'Artagnan said. "We appreciate your hospitality very much, but we don't wish to tax it."

They fell to their dinner, finishing quickly as they were all hungry. Afterwards, Athos carried the monk upstairs and to bed.

"I'm glad Brother Xavier wanted to speak to Father Andreas. It gives us a chance to talk," Athos said.

"I'm glad he didn't recognize Brother Etienne," D'Artagnan added. "He is not on my list of safe people."

"Where is our next stop, tomorrow?" Athos continued.

"Maintenon," D'Artagnan said, reading the letter. "I think all our stops are around five to nine miles apart." He looked at the cardinal. "When he is better, we should be able to make better time."

"If the horse can pull the cart faster," Athos replied.

Chapter Seven

"Hold up!" Porthos called. "It's not a race and we don't have to get there before they do."

Aramis looked back. He was three horse lengths ahead of Porthos.

"Besides, we have something to decide," Porthos went on.

Aramis reined his horse to a walk, waiting for Porthos to catch up. "What do we have to decide?" he asked.

Porthos reined his own horse to a walk as he caught up. "We have to decide who we are. Will I be Georges or will you? Which one of us will be Emile?"

"Oh. That. It really doesn't make that much difference to me. If you want to be Georges, then you can be Georges. Actually, I think Emile is a nobler name."

"Nobler, huh. You don't think Georges is noble?" Porthos looked at Aramis, eyebrows arched.

"Well, Georges is noble enough, but not more so than Emile."

"I beg to differ," Porthos said in a huff. "I think Georges is much nobler. There have been kings of that name. I can't think of any king named Emile."

"Oh, I'm sure there have been. And plenty of nobles of other ranks, as well." Aramis stroked his beard. "Yes. I think I like the name Emile." He looked over at Porthos and bowed, as much as he could from horseback, and tipped his hat. "Good day, monsieur. My name is Emile Gillette."

"Very well. Good day to yourself, monsieur. My name is Georges Moreau."

"I think we should call each other by those names only. If we do that, perhaps we won't use our real names by accident."

"Not a bad idea, Emile."

"Thank you, Georges."

∞ ∞ ∞

A loud knock was heard at the door of the rectory. "What was that?" Athos asked.

"I think someone just knocked on the front door. I'll go look down the stairs to see if it's anyone we should know about," D'Artagnan said.

He arrived at the top of the stairs just as the door was opened. Standing out of sight, he peeked over the banister. He could hear voices, but couldn't make out what was being said for a moment. Then he heard Father Andreas say, "Yes, we have four travelers staying with us. Let me call them down." He turned to the stairs and called, "Allais, Gerard, would you come down a moment, please."

D'Artagnan started down the steps. When he saw who the visitors were, his speed increased.

"You called for me, Father?" he said.

"Ah, Monsieur Dubois. Thank you for coming down." He turned to the other men and said, "Monsieur Moreau? Monsieur Gillette? This is Monsieur Dubois."

Before the priest could say anything else, D'Artagnan strode forward and embraced first Porthos, and then Aramis.

"Georges! Emile!" he said, looking from one to the other. "I'm so glad you could join us. Gerard is still upstairs with Brother Etienne. And here is Brother Xavier," he said as the young monk entered from another room.

"Brother Xavier, my friends Georges Moreau," Porthos bowed, "and Emile Gillette," Aramis bowed. "They will be traveling with us. Father, I hate to ask, but do you have another room available for my friends?"

"I do, but not as large as the ones you and your companions have. But it does have a larger bed."

"That will do just fine," D'Artagnan replied. "My friends, here, are quite used to sleeping on the ground. They may even decide to sleep on the floor of the room instead of the bed. Thank you again."

Father Andreas summoned the housemaid and said, "Roxane, please ask the stable boy to see to the horses of these two gentlemen. They should fit into the stable along with the others and the cart."

"Thank you, Father Andreas, but we must retrieve our belongings first," Emile said. "Georges, why don't you do that while I find our room?"

Porthos almost said something, but caught himself. "Of course. I shall be back soon."

"Monsieurs, we have just finished dinner, but if you haven't eaten, I think we could find something left over," Father Andreas said.

Emile bowed. "We thank you with pleasure. We have been riding hard to catch up with our friends and would welcome refreshments." He turned to Georges. "I will see you down here in a few moments."

"As you say."

D'Artagnan led Aramis up the stairs, followed by the housekeeper to show them the room the new visitors would use. It was next door to D'Artagnan's and the cardinal's room.

"This will do nicely," Aramis said. "It will be for just one night, anyway. Georges and I would have slept on the kitchen floor if needed. Thank you." The housekeeper nodded and left.

"Our rooms are right here," D'Artagnan told him as they went back the way they had come. "These two." He pointed at the doors across from each other. Then he opened the door to the room the cardinal and he would use.

"I thought I heard a familiar voice," said Athos, embracing Aramis. "Is Porthos with you?"

"Yes, he just went out to get our things before the horses are stabled. He'll be right up."

"Would you watch for him, and also watch for Brother Xavier. We have things to catch up on, with the young monk out of earshot," D'Artagnan said to Athos.

Athos left and D'Artagnan went on. "Aramis, this is our patient, Cardinal Richelieu, who we call Brother Etienne. The cardinal is very ill. I'm sure Cardinal Tremblay filled you in."

"He did. How is he doing?" Aramis nodded toward the cardinal.

"Unfortunately, not well. He drifts in and out of consciousness. The journey has not and will not be an easy one."

"Where are we taking him?"

"I have an itinerary in my possession," D'Artagnan answered. "But Cardinal Tremblay asked that I not give out the information of where we are going. To anyone. Tomorrow I will tell you where our next stop for the night is. I'm sorry, but those are my instructions."

Just then Porthos entered, followed by Athos.

"Brother Xavier is back in conference with Father Andreas."

He closed the door.

"There's something Aramis and I decided shortly before we got here that I think we all should do," Porthos said.

"What's that?"

"Well, we were deciding which pseudonym each of us should use: Georges or Emile. We decided I would be Georges and Aramis would be Emile, and we should use only those names. That way we won't get mixed up and use our real names at the wrong time. What do you think?"

"I think that's a wonderful idea. What do you think, Gerard?" D'Artagnan said to Athos.

"I think that's what we should do, Allais," he replied. "Brother Etienne will still be Etienne, of course, and Brother Xavier is the same. He does know about our mission, but not how important it is."

"But why is Brother Xavier here, anyway?" Georges asked. "Why have a stranger along with us?"

"Because he made a fuss to the abbot at the monastery where the cardinal had been taken. He wanted to come along. Fortunately, he had just recently arrived there and the brothers didn't know him very well. He wanted to study or something with the cardinal and asked permission. The abbot decided it was safer to have him with us, since he was convinced he knew 'Etienne's' identity. That way he couldn't let it slip among the rest of the monks who don't know. Whatever the reason, he's here and we can't do anything about it. Unless he poses a threat, of course. Then we'll leave him with the next priest we encounter, telling him that Xavier has been talking treason and not to believe anything he says."

"Well, all right, then. I guess that's that," Georges said. "Where is our room? As much as I'd love to catch up with you, we've been riding hard to do it, and I would like to get some sleep."

"Right this way, Georges," Emile told him. "Would you like the right or the left side of the bed?"

"First I would like the dinner we were promised. Shall we go down?"

"Agreed. We will see you in the morning," Emile said to the others.

Chapter Eight

"Cook, you'll never guess who one of our guests is," Roxanne, the housemaid, said as she entered the kitchen.

"I don't guess, girl, and I don't much care who the guests are as long as they don't make trouble and appreciate our hospitality." The cook, a plump older woman with her gray hair tucked up under her mobcap continued the cleaning she had been doing when the housemaid had interrupted her.

"Well, I'll tell you, then. The older man, the one that's ill, he looks exactly like Cardinal Richelieu, the king's minister. I saw him when I took the plate of food to the young monk."

The cook stiffened briefly, then asked, "And how would you know that, girl? When has the likes of you ever seen the likes of him?"

"It was before I came here. I was sent to Paris to stay with my grandparents for a short time. I'd never been away from home and longed to see Paris, so my parents let me go. It was only for a week, but the cardinal attended the king when he addressed the public while I was there, and I got to be in the first row." The thought of that trip took her back as she remembered the event. "He looked so tall and stern, but I could swear I saw a twinkle in his eyes once. He was so impressive."

"Believe me, there was no twinkle in his eyes. I've seen him, too, and I didn't find him impressive. But never you mind. You keep away from the strangers. You don't know what they're like."

"Yes'm, I will."

∞ ∞ ∞

After her duties were finished for the day, the cook went to her room and thought. If it were true that Cardinal Richelieu was in the house, she had to let her uncle know about it. When she was sure that everyone was asleep in bed, she took an unlit candle and sneaked back downstairs and into Father Andreas' study. Silently, she closed the door, lit her candle and carefully slid a single piece of parchment from the stack on the priest's desk. She took a quill and opened a pot of ink. Then she quickly penned a letter. She let the paper sit long enough for the ink to dry, then waved it back and forth for good measure. She folded it and sealed it with the priest's wax and stamp. Then, last, she wrote the address of her uncle on the outside, put everything away, and left the room, taking the letter.

The next morning, after breakfast, when she went to do the day's marketing, she took the letter with her and gave it to the town's messenger. "Pierre, Father Andreas gave me this to be sent right away."

"Of course." He looked at the address. "And who would this be? I've never seen a letter of his going to this address."

"Why are you asking me? I don't look over his shoulder when he's writing correspondence. Nor does he ask me who to write to. He sounded as if it's urgent, so get on with you."

"Yes, ma'am. I'll be leaving later this morning. Good day to you."

"Good day," she answered, completed her shopping and returned to the rectory.

She was sure her uncle would want to know about Cardinal Richelieu staying at her priest's home. He was no lover of the late king, Louis. Although, since he was just a minor functionary at the palace, no one knew that. Monsieur Gaston was sure to want to find the cardinal, and if he could get word to any of Monsieur's men, the cardinal could be captured and her uncle could be raised to a higher office.

∞ ∞ ∞

The next morning, bright and early, five of the six travelers awoke, readied themselves, and descended the stairs. Porthos carried the cardinal, who had awakened briefly when moved. They had hoped to get away before the priest was up, but their hopes were dashed when he greeted them at the foot of the stairs.

"Good morning, my friends. How are you today? Would you like to join me for the early service before you resume your journey?" he said.

D'Artagnan looked at Xavier, who looked back hopefully.

"I would like that very much," the younger monk said.

D'Artagnan sighed silently. He had so wanted to be away early. "Thank you, Father, we will join you. But, of course, Brother Etienne will have to stay here. Then we must leave right after; we have far to go."

"Of course. I will ask Cook to prepare some food for you to take with you. I know you'll be hungry, and you shouldn't ride on empty stomachs."

"Very generous of you, Father," Athos said. "We are in your debt."

"I will stay with Brother Etienne," Porthos offered. "Should I carry him back upstairs?"

"You may lay him on the settee in my study," Father Andreas said. "And I will not urge you to stay any longer, as I know you want to be on your way."

Their time in church gave them a much-needed rest and a feeling of peace.

"If we ever return to this village, we must attend one of Father Andreas' services," Aramis said. "I felt – peaceful -- in there, as though everything will turn out well. He gave an inspiring sermon."

As they left the church, each left a coin in the collection box for the poor.

They returned to retrieve Porthos and Brother Etienne and were soon traveling on.

After they had been on the road for a while, the cardinal seemed to revive a little. He pushed himself to a sitting position, but then thought the better of it and sank back down. Brother Xavier looked back and asked, "Are you feeling better, Eminence? Or did the bouncing of the cart wake you?"

"Perhaps a little better," the cardinal answered in a slow, soft voice. "But I think the rough road might have caused me to wake. I will try to go back to sleep now."

"I had better pay more attention to the road," Brother Xavier said to himself.

∞ ∞ ∞

"Who did you say sent you this message?" Gaston, soon to be His Majesty, King of France, asked Terrye Jo Tillman.

"It was sent by your man, GBJF." She handed him the message that had been sent by radio.

"I see. Thank you." With that, he left the radio room at his brother-in-law's home in Turin without reading it. He knew that Mademoiselle Tillman had transcribed the message and knew the contents, but that couldn't be helped. He also knew that he would be taking her with him to Paris when he left Turin. She would be his – man? – there, in charge of the radio in the palace.

In the privacy of his suite, after dismissing his entourage, he settled into a comfortable chair and unfolded the paper.

'Possible location found. Stop. Monastery in Clairefontaine. Stop. Person's presence not verified, but most likely there. Stop. Location may change soon. Stop. Will send more information when acquired. End of message.'

He went to his door and summoned his host, Duke Victor Amadeus, the husband of his sister.

"Gaston," the duke said as he entered the suite. At a look from his guest, he quickly added, "Excuse me. Your Royal Highness," and bowed deeply.

"Soon to be Your Majesty, Victor. Don't forget that."

"Of course. Your Majesty," Victor said and bowed again.

Gaston handed him the message he had just reread for the third time. "What do you make of this?"

Victor read it. "Who sent you this?"

"Soissons. A message was sent to him by one of his men, who thought he'd found the cursed cardinal."

He read it again and looked up at Gaston. "Have you sent anyone around the countryside looking for evidence of Richelieu's death? Or life? Did Soissons do that? Has anyone else?"

"Actually, I haven't, yet. But perhaps I should, when I get to Paris. Regardless, if the cardinal is at this monastery, he must still be alive. Blast Vendôme! He told me the order was given to kill everyone. How did the cardinal escape? And did anyone else escape with him?" He had been pacing back and forth as he spoke; now he turned to Victor and said, "Send some men up there to check this place out. I have plans to make."

"Where is this place, Clairefontaine? I don't know how good our maps of France are," he protested.

"Oh, somewhere south of Paris, one direction or another. Someone along the way will know. Just send them!"

∞ ∞ ∞

Some days went by without anything untoward happening. The company had met few other people on the road, and the ones they passed seemed uncommunicative. They had found rooms at inns at every stop, and no one had challenged them. They were feeling too secure, and D'Artagnan was getting worried.

His three friends, the musketeers, were paying less attention to their surroundings, although their lack of attention was a very recent thing.

D'Artagnan beckoned to Athos to join him ahead of the others.

"Gerard, I think we are getting complacent. We have had no confrontations with others, not even conversations, in the last few days. I think we are becoming less attentive."

Athos thought a moment, then said, "I think you may be right. What if someone attacked us? Would we be as quick as we usually are? I'm not sure. What should we do?"

"I don't know. We could talk to Georges and Emile about it. We have to do something to keep alert."

"I agree," Athos said. "But should we call them ahead to join us or wait for them to catch up and speak with them all at the same time?"

"Well, I don't want to embarrass them in front of the monks, but we need to discuss the problem with all of them. Why don't you go back and send Georges and Emile to join me. I can speak to them and then we can all talk to the monks."

"That sounds like a good idea. I'll send them right up to talk to you."

Athos turned his horse back toward the others but stopped with a loud gasp.

"What?" D'Artagnan asked as he also turned. "I didn't think we had ridden so far ahead." The road behind them was empty of cart and riders.

They kicked their horses into a gallop. "Maybe the cart broke down," Athos said. "Or maybe Etienne is worse and they stopped because of that. Or maybe . . ."

"Stop," D'Artagnan cried. "No more speculating. We need to find them."

There was a bend in the road, with trees that blocked their view of the road beyond it. As they rounded that curve they saw no one.

"Where did they go?" Athos said, shaking his head. "I know they were right behind us."

"Here," they heard a feeble voice call. They looked around and saw Porthos trying to stand.

"What happened?" D'Artagnan called. "And where are the others?"

"We were attacked. Taken unawares. I'm afraid we weren't paying as close attention as we should have been." Porthos was searching around him. "I was clubbed from behind, as was Aramis, I mean Emile, I'm sure. My head still hurts. The attackers must have taken the cart with the monks in it. Not to mention our horses."

Athos and D'Artagnan dismounted to help Porthos search for Aramis.

They didn't find him on the side Porthos was on, but when they crossed to the other side they found him lying in the grass with his eyes closed.

D'Artagnan felt his arms and legs to make sure he hadn't been injured when he was knocked off of his horse. He found no breaks, but other injuries would not be apparent until he regained consciousness.

"Did you see anything? Who attacked you?" Athos asked Porthos as D'Artagnan was examining Aramis.

"No. They attacked from behind, and they were so quiet as they approached that we heard nothing." Porthos knelt beside D'Artagnan to see how was faring.

After a moment Aramis showed signs of life. The others began to help him to stand, but he held his head in his hands and said, "Oh, my head hurts! What happened?" as he carefully felt the back of his head.

"We were attacked from behind," Porthos told him, then looked around. "Where is the cart and the monks?"

That question reminded D'Artagnan and Athos that they must search for them.

"The cart and the monks were kidnapped," D'Artagnan told him. "Are you feeling well enough to ride?" D'Artagnan asked.

"I'll live. But we must find the monks." He looked around for his mount, not seeing his or Porthos', "and our horses." He gave a particular whistle, and Porthos did the same with a different one. They waited a moment, but no horses appeared.

"They must be too far away to hear their summons," Porthos said. "They have been well trained to come when called, but if they are too far away to hear it . . ."

Athos and D'Artagnan each took one of the others up behind them, and they rode back the way they had come.

"How were your attackers able to get the drop on you?" D'Artagnan demanded. "Where were the two of you?"

"We were riding a few yards behind the cart. There had to have been at least two attackers. I think we must have been knocked off our horses at the same time, since I didn't see, uh, Emile fall," Porthos said.

"I didn't see Georges fall, either, so he must be correct," Aramis confirmed. "They must have been very quiet, or Brother Xavier would have heard it and sounded an alarm."

"And they must have been very quiet when they attacked the cart, or you would have heard something," Porthos added.

"Or they had help from someone. Perhaps someone in the cart. Perhaps the monk driving the cart," D'Artagnan said.

"Brother Xavier? But he seems so . . ." Athos pointed out.

"Mild? Ineffectual? Not one to make trouble?" D'Artagnan said. "Remember the man who was following us a few days ago? What if he was trying to make contact with Brother Xavier? The young monk did beg to be allowed to go with us. Perhaps he is in league with our foes."

"Then we must find them quickly," D'Artagnan said. "You two go that way," he told Athos, pointing to the road that split off, making a fork. "We'll go this way. If we haven't seen them in thirty minutes, we should return to this place and regroup."

The four men mounted the two horses and parted ways, riding faster.

D'Artagnan and Porthos took the left fork. The road was narrow, with trees overhanging on both sides. The ground, however, was sparsely covered, due to the lack of sunlight, so the men could see easily for a good distance.

"You look to the right, I'll watch to the left," D'Artagnan told Porthos. "If they came this way we should be able to spot them easily."

"How far do you think they could have gotten?" he asked.

"Not too far. We discovered their disappearance quickly, within minutes, I think. We know they didn't go forward or Athos and I would have seen them. There were no other roads branching off before the fork. They had to have gone this way or the other."

"But what if they went across country?" Porthos asked.

"Then we'll see them if they came this way. Be sure to look as far away as you can."

"But if they went the other way? We don't know what the terrain is like that way."

"I should think it is much like this. Athos and Aramis should be able to see as well as we can. Try to keep track of the time so we'll know when to turn around," D'Artagnan said.

They rode on for a while, seeing nothing, before turning back to meet their friends at the fork. When they arrived the other party was not there.

"We'll wait for a few minutes. If they're not back shortly, we should go after them," D'Artagnan said. "They may have caught up to the kidnappers."

"In that case, shouldn't we go after them now? We don't know how many kidnappers there are. Athos and Aramis may be outnumbered. And if Brother Xavier is in with the kidnappers, the cardinal will be alone and injured."

"And in danger. You're right. And it has been several minutes, anyway," D'Artagnan said as he urged his horse onto the right fork. They rode for several more minutes before hearing a commotion at ahead.

"Hear that?" D'Artagnan asked, spurring his horse faster.

"Yes. We may have found them. I wonder who has disarmed more men, Aramis or Athos," Porthos said.

"We shall soon see. Look up ahead," D'Artagnan replied.

Some way ahead, the distance shortening every second, a battle was underway. They could see the cart at the side of the road, with Brother Xavier huddling protectively over the cardinal.

Athos and Aramis were fighting two other men with a third on the ground, bleeding. Then Aramis tripped and fell. The man he had been fighting was about to finish Aramis off when Porthos jumped from the horse he was riding and dashed to Aramis' defense, his sword drawn. He engaged the other man and Aramis was able to get to his feet, adding his sword to Porthos'. D'Artagnan couldn't bear to miss out on the fun and joined Athos in getting the better of his foe.

The four friends made short work of the two attackers, who soon lay dead on the ground near their injured comrade.

"Thank you for preventing my untimely demise," Aramis said to Porthos. "I don't know why I tripped. I'm usually very steady on my feet."

"Perhaps you were still a little light-headed from the blow that knocked you unconscious," Porthos replied. "No matter; you will be back to normal in no time."

Two horses stood under a tree, but the third had vanished. Porthos' and Aramis' horses were nowhere to be seen. Fortunately, the cart horse was still attached to the cart.

D'Artagnan stood next to the injured man. "Should we kill him, too?" he asked Athos and Porthos. Aramis had gone to the cart to make sure the two monks had not been mistreated.

Before they could reply, they heard D'Artagnan saying to the prisoner, "You look familiar. Haven't I seen you before?" He thought a moment. "Oh, yes. You were the one following us a few days ago. Let me see your arms." The man gestured that his weapons had already been taken from him, but D'Artagnan grabbed the man and pulled his jacket and shirt off. Each arm had a slightly healed slash.

"Yes. I see you went back for reinforcements." Noticing the blood on the ground, he continued. "Your blood?" he said, pointing to it.

"My leg," the injured man said. D'Artagnan rolled him over and saw the tear in his breeches and the cut on his leg.

He motioned for Athos to follow him as he walked a short distance away. "Your thoughts on the prisoner's disposition? Keep him or kill him?"

"Well, we might get information out of him, but he also might try, and succeed, to escape," Athos said. "Although that is unlikely, with his new injury."

"True. I'll solicit a suggestion from Brother Etienne, if he is conscious. Also, Brother Xavier must be questioned. We are all in this together, and everyone should have a say. But I get the last word. Agreed?"

"Agreed."

They went to the cart holding the two monks. "How is Brother Etienne? I would like his opinion on the prisoner over there if he is able to speak with me." D'Artagnan waved his hand at the man on the ground, who had started crawling as if trying to get away.

"Por…I mean, Georges, would you keep watch on him, please?" D'Artagnan asked. Porthos walked over and stared menacingly at the man.

"I'm afraid that he is unconscious again," Brother Xavier said. "I hope he is just sleeping, but I'm not sure."

"As you saw," D'Artagnan continued, "his companions did not survive their encounter with Georges and Emile. We have been discussing what to do with him. Did they harm either of you when they abducted you?"

"No, but they did threaten us," Brother Xavier said. "One of them knocked me from my seat and took the reins. I fell backwards but didn't fall onto Brother Etienne, which, considering the size of the cart, was indeed fortunate. One of the others rode behind us and the third rode in front. They didn't say where they were taking us. I am very grateful that you found us."

"Thank you," D'Artagnan said. "We will be leaving soon. Brother Xavier, would you step aside with me for a word?"

"Of course," he replied, doing so.

"Brother, how did you happen to request that you accompany us on this journey?"

"W-Well," he stuttered. "I was talking with a visitor at the monastery who had heard that Cardinal Richelieu was there. I said I would like to learn from him, but that I had heard he would be leaving soon. The man suggested I ask to go with him, so I did."

"And why would the man make such a suggestion? Did he suggest anything else?"

The monk thought for a moment. "Yes. He asked if I would write him about what I learn from the cardinal. He gave me the address of his sister, so that I could write him there."

"And have you written him any letters?"

"No." He hung his head. "I knew this trip was to be in secret, and was afraid to do so openly. And I had not brought anything to write with or on. And I had no money for a messenger to take a letter." He looked up at D'Artagnan with hope.

"It is well for you that you couldn't send a message. Before we left, the abbot told me of the visitor, and that he sneaked away during the night, most probably taking the cardinal's torn and bloodied robe and biretta with him. I suspect he may be aligned with Monsieur Gaston and his quest for the crown of France." D'Artagnan looked at the monk pointedly. "See that you don't do anything suspicious in the future."

"Of course, sir. I will do nothing to endanger this mission."

D'Artagnan just smiled.

Porthos tied their prisoner's hands and feet after tying a cloth around the cut on his leg. He asked one of the others to catch the dead men's horses and attached their reins to the wagon.

"Help me transfer some of these bundles to the extra horses," he asked Aramis. "The prisoner can ride in the wagon where Brother Xavier can keep an eye on him."

"I don't think that would be a good idea," Aramis replied. "He could easily injure Brother Etienne further, perhaps cause his death. It is a very small cart."

"You're right. But what can we do with him?"

Aramis thought for a moment. "I suggest we make sure his hands and feet are tied securely and throw him across the bare back of one of the extra horses. Then tie his hands and feet together underneath. If he slides to the side, we'll know and can try a different way of tying him on the horse."

"What about the dead men?" Athos asked. "Shouldn't we bury them?"

D'Artagnan had just joined them and heard the question. He thought for a moment and said, "Digging graves would take much too long. We don't know that there aren't others following. But we certainly shouldn't leave them where they are."

"Why not?" asked Porthos. "If any are following, they will see the dead men and know their plot was foiled. Perhaps we should move them to the edge of the road, though. We should take their weapons and any money they have on them. They're useless to them, anyway."

When the supplies were redistributed and the prisoner was attached to his horse, D'Artagnan asked Athos to ride with him at the head of the company. Porthos and Aramis would ride at the back on either side of the prisoner and Brother Xavier would periodically look behind and warn them if anyone was approaching from the rear.

Porthos and Aramis each whistled for their horses, who soon came trotting back to their masters, seemingly pleased to see them.

In this manner they rode back to the point of the attack and then rode farther. By that time it was nearing late afternoon.

"I don't know how far the next village is, but I don't think we should ride any farther. We all have had a hard day and need a good night's rest," D'Artagnan told the group. "We have food and drink with us that should be enough for tonight. Let's find a place off the road to camp."

The others agreed and started looking for a good place which would be shielded from the road. About half a mile off the road they found a clean stream with a stand of trees a short distance from it, toward the road. By the stream was a small grassy clearing.

They tied the horses close enough to the stream that they could drink, but in the clearing so they could graze. Since the ground sloped toward the stream, D'Artagnan decided to build a fire, trusting that it couldn't be seen from the road. The cardinal would remain in the cart, but the rest of them would sleep on the ground around the fire.

After preparing a simple meal out of the provisions they had been carrying with them, D'Artagnan motioned for his friends to follow him a few feet away. In a low voice, he said, "That little slip from Xavier means that we must be sure the prisoner doesn't escape. We must question him now."

The others nodded in agreement, and Porthos went to get him.

They took him to a flat place beside the stream where they could sit. Then they sat him down and tied him to a tree.

"If you answer our questions truthfully, we will be lenient with you," D'Artagnan began. "We want to know who you are and why you and your fellows attacked our party."

"My name is Jean DuPont. You must release me at once or suffer the consequences," he said, defiantly.

"Well, Monsieur DuPont. You must answer our questions first. Why did you attack us?"

"I believe you are harboring a fugitive. You must release me and hand him over."

The others laughed quietly for a moment.

"I don't believe you understand your situation, monsieur," Athos said. "You are our prisoner, not our guest. Who do you work for?"

"I work for the rightful king. That man in your cart is an enemy of the crown."

"That man? Why, he is nothing but a young monk travelling on a pilgrimage," D'Artagnan replied.

"The other man, you dolt!" Monsieur DuPont spat at the ground.

"Our prisoner doesn't seem very friendly," Aramis said to the others. "Or bright. If he was smart, he would be answering our questions and begging for his life."

After an hour or so of fruitless questioning, the suggestion was made that they get some sleep.

"Morning will come all too soon," said Athos. "We must be rested, for only the Good Lord knows what will befall us tomorrow."

They all lay on the ground surrounding the cart, the front hitching posts jammed against the tree to keep it level. The prisoner was tied with more rope to the posts as well as the tree. Each man wrapped himself in the blankets he had brought. Aramis and D'Artagnan lay next to each other on one side of the cart, and Athos and Porthos lay on the other side.

"Allais?" whispered Aramis. "How do you think the cardinal is doing? He seems very weak to me. I know the musketeers never got along well with his guards, except for us, of course, but I'm afraid what will happen to France if the cardinal dies."

"I am afraid, also," D'Artagnan replied. "All we can do is our best to keep him safe and alive until we deliver him to . . ." D'Artagnan had almost disclosed their final destination. "I'm sorry, but I can't say exactly where we're going. Now we should try to sleep. I think this will be a long journey."

Chapter Nine

ne of King Gaston's advisors knocked on the door to his private quarters. "Your Majesty, there is another message with news of the cardinal."

"What does it say this time?" The king had received many messages from people insisting they had seen the cardinal in their towns or villages. Gaston thought, as much as he wanted to know where the cardinal was, or if he was even alive, that all the messages were not worth the trouble it took to write them. Or read them.

"It says that a man who looks a lot like the cardinal was seen in the town of La Peage. He and some men who looked like mercenaries stayed a night at the rectory with a Father Andreas. The letter was sent by a Marie Antin. Damien Antin is her uncle and works here in the palace," the advisor said.

"Let me see it." Gaston held out his hand for the letter. He read, "Your Majesty, King Gaston. I have reason to believe that the cardinal, Richelieu, stayed for a night in La Peage at the rectory at Father Andreas' invitation. His party, including a young monk and four mercenaries, will be traveling to the west, I think, when they leave La Peage.   Marie Antin, Epernon rectory"

"Hm. I am aware of her uncle. I know the family has been supporters of mine. Send some men in that direction and tell them who to look for. I want him back alive, but the others may be dealt with however is needed." He handed the letter back to the advisor and dismissed him.

∞ ∞ ∞

A chilly morning came early that day, and with it, a heavy dew. Bird song woke everyone to discover their clothes and bedding were soaking wet. Brother Etienne, by virtue of sleeping in the cart, was dryer, although the air was humid.

D'Artagnan checked first to see if the cardinal was awake.

"How are you feeling this morning, Brother Etienne?" D'Artagnan asked him.

"Still very tired, but now I feel a little hungry. Why are we out here? And who . . ."

Before anyone could answer, the cardinal said, "Oh, wait. I remember now."

"That's good news. I'll see what provisions we have."

"I suppose we should all change into dry clothing," said Porthos. "Riding in wet clothes would not be pleasant."

"Perhaps, since there is a stream here, we should take some time to bathe," Aramis suggested. "Our clothing is already wet, and we are covered with road dust. We could clean ourselves before we dress in dry clothing."

The rest, except for Brother Etienne and Brother Xavier, plunged into the flowing water and rubbed their clothing against their skin.

"Brother Xavier, do you have a dry habit to change into?" Porthos asked when he emerged from the water.

"I fear I do not, Monsieur Georges." Brother Xavier looked uncomfortable at the admission. "I have only what I am wearing."

"Perhaps one of the rest of us has something." Then Aramis said, looking right at Athos, "Gerard? You seem to be about the same size as our young monk. Do you have anything to spare?"

"I do have another shirt, but I'm afraid my breeches might be too, uh, small." Athos looked at Aramis. "Emile? You may be a similar size."

Aramis was already looking through his pack. "I have a pair of breeches that Brother Xavier is welcome to try on." He pulled them out and held them up.

"But, but, they are so small. I can't see how they would fit me," Brother Xavier said.

"Just try them on," Aramis said, holding them out to him. "It's just temporary, after all."

Brother Xavier took them and held them up to his waist. Shaking his head, he leaned against the side of the cart and stuck one leg, and then the other, into the legs of the breeches. Then he stood and pulled them up. Pulling up his robe, he fastened the waist.

"They fit, all right," Aramis said. "I thought they would. Here's the shirt." He handed Athos' shirt to the monk. "Try that on, too."

Brother Xavier took his habit off and laid it over the edge of the cart. Then he pulled the shirt on over his head.

"It fits, too."

The others admired Brother Xavier's new look, to his chagrin, and then started arranging the wet articles around the cart's edges to dry.

"What about our prisoner?" Porthos asked. "He's wet, too." Du Pont had been tied securely to the tree trunk during the night and, although he had tried to break his bonds, had been unable to.

"I say let him be wet. It may loosen his tongue," replied Athos.

"I agree," said D'Artagnan. "Shall we have some breakfast?"

There was a muffled cry from the prisoner, which was ignored.

They all shared what they had, being sure that the cardinal had as much as he wanted first. They offered the prisoner the leavings, which he refused.

"A little more for us, then," Porthos observed.

When Porthos went to get the prisoner, he found the man tangled in the ropes.

"Were you trying to free yourself again?" Porthos asked, leaning against the cart. "You look as though you're caught up in a giant spider web. Well, I would like to leave you here, but that would be a mistake."

He thought a moment, the called out, "Would someone help me with this? Our prisoner may be the intended breakfast for one of those giant spiders I've heard about."

Athos was the closest, and he went around to the tree. "Well, he seems to have got himself all tangled up. Perhaps we could tie him to the other end of the cart and drag him."

D'Artagnan heard what was being said and joined Porthos and Athos. "Oh, my," he said. "Dragging him would be entertaining, until someone came along and saw him. We had best get him untangled and back on the horse."

∞ ∞ ∞

Soon they were ready to get back on the road. D'Artagnan rode ahead to scout the road to make sure no one was there to see them reenter it. At his all clear wave, the rest started across the uneven ground to join him.

Before they got to the screen of trees, though, D'Artagnan started racing back toward them, motioning them to stop and go back. By the time he got to the rest of them, they could hear hoof beats from the road.

"Go back," he told them. "Turn the cart and ford the stream. It sounds like a regiment is coming." When the prisoner heard what D'Artagnan said, he started yelling for help. It was unlikely that anyone on the road would be able to hear him, but Brother Xavier hastily found a scrap of cloth and shoved it into his mouth as a gag.

"But they are passing and will be gone soon," Athos said to D'Artagnan. "Can't we wait them out and go on when they have gotten far enough away?"

"Yes, but there may be more behind them. I think it would be better to go another way and take the chance that others catch up to us."

"But do you know what lies in that direction? There isn't even a road to follow. What if we get lost?" Athos pressed his case.

"Nevertheless, I am the leader of this group, and I think it would be to our advantage to go the way I suggest."

The others finally agreed, and D'Artagnan rode to one side of the cart horse and motioned for someone else to go to the other side. They took hold of the horse's harness and guided it toward the stream. The other two took the pack horses and the horse the prisoner was tied to and followed.

"You two go on ahead," D'Artagnan told Athos and Aramis, who had the pack horses. "We'll follow the way you go so we won't step in holes and spill the cart."

Athos and Aramis entered the stream some few yards apart and went slowly. No one wanted a lame or injured horse. They stepped carefully across the rocky bottom of the stream. Fortunately, the stream was calm at that place, but they could hear rapids in the distance. The water came up to the horses' knees, which was around axle high on the cart. As long as the bed of the cart didn't leak, the bedding in the cart wouldn't get wet, but just to be certain, Brother Xavier and Porthos lifted and placed on the seat what they could. That left the cardinal with very little to rest on.

"I would rather lie on the bottom of the cart for a short time than have to rest on wet bedding for much longer," he said, wheezing a little.

They forded the stream successfully but had some trouble mounting the bank of the opposite side. Porthos muttered curses under his breath, although the others could hear him and several joined in. Finally, three of the men on horseback dismounted and got behind to push.

When the cart was on dry ground, Brother Xavier checked the bed of the cart to make sure it wasn't wet. Then he replaced all the bedding that had been placed on the seat. Aramis held the cardinal while padding was placed where he lay, then he was placed on it and wrapped in the remaining blankets.

"I've never had to push a cart before," Athos grumbled. "But I've never had to cross a stream with one, either. Shall we not have to do that again, please?"

"I think we all can agree with that," Porthos said. "And now we are soaked to the knees. Do you know where we are now?" he asked D'Artagnan.

"I have a very general idea. I know where we were headed, but I don't know exactly where we stopped, or where we can get to without going across the stream again." He rummaged in his saddlebag for the map he carried. "Our next stop was at Ramalard, but we missed it and seem to be headed in an entirely different direction." He had the map out and spread on a flat rock away from the stream's bank.

"I think we stopped here." He pointed to a place on the map for the others to look at. "See, here's the fork. After we rescued the monks and got back to where you were attacked, here," he pointed again, "we rode a little farther, possibly to here." Another point. "Then we camped about here. Sorry; the map is small and the streams are not marked, so this is just a guess. But I'd place us about – here." One more point. "And this is the direction we should be going." The last point.

"Where will that take us?" Athos said. "Will we still be going in the right direction?"

"First we need to find out if we can go in that direction. There isn't a road close by that I can see on the map. If we head in the right direction, we may find a road and we may not. If we do, the road might not be going where we want to go." D'Artagnan scrutinized the map some more. "Perhaps if we go that way," he pointed away from the stream, "we will find a road, or a village on a road, or something."

"At least it's a direction," Athos said. "Let's go."

They all mounted their horses, D'Artagnan keeping his map where he could get to it easily. The way was not smooth, and the cart bounced around continually. Brother Xavier had some trouble staying on his seat, and Brother Etienne prayed until he fell asleep as they looked for a road.

Their prisoner swayed back and forth on his horse and nearly swung underneath several times. Then he started to, slowly, move himself toward the rear of the horse, meaning to slide off and try to escape. He was resting on the horse's rump when Porthos noticed and quickly preventing him from completing the act.

"Allais!" Porthos called to his friend. "Our prisoner is trying to escape."

Porthos was holding the man in place by gripping his clothing.

The other turned to look as Porthos moved the man back to the center of the horse's back, saying, "Your hands and feet are tied together. How far do you think you could get before we noticed?" Porthos looked to the others. "Perhaps we should knock him unconscious." Then he looked back at the prisoner. "Do you think that will be necessary?"

Du Pont just shook his head.

The area they were travelling through was a forest. Fortunately, the trees were widely-enough spaced and there wasn't much vegetation on the ground so that, although the way was rough, they did not have to be wary of running into trees. After a while they came across an animal track, perhaps deer, and followed it.

"Do you think this deer track will lead us to a road?" Athos asked.

"Of course," D'Artagnan replied. "Deer always cross roads. There must be tracks to lead them there. I'm sure this one will lead to a road going somewhere. Don't you think so, Brother Xavier?"

"What? Oh." The monk started at hearing his name. He had been so lost in prayer that he had just about dozed off, perilously close to falling off the cart. "Yes, I believe you're right. I'm sure God is leading us the right way."

Before long the sun was high and they started complaining of hunger.

"Let's stop by this stream," Porthos suggested. "At least it's not going across our path."

They stopped and led the horses to the water.

"Please help me out of the cart," the cardinal requested. He seemed very weak and could barely move. "I must relieve myself." Porthos and Aramis lifted him out and carried him to a large tree, holding him up. Then they carried him back to the cart, where Athos and Brother Xavier had shaken out the bedding and arranged it back in the cart.

After that, they inventoried their supplies. Other than some grain for the horses, they didn't have much. There was some bread, cheese, and dried meat. Athos unearthed a bottle of wine and another of beer. After the last of them had taken his turn behind a tree and returned, they ate their meal.

All that time the prisoner had been lying across the back of the horse.

"Should we let him off for a few minutes?" Aramis asked. "It must be very hard traveling like that."

"He could be dead," Porthos pointed out. "If he wanted to live, he shouldn't have attacked us."

They started out again following the same track. In the distance they could see a small cabin.

"Shall we see if someone is home?" asked Aramis. "Maybe we could get an idea of where we are."

"Perhaps we should conceal our prisoner first," said D'Artagnan. "We don't want our motives misconstrued."

"Is there enough room to squeeze him into the cart without discomforting Brother Etienne?" Aramis asked.

D'Artagnan examined the remaining room in the cart and then scrutinized their prisoner's size.

"I think so. Your Eminence, could you move as close to the side as you can? We'll conceal our prisoner under the blankets and put some of our supplies on top."

They made sure Monsieur DuPont was gagged and well-tied. They then covered him with some of the drying clothes.

"If you make a single sound or motion before we uncover you, your life will be extremely short," Athos warned him.

"Maybe we should knock him out first," suggested Porthos. "That way he won't even be able to move."

"Should we do that, monsieur?" Athos inquired of the prisoner, who shook his head violently.

"No? Then be absolutely silent and still."

When they were near the cabin, they were hailed by a man standing nearby.

"Monsieurs, do you know you are on private property? This wood belongs to the King. You must leave immediately," he said to them.

D'Artagnan dismounted and walked up to the man. "That is what we are trying to do. My friends and I are escorting an injured monk back to his family home to recover. Several miles back and across a stream, we were nearly accosted by highwaymen and had to escape. Because we had been camping by the stream, we thought it best to cross it and change our direction. Thus, we are lost and didn't know we were crossing the King's wood. If you can direct us to the nearest road, we will gladly leave the wood and proceed to our destination."

"I see," the man said. "Can you prove that your story is true?"

"I can, but what would happen if we could not prove it? Or if you don't believe us? All I can do is ask you to speak to Brother Etienne. He will verify the story," D'Artagnan said. He turned back toward the others "Is Brother Etienne awake?"

"I am," came a soft voice.

"Could you please explain to this man our intentions?"

Because D'Artagnan had been speaking loudly, the cardinal had heard and knew how to answer the man's questions.

Straining to hear the monk, the man walked closer to the cart.

"Yes, monsieur, what Allais told you is true. I was being escorted toward my old home near Nantes when we encountered the highwaymen." That was all the cardinal was able to say for a few moments. Then he continued, "We just want to find the closest road so we can find out where we are and which way we need to go." It took several minutes for the cardinal to say this, and he didn't need to try to look ill. He had been chilled during the night, even though he wasn't sleeping on the ground with the others, and he shivered a bit.

The man thought for a moment. He could see he was vastly outnumbered and had no chance of winning if there was a fight.

"Very well. The road is several more miles in that direction." He pointed toward the way they should go. "The road goes east and west. If you go either way, there is a north/south road not far. Please be on your way quickly."

"Thank you, monsieur. May God be with you," Brother Xavier told him.

They rode a ways on and stopped again when they were out of sight of the cabin. D'Artagnan rode up to the cart and moved the wet clothing off the prisoner.

"You did well, Monsieur. We may let you live, yet. Please continue to be silent and still. It will work in your favor."

One or two more miles got them to the promised road.

"We should turn to the left, now. We've been going north, and our direction is to the west," D'Artagnan told the others.

The group entered the roadway at that point. Within a few more miles they came to a village. Without prompting, Brother Xavier turned and began covering Monsieur DuPont with the slightly dryer clothing and the same warning as before.

"We will go on to the other side of the village, and then Gerard and I will come back and acquire more provisions," D'Artagnan told the rest. "We'll also find out where we are. Do try to avoid attention, but keep alert."

They stopped at the west end of the village, pulling off the road and into a stand of trees. Then D'Artagnan and Athos set off on foot back toward the village and the local inn.

The village was typical of small towns in this area: a mixture of houses and businesses with the inn and the church in prominent positions.

"We're wondering if we could procure provisions for our journey," D'Artagnan said to the innkeeper. "We have run low but aren't ready to stop for the night."

"Of course, Monsieurs. What will you need?" the innkeeper replied.

"Gerard, do you have the list?" D'Artagnan asked his friend.

"No, I don't, Allais. I thought you had it," Athos replied.

D'Artagnan covered his face with his hands and hung his head. "Gerard, I know I gave you the list. What have you done with it?"

"As I said, I never had it. Do you remember what we need?"

"Ah, well. I guess we will have to tax our memories. We need dried meat."

"And bread," Athos added.

"And cheese."

"And carrots. Do you have carrots?"

"And wine."

"And beer. Oh, and onions."

"And a sack to carry it in," D'Artagnan finished. "Do you have all that?"

"Oui, Monsieurs. I can furnish that for you," the innkeeper answered, and totaled the charge.

"That much?" Athos asked. "I have only this much." He opened his hand to show a few coins. "How much do you have, Allais?"

D'Artagnan took some currency out of a pocket and displayed it. "This is all I have. Will this be enough with what Gerard has?"

The two tried in vain to figure out how much they had. Before long the innkeeper's head was swimming from trying to keep up and offered them their order for the amount they said they had. Plus the sack, which they loaded with the food, and then argued about who would carry it.

"That was fun," Athos said when they were half a block from the inn. "We should try that again."

"It was, and it saved us some money," D'Artagnan added. "Oh, we forgot to ask where we are." He walked up to a woman who was about to enter a shop and asked, "Pardon me, Mademoiselle, but could you tell us the name of this lovely village?"

The woman giggled behind her fan and replied, "It is madame, kind sir, and the name of the village is Bizou." She giggled again and went into the shop.

Chapter Ten

D'Artagnan and Athos arrived at the edge of town where they had left the others in the group. The cart was in the same place, but Porthos and Aramis were not to be seen. And they saw that the prisoner was no longer in the cart.

"Where are Georges and Emile?" D'Artagnan asked Brother Xavier as they loaded their provisions into the cart. "And where is Monsieur DuPont?"

"They took the prisoner off that way." Brother Xavier pointed toward the woods behind them. "They wanted to question him some more."

"How long have they been gone?" Athos asked.

Brother Xavier thought for a minute and answered, "Not more than a dozen minutes."

"Gerard, you stay here. I'll go after them," D'Artagnan said, and started off in that direction.

"That's fine, Allais. I'll put the provisions away," Athos said to D'Artagnan's disappearing back. "Help me stow this away, Brother Xavier. We can test it for freshness as we go."

D'Artagnan caught up with Porthos and Aramis quickly. The prisoner was lying on the ground in a small copse, bleeding and groaning.

"What happened here?" he asked his friends.

"He was starting to make noise," said Porthos. "We didn't want him attracting attention, so we brought him away from the road. Then he tried to escape. He got his hands free and took my sword. Aramis had to defend me, since I had no weapon."

"Where is your firearm?"

"I left it in my saddlebag. I didn't really think I would need it just now."

At that point, Monsieur DuPont started screaming. D'Artagnan walked over to him and warned him. "Stop right now or you will be of no use to us."

The man continued to scream. Porthos, who had recovered his sword, joined D'Artagnan at the prisoner's side and brandished it menacingly. "Stop it!"

The prisoner, at that, started to get up, but Porthos objected by holding the point of his sword against the man's chest.

"Georges, don't," D'Artagnan protested, but before either of them could do anything, the man lunged against the sword tip, impaling himself. He fell, pulling the sword out of Porthos' hand, and breathed his last.

The three friends looked at him, then hung their heads.

"I didn't want this to happen, but it seems Monsieur DuPont did. Besides, we couldn't have let him go. We need to move his body away from here into that group of bushes over there. Don't pull the sword out yet. We don't want to leave too much of a trail of blood," D'Artagnan told the others.

After they had finished the task and returned to the cart, Porthos told the ones who had waited what had happened.

"We did get a little information. Apparently, he was sent out by one of Monsieur's men to search for Cardinal Richelieu."

Brother Xavier looked like he was about to speak, but D'Artagnan held up a hand to stop him. "He was told to look elsewhere, but he seemed not to believe us. It was just as well that he caused his own death. All the men that attacked and kidnapped you are now dead. Perhaps no one will look in this direction again and we can proceed in peace." He glared at Brother

Xavier as a warning to keep quiet. "We don't want Brother Etienne to be in danger."

After eating some of their new provisions, they continued on the road, hoping to find another inn in another village to stay for the night. No one wanted to be as wet again as they had been that morning.

Not that much later the sky began to darken. Clouds were rolling in, covering the sun, which was low ahead of them.

"We may have to camp again tonight, unfortunately," Athos said, gloomily. "We have no waterproof groundcovers, do we?" D'Artagnan shook his head.

"Then we should change back into our wet clothes so as not to get these dry ones wet, also."

Most of the clothing that had been drying in the cart was dry by then, but they decided to change, anyway.

"I am so glad to be back into my robes. I am, of course, grateful to you gentlemen for the loan of your garments, but I am more comfortable dressed as I am meant to be." Brother Xavier sighed.

They found a sheltered spot and pulled the cart under a large tree away from the road. They were able to light a small campfire fairly close and made a small feast of the bread and cheese left of their provisions.

They moved some of the contents of the cart to the seat and hung the rest from a tree branch to keep them dry. The two monks managed to fit into the cart for the night and snuggled into the blankets for warmth.

"Do you think we need a guard," Porthos asked. "It's unlikely that we will be attacked again, but just in case . . ."

"Yes," D'Artagnan interrupted. "I think that would be a good idea. Would you like to stand watch first? I think two hours apiece should be enough."

"I will. Who will go next?"

Aramis agreed to go second. Then Athos chose third. That left D'Artagnan to be last. Porthos settled in against the tree and the other three crawled under the cart as far as they could manage, to sleep.

Despite the thunder during the night, it didn't rain on them directly. But the dew was again heavy and parts of their clothing were damp when they awoke.

The next morning, Brother Xavier checked on the cardinal. "He seems to be breathing calmly, but his heartbeat is weak. I think he must need food. I'll see if I can wake him."

After changing back to their dry clothes, they got out the stores they had left and looked for anything that the cardinal could eat.

"I found some dried meat," Athos said as he pulled a piece out of a bag. "I can cut it up into fine bits and mix it with a bit of the small beer we have left. That would make a sort of cold soup." They did so.

After Brother Xavier had roused the wounded man, he checked how he was healing, then propped him into a reclining position and began to feed him.

They all ate a sparse breakfast of cheese and bread and got back on the road. The day was overcast, but they remembered the direction they had been going the day before, and headed that way again.

"Allais, get out your map and try to figure out where we are," suggested Athos. "You knew where we were supposed to go the other day. Maybe you can work backwards."

"A good idea, Gerard," replied D'Artagnan, and dug the map out of his saddlebag, along with the itinerary that Cardinal Tremblay had given him. He searched for the town they had been headed to before they got lost. "The last place we stayed, before the attack, was Moutieres-au-Perche. The next night we were supposed to be in Remalard." He thought for a moment. "We turned off the road to our right, didn't we, to camp for the night the first time? That would have been to the north. Then we had to keep going that way to avoid being discovered. We crossed the creek and kept going north. Then we ran into the game warden who directed us to keep going to find a road. The village we stopped in was called Bizou. We then continued west on the road. So we should be around – here." He pointed to a spot on the map. "I think."

"How close to the route the cardinal gave us are we now?" Athos asked.

"Not very close at all. But we seem to be going the right direction. Should we continue on this road or try to go back?" D'Artagnan said.

"Would going a different way get us there faster?" Aramis asked.

"We don't even know where 'there' is," complained Porthos. "Where are we headed, anyway?"

"We are going to, uh," he consulted the itinerary. "Nantes. It's to the west and south from here."

"What's in Nantes?" Porthos asked.

D'Artagnan looked at him pointedly. "Brother Etienne's family home, of course."

They got on their way after rearranging the remainder of their supplies in the cart. The passenger had more room, which could be a problem. It meant that their food supply was getting low and would need to be replenished soon if they had to camp again.

"I hope we can find an inn for the night," said Porthos. "I am so tired of camping."

"I remember when you said you would be willing to sleep on the kitchen floor if you had to," teased Aramis.

"Yes, I would. But kitchens are generally inside a building away from the elements. By the way, when we do restock our food supplies, could we please purchase some good wine? Beer is good. It's wet and better than bad wine, at least, but good wine is the drink of the gods, and I want some."

"Anything else, your highness? A roast capon? Some chocolate? We'll ask the innkeeper if he can provide," Athos taunted.

"All right! Tease me if you will. I have expensive taste," Porthos replied.

"On an ale budget." Athos grinned and slapped his friend on the back. "We'll get what we can get and be happy for it."

They reached a small village around lunchtime, but there was no inn.

"Go on and I will catch up to you. I'll try to buy some food and meet you at the other end of town," D'Artagnan told the others.

After they had gone ahead, he hailed a woman who was walking along the road.

"Madam, have you any food I can purchase? My friends and I are running low on foodstuffs and have a long way yet to go."

She looked him up and down. From his boots and the tack on his horse, not to mention the quality of the horse, she decided he could probably afford to pay well. "I have a bit, but I must feed my family. What are you asking for?"

"Some bread and cheese, if you can spare it, and possibly some wine."

"And what can you pay for it?"

They haggled a bit and came up with a price acceptable to both. The exchange was made and D'Artagnan rode the short way to meet his friends.

"Here we are," D'Artagnan said as he rode up to the others. "I have found a feast."

"Where is your hat," Aramis asked. "Did you pay for the food with it?"

"No, but I did have to leave it as surety that I would return the pitcher I brought with wine in it."

They pulled the cart off the road a few feet and everyone gathered around it. D'Artagnan spread his purchases on the bed of the cart to show them off.

"Bread and cheese" Aramis said. "That's nothing special. Didn't we just have that this morning?" D'Artagnan admonished him.

Another sack was placed in the bed of the cart. He took out a stoppered pitcher of wine. "This is for you, Georges. And the rest of us, of course."

They set to and before long all the bread and cheese had vanished. The pitcher was well on its way to being empty.

"One last drink and we will leave. I'll go return the jug and retrieve my hat."

When D'Artagnan returned with his hat, the company moved on.

The day was lingering and getting hot. The road was not shaded by trees, but was leading them through a field where cows grazed near a pond.

"Beef!" exclaimed Athos. "I wish it was going to be our dinner. Alas, I'm afraid that we will be eating what is left of our stores. Meager pickings."

"We may yet come to a village with an inn," Aramis said. "A real bed would certainly be welcome. A floor in the kitchen for you, Georges, of course. You seem so fond of them."

Porthos just grumbled a moment. He fanned himself with his hat, then shaded his eyes with it. "That may be a village ahead." The haze in the air, plus the lowering sun in their eyes proved to interfere with their sight, but a few yards further brought the village into better focus.

"I think I see the sign for an inn," D'Artagnan said. A little farther, he read "The Blue Whale. A strange name for an inn, or perhaps we are closer to the coast than we thought."

"I don't care if the inn's name is The Depths of Hell," returned Porthos. "I will sleep in its bed and eat its food."

"Then it may be fortunate for us that that's not its name," D'Artagnan replied. By that time they had pulled close to the building. "It doesn't look to be in very good condition. Pull the cart around the back. Gerard, come with me to see about rooms."

"Of course, Allais," Athos replied. "We will be back soon," he called to the others.

"Doesn't it seem strange to you that there are no villagers in the streets?" D'Artagnan asked his friend.

"As a matter of fact, it does. I hadn't noticed before, being rather excited by the village and the inn," he replied. "Maybe they're all inside. Shall we go in and see?"

D'Artagnan opened the door to a dark room. No fire blazed in the fireplace. Though it was rather hot for a fire, most inns had a small fire lit for extra light. They moved through the room toward the bar, calling out in case someone was there. They finally made their way to the kitchen, where there was also no fire burning.

"I think this inn may be abandoned. I wonder why." D'Artagnan turned toward the steps to the second floor. "Let's try upstairs."

That floor seemed empty as well. There were beds and bedding in the six rooms, but no occupants.

Athos, who had accompanied his friend to the second floor, rummaged through the bedclothes on one of the empty beds. Pulling back the blanket, he said to D'Artagnan, "Here's something." He picked up a small book and opened it. "It's a prayer book." He rifled the pages. "And it doesn't look like a proper Catholic one, either." He took it over to D'Artagnan and handed it to him. "This looks like it's Protestant. Why would such a book be left at an inn? Shall we take it with us? If nothing else, we could use it to start a fire."

"I'm sure that Protestants travel, too," D'Artagnan said. "Perhaps we should leave it in case the owner returns for it."

"I want to go back to the kitchen and look around," Athos said. "Something looked wrong to me."

In the kitchen again, they started to actually search the room. The cupboards were bare of anything edible, although there were pots and dishes and cups. In fact, everything a cook would want was there except food to feed the nonexistent customers.

They went out the back door to confer with the rest of their company.

"I don't understand what's going on," Aramis said. They were inside the stable, which held no horses and no grain to feed any. "There is a stream behind here. We should tie the horses there so they can drink. Then we should search the houses."

They led all the horses except the still-hitched cart horse to the stream. There was also sweet grass by it for them to eat.

"What about Brothers Etienne and Xavier?" Aramis asked. "I don't think they should go with us, but they shouldn't be left alone, either. One of us should stay with them."

"I agree," D'Artagnan said. "Would you rather stay here in the stable or in the inn?" he asked Brother Xavier. Brother Etienne was still asleep. "It's cool there since there are no fires burning."

"The inn, I think," Brother Xavier said. "If you can carry Brother Etienne up the stairs."

"Very well. I'll take the horse with the others so it can eat and drink. Georges, would you take the brothers up and stay with them? If the rest of us don't finish searching the village soon, one of us will replace you and we'll keep searching. God willing, we will find a bit of food to buy. Otherwise, we'll be eating the rest of our rations," D'Artagnan said.

The Cardinal's guard and the two musketeers searched the homes and shops of the absent villagers. There were less than two dozen buildings to look through, including homes. Most of the buildings were very small, and most of the houses were two or three rooms with a loft. They found no food and little else there. The only other buildings were a bakery, a butcher shop, a blacksmith and the church with its rectory, set a good quarter mile back from the road, which they went to last.

The door to the church was locked. Banging on it did no good, so they went around it to the back, where another door proved impossible to open, as well. Next they went to the rectory, which near the church, but a small stand of trees screened it from the church. Before they were in sight of the house, D'Artagnan said, "Gerard, you go back for the others and bring the cart and horses and everything with you. We'll wait for you here."

Athos did as asked. It took a while to hitch the cart horse, which had been let loose to graze and drink, saddle the other horses, gather up their belongings and carry Brother Etienne down to it. Then they returned to the spot where D'Artagnan and Aramis were waiting for them.

"Brother Xavier, would you drive the cart up to the house? Then you can knock on the door and ask for sanctuary. Say that Brother Etienne is ill, which is true. The rest of us will approach the house at a distance and spread out around it. Gerard will go to the back. Georges, you go to the right side, and Emile, you go to the left side. I'll be at the front out of sight. Be sure you can't be seen. Maybe, if anyone is in there, if they see just the two monks at the door, they'll open it."

They all took their positions and Brother Xavier knocked on the door.

After several knocks, D'Artagnan saw someone peeking through a window. "Someone is in there," he said, softly. "Brother Xavier, please call out and see if the door opens."

"Hello the house," the monk called. "My companion and I are Capuchin monks and seek food and shelter."

After a moment they could see a crack in the door. A face peered out and looked the monks up and down. "What are your names and where do you come from?" it asked.

"I am Brother Xavier and the man in the cart is Brother Etienne, who is ill. We are traveling from the monastery in Clairefontaine and seek shelter. Can you help us?"

"Ill! No! Leave here at once," the man at the door said. Before he slammed the door, Brother Xavier called out.

"I didn't mean ill. He has been injured. He fell from the cart when we hit a rut. He is not ill."

The door opened a bit farther and another face joined the first. "Who is your Abbot?"

"He is called Abbe' Michel."

"And you are telling the truth when you say he is only injured?"

"On my oath, I tell you the truth," Brother Xavier told them.

The two faces whispered to each other and after a moment the door opened farther. "Are you traveling alone?"

Brother Xavier paused a moment. "No, we have traveling companions. Four men who are seeking employment are traveling with us. They are looking in the village for help."

D'Artagnan heard and headed around the building to gather the other three and sneak back toward the village.

The door opened to let the two monks enter, Brother Etienne being carried by a large, strong man. They were startled to hear the door slammed and barred behind them. Once they were inside, people slowly entered to see who the newcomers were. Brother Xavier thought, *These must be the people from the village.*

"What has happened in this village?? All the buildings were empty. Are these people the villagers? You welcomed us into your home and then barred the door behind us."

A man in a priest's robe pushed his way through the crowd. "Come in; you are welcome here. I am Pastor Alexandre."

Chapter Eleven

The two monks saw a tall, thin man standing in the house's foyer. There were other people standing behind him, dressed simply. The group extended into the next room as well as up the ornate staircase. The man looked similar to Brother Etienne, but much younger and clean shaven.

"Please forgive my people. They are afraid, but with good reason. Yesterday a rider came through our village warning us of a small group of heavily armed men heading our direction. He told us they are looking for an enemy or enemies of the Crown and will search every home and shop in each village they visit. I told the people they have nothing to fear since there is no enemy of the Crown hiding here, but it didn't placate them. So I asked them to come to my home and bring whatever food they have with them so we all can eat."

By this time the man holding Brother Etienne had laid him on a divan in the foyer. There were other chairs with several elderly people sitting in them.

"This is Brother Etienne," Brother Xavier told the men. "He was gravely injured and is being taken to his family home to recover. I can see you are crowded, but is there a bed he may lie in away from the bustle of the people?"

"Of course! Please come with me. I have a room he may stay in." The pastor carried Brother Etienne a short way to a small bedroom on the first floor where the injured man could rest. He went back to the front when he heard a knock at the door again.

Before the young monk got to the bedroom where the cardinal had been taken, he heard D'Artagnan calling, "Brother Xavier! Are you in there? Brother Xavier?"

The pastor opened the door this time. "You are with the monks? What are your names?"

D'Artagnan spoke for all. "I am Allais Reynard. My friends are Georges Moreau, Emile Gillette, and Gerard LeRoi. We have been traveling with the monks for a couple of weeks to make sure they get to their destination safely. May we come in?"

"A moment, please." Pastor Alexandre closed and barred the door, then went to the bedroom to confirm the identities of the men at the door.

"Oh yes, they are the men traveling with us. Please let them in," Brother Etienne said, repeating their names to prove that he knew them.

Once inside, the men bowed to the pastor and thanked him for his hospitality.

"Pastor, could you tell us what has happened here? We were looking forward to a night at an inn instead of on the ground, and found your inn and all your houses and shops empty."

The priest explained the situation to them and then asked if they would like to join everyone for supper.

"We would be delighted, Pastor," D'Artagnan told him. "And we have some food with us that we can share. Georges, would you go out to the cart and get our supplies, please? Emile, please go help and then tether the horses out of sight where they can graze and drink." He turned to the clergyman. "May we store our cart in your stable?"

"Of course, if it isn't large. The stable is small."

"Thank you," D'Artagnan said, and requested that Athos do so.

"The monks have been taken to my bedroom, which is next to my study. Come with me; we can talk there. You are their leader, then?"

"I am, to some extent, but we all have a say in what we will do and where we are headed."

"Does that extend to the monks, as well?"

"Of course. They are knowledgeable, and Brother Etienne, who, as you can see, is injured and sleeps much of the time, has wisdom the rest of us don't possess."

By that time the two had arrived at Pastor Alexandre's study, where he bade the visitor sit.

"And where are you going?"

"Brother Etienne wishes to return to his family home to complete his recovery. Brother Xavier is his companion, and since he has had medical training, his physician while we are on our way. After we have delivered Brother Etienne to his family home, we will continue our journey."

"Where is Brother Etienne's family home?"

"In Nantes, although we know we are far from there. We will be on the road for a long time before we arrive."

"And may I ask where the journey will lead you then?" The pastor sat at his desk.

"Wherever we can find employment. We have all been trained as soldiers."

"And how did you come to be riding with the two monks?"

"You seem to have a lot of questions, sir. But I understand why you are asking and will tell you. I was hired to accompany the two monks as their guard. We came upon my friends on the way and they agreed to ride with us. I have known these men for some time and trust them implicitly."

"Very well, sir. It sounds as if your friends have returned from their tasks. Shall we go to our supper?"

"Thank you." D'Artagnan was glad for the interruption, and hoped there would be no more questions.

They entered the carved-oak paneled dining room to find the simple oak table laden with dishes of food. The townspeople were lined up, taking their turns to fill their plates.

Porthos and Aramis were in the line with the plates from their packs. Porthos handed D'Artagnan a plate and said, "This one's from your pack. The others have gotten their own plates. It seems everybody brought plates with them when they came."

"My thanks," D'Artagnan replied. "Did you bring all our belongings in with you?"

Porthos looked around before answering. "Almost all. We moved the cart into the stable and buried a certain sack underneath it. I have brought some of its contents in with me, as payment for our room and board." He patted a pocket and a faint jingling could be heard.

"Good thinking, my friend. Did we have much food to donate to the cause?"

"Not much, but it was all we had. I didn't want to slight on that. We'll find more after we go on our way." *I hope,* he added to himself.

By that time Porthos had reached the table and began to serve himself. D'Artagnan went to the back of the line with his plate to wait his turn. Then he filled a plate for Brother Xavier and Brother Etienne, although he wasn't sure the older man would be able to eat much, and took it to the room where the monks had been taken.

After all had eaten, Pastor Alexandre called everyone together. They filled the living room, the dining room, and the foyer, with some standing on the stairs.

"My friends, I know you all want to go back to your homes, but there is still threat of danger. As you already know, I haven't enough bedrooms for even each family, so again you will have to bed down on the floors.

Those with the largest families may each take one of the bedrooms to leave more space in the other rooms for the rest. One of our new guests, the injured monk, will need a bed, and I will give up mine and sleep on the floor. Monsieur Allais, there may be enough space on the floor of my bedroom for some of your party to sleep, if not all. You are welcome to it. The rest of you may group by family in all the other rooms of my home except for my study. I will sleep in there. Now, please, pray for our continued safety and that of our travelers as you thank the Lord in your evening prayers. God be with all of you as you go to find your places and retire for the night."

There was much chatter and moving around before the settling down began. By full dark everyone was in place and the candles had been extinguished. The fires in the fireplaces had been banked and all was quiet, except for one or two crying infants, which was to be expected.

The group of travelers were in their assigned bedroom with the door closed.

"We must discuss this situation, but we must also be very quiet about it," D'Artagnan said to them in a low voice. "Brother Etienne," he said to the now awake monk, "we suspect, with reason, that the enemy of the crown who is being sought is you. Don't worry, you are safe, we would never give you up. You are much too important to us and the country for that. But we must leave at first light. I think that even here we must stand guard through the night."

The cardinal nodded, then went back to sleep.

"Do you think the townspeople might think to betray us?" Athos asked. "I think these people may not be what they seem."

"It is a possibility. I believe they do not know exactly who those men are searching for, but I think they would give up any stranger to ensure their own safety. But what do you mean, not who they seem to be?"

"The pastor. He is wearing the robe of a priest, but does not call himself that. His demeanor does not seem to be that of a priest and he isn't wearing a crucifix. Oh, I cannot really explain it, but we should keep on our guard."

"We shall. Georges, will you take the first shift and wake Emile or Gerard for the second? I will take the last and watch for the first hint of dawn."

The two monks fit in the one bed, lying close together. The rest bedded down on the floor while Porthos sat in the one chair. There was barely enough room for all of them, but they had slept in close quarters before and were used to it.

Shortly after the household quieted and went to sleep, three of the townsmen--the innkeeper, the butcher, and the blacksmith--quietly rapped on the study door. Pastor Alexandre opened it and the three men crowded in.

"We must speak to you, Pastor," François, the innkeeper, who also served as the village magistrate, said quietly. "We are worried about these new people. I know that two of them are supposed to be men of God, but how do we know that for sure? How do we know they are telling the truth about anything? They may be the men wanted by the king. And besides that, they claim to be Catholic."

"Yes, Pastor," the butcher, André, bald and the eldest of the three, chimed in. "We all agree that you should wear the priest's robe and be careful around strangers, but they may have suspicions that we are Protestant. We may not be safe from them or because of them. The men looking for them may punish us for giving them aid. We must turn them in if it is demanded of us."

The blacksmith, who was the large man who carried Brother Etienne in earlier, just nodded.

"This is a grave request, my friends. I am duty bound by God, even as a Protestant, to give aid to travelers in need. I am also duty bound to protect my flock. But we may not have to make the choice. We will send them on their way in the morning, and if the King's men haven't arrived by then . . . Well, our consciences will be clear. Go back to your families and get some sleep."

The men left to sleep, but the pastor had trouble finding it himself.

Several hours before dawn, a pounding was heard at the back door of the house. "Open up. It is I, Jacques. I must speak with Pastor Alexandre."

The man sleeping closest to the door looked out the window to verify the identity of the door's assailant, then opened it quickly.

Jacques, panting, dashed in and slumped to the floor.

"What is so important that you wake us in the middle of the night?" he was asked.

"They are coming, they are coming." Jacques caught his breath and rose, heading for the Pastor's bedroom to tell the clergyman. Fortunately, Pastor Alexandre had heard and intercepted him before he could open the wrong door.

"Pastor, Pastor" he called. "I must talk to you."

The pastor pulled the man into the study, closing the door.

"They are coming!"

"So I heard, Jacques," he said, motioning for Jacques to lower his voice. "How far away are they?"

"Not more than one day's ride, I think. I rode as quickly as I could to warn you. What should we do?" The man was wringing his hands in distress.

"First, calm yourself. There is no benefit to being in a panic."

François, the innkeeper, stuck his head in the door. "Pastor, now is the time to decide about the new people. If we turn them in, our village will be safe and so will we. And we may be rewarded, as well."

"What new people?" Jacques inquired.

"Two monks and four mercenaries arrived in the village last night," François told him. "They seemed all right and were allowed in, but then some of us started thinking that they may be the enemies of the crown that are being searched for." He turned to the pastor. "If we don't turn them over to the crown soldiers who are coming to the village, we all might be hurt or killed for defying them."

The pastor thought a moment, then told the other men, "I'll pray about it and let you know by dawn what we will do."

François and Jacques left the room and Pastor Alexandre closed the door. He sat on his chair, deep in thought. He was loath to betray the trust of the newcomers, but the villagers, his people, had to come first. His head bowed, he prayed for wisdom from God to do the right thing. Then he lay down on the bare floor and went to sleep.

The Hunt for The Red Cardinal

Bradley H. Sinor, Susan P. Sinor

Chapter Twelve

At dawn the families were up and about, getting together whatever breakfast they could. François and Jacques knocked on the pastor's door, who was ready for them.

"I have made a decision. I am not willing to just turn over the strangers. Even if they are not the ones being searched for, they would possibly be dealt with severely." He raised his hand to forestall objections. "However, this is what we will do. When the signal is sent that the men are approaching the village, the women, the children and, the newcomers will be sent to the tunnel."

The two men looked at each other. "What tunnel?"

Pastor Alexandre sighed. "It is a long-held secret that there is a tunnel between this house and the church. I found the entrance shortly after I took over."

"But why is there a tunnel?" François asked. "And why has it been kept secret?" Jacques nodded.

"I can only assume. When the house and church were built, there was much fighting and looting in this area, and I suppose the priest used it to hide the church's treasures, although they were not there when I discovered the tunnel. Regardless, it will be a safe place for us to hide. Go get the travelers and bring them in here."

François and Jacques went to the bedroom door and knocked. There was no answer. After another futile knock, François opened the door to an empty room.

"Perhaps they have already joined the rest," Jacques commented.

The two men searched the rest of the house to no avail. Then François said to Jacques, "It looks like they have left. Come outside with me."

They went out the back door to the stable. "No cart in here. But look here; it looks like the floor has been disturbed." He pointed to a place on the floor where the dirt was soft. "Do you think they buried something and then dug it up?"

"Could be. Or haven't dug it up yet. Look around for their horses while I dig there in case they left something," Jacques suggested.

There were footprints and cart-wheel tracks in the dirt in front of the stable. The men searched the area, but found no horses. Likewise, François found nothing, either.

"We must tell the pastor that they are gone. Then we should be able to go back to our homes," said François.

"But the searchers have not come yet," Jacques protested. "When we were warned of them and came to the Pastor's house, the strangers hadn't joined us yet. I don't think it is safe to go back to our homes yet."

"We'll ask Pastor Alexandre."

∞ ∞ ∞

D'Artagnan, who had been watching the house from the branch of a nearby tree, rejoined the rest of his group. "They have discovered we're gone and gone back in to tell the pastor. I think it's just as well we left before the household was up. I could hear through the door that some of them wanted to turn us over. I'm sure the men they were warned of are Gaston's men, or, at least, César Vendôme's. They would do anything to get ahold of the cardinal. I'm just glad that taking Brother Etienne out through the window didn't hurt him."

"But what do we do now?" asked Aramis. "We're not sure what direction these men are coming from. If we continue the way we were going, we could run into them. If we go back the way we came, we could also run into them."

"Then we hide in these woods. I would like to see them for myself, and perhaps get the jump on them, as well," D'Artagnan stated. "The indication was that there were not many of them. There are four of us. I think we could take down eight of them."

"Or ten or twelve, even," put in Porthos. "Let's wait around a bit. Maybe we could save other villages a bit of trouble."

The four riders and the cart moved a little farther into the woods and found a spot where several trees grew together. They hid the cart there and left Athos to guard it, its passengers and all the horses while the other three spread out nearer to the wood's edge, where they could keep an eye on the road.

They waited for some time, until another of the townsmen came running up to the house, declaring again that 'they' were coming. This time the warning was correct, for just minutes later hoof beats could be heard in the distance.

Each of the three watching the road had climbed a tree, hiding in the foliage. Porthos was closest and saw them first. "Twit tu whit" he whistled. It was a pre-arranged signal from years earlier, and told the other two to get ready.

∞ ∞ ∞

Six men rode into the village and spread out. Each went into a different building without even knocking. Homes and shops were treated equally. When all the buildings had been searched, they met not far from the tree Porthos was hiding in.

"I found no one," stated one of them. "They must be hiding."

The rest concurred. "If they haven't run into the woods or somewhere else in the countryside, they're probably hiding in the church," another said. "Abelard, you and Bruno look in that direction." He pointed to the north. "Felix and Eustice, look to the west. Henri and I will look to the south. Don't go in until we are all together again. We will meet back here in ten minutes."

"Yes, Frééric," Abelard said, and they went their appointed ways.

Ten minutes later they got back together and headed for the church. Not being able to enter through the locked door, and not being able to get anyone to answer it, they tried to break the door down. Repeated pounding and battering failed to budge the door.

"We could break a window to get in," suggested Felix, a pragmatist.

"No!" Frdric exclaimed. "We cannot break a stained-glass window in a church just to get in. It would be a sacrilege. Look all around to see if you can find a plain window to break, Felix. The rest of us will go to the priest's house. If no one answers there, we will return to the church and will break whatever window you have found."

By the time the men had ridden up to the church, all but a few of the townspeople had hidden in the tunnel, along with all the belongings they had with them. Only Pastor Alexandre, the blacksmith and the innkeeper were there to answer the door.

"We have been sent by the king," Frdric told the men. "Who are you and where are the rest of the townspeople?"

"Why, I am Pastor Alexandre, and these men are the blacksmith and innkeeper of the village. As to where the rest of my people are, I can only describe the illness that has swept our village recently. Please come in and I will explain."

He opened the door wide and ushered the king's men in, watching two of them go upstairs.

Frédéric looked at the other men, then said, "We have heard of no illness. Where has everyone gone?"

Pastor Alexandre led the men into the main room of the house, sat down and started to tell them a story.

"Not long ago a stranger came into town. He claimed to be sent by our king to look for an enemy of the crown. I asked him who the enemy was, but he would not say. While he was here, he went to each house and shop to see who lived or worked there. I told him I had known all these people for many years and could vouch for their loyalty. Unfortunately, he became ill while he was here. We have no doctor, nor any other kind of healer, and offered to send someone to a larger town to ask for one. While our messenger was gone, the man died. Being fearful that the town would be contaminated, we had to burn his body. Afterwards, we buried his remains in a deep hole in the woods. Shortly after that, some of the townspeople fell ill as well. Several of our families who had not been infected went off to stay with relatives in other villages. The families of the ill ones stayed and fell ill themselves. To make a long story a bit shorter, these two men and I are the only ones left, and we're not feeling so well, ourselves."

The five men looked at each other and Frdric spoke up. "We don't believe your story. Can you prove it?"

"Alas, no, for we had to burn all those bodies, too. They are also buried in the woods. But believe what you will; only we three are left in this village."

"And why are you still here?"

"Where should we go? This is still our home, and some families will surely be coming back."

Before the men had arrived, the pastor, the blacksmith and the innkeeper agreed on what to tell them. They couldn't tell them the truth, of course. That would have been too dangerous for the rest of the townspeople. Pastor Alexandre said he was sure that the Lord would forgive them for the untruth.

While this conversation was going on, the musketeers and cardinal's guard had sneaked back to the stable, and from there quietly drifted to several windows of the house. Aramis could see, through the window of the main living room, the pastor and two townsmen talking to three other men. He knew there should be six, but the other three were not visible. He signaled to D'Artagnan to join him.

"Where do you think the other three are?"

D'Artagnan thought a moment. "We saw five enter the house. The sixth may still be at the church, looking for a way to get in. You go check around the church. Try to be quiet, but if challenged, do not lose." He peeked back through the window and saw that two of the missing men had joined the others. "I'll watch here to see what happens."

The King's man took a paper out of his vest. "This is a warrant for the arrest of the enemies of the crown we're looking for." He passed the warrant over to the pastor.

As Pastor Alexandre was reading the document, a faint noise was heard.

"Do you have an infant here," Frdric asked, looking around.

"No, only who you see here with me. It is probably a cat," the pastor replied.

They heard the cry again, which arose in a wail. Another cry accompanied it, and then another.

"Where are they?" demanded Frédéric. "I know you have people secreted here." He rose and began searching for the sound.

As he walked along the walls, the crying got louder. When he got to the door to a bedroom, the sound seemed very close.

"Whose bedroom is this?" he demanded.

The Pastor told him, "It is my bedroom."

Frdric looked around the room. *I see no crucifix above the bed,* he thought to himself. *And no icons hanging on the walls.* He looked closer at the man who called himself Pastor. *And no crucifix around his neck.* Before he challenged the man, he decided to investigate the noises that seemed to be coming from behind the wall, or from under the floor.

"Is there another room beyond this one?" he asked.

"No. You can see the window right there."

"And underneath the room. Is there a cellar?"

"Of course. But the entrance is in another room."

"Show me."

The demand distressed the pastor, because the warrant described the enemies of the crown as being Protestants; heretics were what they were called by the Roman Catholic Church. He hoped that revealing the cellar would not also reveal the tunnel.

"Come this way." He led the man, Frdric, to the kitchen, where there was a door almost hidden in a corner, which opened to descending stairs. Fréic started down, followed by Pastor Alexandre, who was clasping his hands in silent prayer for the safety of his parishioners

Th noises were louder in the cellar.

"Aha! You do have hidden townspeople." He dashed back up the stairs, calling for the others. "I have found them. And more, I believe, this is the village of Huguenots for whom we are searching. Come with me."

Listening at the door to the stairs, D'Artagnan heard what the man said. "Not us, at all," he thought. He went outside the house, calling for his friends to join him.

When Aramis and Porthos arrived, D'Artagnan told them what he had heard. "They're after Protestants, not the cardinal."

"Then let's go and leave the heretics to their fate," Porthos said, ready to move on.

"That wouldn't be right," protested Aramis. "They gave us shelter without even asking us about our faith. They didn't threaten us or deny us."

"You forget that several of them wanted to turn us over to these men," said D'Artagnan. "But you are right. Remember Christ's teachings, that every man is our brother. Besides, I'm ready for a fight, and these men are asking for one."

"There are only six of them, but Athos, I mean, Gerard, would be very upset if he were left out. I'll dash back and get him. I'm sure the brothers will be all right for a short time."

Aramis was back in moments with Athos. By then the King's men had found the secret door to the tunnel, and were trying to get it open.

D'Artagnan, with his three friends, broke down the kitchen door, rushed down the stairs, and drew their swords.

Pastor Alexandre was standing out of the way with a terrified look on his face. When he saw the four men dashing down the stairs, he tried to conceal himself in fear they were coming to assist the other men in opening the door to the tunnel.

D'Artagnan was the first one to reach the bottom of the stairs.

"Halt in the name of the king," he said. That cry got their attention and they turned to see who made it.

By that time the three musketeers had joined D'Artagnan and all four stood, spread out with their swords pointing at the six men.

"We were sent by the king!" Frédéric said. "Stand away and let us finish routing these enemies of the true church." He and his men turned back to their work.

"No, I think we will join you. Or perhaps separate was the word I was looking for." D'Artagnan swung his sword, slashing the other man's sword arm and pushing his sword out of the way. The man quickly recovered, though, switching hands and swinging again at D'Artagnan, slicing his sleeve.

Porthos took the next man and disarmed him by tripping him, causing him to fall to the floor. Aramis followed suit with the third man, pinning him to the wall.

Athos was about to follow the lead of the others, when a voice rang out. "May I join the party?"

Everyone turned to see a small, simply dressed fellow. D'Artagnan was the first to recognize him.

"Monsieur Montaigne. I haven't seen you in quite a while. I'm sure you remember my friends, Gerard, Georges, and Emile. But we can catch up later. Are you here to help us or them?" He waved his sword at his opponents.

"Depends on the reason for the fighting. For instance, are these men looking for Huguenots in order to rid the country of them? Or are you the ones doing that?"

"Answer that questions for yourself. Then we will decide if you may help us stop these men from killing many innocent townspeople or kill you for helping them do the same."

"That answers my question, so I will join you, although I think you don't really need my help." Montaigne drew his sword and lunged at the next in line.

During the conversation the men under attack had stopped trying to open the tunnel door. But at the resumption of the fight, they turned back to it.

As it was close quarters, and Frédéric and his men were backed against the door to the tunnel, the two at the back started trying to open the door again in order to escape.

Abelard finally discovered that the door slid to the side to open. He opened it just to discover that no one was there. He turned to the others and cried, "They've escaped to the church! Follow me!"

They rushed into the tunnel with Frédéric, at the back, going backwards to keep Porthos from killing him. Aramis followed Porthos through the tunnel while the other four, including Pastor Alexandre, dashed outside for the church. The pastor had the key out, ready to unlock the door which had held against pounding by two different groups.

"Follow me," said the pastor as he led them to the back of the church where the tunnel ended. The townspeople had gotten in and were trying to hold the tunnel door closed against the others.

D'Artagnan indicated to them that they should back away and let the door be opened.

"The three of us will attack on this end while our friends will attack from behind," he told Pastor Alexandre. "If you'll have everyone leave the area . . ?"

The people started moving out, going to the sanctuary, and when the last of them was gone, D'Artagnan, Athos, and Montaigne, who had been holding the tunnel door shut, backed off themselves. The men in the tunnel burst out, only to face the weapons of three men in front and those of two others behind. The five men made short work of the five others, killing four of them and capturing the fifth.

D'Artagnan quietly asked Porthos to go and report to the brothers what had happened and to bring them back to the stable.

Then he said, "Pastor, we need to move the dead men out of the church. Could your people see to that? We'll keep the other one for interrogation and deal with him later."

"Of course, and you may have the church's office to talk to this one. I'll show you where it is."

He asked the blacksmith and several other townsmen to dispose of the dead bodies and led the way to the office.

The pastor started to leave the office, closing the door behind him, when he heard "Pastor, you may stay to hear what is said."

He looked back into the room, then went back in and closed the door.

D'Artagnan started to speak, but Montaigne held his hand up to stop him.

"I have been chasing after these men for over a week, watching them destroy homes and families in their search. I would like to ask the first question." He turned to the leader, Frédéric, and asked, "Who sent you on this mission?"

Frédéric refused to answer, saying only, "We have a warrant."

Then D'Artagnan asked, "Where is the other one of your people? We know there were six of you, but only five came out of the tunnel."

Frédéric only shrugged.

"Emile, please try to find the other one," D'Artagnan said. "You may bring him here or send him to join the others, whichever you want." He turned back to the prisoner. "Now, where were we?"

Pastor Alexandre remembered that he still had the warrant, and handed it to D'Artagnan.

"Ah," he said as he read it. "A warrant for Protestants. And from the king. Well, everyone knows now that the king was murdered by outlaws, so who is this really from?"

Frédéric kept his mouth shut.

"I expect it was Gaston, the pretender," Montaigne said. "He has always wanted to be king."

"He is the rightful king," shouted Frédéric. "He will rid this country of heretics. We will kill them all!"

"Ah, now he speaks. How many heretics have you killed so far? And how many of them have actually been good Catholics? And of those who weren't, how many had been good men, anyway?" Montaigne turned to D'Artagnan.

"Any more questions?"

"Yes. How many more of you are roaming the countryside, terrorizing the citizens?"

"Many," Frédéric proclaimed.

Just then a knock on the office door was heard. The blacksmith stuck his head through the door and dragged another man in with him.

"Is this the one you're looking for?" he asked D'Artagnan.

"As a matter of fact, he is. Thank you for finding him. Now take him out and slit his throat."

"You can't do that!" protested Frédéric. "We are agents of the king."

"Not the rightful one," said Montaigne with a wink to D'Artagnan. "Who wants to take this one," he pointed at Frédéric, "to join the others?"

The blacksmith volunteered for that chore also, and took Frédéric to join his compatriots.

After being profusely thanked by the pastor and townspeople, and being given what provisions the town could spare, the group of, now, seven, set out again.

Just before they left the church, Pastor Alexandre said, "We have been afraid for a long while that we would be found. We are very fortunate that you are the ones who found us. This proves that not all Catholics hate us and wish to rid our country of us. Thank you."

"We all worship God, the same God, in different ways. We harbor no ill will toward you because we know you are good people," D'Artagnan explained to him as they were leaving to go on their way.

On the way from the church to the stable, D'Artagnan explained what their journey was all about. Of course, Montaigne already knew about the attack on Cardinal Richelieu's party and the death of King Louis. He brought the others up to date on current events.

In the stable, Montaigne was formally introduced to Brother Xavier, who had never met him before. Cardinal Richelieu woke long enough to recognize him before going back to sleep. "We're calling him Brother Etienne if anyone else is near."

D'Artagnan and the three musketeers had worked with Montaigne in the past. In fact, the first time they met was the time that D'Artagnan had first met Athos, Porthos, and Aramis.

Montaigne nodded to D'Artagnan, then he bowed to the cardinal, saying, "Your Eminence."

As they rode away, Montaigne told the group, "Gaston has had himself installed as king. Everyone knew that would happen. And no, before you ask, I do not know the gender of the child of Louis and Anne. I heard that they, Anne and the child, escaped to another country. I've heard rumors of Spain, Italy, Switzerland, Germany and the Low Countries. I have no idea which, if any of them, is true. For all I know, she has boarded an up-time ship headed for the New World."

"Speaking of rumors," D'Artagnan broke in as they rode slightly ahead of the others, "the spreading of rumors of the great cardinal's whereabouts is something that needs to be done. Before leaving on this journey, I was told that this would be done all over France. What direction will you be heading when you leave us?"

"Well, now that I've caught up with that bunch back there, I suppose I could go wherever I want. I was not directed to report back immediately, so I suppose I could go south toward Spain, seeing my former master at each stop."

"It's fortunate that few people outside of Paris actually know what he looks like," D'Artagnan said. "It is the same for us," he added, indicating his three friends. "And in our case, people have never even heard of us. It is also fortunate that the book about us wasn't, er, won't be written until 1844."

"By then that writer will have a very different story to tell," said Montaigne. "Now I must be off on my own errand. Have a safe journey."

"You, as well, my friend," D'Artagnan said. "May God be with us all."

The two friends had slowed, letting the others catch up to them.

The cardinal had awakened just in time to hear that Montaigne was about to go his own way. "Monsieur Montaigne, would you mind travelling with us for a while?" he asked. "I would enjoy your company again." The cardinal seemed more alert than he had for days, and seemed to feel better, as well.

Montaigne looked at the rest of the group, questioningly. "I suppose I could, if no one objects."

D'Artagnan spoke up. "Of course not, if that's what the cardinal wants."

"Excellent," the cardinal said. "Come ride beside me so we can talk."

Athos rode up to D'Artagnan and asked, "Where do we go next?"

Chapter Thirteen

Simon Cordonnier, a short, balding, middle-aged cobbler, walked along the road next to the river, toward his home in the village of Soissons. The sun was dipping in the west, and the breeze was cooling from its warmth earlier in the day. His steps were slower than usual due to the heavy bundle tied to his walking stick. He had fished it out of the river, which meant his legs were wet from the knee down. Fortunately, the bundle had caught up in a bush whose branches touched the surface of the slow-moving river. He had then taken it to rest on a stump in order to open it and examine the contents. It was wrapped in brown cloth which looked very much like a shirt. The contents were a red, watered-silk robe the likes, it appeared, fit for a wealthy nobleman, or, perhaps, a cardinal of the Church. Next he saw a strange-looking hat. Cardinals wore hats like that, he had heard, never having actually seen a cardinal before. It was four-cornered with a ball of some kind on top in the middle. He thought they were called birettas. No matter. It looked like the bundle could have been in the water for several weeks.

He thought about wrapping it back up and throwing it back in the river, but it was unlikely that anyone would be looking for it here, and the fabric was beautiful where it wasn't torn or stained. He decided to take it home where his wife could repair it.

He hoped his dinner would be ready when he arrived. His day's work had been tiring and he was hungry. He enjoyed making and repairing shoes, but when he had to leave his shop to visit a customer, he had to walk there. *I'm too old to walk this much*, he thought as he trudged on. *If only I had a horse. Oh, well. We do what we have to. And walking is what I have to do.*

Fortunately for him, he arrived at his home shortly thereafter.

"My dear, I'm home," he called as he entered his house. "Is dinner ready? I'm starving."

His wife, Marie, short and plump with graying hair, met him at the door. "Soon, soon," she said. "What is that – thing – hanging from your walking stick? It's wet! Quick, put it outside before the floor is flooded." She pushed him back through the door, where he set the stick down and untied the bundle from it.

"It was in the river."

"What?"

"I was curious to see what it was. You won't believe it, so I'll have to show you, but not here outside where any passerby could see." Simon took her arm and pulled her with him. "Come around the corner of the house."

He carried the dripping bundle with them around the side of the house to the back and stepped behind a large bush which would screen them from view. Untying the string from around the bundle, he spread the cloth covering flat and gently raised the robe for his wife to see, letting it hang loose.

"Where did you get that? It looks like a cardinal's robe," she gasped. Then she saw the hat. "And that, that's a biretta."

"Aha, I thought so," Simon said.

"But what are you doing with it? This can't be good. The likes of us should not have anything like that."

Simon shrugged. "I told you, I found it floating in the river. I thought, it's wet, but it will dry. And the material is still in pretty good condition, if you don't count the tears. Maybe you could get the stains out and make yourself a nice dress."

"Simon, what were you thinking? We must take this straightaway to the priest in the village. Father Benedict will know what to do with it," she said.

"But shouldn't we let it dry, first? And have our dinner? I told you I'm famished."

At that, she relented. "But we mustn't leave it out here. We'll take it in the house and lay it over the backs of two chairs to dry while we eat."

"And let it drip all over the floor? Besides, we have only two chairs. Where will we sit to eat?" Simon asked.

"We can stand. That robe is more important than we are. But you're right; it would drip all over the floor. We'll bring the chairs outside where the sun can dry it faster."

"But what will we sit on?" Simon asked.

"We don't have so much food that we can't stand up to eat it," she replied.

"We could always sit on the hearth."

After moving the chairs and carefully laying the wet robe over their backs, they went back in to eat.

Half an hour later, Marie said, "Well, it must be dry by now. I have some white material to wrap it in and a basket to carry it in to the village church."

But when they went out to retrieve the robe, it was gone. The two chairs were still where they had been placed, but no red robe was draped across them, and the biretta was nowhere to be found. Marie and Simon looked all around the yard for it.

"The wind must have blown it away," she said. "We have to find it!"

They looked, again, all over their yard, in the neighbors' yards and then went to the front of the house and looked all around there.

"This is terrible," Marie said, her head in her hands. "What will we do? What will we tell Father Benedict?"

"Nothing," Simon told her. "No one knows we had it. If it has blown away, someone else will find it. Don't worry."

"But the biretta is gone, too. I don't think the wind could have blown it away. Someone must have taken it."

"If someone took it, it's their problem now. Just pretend that I never found it, that I never brought it home. Now, let's bring the chairs in."

∞ ∞ ∞

A tall, loose-jointed, middle-aged man wearing a wide-brimmed black hat walked jauntily across the meadow. *What a find I have made*, he thought, *a beautiful red robe and a funny-looking hat.* He was surprised that anybody would leave the garment outside for just anyone to take. It did have some tears in it, and there were some stains, but no matter. That didn't bother him.

He had folded the robe into a small bundle and put it around the hat. Then he put it into his large leather pouch, so no one would see it. He wouldn't put it on until he got home to his hut.

Or would he? He decided he should be wearing it right then. *What good is finding something special if you don't wear it?* He stopped and took the bundle out of his bag, putting the biretta on his head – a good fit – and carefully unfolding the robe and putting it on right over his clothing. It had obviously been wet, but seemed to be almost dry. *A little dampness won't hurt me,* he thought.

The route to his house took him across a stream with a steep bank. He had never had any trouble crossing the stream before, but he had never been preoccupied with this good a find before, either. As he daydreamed his way down the slope, he tripped on a stone and fell into the swiftly moving water. Never having learned how to swim, he floundered, being dragged by the current, until a fallen tree branch snagged him. The branch caught the robe pulling his head underwater. He tried to get free, but the branch held him firmly and he couldn't raise his head above the surface.

The Hunt for The Red Cardinal

∞ ∞ ∞

Some short time later another traveler, in ordinary dress, walked past the place in the stream and saw something red fluttering in the current of the river.

"I wonder what that is," he said to himself, and went down the bank to see. After pulling on the red fabric he could see that it was attached to a dead man. He was able to disentangle the man from the branch and pull him onto shore. He laid the man on his back and arranged his clothing in order to see what the red garment was.

"Oh, my," he said to himself. "That looks like the robe an important church man would wear. I don't want it to get into the wrong hands." He removed the robe from the dead man, and, glancing back at the water, saw another red garment trapped by the branch. After fishing it out, he said, "Yes, that is the hat that goes with this robe. Better not leave these lying around."

He took the robe and, because it was dripping wet, carefully squeezed as much of the water out as he could, folded it into a small bundle and stuffed it and the hat he had rescued from the stream into the traveling bag he was carrying and went on his way. He told himself he would report the dead man when he got to the next village.

"I fished a drowned man out of the stream a couple of miles back that way," the man told a shopkeeper in the village, pointing the way. "I didn't know him, but you might. I wasn't going to bring him with me; he was too heavy and soaking wet. But I thought I should tell you in case this village is missing a tall man." He started out the door, saying, "I must be on my way."

The man lived a couple of villages farther on, but decided to stop for the night at the next one. It was getting dark and he didn't want to be walking all night. There was a small inn where he could get a meal and share a room with other travelers, so he stopped.

The food was decent, though the portions were small, but, he figured, you get what you pay for. The room had four narrow beds, and he would be sharing it with three strangers, which was nothing unusual. His trip had been somewhat profitable, and he could afford to spend that small amount of his money.

He took the bed by the wall farthest from the door. He didn't want anyone catching a glimpse of what he had in his bag. He shoved the bag under the bed and went to find the privy going down the back stairs.

While he was out, one of his roommates entered and chose the next bed. No one else had come into the room yet, so this man decided to look around. He spotted the bag under the other bed and pulled it out to see what was in it. Setting the bag on the bed, he opened it enough to see that there was something red, and wet, in it. He pulled out the bundle to see it better.

He pulled the wet fabric out and started to unfold it, when he saw another red article. He picked up the biretta and examined it.

"I know what this is," he said to himself. Then he finished unfolding the robe. He could see the rents and stains on it, and another thought came to mind. It had to be the robe that Cardinal Richelieu was wearing when he was injured during the attack when the former king, Louis, had been killed. The man knew someone who had been involved in the attack. He also knew that the cardinal had not been killed but had escaped. *Perhaps the owner of the bag that holds the robe knows where the cardinal was taken,* he thought. He laid the wet robe across the other bed and stood behind the door. When the man came back in he would confront him.

After just a moment, he heard footsteps outside the door. The traveler entered and turned toward the bed he had claimed. He stopped short when he saw the robe lying across it and whirled around to see the other man pointing a flintlock pistol at him.

"Where did you get that robe?" the man with the pistol said.

"I don't know what you're talking about. How did that come to be on my bed?"

"Don't be stupid. It came to be on your bed because I found it in your bag and put it there. Now, where did you get it?" He brandished the pistol.

Realizing he actually had nothing to lose, and maybe something to gain, the traveler said, "I found it floating in a stream and fished it out." He said nothing about the dead man who had been wearing it at the time.

"Really," the other man said, disbelievingly. "Which stream was this?"

"I don't know what it's called. It's just east a ways from the town. I thought it might be worth something and thought I could sell it. Are you interested?"

"I am, but not in buying it. I know who it belongs to and wish to return it."

"As a matter of fact, I know who it belongs to, also. I will return it." He reached around himself and brought his own flintlock pistol out, pointed at his adversary.

Just then, the door started to open again, creaking as it swung. It startled the men, who had their pistols pointed at each other, causing both to pull their triggers.

The gunshots startled the man coming in the door, and he staggered back into the corner next to the bed with the robe on it.

He quickly recovered when he saw the robe. His eyes got wide and he gasped. *I know who that belongs to,* he thought to himself, then quickly folded it and put it in the bag he was carrying, along with the biretta, and left the room.

A moment later the innkeeper dashed up the stairs. He was sure he had heard a gunshot. If someone was injured, he needed to get help. If someone was dead, he needed to clean up whatever mess had been made and get rid of the body.

When he saw two bodies, he was dismayed, but only for a bit. He was a shrewd man, always concerned with his own situation. He snatched up the pistols and hid them in the waistband of his pants. He moved one of the dead men to parallel the other, as if both were killed by another man, and ran back downstairs to alert whatever authority he could find.

By that time the third man, who had the stolen robe, had gotten to the stable, taken his horse, and left town. He didn't care that he had paid for his share of the room already. That was a pittance to what he could get for the robe that Cardinal Richelieu had probably been killed wearing. He had been going back to his village, but he decided, after that, to travel a little farther, where he knew of someone who might pay for what he had in his bag.

Since the man wasn't married and had no children, he was free to go about his business as he wished. He told his landlord he might be away for a few days and paid him in advance to keep his room for when he returned.

"Certainly, Monsieur Baudin. But if anyone is looking for you, what should I say?"

"Nothing, Monsieur Borde. You might even deny that you know me at all. I will leave tomorrow."

He went up to his small room and packed his bag with what few things he would need, after taking the robe and biretta out of the bag they were in and laying them out on his table to complete drying. He also laid out changes of clothes and all of his money. He went to bed early, but tossed and turned, knowing that he had a long ride ahead of him, so he rose before dawn. He was able to get his horse without anyone hearing and went on his way.

He rode southwest, aiming for Paris. He knew someone there who would be very interested in his find, someone who might pay well. He rode swiftly as long as his horse held out, then he had to stop. The sun was coming up, and he found that he was hungry. He had no provisions with him and he didn't know if there was another village near, but his horse had to rest and graze. He would get nowhere without a horse. He moved away from the road so as not to be seen, leaning against a tree to wait until he could ride again.

Because he had gotten little sleep that night, his head began to droop, and soon he dozed off. Then he fell over, but instead of waking, he squirmed around to get comfortable on the ground. He was a deep sleeper, so when he finally awoke it was late afternoon. He went to get his horse and then looked around for his bag, which was nowhere to be found.

"It must have been stolen!" he said to himself. "The thief cannot have gotten very far, but which way would he have gone?" The thought of going after the thief was too much for Monsieur Baudin, so he decided to go back home and tell his landlord that his plans had changed. At least his rent was paid for a week.

Meanwhile, the latest thief of the robe and biretta was continuing in the same direction as Monsieur Baudin had been. He promised himself that he would not stop for any reason until he got to his destination. He had to break that promise several times during his journey, but he kept the items with him at all times.

That is, until his horse stepped in a hole and stumbled and he was thrown, hitting his head on a large stone. The bag containing the items had been tied to the horse's saddle. The horse recovered from his stumble and abandoned his rider. The horse was hungry and knew the way back home. He turned around, going back the way he had come, and eventually overtook Monsieur Baudin.

Monsieur Baudin heard a horse galloping up behind him. He turned to see who was about to catch up to him and saw a riderless horse. He angled his horse so that he could grab hold of the reins as the other horse passed. Then he saw the bag tied to the saddle.

It wasn't hard to catch the horse, but it was hard to hold him. It seemed as if the other horse was on a mission and wouldn't be delayed. Monsieur Baudin urged his horse to keep up with the other and held onto the reins, slowly bringing both of them to a stop. He leaned over and untied the bag, peeking inside to verify its contents. *It's the bag that was stolen from me! I must be meant to take it somewhere, but to whom? Perhaps I should take it to the next church and give it to a priest. I could say I found it. After all, I did find it.* He tied it to his own saddle letting the other horse go on his way.

Monsieur thought a moment. Should he go back to his village or turn around and go on to Paris? After another moment, he decided. Paris, it was.

It was starting to get late, again, but Monsieur Baudin wasn't sleepy, or even tired. He was excited to have found his bag again. He kept riding and soon came to a village. He was hungry, so he decided to stop for a meal.

The inn was small and busy and hot. It was approaching late May. The air was warming, the trees were full and many flowers bloomed along the road. But inside the inn, Monsieur Baudin would have been quite comfortable in early January. He took off his jacket and draped it over the bag he was carrying. He found a small table just vacated in the middle of the room. He would have preferred a dark corner, but there wasn't one. A large chandelier hung from the ceiling and all the candles were lit. The windows were small, and even though they were open they didn't admit much breeze.

He put the bag at his feet and his hat on the table. Soon a young woman arrived to take his order.

"Ale and supper," he told her.

"No room?" she said, frowning. "I'm Mariette, and I think a strong, handsome man like you needs his sleep."

She looked promising, but he declined. "Just what I asked for."

Soon she returned with a mug and plate. Setting it on the table, she leaned over, letting her cleavage show. "You sure?"

He looked, then shook his head, saying, "I must be on my way. Important business in Paris," and gave her a coin in payment for the meal.

The ale wasn't too bad, for the price, and the food was no more than it needed to be. He ate and drank quickly, and while he wasn't looking, Mariette refilled his mug. He lifted it and took a drink before he realized it was fuller than it should have been. After a second drink, a man at the next table called out to him.

"Just passing through, are you? Where are you headed?"

"Paris," Monsieur Baudin replied.

"Ah, Paris. Big city, that. Don't get lost in it, now." He lifted his mug in a toast. "Here's to the King!"

Monsieur Baudin felt obliged to answer the toast with a hearty, "The King!" and drain his mug. While his back was turned, Mariette brought another full mug, whisking the empty one away.

He looked at it, shrugged, and took another deep drink. He was starting to feel wobbly and decided he needed to leave, but before he knew it, Mariette and a large man had him on his feet and up the stairs. He struggled as much as he could, but the man punched him in the head and he lost consciousness.

After Monsieur Baudin had been removed from his table, the man with whom he had toasted the king slid out of his chair and onto the one at the smaller table. As if he had been sitting there all along, he took a drink from the mug that had been left there. Then he put on the hat that Monsieur Baudin had left, picked up the jacket-draped bag and left the inn. The horse that must have belonged to the man was tied to the rail in front of the inn. The man mounted the horse and rode on toward Paris.

At the inn, Mariette and the large man removed the contents from Monsieur Baudin's pockets before removing him from the inn.

The next morning Monsieur Baudin found himself in a meadow, without bag, horse or money. However, he saw a large bull not too far away which seemed to be taking an interest in him.

Chapter Fourteen

Monsieur Faucher, the man now in possession of the bag, stopped some distance away from the village to inspect its contents. He had no knowledge of what was in the bag, but he thought he might be able to make a profit with whatever it held. He stopped behind a tree off the road for privacy and set the bag on the ground. He undid the clasp and opened the bag as wide as he could.

"What?" he said as he pulled the red garment out. He held it up, shaking out its folds. A red hat fell out. He could see stains and a large tear in the robe. He turned it back and forth and held it up to himself to gauge the size. He'd seen something like it before, in a cathedral in Paris. *It's a cardinal's robe,* he thought. *Why would the robe and hat of a cardinal be in this bag? And why would it be torn and stained.* He thought a moment and a glimmer of memory came to him. *Cardinal. THE Cardinal. He was hurt awhile back, I think. Shot? Maybe. Could this be his robe? But how did it get here, to me? Maybe it's supposed to be mine. Yes! Maybe I'm the new cardinal.* He carefully pulled the robe over his clothing and put the biretta on his head. They seemed to fit. He took them off again and carefully pulled his own outer garments off, stuffing them in the bag. Then he put the robe back on.

"I'm the cardinal now," he said to no one.

He headed back to his home, which was in a village outside of Paris. It was early morning when he arrived, still dark, and no one was out and about yet. He found his way to his small cottage and went in, taking care not to wake his wife. She would be quite incensed at his late arrival. He stopped just inside the door and took off the robe and biretta, which had completely dried along the way. He folded them back up and put them back in the bag, put his clothes back on and hid the bag in a corner under a chair.

"Pierre, is that you?" his wife, Annette, called from the second room, where they slept. "Are you just getting home?"

"Oh, no. I'm just getting up. I wanted to let you sleep, since you work so hard."

"Hmmph," she said, entering the room. "And did you bring back money?"

He pulled some coins from a pocket. "I brought this."

She counted them and looked at him. "I'd hoped you'd bring back more, although I know the horse wasn't worth that much." She looked around the room and saw the bag, which hadn't been hidden as well as he thought it had been. "What is that?"

Pierre thought fast. He looked around at what she was pointing to, and said, "Oh, that. I'd forgotten about it." Although he was loath to show it to her, he knew she would find out its contents anyway. "It's something I found along the way. I haven't even looked inside yet."

"Found along the way? Stole, more likely. But let's see what's inside first, before I pass judgement." She pulled the bag out from under the chair. Opening it wide, she pulled the robe and biretta out and held them up. Then she gasped, looking at her husband. "Do you know what this is?" she said, excitedly.

He looked it up and down, as if he'd never seen it before. "I'm not sure. What is it?"

"Well, of course you wouldn't know. You've never seen a cardinal before. I saw that dead cardinal, Richelieu, once when I was in Paris visiting relatives. I think it is his robe." She spread it on the table. "See, this tear is where he was injured. It looks like it has been ill-treated, maybe wet. Someone must have stolen it from wherever he was after it was removed from his body."

"How do you know he's dead? I haven't heard anything about it."

"Well, he must be by now. No one's heard a word from him. And the new king hasn't posted notices that the cardinal has been captured." She thought a moment. "Do you think he may still be alive and in hiding? Perhaps he plans to raise an army and try to overthrow King Gaston." She looked at her husband. "You stay away from anyone who has authority, and don't tell anyone about this. We could be arrested if anyone thinks we stole the cardinal's robe."

"Of course, my dear. Now, how about some breakfast? I'm starving."

"In a minute. I'm going to hide this where no one can find it. Then I'll decide what to do with it."

She bundled it back into the bag and shoved it as far under their bed as she could, placing a few other items in front. Then she got dressed and fixed them both breakfast.

"I'll take that money now. I need to go to the market since we're almost completely out of food." Putting her hat on and the money in a pocket, she went outside. "Where did this horse come from?" she asked as she stepped back inside.

Her husband grinned and said, "I found him, too."

"He's a much better horse than you sold yesterday. We could get much more for him."

"I'd like to keep him for a while," Pierre said.

"Then take him around back where there's grass and he won't be seen. I guess we'll have to bring him water in a bucket." She went off to do her marketing.

"Take him around back. Bring him water," Pierre said to himself in a whiney voice. "Maybe I should sell him. I could tell her he was stolen and keep the money." He thought a minute. *And I could take that bundle and sell it, too. Tell her that thieves broke in and stole it and the horse.* After debating with himself for a few minutes, he went inside and took the bundle. Then he led the horse to the back of the house, mounted it and rode off toward Paris, holding the bag in front of him. He knew a man who would pay well for something as valuable as what he wanted to sell. After winding through the streets for a while, he found the man's shop.

"Thomas," he called to his friend as he entered. "I have something you will want. And a horse, too."

"Pierre, good to see you. Show me what you have," Thomas answered.

Pierre went up to him, saying, "In private. You won't want anyone else to see."

"What could you have that would be that valuable, huh? Come back here and show me."

They went behind a curtain that shielded the back of the shop from the public area.

"Just look." Pierre handed Thomas the bag. Thomas opened the brown bag and picked up a rag, then another and another. He looked at Pierre questioningly. Pierre stared at the rags.

"That wife of mine has tricked me," he said. "I'll go back and get what I meant to bring."

"What about the horse?" asked Thomas.

"I'll bring him back, too. Right now I'm in a hurry and need to ride rather than walk." He left the bag full of rags and ran out of the shop, mounted the horse, and left for his home.

Pierre's wife returned from the market with a basket of vegetables, bread, and cheese, only to find him and the horse gone. She hurried inside to check on the bag she'd hidden. Sure enough, the bag was gone. *It was a good thing*, she thought, that she had removed the robe and biretta and put some old rags in the bag, putting the original contents under the mattress.

"It will serve him right when he finds that he doesn't have anything to sell, after all."

Pierre's wife took the robe and biretta and placed them in her market basket after she put her purchases away. Then she covered it with a white cloth and took it to the village priest.

"Father Matthias, I found these next to the stream when I went to gather herbs. I think I know what they are, and I want you to have them."

"Annette, what do you have?" She handed him the basket, uncovering the contents. Father Matthias picked up the robe and shook it out. "Annette, where did you get this?"

"Where I told you, Father. By the stream. Someone must have dropped it there unawares."

The priest looked the robe over carefully, noting the tears and stains.

"You said you thought you knew what it is. Tell me what you thought."

"We heard, of course, about King Louis' death and that Cardinal Richelieu was injured. This looks to me like the robe of a cardinal. And the hat, the biretta, could those have been his?"

Father Matthias thought a moment. "I haven't heard any more than you about the Cardinal, but these do look like the robe and biretta of one. And the damage to the cloth could mean it belonged to Cardinal Richelieu. Leave them with me. I will take them to where they should go."

"Thank you, Father.

When Pierre returned to his home, his wife wasn't there. He looked under the bed, but didn't find what he was looking for. Then he looked every place he could think of, which didn't take long. The house was small and they didn't have many possessions. Then he thought, "She's taken it to the priest." He left for the village's church and met her on her way home.

"What have you done with it?" he demanded.

"I gave it to the priest, as should have been done right away," she retorted, passing him on her way. "He'll take care of it and we won't be in any trouble."

"I could have gotten a lot of money for it," he said in a low voice so as not to attract attention.

"I had to lie about where it came from." She whispered back. "Now, if you want money, sell the horse."

Father Matthias, who had given Annette back her basket, took the robe and biretta and wrapped them carefully in a spare alter cloth. He wrapped the package in a piece of woolen fabric and tied the bundle with string. Then he locked the church's front door, went to a neighbor's home and asked to borrow a horse.

"I'll be back before dark. I have to visit a parishioner in the country." He didn't explain further, but took the horse, attached the well-wrapped bundle to the saddle, and left for Paris.

He reached Paris within two hours and headed for the residence of a long-time friend. When he got there, he led the horse around to the back where he could give it some water. Then he knocked on the rear entrance.

The door opened and a young woman looked out. "Oh, Father Matthias! It's good to see you again."

"Good day, Audrey, I must see the cardinal as soon as possible. I have something I think he's been looking for."

"Come in, Father. I will get Pascal."

Father Matthias waited inside for just a moment, until his friend's secretary appeared.

"Father Matthias. Audrey said you were here to see the Cardinal. I'm afraid he is – unavailable -- at the moment. Could I help you?"

"I have brought an important item to him, one I think he would like to have. When might he be available?"

Pascal thought for a moment before motioning Father Matthias to follow him. He led the priest to the room upstairs in which the Cardinal had spoken to the guard and the musketeers.

"I'm afraid that he will not become available for some time. He has been arrested by the king. King Gaston, I mean."

"What? Why was he arrested?" The priest was shocked that a cardinal of the church had been arrested.

"They said for conspiring against King Gaston by keeping Cardinal Richelieu's whereabouts secret. I don't know when, if at all, he will be released." Pascal looked at what Father Matthias was carrying. "That is something you brought to give him?"

"Yes. Although now I don't know what to do with it." He looked at the secretary. "Perhaps here would not be a good place to leave it."

"May I know what it is?" the secretary asked.

"I suppose so. This morning one of my parishioners came to me carrying a basket with this wrapped inside." He unwrapped the wool covering and set it aside. Then he unwrapped the alter cloth and spread the contents out on the table.

Pascal looked at it and gasped. "Is it Cardinal Richelieu's?"

"I believe so. She said she had found it beside a stream this morning, as if someone had dropped it. I don't know; it may be true. But her husband is known to 'find' things that belong to others."

"I see." The secretary thought for a while. "There is a place I know of that items can be put for safekeeping. If you will trust me, I can put this there and tell no one until Cardinal Tremblay is released or you come for it. Do I have your permission to do that?"

Father Matthias thought for a moment. He figured that if Cardinal Tremblay trusted Pascal, he had no reason not to trust him.

"All right, I will give it into your safekeeping and pray that the Cardinal will be at home in the near future." He would also pray that Pascal was indeed trustworthy.

Pascal escorted Father Matthias downstairs and back out through the servants' entrance. When the priest was gone, he wrapped the package back the way it had been and took it to the cellar. There he pulled a cabinet away from the wall, then pulled four bricks out of the wall. He pushed the package into a recess behind the bricks and replaced them. Then he replaced the cabinet and returned upstairs. "It should be safe there," he thought. Then he thought, "Perhaps I should go to Clairefontaine and talk to the abbot." He didn't know much about what had happened to Cardinal Richelieu, but he knew where he had been taken after the attack that killed the king.

"Audrey," he called to the maid. "I need to be away for a while. I should be back by tomorrow night."

"Sir? Is something wrong?" she asked him.

"No, no. I just need to talk to someone who lives a short distance away. I'm sure everything will be fine. Don't worry."

Then he went back to the cellar and got the bundle he had just hidden away. He put it in a traveling bag and went out to get his horse ready for the journey.

He arrived at Clairefontaine after a tiring ride for both him and his horse. The sun was just about to peek above the horizon when he knocked on the door of the monastery. The monks were at Morning Prayer when he was let in.

"I must speak to the abbot at once," he said to the monk at the door.

"He is at prayer, but come in and join us. It won't be but a moment until we have finished," the monk told him. "I am Brother Paulo."

Presently, the monks finished, rose from their kneeling positions, and filed back into the chapterhouse.

"Come eat with us," Brother Paulo said to Pascal.

"Thank you, but I must speak with the abbot."

"Of course. Come with me."

Brother Paulo led him to the door of the abbot's office. Knocking, he opened the door for Pascal to enter.

"Abbe', I am Cardinal Tremblay's secretary, Pascal. I have an item that I would like you to look at to verify its identity." He pulled the bundle out of his bag and unwrapped it, spreading it out on the desk.

The abbot looked at it, then stroked it, smoothing the wrinkles.

"It is the cardinal's robe which was stolen from us weeks ago." He looked at Pascal. "Where did you find it?"

"A priest from a village near to Paris brought it to me. He said a parishioner had found it by a stream, as though it had been dropped accidentally and left there. That may or may not be true, but it doesn't matter if it is really the Cardinal's robe."

"What does Cardinal Tremblay say about it?" the abbot asked.

Pascal hemmed and hawed for a moment before saying, "He wasn't there when the priest brought it. I'm not sure when he will return, and I thought I should bring it to you just to be sure."

"It has come back to us, then, where it was stolen. I wonder what happened to the man who stole it. That doesn't matter, now. Will you take it back with you?"

"Perhaps I should leave it here. I'm sure you have a place it can be hidden in case someone comes asking about the cardinal."

"We have already been questioned by one of King Gaston's men about the cardinal's whereabouts. He isn't here, and hasn't been for weeks. I don't know where he has gone."

"I see," Pascal said. "I will leave it with you anyway. If Cardinal Tremblay, when he returns, wants to see it, I'll return for it. Keep it safe."

Pascal went to eat with the monks and then started his journey back to Paris, satisfied that the robe had returned to the right place.

Chapter Fifteen

Two old men sat in a tavern in Toulouse, drinking ale. One of them said, in a loud voice, "Wasn't it that cardinal we saw yesterday at the inn? You know, King Louis' minister, what was his name? I thought he was dead."

"You mean Richelieu? No, I'm sure it wasn't. I thought he was dead, too," the other one said, equally as loud. "But maybe . . . do you think he survived and is hiding? It did look a lot like him."

"I saw him many times when I lived in Paris. This man looked just like him. Why do you think he's here?"

"Hiding out, like I said. I'll bet he's going to raise an army to overthrow King Gaston."

"Yes. We know Queen Anne had a child awhile back. Suppose it was a boy? He would be the rightful heir, wouldn't he?"

"He would. Maybe Richelieu is going to try to bring Queen Anne back as regent for the infant and will advise her."

"Should we tell anyone?"

"Who would believe us? We're just two old men. What do we know?"

∞ ∞ ∞

The companions' travel was uneventful for the next few days, except for Porthos' complaining of hunger.

Finally, after being questioned about their location and destination yet again, D'Artagnan took out his map, spreading it over his horse's neck. He looked at it, tracing what he thought their route had been with a finger. "I think we're about here." He pointed to a location on the map. "We're going – here – if we can find our way there." He pointed to Renne. It was one of the towns pinpointed on the map. There were no roads drawn in, though, so finding their way there might not be direct.

"We should continue in a westerly direction, as best we can. With luck, we'll find villages and towns on our way where we need them. I, also, have had enough of camping."

"I thought we were going to Nantes," said Athos.

"Yes, but Rennes is on our way, and closer."

The seven men set out again. Eventually, the sky grew dark with clouds blocking out the sun.

Porthos had been watching the clouds grow darker toward the west. "I hope we reach a village soon. It looks as though it could rain at any time. I've had enough of being wet."

"Well, if it does start raining, we will find a large tree and take shelter under it," Athos told him. "I'm sure we will be fine."

"I suppose so, but I wish we had something to cover ourselves with when it rains. All we have are a few blankets, which will soak through and be worse than useless in rain."

"Well, think about it for a while. Maybe you will invent something."

The cardinal was awake, and he and Montaigne were deep in conversation, when Aramis, who was in the lead, spotted buildings ahead.

"We may be coming to a village soon," he called back to the others.

D'Artagnan rode up to join him. Pulling his hat down to shade his eyes, he said, "I hope you're right. We need to replenish our stores, even with the provisions the good pastor gave us. We will need more, with the extra member of our group."

"Do you think it was wise to allow Montaigne to join us?" Aramis asked.

"The cardinal wants him with us. We must take our cue from him. But you're right that we must keep our guard up. It has been a while since you have seen him, but not as long for me. We worked together more recently in Italy."

They were nearing the village and spotted what looked like a sign for an inn.

"The Spotted Cow," D'Artagnan read as they got nearer. "We should stop there. It's near time for dinner, so shall we stop for the night?"

"I like that idea. Let's go back and tell the others," Aramis said.

They turned and waited for the rest to catch up to them.

"We'll stop here for the night," D'Artagnan announced. "Stay at the edge of town while I inquire about accommodations. Monsieur Montaigne, would you come with me?"

"Certainly," the new member of the group said, and the two men rode off.

They entered the inn and looked around. "This is better than the last inn we wanted to stay at," D'Artagnan said.

Inside it was warm and noisy. There was a low fire in the fireplace, and all the windows were open to let cooler air in. D'Artagnan went to the bar and asked about rooms.

"We'll need at least two, if each has two large beds. If not, we will need three."

"How many will be sleeping?" the innkeeper said.

"There are seven, all men."

"That's quite a few. Are you sent from the government to find a fugitive?" The innkeeper whispered behind his hand. He was a curious man; you could even call him nosy. You could definitely call him gossipy.

D'Artagnan stared at him for a moment before answering. "You could say that."

"I'll show you the rooms for your approval right away. Follow me."

He took them up the stairs to the end of the hall. There was a stairway beyond that which led down past the kitchen and private quarters.

The room on the left had four narrow beds, and the one on the right had two beds wide enough for two to sleep in each.

"These will do nicely. We will go back and get the rest of our party. Do you have room in your stable for eight horses and a small cart?"

"I'm afraid not. But I have a fenced pasture with a pond behind the stable, if you would be willing to put the horses there. I could fit the cart in the stable if it is not too big."

"Show us, please."

The pasture was as the innkeeper described. The fence seemed secure, the pond was fed by a stream, and the grass looked lush.

"This will do. Monsieur Montaigne, would you stay behind while I fetch the others?"

"Of course, Monsieur Dubois." Montaigne walked back inside with the innkeeper.

D'Artagnan rode back to the edge of town, which was only a few buildings away.

"We have two rooms for ourselves and a fenced pasture for the horses. The cart will be put in the stable," he said as he led them to the inn. "We will bring our supplies to our rooms. Brother Xavier, please drive the cart back to the stable. We can carry Brother Etienne up the back stairs, as our rooms are next to it on the second floor."

They all proceeded to the back of the inn, where the stable master unharnessed the cart horse, then stowed the cart in the stable and removed saddles and bridles. After rubbing down the horses, he turned them into the pasture.

Porthos carried Brother Etienne through the back door and up the stairs while the others carried what supplies they had left.

Montaigne was waiting for them at the top. "I informed the innkeeper that one of our party is injured and requested that we take our meals in our rooms. He said he was short on staff and asked if we could bring them up ourselves."

"That's acceptable; we've done that before." D'Artagnan opened the rooms' doors. "We should decide who stays in which room."

Athos spoke up. "The three of us could stay in that room." He pointed to Porthos, Aramis and the room with four beds.

"Then Montaigne, Brother Etienne, Brother Xavier, and I would stay in this one." He indicated the room with two beds. "Any other suggestions?"

They all looked at each other and shrugged.

"All right, then, let's choose our beds. Gerard and I will go downstairs to see when the food will be ready and be back in a moment," D'Artagnan told them.

The group dispersed to claim their beds and put their belongings on them.

"Would you and Georges eat down here to listen for gossip we should know about?" At Athos' nod, he said, "I'll send him down shortly."

After notifying the innkeeper that they were waiting for the food to be ready, they sat at a table to watch the room. When the barmaid arrived, they ordered wine for themselves and two pitchers to take to the others.

"How much longer do you suppose our journey will take?" Athos asked.

"Hard to tell. How many more times will we be attacked? How many times will we have to change our route to avoid being captured? Or stop to help people in need? I would rather be doing other things, but taking an important man to safety is what we are needed for now."

"Your plates are ready now, gentlemen," the innkeeper said.

"Thank you. We'll take two each, then come back for more. My friend, here, and another will eat down here." D'Artagnan and Athos picked up the plates and went back to their rooms.

Everyone was waiting in the smaller room with the two beds. The cardinal was in one of the beds, propped up on pillows, with Brother Xavier sitting on the bed with him. The others were sitting or standing where they could find room.

"Georges, come down with me. We'll eat downstairs," Athos told his friend.

"I'll go down with you to get my own plate," D'Artagnan said. "And bring it up here with two pitchers of wine."

They went downstairs, where Gerard and Georges found a table in the center of the room. They ordered wine to drink with their dinner and settled in to listen intently.

Back in the room, D'Artagnan sat on the second bed to eat while the rest, who had already finished eating, enjoyed their wine.

"How are you feeling, Your Eminence? Is your wound healing well?" All eyes were now on him.

"I think I'm doing well," he replied, although his voice was still weak and breathy. "Brother Xavier has examined me and pronounced my wound to be healing properly. I should be stronger before we get to our destination. Where is it, anyway?"

D'Artagnan looked at him pointedly. "Nantes, as I have said several times. That belongs to your family, does it not?"

After a moment's hesitation, the cardinal said, "Of course. My apologies for forgetting. With God's help, we will arrive there soon."

"Indeed."

By that time, all had finished their dinners and were well into finishing the wine.

"I'll take the dishes back downstairs and retrieve Gerard and Georges," D'Artagnan said, gathering the empty plates in one hand and the cutlery in the other.

After turning the load over to a barmaid, he found his two friends at their table.

He joined them and asked, "What have you learned from eavesdropping on this motley group?"

"Quite a bit," said Athos. "But probably nothing very helpful. We now know a lot about daily life in this village, and something about the travelers passing through, but have heard nothing about what goes on in Paris currently."

"Ah well. Perhaps the lack of news is itself good news. Come back upstairs. We should get an early start tomorrow."

"A moment while we finish our drinks. We'll join you shortly," Athos said.

D'Artagnan went on, but before he reached the stairs, an obviously drunken man approached him, saying, "You look familiar. Don't I know you from somewhere? Let me see . . ."

D'Artagnan recognized him right away as a former Cardinal's Guard who had been dismissed due to his drunkenness. He turned away and said, "No, you don't know me. I've never seen you before."

"Oh, I'm sure I do. Now where were we?" He held his chin in his hand and closed his eyes.

When he opened them again, D'Artagnan had dashed up the stairs. His eyes widened with the memory of the identity of the man he had spoken to.

Safe upstairs in the room with four beds, where Montaigne and Aramis were, D'Artagnan told them what had happened. Montaigne asked, "Do you know him?"

"Unfortunately. His name is Henri Lamar. He used to be a fellow guard, until his attitude and carelessness, and drunkenness, got him thrown out. He, of course, thought that was quite unfair, and vowed revenge."

"Do you think he remembered you?" Porthos asked. "And if he did, what do you think he will do?"

"I wish I knew the answer to both those questions. But we must assume he will, and seek revenge on me. We must post watches in both rooms. He is bound to have a room on this floor." D'Artagnan turned to Aramis. "Have the monks gone to sleep?"

"Yes. That is why we're in this room."

"Someone must stay in the room with them at all times until we leave in the morning. Montaigne, would you go downstairs and watch the man until he comes up?" He described the man in question.

"Of course. You've always told me that I'm the perfect spy; no one ever remembers seeing me. When he comes to his room, I'll join you in the other room. I'll take the first watch. Then I'll wake you for the next watch."

Athos and Aramis passed Montaigne on the stairs as they went to rejoin their group. D'Artagnan was still in the room when they entered.

"Was that man a friend of yours?" Aramis asked. "Could he be a problem?"

D'Artagnan repeated what he had told Montaigne and Porthos. Then he said, "You three sleep in here and put the fourth bed across the door. Even so, one of you should be awake at all times."

D'Artagnan went back across the hall to the other bedroom. Brother Xavier was asleep in the other bed, so he crawled in with him, but stayed awake. Although he depended on Montaigne to watch the former guardsman, he felt the need to keep watch in the room.

A little while later, D'Artagnan heard a knock on the door. It was one he recognized from years past, when Cardinal Richelieu had assigned him to travel with Montaigne.

The door opened enough for Montaigne to slip in.

"Your friend has gone into a room down the hall by the stairs. I bought him a few drinks and had practically had to carry him up the stairs. I don't think he'll be a problem for us tonight."

D'Artagnan lay back with a sigh. "But even so, one of us needs to be on guard."

"I'll take the first shift, as I said. I only pretended to drink. I'll wake you up in a few hours." Then Montaigne moved one of the two chairs in the room against the door and sat down.

After Monsieur Lamar was deposited in his room and left alone, he quietly peeked through the door. The small man who had bought him drinks had disappeared. He slipped out of his room and down the stairs.

"Jules," Lamar whispered to a man sitting at a back table, "I've found D'Artagnan."

Jules looked up at his friend. "Excellent. He is staying here, I presume. Alone?"

"No. He was with two others. They went upstairs together. Moments later another man came down and engaged me in conversation. I continued to play drunk, and he bought me more drinks. Luckily I was able to dispose of most of them without his knowledge. He almost carried me up the stairs to the room! I believe he's in with D'Artagnan and his friends." By the time he finished speaking he sounded enraged.

"Calm yourself, Henri. I know you blame D'Artagnan for all your troubles, but rage begets carelessness, and carelessness loses the fight." Jules patted Lamar's shoulder as he would a child who was having a temper tantrum. "We will watch for them to leave in the morning and follow them. You'll get your chance." He rose from the table and took his friend's arm. "Let us go up to bed. I will wake early and go down to watch for them. They won't even see me."

D'Artagnan had taken the second watch, and woke the others before dawn. A coded tap on the door of the other room told the occupants to get ready to leave.

"I was recognized last night by a former guard who bears me ill will," he told the monks. "I'm certain that he will try to exact revenge. No, Your Eminence, you knew nothing of the circumstances. It was all handled when you were away with the late king. As far as I know, he knows only that I am with Gerard and Georges." He turned to Montaigne. "Would you go back down and watch for Monsieur Lamar? The rest of us will leave down the back stairs." He took a few coins out and handed them to Montaigne. "Please buy some provisions from the innkeeper for our breakfast and lunch. Perhaps more in case we don't find another inn for tonight." He passed over a few more coins. "I'd expected to do that this morning, but things have changed."

There was a tap on their door, and a voice asked, 'may we enter?' Montaigne opened it a crack, then wider to let the other three in as he exited. "I'll meet you down the road heading west in fifteen minutes," he said as he left.

"Georges, would you go down and ready the horses and cart? Go the back way. I believe someone may be waiting for me in the front. And be as quiet as possible. Gerard, would you go with him to help?"

Porthos and Athos took their saddlebags with them and did as requested. The stable boy was already awake when they got there and agreed to help catch the horses and saddle and hitch them.

D'Artagnan carried the cardinal down while Brother Xavier and Aramis carried the rest of their belongings.

Within minutes the group was ready to leave. After giving the stable boy a small tip for his help and his silence, D'Artagnan led the way along a grassy trail that went behind the adjacent buildings.

"Montaigne should be waiting for us just past the edge of town. Or he should be there shortly," D'Artagnan told the others. "And he should have breakfast with him."

Chapter Sixteen

Montaigne glanced around the common room to see if anyone was there. He could see a man sitting in a shadowy corner who he thought he might have seen the night before, but otherwise there were no other patrons. Looking away nonchalantly, Montaigne signaled the innkeeper, asking to buy provisions for the road, and followed the man into the kitchen.

"Do you know the man sitting in the corner? He looks familiar, but I can't place him," he said to the innkeeper.

"Do you mean right now? I didn't see anyone. Last night I saw a man sitting in the dark. Later, the man you helped upstairs came back down and talked to him. But I don't know who he is."

"Really? Thank you for the information." Montaigne asked for the foodstuffs he wanted, including two bottles of wine and a bag to carry them in. After paying for the items, and giving the man a tip for the information, he took them back into the common area and left through the front door. He strolled down the street, looking around, and casually looking back to see if he was being followed. Shortly, the other man left the inn and started walking in the same direction as Montaigne, who went around the side of a building and waited for the man to catch up.

"Good morning, monsieur," he said as he reappeared from around the corner. "And a fine morning it is, isn't it? Listen to the birds singing. Such a beautiful sound."

"Good morning," the man said as he walked past.

"I saw you at the inn, I believe. Are you traveling through this fine village?"

"Ah, yes, I am."

"But don't you have a horse and belongings? It will be a long walk to wherever you're going."

"I'm not continuing on my journey yet. I just like to walk in the fresh morning air. By myself. I do like solitude some of the time."

"Of course, of course," Montaigne said. "I feel the same, myself. Then I will let you be and go on alone." He waved a salute and went back around the building, and returned to the inn from behind. There, he retrieved his horse and followed the route the others had taken.

Jules had noticed which way Montaigne had taken when they parted ways. He followed at a distance, stopping when Montaigne arrived at the inn, mounted his horse and rode on. Then Jules went back into the inn and up to his room, where he found Henri waiting.

"I found your drinking friend and followed him. They're riding west. Come on; we must hurry or we might lose them."

Montaigne caught up to his friends a short way west of town.

"I had a brief meeting with the friend of your friend on the street just now. He didn't tell me that they were friends, the innkeeper did. He said he was out for a walk, but when we separated and I headed back to the inn, I saw that he followed me. I'm sure he didn't notice that I noticed him, but I'm also sure that he stopped to pick up the other man and set out after us. We need to move on quickly, perhaps changing direction at first chance."

"A good idea," D'Artagnan said. "We'll ride ahead and turn at the first fork in the road we find."

They moved ahead, eating their breakfast on the way. The cardinal was propped up in the back of the cart eating more than he had been able to since the journey began.

Shortly they came to what looked like a path going off to the right. It was grassy and wouldn't show the marks of horse hooves or cart wheels for long, and the surrounding area was thickly wooded. The only sounds they made were hoof beats and creaking wheels.

D'Artagnan moved closer to Porthos and spoke in a whisper. "Would you ride into the trees and watch to see if they follow us onto this road? If they do, wait until they pass and get behind them. And sound the alert so we'll know they are there." He meant the bird sound they used in the village of the Huguenots.

"But if I don't see them very soon, should I wait longer?" Porthos asked.

"If you don't see them within half an hour, catch up with us. If you do, and we've gone too far ahead, do what I said before. I'm sure they will catch up with the rest of us quickly. Just don't forget to sound the signal."

Porthos complied, and D'Artagnan rode back to the others and repeated what he had told Porthos. "Brother Xavier, if we do get in a battle, please drive the cart on and don't wait for us. We must keep Brother Etienne safe."

A few moments later, they heard the "twit tu whit" call that told them to be ready.

"Into the trees," D'Artagnan called softly to the others. They moved to either side of the road in pairs, leaving the cart to go on. Presently, the two they were expecting rode into view. They waited until the newcomers were several yards past them, then Montaigne and Aramis dashed out behind. When D'Artagnan and Athos dashed out in front, Henri and Jules saw their quarry and spurred their horses on. Then Porthos arrived to complete the circle.

Henri and Jules looked astonished that they were surrounded by so many. They had expected no more than two or three men accompanying D'Artagnan, but here were four more with him.

"Why are you following us?" D'Artagnan said.

"We are not following you," Henri said defensively. "We just happen to be going this way."

"Really? And what lies in this direction?" D'Artagnan wasn't convinced of his story.

"You are going this way. Don't you know?" Jules was trying to get through the barricade of horses.

"Enough! Henri Lamar, I know it is you. And I know that you know who I am. Don't try to blame your dismissal on me. You did it to yourself, being a drunkard and a liar."

"And I know you are wanted by the Crown as an enemy of the state, Charles D'Artagnan. Give yourself up to me and you may live. If not, I will take your dead body back with me."

D'Artagnan stared at him for a moment, then burst out laughing. "Look around you, Lamar. There are five of us surrounding the two of you. What do you think your odds are? Let me introduce my friends to you." Pointing to each one, he spoke his name. "Athos, Porthos and Aramis of the king's Musketeers. The previous king. And Monsieur Montaigne, who is a great and helpful friend."

At the mention of the musketeers, while the others were distracted, Jules spurred his horse, which leapt between Athos and Porthos and out of the circle.

The two musketeers wheeled their horses and chased after him. Henri was taken by surprise and quickly captured by Montaigne, while Aramis and D'Artagnan joined the chase.

The cart had been going on, as D'Artagnan had instructed, and had just rounded a curve in the road when Jules, who hadn't seen the cart as he raced along the road and navigated closely around the curve, barreled into the left side, knocking the cart off balance and frightening the horse. Athos and Porthos were right on his heels and couldn't avoid the collision either. Those actions caused the cart to overturn, throwing the cardinal and Brother Xavier out and spilling all the provisions and belongings that had been resting inside. Brother Xavier fell on soft grass, but the cardinal fell closer to the road and hit his head on a bump which turned out to be a rock covered with grass.

Jules was quickly recaptured before they noticed the rest of the accident. By that time the rest of the group had caught up. Fortunately, the other two had been riding in the middle of the road and missed colliding with anyone.

Aramis was the first to notice the two monks on the ground.

"Brother Etienne," he called out as he quickly dismounted and ran to help. "Are you all right?"

Brother Xavier, who had quickly crawled to the cardinal's location, spoke up. "He hit his head on this hard rock and was knocked unconscious. Help me get him back into the cart."

The two men quickly raised the cart back upright and carefully lifted the cardinal and placed him on the cart floor, cushioning his head with a sack of grain and covering him with the blankets. Then they began replacing everything else that had spilled out on the ground.

"Eminence! Can you hear me?" Brother Xavier said. He looked up at Aramis. "He seems to still be breathing. What should we do?"

"I would say to let him rest. We still have to deal with these two." He pointed at the two prisoners.

"Who are they?"

"One of them is someone Allais knew from before. The other one seems to be a friend of that man. Now that they have seen the two of you, we don't have much choice. We can't let them get away and tell anyone where we are."

D'Artagnan walked up right then, and asked, "How is he?"

"Unconscious, but still breathing, thank God," Aramis told him. "Brother Xavier will keep watch over him and let us know if anything changes."

The two men walked back to where the others were. They had been disarmed and each tied to a different tree. Athos and Porthos stood a short distance from them, watching them carefully.

"What should we do with them? They know where we are and surely know who we have with us. I wouldn't trust either one of them not to go back to Paris with their story of how we attacked them while we were kidnapping the cardinal," D'Artagnan said.

"We can't keep them and can't let them go. I don't see any choice. They did attack us, did they not?" Porthos clearly knew what he wanted to do with them.

"They would have, if we hadn't seen them coming."

While the five men were discussing the situation, the two prisoners tied to trees had been trying to get loose. They broke free at about the same time the others finished their conversation and started for their horses.

"Look! They're getting away." Porthos cried, mounting his horse and dashing after them. Athos did the same and Montaigne followed.

When Porthos caught up with them, Jules pulled out a pistol he had secreted in his saddlebag. He had just enough time to get off a shot, which went wide, before Porthos caught up with him.

Jules then pulled out the sword that had been left sheathed on the saddle. Porthos already had his sword ready and defended himself from Jules' attack.

Henri, instead of mounting his horse, had grabbed his sword from the saddle and turned on D'Artagnan, who had his sword at the ready.

D'Artagnan and Henri knew each other's strengths and weaknesses. Fortunately, D'Artagnan had more strengths and Henri had more weaknesses. Before long, D'Artagnan had the upper hand and Henri was falling back, until he tripped on an exposed tree root and fell. He tried to scramble up, but D'Artagnan held him down with the point of his sword at Henri's throat.

"It is not my wish to kill you, but you have put my friends and me in a precarious position. As I was reminded, we can't let you go and we can't take you with us."

"Was that Cardinal Richelieu I saw in the cart? I thought, we all thought, he was dead. I know what's been happening in Paris. I know people are looking for him. I can help take him to safety," Henri said.

"I'm sure you have no love for the cardinal, or for me. You were dismissed from the guard for being a drunkard and a liar. Why should I trust you now?"

Henri looked blank, his eyes shifting back and forth as if he was trying to come up with an acceptable answer.

"Just as I thought. You would send word back to Paris and try to have us arrested in the next town."

At that, Henri scooted back and tried again to rise with his sword held high. Before he could even attempt to attack D'Artagnan, he was struck through the chest with the sword that had been held against him.

D'Artagnan turned to see what was happening behind him just as Porthos finished with Jules, whose body lay sprawled on the ground.

Brother Xavier said, "Please, I must attend to them, since the cardinal can't."

D'Artagnan nodded and went to watch over the patient.

After Brother Xavier had done what he could for the dead men, they were carried into the woods and buried under bushes.

The group gathered back on the grassy road after that was done. "How is Brother Etienne doing?" asked Aramis.

Brother Xavier spoke up. "His heart seems to be beating regularly, but he is still unconscious. Where can we take him?"

D'Artagnan consulted the documents Cardinal Tremblay had given him: the map and the list of sympathetic nobles and churchmen on their route. "There is no one that is living nearby who Cardinal Tremblay deems sympathetic to our cause. We must trust in our safety wherever we find ourselves, or find another place to go." He looked at the map again. "Rennes is much closer, although there is no one there on the list, either."

Aramis spoke up. "Rennes is the closest city of size. I think we must trust that we will be safe there. We must get the cardinal to a physician as soon as possible."

"I'm afraid you're right," D'Artagnan said. "We must get on our way."

"What should we do with these two extra horses? We already have more than we need," Porthos said.

D'Artagnan thought a moment, and said, "Brother Xavier, drive the cart onto the road and turn to the west. Montaigne, would you and Gerard accompany him, please? The rest of us will deal with the horses and catch up to you."

After the cart had rounded the corner, Porthos said, "We could sell them in Rennes. No one would know they weren't ours. We could also sell the tack and one of the pack horses, too"

"We can try. Let's catch up with the others."

Chapter Seventeen

After another uneventful, and somewhat boring, journey of several days, they arrived in Rennes. They had had to camp two of those days, which caused many complaints and some bickering. Fortunately, it hadn't rained, for which they were eternally grateful. The cardinal had twitched and jerked along the way, but had not awakened.

They had passed no settlements large enough to support even a healer, but the patient was breathing normally and didn't show signs of distress even though he had not awakened.

Aramis was taking his turn driving the cart when they arrived, so that Brother Xavier could keep watch over the patient.

"I think there's an inn up ahead," said Athos. "Shall we try for rooms there?"

"Come with me to inquire if they have two available," D'Artagnan replied after locating what looked like the inn that Athos mentioned. "The rest of you, try not to draw notice. We shouldn't be long."

"I'm an expert in being invisible," Montaigne said, as D'Artagnan and Athos rode off. "First, we must try to be quiet and not look around at the sights, such as they are. Next, we must find another place to stop. Stay here and I'll look around for a likely place." He rode back the way they had come, looking for a side street or a stand of trees they could hide behind. Not too far back was an alley, so he directed them to pull the cart in there.

D'Artagnan and Athos rode forward toward the inn. It was called The Black Dragon and looked well-kept. Leaving their horses tied to a post in front, they entered the establishment and looked around.

"It looks all right," Athos said. The windows were open to let in light, although there was a small fire in the fireplace and candles hanging from the ceiling to help. They looked around for the innkeeper or a barmaid.

"May I help you gentlemen?" inquired a small, rotund man wearing an apron. "I am Jacques Boucher, the innkeeper. Are you looking for a meal, a room, or both?"

"A room, if you please, Monsieur Boucher, with meals. Or, rather, two rooms. There are others with us waiting outside," D'Artagnan told him. "And a stable for several horses and a small cart?"

"How many in your group?"

"There are seven, and one is ill. Is there a physician in this town to examine him?"

"Ill?" Boucher said in a voice bordering on panic.

"Actually, he is injured, not ill. I misspoke. He fell and hit his head."

"Well," the man replied, sounding relieved. "We do have a physician. I can have him sent for."

"Do you have the rooms, preferably together or across the hall from each other?"

"I do. I have one room with two large beds and one next door with four beds, if those will do."

"Those should do nicely," D'Artagnan told him. "We'll look at the rooms, and if they are suitable, my friend will go back for the others."

Athos and D'Artagnan followed the innkeeper upstairs. It looked remarkably like the inn they had stayed in previously. "Very good," D'Artagnan said. "Do you know where we could sell some horses and their tack?"

The innkeeper thought a moment and said, "We have a stable here, of course, but there is a general stable a couple of blocks farther west. The stable master might be interested. Other than that, I don't know."

"Thank you. I'll try there." He turned to Athos. "If you'll go for the others, I'll order meals." He turned back to the innkeeper. "You said you have a stable here? And will it hold eight horses and a cart?"

"That's quite a lot. I think we have room for two or three horses, but the cart won't fit inside. It could be put around back, though, if that would be all right."

"That will have to do. And the rest of the horses?"

"The general stable should have room for them," the innkeeper told him. "How long will you be staying?"

"I'm not sure," D'Artagnan answered. "It depends on when our companion regains consciousness. If he has no other injuries, we will be leaving immediately."

"Very well." The innkeeper handed D'Artagnan keys to the two rooms in exchange for payment for three days.

They went back down the front stairs and met the rest of the group coming in. Porthos carried Brother Etienne, while Aramis, Athos and Brother Xavier carried their belongings, and Montaigne stayed with the cart and all the horses.

"My friends," D'Artagnan said. "We will have to stable several of the horses elsewhere. Let's go up to the rooms and then I'll check out the stable here and the other one. Oh," he said, turning to the innkeeper. "Would you send for the physician as soon as possible? You can see the state of our companion."

The innkeeper looked closely at the monk, trying to lift the hood of his habit get a better look.

D'Artagnan said, "Don't remove the hood, please. He is sensitive to light and we don't want to wake him."

"Of course," Monsieur Boucher said. "I'll go send for the physician."

Porthos carried Brother Etienne up the stairs and got him into bed quickly. Brother Xavier and Aramis stayed in the room awaiting the doctor, while the others stowed their belongings and went back down to join Montaigne and take care of the horses.

"The cart can be put behind the stable, and the cart horse and one or two others will fit inside," D'Artagnan told them. "The rest, including the ones we want to sell, we'll take to the other stable a little farther west."

"I don't like splitting up the horses like that," Montaigne said as they took the cart and horses toward the back where the stable was.

"I don't, either," said D'Artagnan, "but we were told there wasn't enough room in this stable for all of them. We'll see soon enough."

The inn's stable was not overly large, but without the mounts of other guests of the inn, it still wouldn't have held all of their horses, including the ones they wanted to sell. With those other mounts, there was room for only three.

"We should leave the cart horse here, I think, and two others. But we have to decide whose horse will stay," D'Artagnan said.

"You are the leader, so I think it should be yours," said Montaigne, and Athos nodded agreement.

"Very well, but the third should be yours." D'Artagnan replied to Montaigne. He called for the stable master. "We have rooms at the inn and wish to leave these three horses here." He pointed to them. "We will take the others to the stable the innkeeper recommended. He said to put the cart around back."

After the cart and horses were secure, fed and watered, D'Artagnan and Montaigne took the other seven on down the street to the larger stable. It looked to be quite large, since it needed to house both the mounts of many of the town-dwellers and those of visitors.

D'Artagnan was able to sell the horses and their tack with some haggling for a good price.

When they returned to the inn, D'Artagnan said, "I'm sure you're all getting hungry. I am, myself. But first we must check on our patient."

They went up to their rooms as soon as they returned to the inn. The physician had arrived and was examining the monk.

"He is breathing sufficiently, seems to be comfortable, and his heartbeat sounds normal, but he is still unconscious. I can do nothing more until he awakens," the physician said. "If, I mean, when he awakens, send for me. I have other patients to see today." Then he left.

Before the physician left the inn, he conferred with the innkeeper in private. "Do you know who your new customers are?"

"I got only one name. Their leader or, at least, their spokesman, said his name is Allais Dubois. Why do you ask?"

"Their friend who is unconscious looks familiar, but I can't think of who he might be. Oh, well. Dubois' name isn't familiar. I'll think about what the patient's name might be," the doctor said as he left.

D'Artagnan said to the others after the physician left, "Well, there seems to be nothing to do except to watch over him. We can each take turns during the night so that everyone gets to sleep. It looks as if tonight will be a repeat of last night, except for keeping watch for trouble. I hope."

"I will go down to inquire about our meals," said Athos. "Who would rather eat up here and who would like to eat downstairs?"

Brother Xavier spoke first. "I will take my supper watching over the cardinal and will stay with him."

"I will stay with the good brother, as well" said Montaigne. "Why don't the rest of you eat downstairs? That way there will be many ears to listen for information."

"Done," D'Artagnan replied. He and the musketeers left, saying that plates would be brought up to the others.

As there was no available space at the boards that would seat the four of them far enough away from other ears, they found separate space in different areas of the room.

"That way we can overhear twice as much," D'Artagnan explained.

Just then their plates were brought, with two extra for the others. Athos and Porthos volunteered to take the meals, along with a pitcher of house wine, upstairs and then returned to eat their own meals.

During the time downstairs, they spoke little and listened intently, but heard nothing of interest until another traveler entered with news.

The traveler went to the bar and ordered wine. Speaking loudly, he told the innkeeper, "I hear a rumor that the king has sent men riding to all parts of the country, searching for citizens who are still loyal to the late king and his wife, the former queen." He turned around speaking to all the customers in the inn. "Now, I know everyone here is a supporter of King Gaston, so I'm sure no one is in danger. I just thought I should mention it."

The four friends looked at each other from across the room. How were they to get Brother Etienne to safety without endangering him? Where could they hide him?

"Do you think any of these men would know who we are?" asked Athos.

"I think any men that Gaston sent to search for us or for anyone who doesn't support him would be his own men and wouldn't recognize us." D'Artagnan said. "He said it was a rumor, but I doubt that it was unfounded, and I think we should look for a safer place to hide until Brother Etienne is well enough to travel again."

"I suppose there must be some safe place in this city, but how will we find it?" said Athos.

"Montaigne. He knows many people, but not so many know him," D'Artagnan said, looking around to see if anyone was close enough to hear.

"He is the perfect spy. If anyone can find a safe place to stay, it will be him."

They finished eating, bought another pitcher of wine, and went upstairs to their rooms. There had been no change in the patient, but at least he hadn't gotten worse. Montaigne and Brother Xavier had finished their dinners and were drinking from the pitcher that had accompanied the meals. D'Artagnan pulled Montaigne into the other room.

He told Montaigne about the announcement, mentioning that it was a rumor, but that they should take it seriously, anyway.

"I concur," said Montaigne. "I never treat rumors lightly. There is always a grain of truth in them, unless they are spread maliciously and are totally untrue. And I don't think this one is."

"Then we need a safe place to stay until our friend has recovered. This inn is unsuitable, and we know no one here. I'm asking you to walk the streets to see if anyone you know and trust is here and knows of a safe place to stay."

"Of course. As you always say, no one recognizes me," Montaigne said.

"But you recognize everybody," D'Artagnan finished with him. "Excellent. It's late, so you should get a good night's sleep and start tomorrow morning."

∞ ∞ ∞

The next day Montaigne was up and out early. The patient was showing signs of movement, with small jerks of his hands and head. His eyelids occasionally fluttered, as if he was trying to wake up.

"Should we call the physician back?" asked Brother Xavier. "I have never had experience with this sort of injury."

"It might be a good idea. I'll have the innkeeper send for him when I go down to order our breakfasts," said D'Artagnan. "I'll bring yours up with mine, but the others should eat downstairs."

They all went down for breakfast except for Aramis, who would join the rest when D'Artagnan returned to the room.

"Where is Montaigne this morning?" asked Porthos as they descended the stairs.

"I asked him to look for a better place for us to stay," said D'Artagnan. "He's looking for anyone he knows and trusts who might be here in Rennes. As you know, he knows a lot of people."

The room was not full. Two tables were occupied, and the musketeers chose one in a corner where they couldn't be overheard easily. When the meals were served, D'Artagnan took two plates up to the room and sent Aramis down for his.

"We may have a problem, with Brother Etienne's condition being what it is," Athos said to the others.

"I think you're right," replied Aramis. "If he doesn't get well enough to travel, and Montaigne can't find us another, safer, place to stay, this whole mission could be jeopardized."

"What should we do about it," asked Porthos after swallowing a bite of bread.

"Perhaps we should be out looking for a new location, as well." Athos ate a bite of fairly good cheese. "If we stay here and those men come to Rennes searching for us, we might not be able to escape."

"After we finish eating, let's go up and check on the patient. He might be awake and able to travel again." Porthos hurried to finish his meal.

When they got back upstairs, the doctor was there examining the monk, who had opened his eyes, but seemed to not know where he was.

"I won't know if there's any damage to his mind until he's fully awake and talking. I have other patients to visit, so I must leave. I'll be back this afternoon."

He left as the musketeers were returning. Porthos, seeing that the cardinal was awake, said, "Brother Etienne, I'm so glad you're awake again. How are you feeling?"

The monk looked at him, then looked at the other men standing around him. He opened his mouth, but nothing came out. He coughed and tried again.

"Who are you? And why am I here? I can't remember who I am," he spoke slowly, wheezing a little.

D'Artagnan was about to tell him, since he seemed to have lost his memory, that he was Brother Etienne, to make sure he didn't slip up and say who he really was, but Brother Xavier was quicker, saying, "You are Cardinal Richelieu, Your Eminence. You have been injured and have been unconscious."

The cardinal looked around the room. "Then what am I doing in this room?"

D'Artagnan took up the story. "You were gravely injured weeks ago when King Louis was killed."

The cardinal tried to shout in alarm, but it sounded as though he was croaking. "The king? He's dead?" he finally managed to say. He struggled to sit up, but fell back, exhausted.

"I'm afraid so, Your Eminence. You were attacked at the same time. His brother, Gaston, has taken the throne and is searching for you, and we are taking you to safety."

"And I've been injured? Oh, my head hurts and I can't remember things. And I feel so tired. Why is Gaston searching for me?"

"You exiled him, Eminence. You sent him away, and he hates you for it, remember?"

"I did? Oh, yes. I think I remember now. Who are these other people?"

D'Artagnan thought fast, deciding to use their assumed identities. "I am Allais, a former Cardinal's Guard, and these three, Gerard, Georges and Emile, are former King's Guards. We are posing as mercenaries escorting you to your family estates to recover." He pointed to the young monk. "He is Brother Xavier, a monk with medical training who offered to come along to care for you." He looked at the others, warning them with his look to not contradict him.

"I thank you for that, but what happened to make me unconscious? And to not remember things."

"You were knocked out of the cart you were riding in and hit your head on a rock. We were attacked by two men who were looking for me and one of them rode his horse into the cart while you were lying in it. Those men won't bother us again, but we have heard that the new king has sent men to search for you. We are at an inn now, but need to find a safer place to stay until you are well enough to travel."

Cardinal Richelieu had been lying quietly until then. "I feel well, except that my head hurts, as does my side, right here." Pointing at the place he was shot, he started to sit up again and winced. "I think something else has been injured. When I moved just now my knee pained me very much."

"Which knee?" D'Artagnan asked, looking concerned. "Someone go down and send for the doctor again. May I look at your knee?"

"This one," the cardinal said, pointing to his right knee.

At the cardinal's nod, D'Artagnan sat on the edge of the bed and turned the blanket back to reveal the knee. It looked swollen and red, and when he touched it, the cardinal winced. "You may have broken it in the fall. Since you were unconscious until now, no one knew of the injury." He pulled the blanket back over the cardinal's legs.

"There's something I need to explain to you, Eminence. Because of the danger from Gaston, we decided to call you by an alias. It would be a bad idea to let the public know where you are, so we decided to call you Brother Etienne in order to conceal your true identity."

The cardinal looked exhausted, terrified, and curious. "Tell me what has happened since the attack you told me of. Where was it?"

"You were on your way to visit Queen Anne. She was about to give birth to the heir, and King Louis decided to go with you dressed as one of your guards. You were part of the way there when your company was attacked. They killed everyone except for your secretary and a young guard, who were able to get you to a nearby monastery. You had been the victim of a gunshot wound, and the brothers there took care of you until you were able to travel."

"So much has happened that I don't remember. Where are we now? And where are we going?"

"We are currently in Rennes," D'Artagnan told him. "And we are headed to a safe place. It was suggested by your friend, Cardinal Tremblay, who asked that I not reveal it to anyone. I must abide by his instructions."

"You can tell no one? But what if we are attacked again and you are injured, or killed? How will your friends know where to take me?"

"If something happens to me, the information is hidden among my possessions. My friends will be able to keep you safe."

The patient had been looking very tired for a few minutes, and now his eyes were closing. "I think I must sleep now."

D'Artagnan motioned for the others to follow him into the other room, with the exception of Brother Xavier, who stayed to keep watch.

"We must try to keep him calm," D'Artagnan told them. "It's bad enough that he can't remember anything, but a despondent or hysterical cardinal could be dangerous, for us and for him. We must keep his spirits up, the optimism that he will recover fully and that we will get him to safety."

The door to the room opened and Montaigne walked in. "I have found a place for Brother Etienne," he said. "Is he awake yet?"

"He is," D'Artagnan said. "But there is a problem."

Montaigne sat on his bed and pulled his bag out from under it. "What problem?"

"He has lost his memory. And his right knee has been injured, as well." D'Artagnan sat on another bed. "If it was just his memory, we could go on. But now, we must stay until his knee has healed."

"You have called the doctor, I assume. Has he arrived yet?"

"He was here earlier, before Brother Etienne woke. He said he would be back this afternoon. We didn't know about his knee until a few minutes ago, and Emile went to send for him again. Another thing: he knows who he is and what has happened. I told him what name we call him, and why. Now he is asleep with Xavier sitting with him. Tell us about the place you found."

"All right," Montaigne said slowly. "That's not good news, but I have become quite accustomed to bad news." He walked to the door and checked the hallway, seeing no one. "I became acquainted with a merchant in this town some time ago. He owed me a favor, so I have called it in. He has a small warehouse behind his shop that is vacant. He will rent it to us for a small amount for a while."

The others looked at each other. He could see questions rolling around in their heads.

D'Artagnan asked the first one. "Where is it?"

"On the outskirts of town to the north. It backs up to another vacant warehouse behind a shop on the next street. That part of town is becoming rather seedy, but the merchant swears that we will be safe there."

"Do you trust this merchant?" asked Athos.

"I do. It was a rather large favor I did him, and I told him that this would pay it in full." He sat back on his bed. "Also, he has a distant cousin who was a retainer to the late king. The cousin was executed by Gaston. He has no love for the new king."

D'Artagnan looked at the others. "Take me to see this place. Gerard will go with us while Emile and Georges will stay to be here when the doctor arrives."

They heard a knock on the door of the other room. Athos peeked out to see Brother Xavier opening that door to the doctor.

"He's here now."

They all went to see what the doctor would say.

"Hm," he said after uncovering the injured knee. "When did this happen?"

"It must have happened when he fell. We didn't know about it because he was unconscious at the time," D'Artagnan told the doctor. "We just found out when he woke up."

"Yes. And how are you feeling today Monsieur, er, Brother, er, Father…?"

"You may call me, uh, Brother Etienne."

The doctor looked at him for a moment, then said, "Very well, Brother Etienne. How are you feeling?"

"I feel wretched, except for my knee, which feels worse. But I can't remember anything."

"Not even your name?"

"No. My friends, here, have told me who I am and what has happened to me. When should I get my memory back?"

"I can't say. Not much is known about loss of memory yet. We call it amnesia, from the Greek word for forgetfulness. But let me examine your knee," he went on. "It might be bruised or sprained." He pressed on different parts of the knee, exacting groans from the patient. "I don't believe it's broken, but just a sprain, so I suggest you stay in bed for several days to a week. Maybe more. If you must get up, have these gentlemen assist you. But it's best to keep the knee elevated. I will check back in several days to see how you're doing." He nodded to them all as he left.

"Well, this could be a problem," Montaigne said.

"Yes, it could," said D'Artagnan. "I'm not sure what we should do."

Brother Etienne looked at them and said, "Why? I'll try not to be a burden; I'll just lie in bed until my knee heals and we can travel again."

"Because," Montaigne said, "We need to move you away from the inn as soon as possible. I found a safe place for us to stay until you are well enough to travel, but we must be out of here before Gaston's men, who we were told were coming, get here."

"Who are you? You weren't here when I awoke."

"My name is Montaigne, and we have known each other for quite a while now. I have worked for you in the past. Now we need to make plans to relocate."

"Are those men looking for me? Shouldn't we wait for them?"

"Believe me, they are not friends of yours. King Gaston is your enemy. We think he orchestrated the attack against you, killing Louis by accident. He doesn't mind that, of course, since that makes him king now."

"I seem to remember hearing something about an heir. Would that be King Louis' child? Wouldn't he be the new king?"

"If it was a boy. We don't know, and Queen Anne has gone into hiding for fear that Gaston would have her and her child, of either gender, killed."

"Oh, of course."

"Perhaps we should move, regardless. I didn't like the way the doctor peered at him, as though he was trying to remember where he had seen him before." D'Artagnan turned to the cardinal. "If he does suspect who you really are, he could send word to the king."

"You're right," Athos said. "We could sneak him out at night, and then in the morning we could leave separately. How many days did you pay for?" he asked D'Artagnan.

"Three, to start off with. I said that after that I'd pay on a day-to-day basis," D'Artagnan said, leading him to the opposite corner of the room.

He went on in a soft voice. "But I don't really like the idea of sneaking him out at night. So much could go wrong. We need to think of a plausible excuse for leaving sooner than expected."

"Well, we could just tell the innkeeper the truth, or a variation of it. We could say that you encountered a friend or family member who lives here and offered to put us up for a while," Athos said.

"That's not a bad idea. We shouldn't have to come up with a name, and if we do, this town is rather large. No one could be expected to know everyone who lives here." D'Artagnan beckoned Montaigne to join them. "What is the name of your, uh, friend with the warehouse."

"François LeBeq. Why?"

"Because we will use him as a friend who has invited us to stay with his family while we're here. That will be our excuse to leave early. We won't use his name if we don't have to, though."

"Think of another name. LeBeq is known by many in this town, possibly including the innkeeper. How about Conard?" Montaigne said.

"That would be fine. Who is LeBeq, anyway?"

"He is not what you would call a model citizen. His shop is frequented by low-lifes, scoundrels, and other unsavory characters. My threat to him if he didn't come through is to report him to the authorities. I will continue to hold that over his head."

"Then we will stay another night and leave tomorrow. Right now, take Gerard and me to this warehouse so we will know what we will need to purchase for it." He turned to the others and said, "Montaigne, Gerard and I will visit this place. We will leave tomorrow morning after breakfast and move to this warehouse until Brother Etienne has recovered."

Porthos spoke up then. "As it is midday, we are hungry. And I'm sure that Brother Etienne is hungry as well, as he has not eaten for more than a day. I will go down and see to meals for the rest of us."

"Excellent idea," D'Artagnan told him. "We will find some lunch while we are out."

At that, they went on their way.

Chapter Eighteen

D'Artagnan, Montaigne, and Athos walked through the town, pretending to be aimless visitors to the city out to explore, looking at shops and businesses along the way. Montaigne took them a circuitous route which ended on the street behind their destination. They went around the building which fronted that street and past the warehouse behind it, arriving at the place where they might spend several days, or until the cardinal was able to travel again.

The warehouse, which was a small square wooden structure, wasn't locked, although it could be barred from the inside. It had two doors, one at the front and the other in the back, which opened outwards to let carts fit through them.

"It's empty," Athos declared. "And quite dirty. How can we stay in a filthy place with no furnishings?"

"We can clean it and find what furnishings we need in the marketplace," D'Artagnan replied. "We should be able to furnish it with everything we need with the money from the sale of the horses." He looked around, calculating what would need to be purchased. "Pallets for all of us, but a bed and bedding for Brother Etienne. Chairs for us and two or three tables, depending on their size. That's all we really need, I think. Shall we go shopping?"

The three of them left the way they had come, looking for shops that sold second-hand merchandise. They found what they were looking for a couple of blocks away, a spacious building filled with furniture and other items for resale.

"How may I help you, Monsieurs? Are you seeking something in particular?" the shopkeeper asked. "I am Monsieur Allard."

"Seven featherbeds and one bedframe, please, Monsieur," D'Artagnan told the shopkeeper. "And six wooden chairs and two or three tables, if you have them."

"Look around in here," the shopkeeper said, "while I check in the back."

They spread out to cover the space quickly.

D'Artagnan found a medium-sized table with four chairs right away. Athos called out that he had found another table which was a little smaller than the other and was looking for chairs. Then the shopkeeper came back in.

"I have five featherbeds in the back. I don't think I have any more. I do have a bedframe, though."

"Will one of the featherbeds fit it?" asked D'Artagnan.

"Yes, one should. Have you found the other things you're looking for?"

"We have two tables and four chairs, but need two more chairs."

"I found one," called Montaigne, carrying it to join the others. Athos had brought his table to the front and was returning with the last of the chairs he had found.

"We'll take the beds, tables, and chairs. What are you asking for them?" D'Artagnan said.

The shopkeeper named his price, which Montaigne thought was too high.

"I see," Montaigne said. "How much for just the beds and the frame? We can get the tables and chairs elsewhere, since you don't have enough beds and we'll have to go somewhere else anyway. Or we could get everything somewhere else."

The shopkeeper, not wanting to lose a sale, reduced the price.

Montaigne, D'Artagnan, and Athos put their heads together to confer. Seeing this, the shopkeeper reduced the price a bit more.

The three customers conferred a moment more. "That will be acceptable," said D'Artagnan. "Gerard, would you stay here while we go back for the cart?"

"I can deliver it to you," said the shopkeeper. "It will be only a small extra charge."

"No need. We can transport it ourselves." Then D'Artagnan gave him half the total.

"I will pay you the rest when we return to collect our purchases."

D'Artagnan and Montaigne left while Athos stayed and continued to look around.

"You must have a large family," the shopkeeper said to make conversation.

"No larger than most," Athos replied.

"Just moving to town?"

Athos moved away toward the other side of the shop. He saw a stack of blankets piled on a table. "How much for these blankets?" he called to the shopkeeper.

Eager to sell more, the shopkeeper called out a small sum. Athos returned to the front, carrying the blankets. "Are they clean?" he asked.

The shopkeeper hesitated, then said, "Clean enough. There is a laundress down the street where you can get them washed, if you want."

Athos pulled the coins from an inside pocket of his vest and paid for them. Then he sat on one of the chairs to wait for the cart.

D'Artagnan and Montaigne returned to the inn and went back to the stable for the cart and horse. When the stable master asked if they were leaving, he was told, "We agreed to help someone move some items. We'll bring it back in a while."

They set off for the shop and loaded what would fit into the cart. The bedframe broke down into several pieces, so it went in the cart first. Then they placed the featherbeds on top. That filled the cart.

"We'll be back for the rest," D'Artagnan said to Athos. "Will you stay here until then?"

"Of course. The shopkeeper and I are having a wonderful conversation."

On the way to the warehouse Montaigne saw a shop where they could buy a broom to sweep the floor.

"Let's buy two," D'Artagnan said. They did, and soon arrived at the street behind the warehouse. There was just enough room to drive the cart between the buildings.

First they swept a large area near the door and placed the bedframe and featherbeds in that area. Then they returned to the shop for the tables, chairs and blankets.

Then the three men went back to the warehouse and began sweeping. They swept the rest of the floor, put the bedframe back together, and stacked the featherbeds and bedding on top of it.

"Now we need to find two more featherbeds, a chair and, whatever else we think of that we'll need," said D'Artagnan.

They took another direction going back. When they stopped for some lunch, Montaigne asked the serving girl, "Do you know of any second-hand furniture shops near here?"

"Yes, sir," she said. "Two streets south and a block west there is a shop that has a lot of household goods, as-well-as furniture. You might try there."

"My thanks. We will go there right away."

"After you eat."

"Yes, after we eat."

Their meals were brought to them right away.

"This is quite good," Athos commented. "It would be nice to be able to linger a while, but I know we have much to do." They finished quickly and left to find the shop suggested to them.

The shop they were directed to did have everything they needed. They found the two beds and a chair, which they loaded and took back to the warehouse. They also bought a supply of candles and holders, two of them lanterns, so they would have light after the sun set. Also during the day, since the warehouse had no windows and was very dim.

After everything was set out and ready for the rest to get there, D'Artagnan, Montaigne, and Athos went back to the inn to check on the others.

Brother Etienne was about the same. Porthos and Aramis had been filling him in on things that had happened to them along the way.

"Really?" he said. "I suppose I shouldn't be surprised. I'm sure many are after me, now that Louis is dead. I was his most trusted advisor, after all. Or so you tell me. I just wish I could get my memory back." His voice seemed to be getting stronger.

"I'm sure that will happen soon," said Aramis. "We'll continue to pray that it will."

"Indeed," said D'Artagnan as he and the others entered the room. "We have a place to stay, such as it is. And we have furnished it, sparingly, but adequately."

"Where is it?" asked Brother Etienne, "the house of a friend of one of you?"

"It's a place where you will be safe," D'Artagnan told him. "We'll take you there tomorrow. It's not what you're used to in your residence, but it will have to do until we can resume our journey."

"It's just about time for dinner," said Porthos. "Why don't we order our meals? I will stay up here with the monks, if the rest of you want to eat downstairs."

"I will stay, as well," Brother Xavier said. "I don't like to leave the cardinal."

"I know. I was including you," Porthos told him.

"Very well. Georges, why don't you come down with us and you can bring the plates back up with you," D'Artagnan suggested.

After they had placed the orders, they sat at a table in an isolated area of the common room. No one was sitting close by, so they felt it safe to discuss matters.

"What will we do if the, er, Brother Etienne isn't able to travel for weeks?" Athos asked. "Will our funds last?"

"If we use them sparingly," D'Artagnan said. "Fortunately, we are not that far from our destination, so when we leave, the remaining journey will be short."

Just then a man came wandering toward them. They had stopped talking about anything they didn't want anyone to overhear, but they stopped their conversation until the man had passed their table, watching him as he made his way across the room.

"But we will all be together in the warehouse with nothing to do," Athos continued.

"Don't worry," Montaigne said with an evil grin. "There will be enough to keep us busy. I have brought some cards."

The meals arrived just as Montaigne finished speaking, and they turned their attention to the food, Porthos and Montaigne taking plates upstairs for Brother Xavier and Brother Etienne.

The patient was asleep and Brother Xavier and Porthos were talking softly when the others returned.

"How are we going to transport our patient without causing him great pain?" Brother Xavier asked.

"It would be best if he were asleep. Perhaps a sleeping draught?" suggested Athos. "We should ask if there is an apothecary nearby."

"A good idea," D'Artagnan said. "I'll go back down and ask the innkeeper."

D'Artagnan returned quickly, saying, "There is an apothecary not far from here. I'll go over now to see if I can buy a sleeping draught. Gerard, would you like to come with me?"

"Of course," Athos replied, and they left.

"Is the sleeping draught for me?" asked Brother Etienne. "I really haven't had trouble sleeping."

"It's for tomorrow, when we leave. We don't want you to be in pain when we carry you to the cart and then into the place where we'll be staying. The draught is for that," Aramis told him.

"Oh, of course. How kind of you. But if I take it tonight, will it keep me sleeping through the morning when we leave?"

"Well, we could wake you up in the middle of the night to give it to you," Aramis replied. "That should keep you asleep until you wake up in your new bed."

Before too long, D'Artagnan and Athos returned with a small bottle of liquid.

"The apothecary said it should work for eight to ten hours. We'll give it to you a little after midnight. That should be long enough to keep you sleeping until we get there," D'Artagnan told Brother Etienne. "Perhaps we should all retire for the night, or until our turn to stand guard."

"Agreed," Athos said. "I'll stand first, since I'm wide awake right now. Who will stand second?"

"I will," said Montaigne. "And I'll wake Brother Etienne to take the draught. That should be soon after midnight."

"I'll take third," said D'Artagnan, "and wake the rest of you in the morning. We should get an early start. I'll watch for the sun to rise, since I'll be able to see it through the window."

The rest went to their beds, Brother Xavier and D'Artagnan with the patient and the others in the other room. Athos took a chair and put it inside the room by the door, opening the door a fraction so he could hear and see anyone who might be walking down the hallway.

It remained quiet through the time Athos was on watch. When the church bell tolled midnight, he quietly woke Montaigne and went to his bed.

Montaigne woke the monk, who drank the draught and went directly back to sleep. The night remained quiet, and at four o'clock Montaigne woke D'Artagnan.

"When the sun is up, I'll wake the rest of you so we can harness the cart horse and claim our horses. Then we can carry Brother Etienne down and leave."

"That will be fine. If you like, you can harness the horse and bring the cart around to the front, along with our horses," D'Artagnan told him. "I'll make sure all our belongings are packed and brought down. Get some sleep."

In the morning, D'Artagnan left the monks sleeping and went across the hall to wake the others.

"Time to make our escape," he told them. "Georges, you, Gerard, and Emile make sure everything is packed and ready to go. Montaigne will harness and saddle the horses and bring them around front. We should leave as soon as we can."

They went to their duties, accomplishing them quickly, and met back in the monk's room. Brother Xavier was awake by then and had packed his and Brother Etienne's things. He, of course, still slept.

"How are we going to do this?" Porthos asked.

"Since your horses are still stabled elsewhere, we will put your packs in the cart. Then we will place Brother Etienne there and Brother Xavier will drive," D'Artagnan explained. "Then you three can walk to the other stable while the rest of us follow you. Tell the stable master that you will bring all our horses back later, since we have no place to stable them where we're going. Unless, of course, you'd prefer to follow us on foot."

After some discussion, the rest of them decided to ride there this time and return the horses to the stable after fixing the location in their memories.

"Georges, will you carry Brother Etienne down again?" D'Artagnan requested.

When they went down, the cart and horses were waiting for them. It took just a short time for belongings to be stored in the cart and the monk laid there. D'Artagnan and Montaigne stored their things in the saddle bags, which left more room in the cart.

D'Artagnan went back in to inform the innkeeper that they were leaving.

"Is your friend able to continue your journey already?" he asked.

"He is better, but we're just moving to the home of a friend who offered to let us stay awhile."

"You have paid for another day."

"Yes. May we use that to pay for our breakfasts? If so, could you wrap the food so we may take it with us?"

"That is unusual, but I think I can do it. Where is it you are going? I may know your friend."

"Conard," D'Artagnan mumbled. "He is a friend of another in our party. Very generous, as well."

The innkeeper left for the kitchen with a musing look on his face. When he arrived, he asked his wife, "Do we know anyone by the name of Conard?"

She thought for a moment and answered. "Isn't he an acquaintance of your cousin Anatole? The name does seem familiar."

"Bah. Anatole is a reprobate. Our guests seem much more refined. He must be someone else."

The innkeeper soon delivered the food wrapped in a piece of heavy cloth.

"We thank you for your hospitality. Farewell," D'Artagnan said as he was leaving.

Athos, Porthos, and Aramis had already left for the general stable to collect their horses when D'Artagnan left the inn.

"Shall we go? We'll go a different way to our destination and meet the others there, since Gerard knows the way," D'Artagnan said to Montaigne and Brother Xavier. Brother Etienne was still asleep and seemed to be resting comfortably in the back of the cart. The cart slowly traveled the streets in a roundabout route to the warehouse, while the other riders went in a different direction.

Before long they all met on the street behind the warehouse and went together between the buildings.

"Here we are," D'Artagnan announced, spreading his arms wide to encompass the building.

"It doesn't look like much," said Aramis. "But we must take what we can get. Let's look inside."

"We'll leave the cart here, but there's no way we can keep the horses with us," D'Artagnan replied. "We can pull the cart inside through the double door. It should be wide enough for the cart to fit, and then we can bar it."

"I told the stable master that we would be back before the end of the day and would have seven horses to board," Athos told D'Artagnan when they had all arrived at the warehouse.

D'Artagnan and Montaigne opened the doors so they could enter and pull the cart inside. Porthos carried the cardinal to his bed and pulled a blanket over him.

"Thank the Lord he is still asleep," said Brother Xavier, "and has felt no pain on the way."

"Indeed," said Montaigne. "Georges, would you help me unhitch the horse from the cart and take it outside? Then we can eat our breakfast before we return the horses to the stable."

"Since we have seven horses," D'Artagnan said while they were eating, "only three need take them. Montaigne, would you, Georges and Emile take them? One of you can lead two of them. The rest of us can get settled here while you're gone."

"Gladly," replied Montaigne. Porthos and Aramis nodded their agreement. "But since we will keep the door barred at all times, we need a way to be let back inside."

D'Artagnan thought a moment, then said, "A special knock will let those inside know that those who are outside belong to our party. How about three knocks, a pause, and then two knocks? If no one comes to let you in, repeat the knocks."

"That should suffice," Montaigne answered, then repeated, "three knocks, a pause, then two knocks."

Chapter Nineteen

y the time the breakfast fare was laid out, the cardinal was awake. He had slept longer than anticipated, and Brother Xavier had been concerned.

"What if he drank too much of the draught?" he had asked D'Artagnan. "What if he won't wake up?" The monk was beside himself with worry. "Are you certain you got the right thing?"

"Yes, I'm certain," D'Artagnan assured him. "Don't worry."

"We are here," the cardinal said, looking around. "Not as nice a place as the room at the inn, but I suppose it will be sufficient until I'm well enough to continue on our journey."

At that, Brother Xavier breathed a large sigh of relief and all but embraced the cardinal.

"We will do our best to keep you comfortable," Brother Xavier assured him. "We must keep hidden to prevent capture by King Gaston's men."

"Of course. As a humble man of God, I should not complain about our lodgings, since I can't remember any previous ones." He took the food that was handed to him and began to eat. "I must keep that in mind."

After the meal, Montaigne and the others left to stable the horses, which had been tied to a pole outside the warehouse. The rest of them began to look around their new accommodations.

"It's not very big, is it?" the cardinal observed. "We will all be in close quarters."

"No," D'Artagnan said. "But that is not a bad thing. It will be more defensible if needed."

"So how should we arrange the tables and chairs?" Athos asked. "I think the smaller table should be next to Brother Etienne's bed, with a chair for Brother Xavier to sit on."

"That sound good. We can put the other one near the center of the room. It should be large enough to put the other five chairs around it," D'Artagnan replied.

Athos walked around the inside of the building. "It's <u>not</u> very big, but I suppose it's big enough. We don't really need much room."

"And it is much better than camping," added Brother Xavier. He went to the pole in the middle of the warehouse and said, "Will we leave the cart outside?"

"I think we must bring it inside to not call any attention to someone being here," said D'Artagnan.

"But aren't the shafts of the cart too long?" asked the monk.

"I think that if we tilt the cart to the back it won't take up much room. The roof is certainly high enough," Athos pointed out.

∞ ∞ ∞

At the stable, Montaigne found the stable master. "As you can see, I brought our horses back with three additional ones. There may be a time when one of us will need his horse for a short time. In that case, if it is not myself that comes, my name will be used. We don't know when we will be leaving again; one of our party is injured and not able to travel."

"I understand," the stable master said. "Anyone who needs one of the horses is to use your name instead of his own."

Montaigne gave him more money to cover a few more days, and they returned to the warehouse.

"Have you chosen your sleeping pallets, or did you wait for us?"

"We waited," Athos told him. "Now come pick your space while we choose ours. We don't all have to sleep close by each other, but I think someone should sleep near each door. They will be bolted, but they should be guarded even though the guard is asleep."

"That's a good idea," D'Artagnan said. "Since we're sleeping on pallets instead of bedsteads, we can move them around. I will take the first night, then one of you can take the second. The five of us can guard once every five days."

"Don't you think my bed should be placed farther from the door?" Brother Etienne asked.

"Actually, there is another door opposite this one, although it is hard to see. If we move the cart to block that door, we can move the bed farther in that direction," said Aramis.

"But doesn't the door open out?" Athos asked. "What good would the cart do against that door?"

D'Artagnan went to look at the door. "It does bolt on the inside. The cart would be another layer of protection. If an intruder broke through the door, he would still have to get past the cart and the man sleeping by it."

That made sense to Athos and the others, so the cart was pulled next to that door and pushed tightly against it.

"Then might my bed be moved to the corner?" the cardinal repeated.

"But you are awake now, and will feel the pain of your knee if you have to get out of the bed," protested Brother Xavier.

"That's easy," said Porthos. "Some of us can carry the bed with him in it. Which of us are the strongest?"

"First let's move the cart; then we can decide who is strongest," said D'Artagnan.

Porthos and Montaigne moved the cart against the opposite door even though the door was barred on the inside. Then they went to the bed. With one at the head and one at the foot, they tried to lift it. It came barely off the floor and wobbled when they moved it.

"Gerard and Emile, come help us. Four should be enough to move it smoothly," Montaigne said.

With their help, the bed was moved to the back and set with its head in the corner so each side would be accessible. Then they moved the pallets to different places so they were spaced out around the room, with D'Artagnan putting his in front of the other door.

"I think it's time to go in search of some lunch," Porthos said. "Two of us can go out and bring the food back here. Or maybe three of us. It may be hard to carry that much."

"Why don't we buy a basket while we're out, and maybe some plates and cups," Athos suggested.

"We have the plates and cups in our packs," reminded D'Artagnan.

"Of course. We haven't used them since we stayed with Pastor Alexandre, so I rather forgot."

"A basket is a good idea, though," said D'Artagnan. "Why don't the two of you go? Gerard has some knowledge of the area and should be able to find the way back here. Then, for dinner, Emile can go out with Montaigne so he can also learn his way around."

"We shall return," Porthos said as he left with Athos following.

They went up and down several streets, looking for a place to get food to take with them. Most places didn't provide the means to carry food out to be eaten elsewhere. They bought a decent-sized basket and a cloth with which to cover the food they would put in it.

It looks as if we are going on a picnic," Athos commented.

"A picnic sounds like fun, except when you have no other place to eat," Porthos told him. "I do not like to camp out in the elements and eat cold food that's been transported in a cart."

By the time of their return, the room had been further tidied and arranged. The pallets of the five of them, D'Artagnan, Montaigne, Athos, Porthos, and Aramis, had been spaced out evenly around the room to each side of the bed. Brother Xavier's pallet was near the bed, and the tables and chairs were toward the center.

Porthos set the new basket on the table, where the plates and cups from their packs had been placed, and took out bread and cheese. Then came two bottles of wine and a piece of cooked meat wrapped in cloth.

"We should be able to save some of the bread and cheese for tonight, but the meat might not keep as long," Athos told them. "Later, someone else can go out for additional food."

Brother Xavier fixed two plates for Brother Etienne and himself and took them to the corner with the bed, where he had already set a chair.

Aramis took two cups of wine to them. "I'll be back in a little while to refill your cups. Enjoy your lunch."

Brother Xavier was able to urge the cardinal to eat and drink a little, but before he had finished his plate, he went back to sleep.

"I'll save the rest of his food for his supper," Xavier told the others. "I don't want to waste any of it."

The rest of the group had gathered around the two tables and filled their plates.

"Did you see or hear anything of the king's men while you were out?" D'Artagnan asked Athos and Porthos.

"No. But perhaps one or two of us should eat elsewhere this evening," Porthos said. "Maybe there will be talk that could be overheard."

"I'll suggest that to Montaigne and Emile. Where did you get this food?"

"There is a small place a few blocks away. It's not an inn, just a place to eat. The family seems nice; they didn't ask any questions. It's on the first floor of a house," Porthos answered.

"Is it very big? I think a large place might have more customers who might talk."

"It's big enough. Of course, the place wasn't full when we were there, but I think it might be for the evening meal."

"All right. Tell Montaigne where it is."

Porthos went to talk to Montaigne and D'Artagnan went to talk to Athos, who was reclining on his pallet.

"Georges told me where you went for the food and that there weren't many customers at the time. Do you think there might be more for the evening meal?"

"Yes, I think so. It was a nice, clean place, but rather small, at least compared to an inn. The food seemed good. There probably will be more tonight."

"Good. I'll suggest to Montaigne that he and Emile eat there and then bring food back for us. They can listen for gossip and information that we should know."

Later, after eating their dinner, Montaigne and Athos returned bearing additional food, enough to last through breakfast the next day.

"Our dinner was very informative," Athos reported. "We now know much more about this neighborhood and a bit about the surrounding area."

"I spotted our benefactor there," Montaigne added. "When he saw me, it looked as though he would come to our table, but I warned him off with a scowl. I don't think we should be seen talking together."

"Montaigne is famous for his scowl," D'Artagnan said, chuckling.

"It would stop a charging bull," put in Porthos. "I have seen it happen."

"Anyway, we learned much of little importance. But things of little importance now can turn into a possible catastrophe or a Godsend. We shouldn't ignore information just because we think it's of no use," Montaigne said.

"Indeed," D'Artagnan said. "Did you hear anything we should know?"

"Well, we heard nothing of Gaston's men looking for anyone. However, not hearing something bears little weight," Montaigne said. "A different pair should dine there or somewhere else tomorrow night, and a third pair the night after."

"Excellent idea!" said D'Artagnan. "In fact, two pairs can eat at two different places, leaving someone here with the monks each evening. If we spend frugally, we might have enough to continue this journey to its end."

"Fine. But now I'm going to bed," Porthos said. "If the rest of you want to stay up talking, please go to the other side of the room."

"I'm ready to sleep, myself," added Montaigne. "I'll take the pallet near Georges."

The rest agreed that sleeping would be a good idea, with D'Artagnan reminding them that he would stay up to guard them.

"Even if I drop off to sleep, the noise or movement of someone trying to break in will wake me. Then I'll wake the rest of you. Be sure to keep your swords by you as you sleep."

They all bade good night to each other and retired.

∞ ∞ ∞

Several days went by without anyone seeming to notice that they were there. Each evening four of them went out in pairs to eat at two different places, listening for information about Gaston's men coming to town. Each night they learned things about the other customers and the town, but little else.

In the afternoon of the fifth day, they all gathered around Brother Etienne to see if he was able to be moved.

Brother Xavier helped him to sit up on the edge of the bed so he could check the man's knee.

"It isn't as swollen as it was when we got here," Brother Xavier said. "How does it feel, Eminence?"

He moved his foot side to side, then front to back. "It still aches a little, but it is much better. I think I can travel without much pain now."

"But you still can't remember anything from before your fall?" D'Artagnan asked.

"No, but I'm getting used to that. Brother Xavier and I have been talking, and he's told me some of the things I should know about my past." He moved back around and lay back in his bed. "I will try to stand tomorrow to see if I'm able to walk. If I can walk, we can continue our journey."

"But what about the injury to your side?" D'Artagnan asked. "The doctor didn't examine it because we didn't want anyone else to know about it. Have you checked it, Brother Xavier?"

"I have been checking it every day, and sometimes twice in one day. It seems to be healing, but I am still worried about it."

D'Artagnan thought about it for a moment, then consulted Montaigne. "Do you think you could find a healer that deals in herbs and things? Perhaps something like that would be more useful than what a physician could do."

"I'll ask around tomorrow."

The next day, Montaigne returned in the afternoon with an ointment that he smeared on the cardinal's wound.

"What is that?" Brother Xavier asked him. "And where did you get it? I hope it was from a reputable healer. I have heard of people being poisoned by herbs used improperly."

"I assure you," Montaigne replied, "that I was very careful to determine the safety and efficacy of this salve."

"Yes, yes, I'm sure you were," the young monk assured him. "I just worry about his health at all times." Then he went back to watching the cardinal sleep.

That evening, D'Artagnan and Montaigne, and Athos and Aramis went out to eat.

"If we leave tomorrow, we should bring enough food with us to get us to the next town," D'Artagnan said to Montaigne.

"What would that town be called," asked Montaigne. "Will it be large enough to have an inn?"

"I'll have to look at my map, and I don't know. This wasn't the route we were supposed to take, and my map may not have anything marked the way we will be going."

"I can ask around later for the best route going . . Where are we headed?"

D'Artagnan thought a moment. He had been sworn to secrecy by Cardinal Tremblay, but circumstances had changed since that time.

In a very low voice, D'Artagnan said, "I have decided to trust you with the direction we need to go, despite my promise to tell no one before we leave. We'll be going north to a location on the coast. We should aim for northeast. I think."

"I will find out which way to go and what towns are on the way. Also, how far apart they are. I know we can't travel very fast with our injured passenger." Montaigne took his leave, and D'Artagnan finished his dinner and also left.

Athos and Aramis had returned by the time D'Artagnan got back.

They pulled D'Artagnan to the side when he entered.

"We heard something while we were eating," Athos said. "It seemed to be just gossip, but it is information we should pay attention to."

Aramis took up the story. "A man at the next table mentioned Gaston by name. He said he had heard that his men had been seen in Laval and thought they would be coming here next."

D'Artagnan thought for a moment. "So our choices are to leave quickly or to stay well-hidden until they leave. And we don't know how long they will stay here or which way they will go when they leave."

"Perhaps, then, we should stay where we are until then," said Aramis.

"But that could take another week or more," Athos said.

"That would be better than getting caught and taken back to Paris, or killed where we are," said Porthos, who had joined the conversation. "Where is Montaigne?"

"He has gone seeking information for us," D'Artagnan told him.

"Ah. His specialty. Shouldn't we include them," Porthos pointed to the monks, "in the discussion?"

D'Artagnan looked thoughtful. "I suppose we should, but let's wait until Montaigne returns. Did you bring food back with you? There wasn't enough left for their dinner and our breakfasts."

"Yes, we brought more bread and cheese, two onions, and more wine," Athos said.

"I brought a joint of mutton, which should be eaten tonight." D'Artagnan opened the cloth it was wrapped in.

The four men took their bounty to Brother Xavier and Brother Etienne. Since Porthos had been the one to stay in, he joined the feast. They finished the mutton and part of the bread and cheese.

Before too much longer, Montaigne returned. "I have news," he told the rest. "Gaston's men have been seen coming this way. I believe it is too late for us to get away safely before they get here since we will be traveling slowly."

"We were considering our choices before you returned," D'Artagnan said. "We think that the others should be included in the decision."

"By all means," said Montaigne, and started toward the bed, motioning the other to follow. "Brother Etienne, Brother Xavier, we need to discuss the current situation."

"Of course, my son. Please share with us what you know." Brother Etienne seemed a bit stronger and more aware, perhaps ready to continue traveling.

"I have found out that Gaston's men are headed this way, and getting closer all the time. Since we don't know when they will get here, which direction they will go from here, or how long they will stay in Rennes, the question is: do we stay or do we go?"

D'Artagnan replied, "I think we should stay and wait until we know in which direction they will go when they leave. Remember, we will be traveling much slower than they will. If they decided to go the same route we plan to, we would be discovered quickly."

"That will mean delaying our trip for an unknown length of time," added Athos.

"I am feeling much better," Brother Etienne said, sitting up in his bed and turning to get up. "See, I can stand without much pain now."

"How long would you be able to stand?" asked D'Artagnan? "And I'm sure the road will be rough. Could you stand being bounced in the cart? It could be more than a week until we get to our destination."

"I feel well enough, I think, to ride a horse." Brother Etienne was cheerful and sure he was almost completely recovered from the accident. Then his attitude changed. "Or maybe not. I think I should sleep now." He was helped back into bed and was asleep before the bedclothes had been replaced over him.

Chapter Twenty

everal days after his previous guests had moved on, Monsieur Boucher, the innkeeper, looked up as several men entered the inn.

"May I help you gentlemen? Would you like rooms or meals?"

One of the men stepped to the counter and said, "Both, I think. Your establishment looks clean and well taken care of. What rooms do you have available?"

"Just recently a group which had two rooms left to stay with a friend. Their rooms are still available. Are there just the three of you?"

"There are two more of us. How many beds do the rooms have?" asked the man who seemed to be the leader of the group.

"One has two beds, and the other has four. They are next door to each other," the innkeeper told him.

"Let me talk with the others and I'll let you know. First, could we have a meal?" The man motioned to another to get the remaining men in their party.

"Of course. Would you rather have wine or ale with that?"

"Ale, I think. We'll take that table over there." He pointed to the large one in the far corner.

"Yes, sir."

"By the way," the man said, pulling a sheet of paper from his pocket. "Do you recognize this man? I know it's just a sketch, but it is a very good likeness."

The innkeeper looked closely at the drawing.

"It looks a bit like the injured man in the group that left. I got only one good look at him, and he was asleep at that time, but it could be him."

"What was his name?" the other man asked.

"Oh, I never heard his name. They took him up to the room and he didn't come back down until they left. When they came in he was unconscious. I believe he'd fallen and hit his head. And when they left he was asleep because the fall had injured his knee."

"Do you know the names of his companions?"

"I think they called each other by the names Gerard, Georges and Allais. Oh, and Montaigne. I never heard the names of the others. Who do think the man might be?" The innkeeper looked at the man expectantly.

"It is not important. Do you know where they were going?"

"Hm," the innkeeper replied. "I think the name is Conard. I don't know the family, though there is a chance my cousin does. His name is Anatole Boucher. He lives on the other side of town. We are not close; in fact, I don't associate with him, so I can't direct you exactly to his house. I'm sure if you ask around, someone will take you there."

By that time the rest of the party had arrived and were seated at the table.

"I'll get your drinks. Your meals should not take long." The innkeeper bowed to the men and left for the kitchen.

∞ ∞ ∞

"But if we leave now, we may be caught up by Gaston's men," said Athos the next morning.

"Have they arrived already?" Brother Etienne wondered.

"I have not heard so, but they may have." Montaigne turned to leave. "I'll go out and see what I can find out."

"I'll go with you," Aramis told him. "Four eyes and ears are better than two."

"We won't be long, and if we find out anything important, at least one of us will return."

"And you'll bring something more for breakfast with you?" Porthos said.

"Yes, pig, we'll bring more breakfast," Aramis told his cousin.

Montaigne led the way out of the warehouse, and Porthos barred the door behind them.

"Perhaps we should go two different ways," said Montaigne.

"That way we might get information faster," agreed Aramis. "Although, would the men Gaston has sent recognize you?"

"I don't think so. I keep my head down and try not to be seen when I'm working. Do you have an idea who Gaston might have sent?"

"No, but surely they will be his men who have been in exile with him."

"He did have his own sympathizers in France when he was exiled. Maybe he has sent some of them."

"Then we should both be very careful," Aramis suggested.

They had reached the next street by then and parted ways.

"We should meet again at noon," Montaigne told Aramis, indicating the warehouse.

∞ ∞ ∞

Five men walked through the city of Renne, France, looking for two people.

"If we can't find this Conard person, we will have to locate the innkeeper's cousin, Anatole Boucher," one of the men said.

"Where did the innkeeper say to look?" asked another.

"Just across town. He claims that he and his cousin are not close, but, even so, I would think he would know where the man lived."

A third man pointed to a nearby shop, saying, "Why don't we ask in there? The shopkeeper might know one of them."

The first man said, "I'll go in; you wait out here."

Inside, the man approached the shopkeeper and asked, "Do you know where Anatole Boucher lives?"

"Bah, that reprobate? I wouldn't allow him or his cohorts in here if I saw them coming. Ask somewhere in the northern part of town."

"If not him, how about a man named Conard?"

"Sorry, I've never heard of anyone by that name, but if he is a friend of Boucher's, I wouldn't. I don't do business with men who deal with merchandise which doesn't belong to them." The shopkeeper said. "However, I do know of a man who Boucher knows. His name is LeBeq, and his business is somewhere in the northern part of the city." Then he turned away to tend to a customer, dismissing the other man, who went back outside to report to the others.

"The shopkeeper didn't know of anyone named Conard, but he mentioned one named LeBeq who the innkeeper's cousin knows. Apparently they both are unsavory characters," said the group's leader when he returned. "Just the men we need to talk to."

∞ ∞ ∞

Monsieur LeBeq looked up as the door to his shop opened.

"Ah, Anatole. What are you doing here?"

"I need to talk to you, François. There are men looking for you, King Gaston's men."

"Looking for me? Why? What would they want with me? What did you tell them?"

"Nothing, but someone told them that you might know something about some men they are looking for. That person also told them that I could lead them to you."

"Did you?" LeBeq cried. "Are they outside right now?"

"No. I put them off by sending them back to my cousin, Jacques. He's the one who sent them to me. Do you know who they are asking about?"

Monsieur LeBeq thought quickly. "I don't know what they're talking about, or who they're looking for. Please do not tell them how to find me."

"They may find you by asking someone else," Anatole pointed out. "You can't blame me for that."

"No, of course not. But do try to keep them away from here if you can. Please!" LeBeq tried to keep from appearing nervous. "Don't come back here while they are in town. I don't need to be questioned by anyone with ties to Gaston. I have no love for our new king."

Anatole left after assuring his friend that he would do as asked.

Minutes later another of LeBeq's acquaintances entered the shop.

"Good morning, François," he said.

"Father Jean," LeBeq exclaimed to the small man who was the priest of his church. "How may I help you today?"

"François, I have a problem."

"What can I do to help, Father?"

"Our church is being threatened by those who say they will destroy it if they are not paid a tithe of their own. Do you know of someone who I could hire to protect us?"

Monsieur LeBeq thought for a moment. *This could be the way out of the danger Anatole told me of, but I must hurry.*

"Father, I do. But I must talk to them first. And if they agree to it, they will have to hide in the church until their task is completed."

"They? How many are there? There are accommodations for only a few."

"Just let me take care of it. I will let you know when I have talked to them. Don't worry, Father. It will be all right."

Monsieur LeBeq had been keeping an eye on the goings and comings of the people staying in the warehouse, but it had been difficult since they had been using the door on the opposite side from his shop. After his conversations with his friend, Anatole, and his priest, Father Jean, he thought he knew how to solve his dilemma. Since no one was using the door closer to his shop, he felt confident enough to listen at the door for anything he could hear, any information he could get about who was inside. He knew his–friend–Montaigne was with a group of travelers who needed to hide from someone. He just didn't know who they were. However, knowing that King Gaston's men were searching the city for someone, he had a better idea of who they were hiding from.

Through the narrow gap between the double doors he could see the underside and wheels of what must be their cart, but by kneeling on the ground and looking to the side he could see the legs of the men staying in his warehouse.

Ah, there's Montaigne, he thought. And who else is with him? Four young men. They seem strong. But why would they need the cart if no one was ill or injured? Or in custody? That might be it; they are taking a wanted man somewhere. But who would the man be wanted by, if they are hiding from King Gaston's men? He tried to see more in the room, but the corners at that side of the building were out of sight. Then he heard a voice.

"Eminence, how are you feeling tonight?" an apparently young man asked.

A reply followed. "I am feeling much better. I'm sure I can walk a short distance, but certainly not very quickly. And about riding a horse, I'm thinking better of it. I'm sure I couldn't ride for long, either."

A different voice spoke. "That's good, Eminence. It will be better to wait here until Gaston's men have left the city."

So, LeBeq continued to himself. A cardinal is injured and running from the king. I think I know a way.

∞ ∞ ∞

The next morning when Montaigne left the warehouse to search for information, LeBeq was waiting for him.

"Monsieur Montaigne, may I have a word?"

"Ah, LeBeq. Spying on me?" Montaigne was not happy to see the man.

"No, no. Not spying, but I do know you are traveling with some men and trying to avoid someone. Would that be men sent by King Gaston to find people not loyal to him?" He paused, then continued. "I, myself, am not a lover of the man. Some of my family have been treated badly by him. But I will not do anything to advertise that fact. I do understand your predicament. King Gaston's men are here, looking for you. You have someone with you who must not fall into his hands." He looked directly at Montaigne. "The priest of my church is in need of protection, too, but from those who are demanding money, and will destroy the church, they say, if they don't receive enough." He shook his head. "I have been informed that these men of Gaston's have been given my name as someone who might know the whereabouts of men trying to avoid them. Namely, I think, you and your friends."

"Are you trying to blackmail me, LeBeq? You should know better that to try something like that," Montaigne calmly stated.

"No. I am trying to tell you that there is a better place for you to hide until the king's men leave to torment another town. I can lead you all to the church safely, where you can hide until you can leave. But you must promise to defend the church while you stay there."

Montaigne thought a moment. "Take me to the church and I will talk to the priest. We may be able to work something out."

∞ ∞ ∞

"Allais, I must speak with you for a moment," Montaigne said as he was let into the warehouse. He motioned D'Artagnan to follow him to a corner away from the others.

"We need to move, and move quickly. Gaston's men have been given LeBeq's name, and even if he denies knowing me, they won't give up. I talked to him earlier, and he suggested a safer place to hide. Our skills in fighting may be called upon, though."

"Where is this place, and why might we have to fight," D'Artagnan inquired.

"His priest talked to him yesterday, asking for help in defending his church. LeBeq swears that neither he nor the priest has any love for Gaston, and we could be hidden in the cellars of the church long enough for those men to leave town. Then we could plan our route to avoid them if they go in the same direction we will be going."

"Have you been there and talked to the priest?"

"I have just returned from there. The priest, Father Jean, is sincere in his fear of attack. And I was shown the cellars." He shrugged. "They're cellars. What would you expect? But they would do for the time being. Father Jean promises to hide us, feed us, and take care of our ill companion."

D'Artagnan began to protest, but Montaigne assured him that the priest had never been farther east than Rennes and had no idea what the cardinal looked like.

"Even if he had a suspicion of the true identity of Brother Etienne, he would not betray us. I am sure of that. It's not far from here; we can walk to it. We can take Brother Etienne over in the cart, which we can hide in the church stable along with the horse. Also, we should leave after dark. He said it would be safer then."

"Do you think we should leave tonight? We don't have much and could be ready to go quickly. But what about the bed? We would have to leave it here."

"We could break it down the same as when we brought it here. We will need to bring everything and leave the place completely empty. We should probably sprinkle dirt around so it will look as dirty as before. But we must talk to the others first."

They placed the tables and chairs close to Brother Etienne's bed and gathered everyone around.

"We will be leaving tonight, but not the city. We will be relocating to a safer place until Gaston's men have left. This warehouse is no longer safe. Montaigne has been told of a small church nearby that is being threatened if money is not given to those who are threatening it. We will move to it and stay in the cellar. If the church is attacked, we will defend it. We will need to take everything with us, including the cart and its horse. They will be stored there until we leave. The rest of the horses will remain in the city stable until then," D'Artagnan told the rest.

Montaigne picked up the story. "I will go get the cart horse and bring some food back with me. We will break down the bed and load it on the cart, along with as many of the pallets as will fit. That will be in the early evening. After it gets dark, Brother Etienne and Brother Xavier will go there along with our personal possessions. Then the cart will return here for the remaining items. By morning we will all be in the church and this warehouse will be empty and, we hope, as dirty as it was when I first came here."

"I know you have questions, but please keep them until later. We have to do this, and we will figure out the situation as we go," D'Artagnan added.

This group of men had been travelling together for weeks and, having been trained to fight and move, knew exactly what to do. Nothing had to be done until Montaigne returned with the cart horse and food. Until then, each member of the group made sure that his own possessions were gathered and packed.

Before long, Montaigne returned. The horse was brought inside and hitched to the cart. The food was spread out on the tables and everyone ate.

When the food was gone, the cardinal was helped to rise and sit in a chair while the bed was broken down.

"How are you feeling, Eminence?" asked Brother Xavier. "Does your knee still hurt?"

"A little, but I'm sure it will soon be better. This wound on my side that you said I got when I was attacked by Gaston's men outside Paris seems much better. It doesn't really hurt anymore. I think I'll be fine traveling tonight, and probably better when we leave the city."

"I'm so glad to hear that, Eminence. It won't pain you to sit for a while in this chair, then?"

"Not at all. I will enjoy watching my bed being taken apart. I do like to know how things are made." He said in a softer voice to Brother Xavier, "If I hadn't been promised to the church, maybe I would have been a carpenter, like Joseph."

Quickly, they packed the bedstead, tables and pallets in the cart, filling any gaps with smaller items. The sun had dropped below the horizon when the doors were opened and the cart pulled out by the horse. Montaigne, Porthos and Athos went with the cart, D'Artagnan and Aramis staying behind with the monks.

Within an hour, Montaigne returned, driving the cart.

"I left Gerard and Georges there putting the bed together. We can place this last pallet in the cart and lay Brother Etienne on it, covering him with the blankets. The chairs should fit around him. I will drive the cart to the church, entering the grounds a less visible way, and then bring it back for the rest of the furniture. That will be the last trip."

"Oh, but I can ride on the seat," objected the cardinal.

"Eminence, I don't think you should try to climb that far up," protested Brother Xavier. "You might hurt your knee again."

"He's right, Eminence," Montaigne said. "You ride in the back and I'll drive."

The cardinal looked from one to the other, then nodded. "I'm sure you're right."

Montaigne said to D'Artagnan, "Try to dirty the floor again. It should not look as though anyone has been here. I'll walk back to guide you to the church when Brother Etienne has been settled." At that he drove the cart out of the warehouse and disappeared from sight into the darkness.

D'Artagnan and Aramis got busy sprinkling dirt on the floor and spreading it around. The lanterns would be the last of their possessions to go, since they needed them to light their work.

"This has been quite a journey, hasn't it?" Aramis said. "The day before we left to join you I wouldn't have expected that I would be traveling this far with such an important passenger. And the trip isn't over yet. Where will it end?"

D'Artagnan replied, "It will end when we get to where we're going. It shouldn't be too much longer, though. We are taking him to safety and then we may leave and do whatever we need at that time."

They had finished their chore by the time Montaigne returned. They gathered the few things that were left and took a last look at the place they had stayed in for the last week, then the three friends walked away, closing the doors behind them.

They shuttered one of the lanterns and extinguished the other. The shuttered lantern would give sufficient light for them to make their way to the church.

"I have found a shorter way to get to the church on foot. If we're quiet, we can go between the houses and shops."

The three friends walked as silently as they could along the road leading to the church. At one point, Montaigne directed them along the side of a small house.

"This is a short cut I found earlier and will take us to the rear of the church grounds," he said.

Right then Aramis stepped in a depression in the ground, stumbling and uttering an epithet in too loud a voice. A dog began barking from a nearby house, causing the homeowner to run out of the house in his nightshirt, brandishing a pistol and shouting.

"Who's there?" he cried. "Leave my chickens alone, you thief!"

That woke some of the neighbors, who ran from their homes, shouting.

Montaigne, D'Artagnan and Aramis were able to avoid the irate homeowners by backtracking and crossing in front of the houses while the homeowners were searching behind.

They arrived, out of breath, at the back of the church soon after and Montaigne used their signal knock at the door.

"We are all finally here," said Athos as he let them in. "Come with me. Father Jean wants to meet you."

After Montaigne introduced the new men as Allais and Emile, the priest said, "I want to thank you for agreeing to help me. This is an old but small church, and I don't have much help. Certainly no one who can defend it against thieves."

"We are glad to do so, Father," D'Artagnan said. "We needed a safe place to stay until we may leave Rennes without fear. But we can stay only until the men that King Gaston sent are gone."

"Of course. However, I think the men threatening the church will come back soon. That's why I needed help now. But first, are you hungry? There is food saved from my dinner that you may have."

"Father, we can't take your food. We ate just before leaving our former refuge," said D'Artagnan.

"I insist. I ate my fill; the rest might not keep until tomorrow. Why don't all of you share what is left?"

"Our thanks, Father." D'Artagnan turned to Montaigne. "Let's go check on the rest of the group.

"Follow me," Father Jean said after he had gathered up the leftover food, and he led them through a doorway in a small room and down a staircase. "Brother Etienne's bed is down here in an alcove. He is resting comfortably with Brother Xavier in attendance. Your other friends have placed all the pallets nearby. I have some extra blankets for you, since it is colder in the cellar than in the upper part of the church."

They reached the cellar floor and were led through a corridor to a small room around a corner. The bed, with the cardinal in it, was set in a corner and the tables and chairs were set close to the opening to the room. The pallets were stacked in a vacant area.

"About time you got here," cried Porthos. "Is that food you're carrying?"

The rest of the men laughed, but Father Jean just looked at them questioningly.

"Georges is famous for his appetite," Athos said. "He is the one who always suggests that it is time to eat."

"Yes, it is food, but there isn't much. It's just what was left from my dinner tonight, but you are welcome to it." He spread the food out on the table that had been brought from the warehouse.

It wasn't much, just some bread, cheese and a few vegetables. There was also a pitcher of red wine.

"I suggest we give most of this to Brother Etienne," D'Artagnan said.

"No, no," he protested. "I am not hungry. You all have done all the work; you should eat."

"I'll take a bite of cheese," said D'Artagnan. "Each of you take a bite of something, and the rest we will give to Brother Etienne." He looked at the monk. "No argument. You have been ill and injured; you need to keep up your strength."

Brother Etienne bowed his head in acquiescence.

After everyone finished eating and had drunk his share of the wine, D'Artagnan suggested sleeping arrangements.

"Since Father Jean is expecting an attack tonight, two of us should sleep upstairs near the back door. I suspect they will come into the church that way. On the chance they try to come in from the front, two others should sleep near it." He thought a moment, then turned to the priest.

"Father, is there a chance they might break into your home to rob you?"

"There may be a chance of that."

"Then, Montaigne, why don't you stay in the rectory to protect him."

They all nodded agreement.

"It is late, so let us all go to bed."

"But is it safe for Brother Etienne and me to be here alone?" Brother Xavier asked.

"It's doubtful that anyone will come down here during the night with the rest of us keeping watch upstairs," said D'Artagnan. "Don't worry. We will be down to check on you in the morning."

The rest of the night passed quietly. No one tried to break in the church or the rectory, and everyone slept well. Shortly after dawn, the five friends rejoined the monks, with Father Jean bringing their breakfast down with Montaigne's help.

"Since today is the Sabbath, I do not have much time to talk to you. I must prepare myself to say Mass. I just want to thank you again for guarding the church and the rectory. And if any of you wish to attend my service, you are certainly welcome."

"Thank you, Father. I think we will," D'Artagnan said while looking at his friends as they nodded. "But I believe Brothers Etienne and Xavier should stay below. We have all brought our bedding back down, and they may use the blankets if they get cold."

"Wonderful. I'm delighted to have you join us. But please, leave your weaponry down here."

"Of course, although there is a chance of an attack during the service," pointed out D'Artagnan. "Perhaps one of us should stay armed, and hold the weapons of the rest of us, but not be in the sanctuary."

"I will do that," Montaigne offered. "I should be able to hear well enough from behind, where we entered last night."

"Very well," Father Jean replied. "If you hear shouting or screaming, please come forth to inquire if we need you. I must go now."

"Are you sure you don't mind?" Aramis asked Montaigne after the priest had left. "We have been able to attend very few services on our journey."

"Don't worry about me," Montaigne replied. "I can worship God wherever I am."

"I really think I should attend," Brother Etienne said. "I know Brother Xavier would prefer to be up there during the service."

Aramis looked at the others before speaking. "Your Eminence, you are a cardinal. I'm sure you know the litany and can say the Mass with Brother Xavier's help. I'm sure God will understand."

"But I don't really remember it," he said to the backs of the retreating members of the group. "Oh, well. You and I can do our best, Brother."

The service went peacefully. The musketeers and cardinal's guard felt renewed in their faith, ready to go on with their journey when the time was right.

After all the parishioners had left for their midday dinners, Father Jean offered to bring meals to his protectors.

"Gerard and I can help you," D'Artagnan said to the priest. "Montaigne, would you and Georges stay behind up here, and will you, Gerard, stay with the car, er, Brother Etienne and Brother Xavier in case the attack comes before we return?"

They all agreed and took their stations. D'Artagnan and Aramis followed Father Jean to the rectory.

"My cook is a marvel in the kitchen. I'm a lucky man to have meals of such quality," he told the two men. "Come in. I'm sure you won't have to wait long."

The two friends found chairs in the foyer and sat. The priest went directly to the kitchen, calling out, "Madame LeBeau, is our repast ready? I will help preparing plates for our guests."

Aramis looked around nervously after the priest had left to help the cook. "I know he's a priest, but are you sure that this isn't a trap? Divided as we are, an attack by enough men could prove the end of our travels, and our lives."

"No, I can't guarantee that we are completely safe, but I believe Montaigne wouldn't lead us astray. Not that I doubt that LeBeq would, though. We must stay on our guard at all times."

After a short time, Father Jean and his cook brought two trays out and handed them to D'Artagnan and Aramis. He and Madame LeBeau followed with two more.

"We'll come back for the other three after these are delivered," he said.

Before the group arrived at the church, they were surrounded by six young men with swords.

"Have you our money?" the apparent leader asked.

D'Artagnan looked at the men threatening them, and thought to himself, *this shouldn't take long*. He put the tray he was carrying on the ground and motioned for the others to do the same. Then he whistled. It was the coded whistled they had used before.

Inside the church, Montaigne and Porthos heard the whistle.

"Is that what I think it is?" said Montaigne.

Porthos peeked out the window which overlooked the back of the church.

"It sounded like it," he said. "Let's go."

They gathered up the swords the others had left there and rushed out the door, leaving one behind for Athos.

Montaigne looked around and said, "Well, what do we have here? More for dinner? I'm afraid we haven't enough for six more."

"Who are you?" called the leader. "Go away. This is no concern of yours."

"No? We are guests of the good Father. I believe it *is* a concern of ours."

He tossed a sword to D'Artagnan while Porthos sent the other one to Aramis. Then the four of them stood in a ring around the priest and his cook.

The leader of the gang laughed and said, sneeringly, "Four against six? You are not very good at arithmetic, are you?" Then he brandished his sword and lunged at Montaigne.

Montaigne stepped back drawing his opponent out of the circle. *The young man had been well trained,* Montaigne thought as he disarmed him, leaving a deep slash on his right arm.

"I may not know arithmetic, but you and your cohorts lack proficiency in swordsmanship," he laughed. He picked up the young man's sword and thrust it in the ground next to the priest, point down. "Now it is four against five."

The other youths threatened D'Artagnan, Aramis, and Porthos, who easily disarmed the rest of them.

D'Artagnan told the priest to take the cook, go back inside the rectory, and lock the door securely.

"Shall we go somewhere that is not holy ground to end this disagreement?" D'Artagnan suggested. "Somewhere secluded, where no one will find your bodies for days or weeks. Maybe years?"

The defenders herded the others, who looked frightened, away from the church and toward a dense wood not far away.

"Now then," Montaigne growled, angrily scowling as the young men were gathered together, faces drained of color and surrounded by the others. "What is this all about? You threatened the priest with vandalism if he didn't give you money? What kind of behavior is that for what looks like young gentlemen? You don't look poor, or like lowlifes. Why are you really doing this?"

The stern demeanor of the older man frightened even D'Artagnan. He had never seen his friend act like that before. He'd seen Montaigne kill people; he'd seen him turn people in to the local constabulary, but he'd never seen him act like an angry father.

The six young men huddled together, surrounded by only four men, but acting like they were in the middle of an enemy army.

"I said why?" Montaigne thundered.

Finally, the leader stepped out and said, "Yes, we are all of high social rank. That church is full of derelicts, criminals and sinners. We want to rid the city of these people. We believe that is our calling."

Montaigne laughed. "A church is full of derelicts, criminals and sinners? Do you think only those who are wealthy and above reproach should attend church? Who do you think church is for?" He shook his head at the naiveté of the boys. "Church is *for* the poor, downtrodden sinners that *you* want to drive away. But for your high birth, you could be one of them." He waved his arms. "Now, go home and do not threaten the church of Saint John the Beloved again. I will find out who you are, and if you ever return, you may not get off so easily."

The leader bravely demanded, "Give us back our swords, then, and we will go."

"No." Montaigne brandished his sword at them, and they ran.

"Do you think that was good enough?" Porthos asked. "Maybe we should have made an example out of one of them."

"I will speak with the priest and with LeBeq. They will find out who they are and know what to do if it happens again," said Montaigne.

When they returned to the church, all the trays had been taken inside and the three men there had begun eating.

"What happened out there," Athos asked. "Father Jean told us that you led the men away from the church, but not what you did to them."

"They were only boys, barely old enough to grow a beard," Montaigne told him. "And we did nothing but talk to them."

"Montaigne talked to them like an angry father," Aramis added. "But we will learn their names and warn the authorities."

"Our former 'benefactor' will take care of them," Montaigne said. "Now, enough talking about that. They certainly will not try anything while we remain here. Shall we have our dinner?"

Bradley H. Sinor, Susan P. Sinor

Chapter Twenty-One

The rest of the day was peaceful. Montaigne and Aramis went to a tavern nearby to gather news, while D'Artagnan and Porthos went to one farther away for the same reason.

Later that evening, when everyone was back at the church, they gathered by the bed for a discussion.

"How are you feeling now, Brother Etienne?" asked D'Artagnan when they were all together.

"I am feeling better, thank you. I feel a bit stronger, too. I think I should be able to walk around down here, and I think I could even climb the stairs." The cardinal turned as though he was going to get out of bed. "I'll show you."

"That's not necessary," D'Artagnan protested.

"Nonsense," the monk said. "I wish to demonstrate my physical condition to assure you that I am able to continue our journey at any time. You needn't coddle me, sirs."

"Of course not, Eminence," Aramis told him. "But we don't want you to be injured again. We'll feel much better if you let us take care of you while we travel."

"Oh, all right. I suppose it won't be that much longer." The cardinal, who had been about to stand up, said, lying back down.

"Now, what have you discovered while you were out," asked Athos.

Montaigne began the report. "We heard that Gaston's men have been here for several days, and have been asking at inns and taverns for, and I quote, 'enemies of the Crown.' I suppose that would be us, just as we thought."

"We heard much the same," said D'Artagnan. "I think we will be safe here, though. I believe the men will be moving on in a day or two. Montaigne, would you go out tomorrow and wander around for a while, looking for them?"

"Of course. I might even strike up a conversation with one of them."

The next day they all stayed in the church, except for Montaigne, who went out as D'Artagnan had asked.

There wasn't much to do except to watch in case the boys who had attacked the church came back. The priest spent some time in the cellar with Brothers Etienne and Xavier. The others left them alone to converse.

"Let's practice fencing," suggested Athos. He waved his arm, saying, "I know we don't carry rapiers. Let's just use the swords we have. Or maybe the swords those boys gave us."

The others concurred and they went outside behind the church to practice.

While the four friends were outside, Father Jean and Brothers Etienne and Xavier were in the cellar, talking.

"It's very kind of you to come down to talk to us," Brother Etienne told Father Jean. "We have kept moving and haven't even stopped for Mass on Sundays. I would so like to attend the next time you say Mass."

"I do that every day, Brother Etienne. If you feel well enough tomorrow, you should come up in the morning. I'll come down here to tell you when that will be," the priest said.

"Excellent!" the monk responded. "I'm sure I will be able to climb the stairs tomorrow."

"I look forward to it," said Father Jean. "Wait! Did you hear something?" He listened for the sound again. Lowering his voice, he continued. "It sounds like someone is farther back in the cellar." He took his lantern and moved a short way toward the sound.

Before the priest had gone far, Montaigne arrived.

"Father, I just want to warn you that the men we are trying to avoid are coming this way. The others are watching them and will try to distract them from coming here. But we should move farther into the cellar." He turned to the cardinal. "Will you be able to walk a short distance?"

"Of course," he said. "I'm getting stronger every day. My voice is much better, too, I think. I'm not getting so winded. Are we going there now?" He turned to get up. "Oh, I will need my shoes."

Brother Xavier rummaged in the bag of the few possessions the cardinal had with him, pulling out a pair of sandals.

"Here you are, Brother Etienne. I will help you walk the distance."

"I will take chairs for you to sit on while we move the bed," Montaigne said, picking up two of the chairs.

"I will take the other two chairs, and then we can get the tables," Father Jean told them. "We should leave nothing in this room to show that anyone was staying here."

"Of course," Montaigne answered. "After we clear the room, we can move the bed. Do you think it will fit through the doorway still put together?"

The priest and Montaigne looked at the bed, then at the doorway. "We can try," said Father Jean.

Brother Xavier helped the cardinal to stand, but he swayed and his knees gave out so that he had to sit back down.

"Montaigne, would you help me to move the cardinal?" Brother Xavier asked.

"Of course, but first let me move a chair there for him to sit on."

After everything but the bed had been moved, the two men went back to the room, leaving Brother Xavier to care for the cardinal.

"If we each go to a side and try to lift it that way, at least we can move it to the door," suggested Montaigne.

They did that, discovering that the bed was a little too heavy for just the two of them. Then they dragged it to the door.

"It just might fit, if we weren't standing beside it," said the priest. "We can go through the door and pull it behind us."

"It's worth a try," said Montaigne.

All the bedding and the pallets had already been taken to the new location, so it was just the frame they had to move. Being solid oak with head- and foot-boards, it was heavy.

Montaigne had a thought. "Do you have an old blanket that you don't really use anymore?"

"I think so. We don't throw old things away, since they might have other uses. I'll go see what I can find."

Presently he returned with just what they needed. They spread the blanket out underneath the bedframe, then lifted each corner in turn to put a section of the blanket under the legs. It moved easily when pulled through the doorway and on down the corridor. Shortly they arrived where the bed would be set.

"You didn't have to take it apart," exclaimed Brother Etienne disappointedly. "I was hoping to watch you put it together."

"I'm sorry, but it took much less time this way," Montaigne told him. "I need to go out and check on our friends. Will you be all right?"

"Yes, I'll be fine now. Thank you for taking such good care of me. Would one of you help me into the bed? I'm feeling quite tired all of a sudden."

"Of course." Montaigne and Brother Xavier both assisted the cardinal to return to his bed.

The monks had been moved farther down the cellar hallway than the priest knew existed.

"We're not even all the way to the end. How much farther is there?" Brother Etienne asked Father Jean.

"Not much farther, I think. I haven't exactly gone all the way to the end."

"You haven't? Aren't you curious how far it goes?" Brother Xavier interrupted. "I don't think I could help but explore the whole length. What if it's a tunnel that ends a mile away? Or at another building? Or at your home? Have you checked in the rectory cellar? Maybe this leads there and you could come through it when the weather is bad."

"How interesting!" The priest paused a moment. "I haven't explored the cellar of the rectory. I'm somewhat afraid of spiders, and I'm sure there are many down there. I use it only for storage. Perhaps I can ask one of my parishioners to look."

Another sound came from farther into the cellar. Father Jean looked alarmed, but Brother Xavier said, "It could just be a small animal. I could go look, but I'll need to take the lantern."

"I'd rather you stay here," Brother Etienne told him. "I don't want anything to happen to you."

Brother Xavier bowed to the request, saying, "Of course. Perhaps one of the others will return soon and he can investigate."

Moments later, Porthos arrived, carrying the second lantern down from upstairs. "Montaigne said you'd moved farther in. He asked me to come stay with you until all is safe again."

"We're glad you came," Brother Etienne said. "We have heard a sound from farther along the corridor. We had been speculating how much farther it goes and where it ends. Father Jean hasn't explored the full length yet. I would go, but they won't let me." He motioned to the two other men. "They said it might be too dangerous. Would you go, instead, and report what you find?"

"Certainly, Brother Etienne. I will take the lantern with me and go now. You said you heard a sound? Can you describe it?"

Father Jean turned to him. "It was a rustling sound. It may have been a small animal. I don't know if, at the end, it opens to the outside. If so, an animal may have entered for shelter. Thank you for checking it out for us."

Porthos took the lantern, lit the second lantern with it, and then left to explore farther.

"We forgot to ask him what news there is," said Father Jean. "But if we hear anything, I will take this lantern farther down and shutter it. Then we must be very quiet to not call attention to ourselves."

The small group sat without speaking for a few minutes, then the cardinal whispered, "I wonder if Georges has found anything."

"We should know soon," Brother Xavier whispered back to him.

A few moments later Porthos did come back, with another man in tow. He stopped far enough away from the bed that the small group was in darkness.

"I found someone hiding at the end of the tunnel, for tunnel it is. There is a door at the end that opens into the cellar of the rectory. He says his name is Pierre LeFou."

Brother Etienne said to Father Jean. "I suggested that to you, didn't I?"

"Can you tell me where the door opens into? I haven't been in much of the cellar yet."

"There is a door behind the cellar stairs, but it is blocked from casual sight. This man says he knew of the access to the tunnel and hid there." Porthos turned to the man. "You tell your story."

The man in question stepped forward, but was pulled back so he couldn't see them.

"I have been hiding from Gaston's men. As soon as I heard they were in town, I knew they were looking for me, so I hid in the safest place I knew, this cellar. When I was young, my family attended Mass here. I was a friend of the son of the priest's cook, and he showed me all the hiding places."

"Why do you think those men are after you?" Porthos asked.

"They are after my father, but he died recently. I know that if they can't get to him, they'll find me."

"But what could your father have done to make them search for him?" asked Father Jean.

"My family has lived in Rennes for generations, until a few years ago. My father was in service to the king, the former king, that is. A few years ago he was injured in the line of duty, and was sent to stay with relatives in the southeastern part of France, where it is warmer, in a small town. While there he made friends with a man who turned out to be one of Gaston's men. Our family has always supported King Louis, so my father, knowing that the king and his brother were not on good terms, took it upon himself to do some mischief. More than mischief, really. He killed a close friend of Gaston's. I don't know who that was, but it made Gaston angry enough to look for my father. But my father was able to slip away and make his way back to Rennes. The trip was too much for him. He had enough breath to tell me his story before he died. He said that Gaston would find our family and kill us all. Unfortunately, there was no more family but me. So when I heard that men sent by Gaston were coming here, I got as much food as I could and came here. I was able to enter the rectory undetected and found my way to the tunnel."

"How long have you been here?" the priest asked. "You must be cold and hungry."

"I brought as much of my possessions as I could carry: some clothes and blankets, as well as the food. When I know the men have gone, I can go back to my family home. Are they still here? I have heard no news for several days, since I got here."

"They are still here," Porthos said. "In fact, they have been sniffing around this neighborhood, especially the church. You stay here while I go look for my friends."

He took the lantern to the priest. "Keep watch until I, or one of the others, returns."

After Porthos had left, the young man, Pierre, said, "If I may ask, why are the three of you down here?"

The three churchmen looked at each other. They didn't know what to say. His appearance had caused a problem.

"It is a private matter we are dealing with," Father Jean told Pierre. "It is not up to me to talk about it to anyone."

"Perhaps I could speak with one of the others? I would like to help with your problem, whatever it is, since I have yet to be reprimanded for trespassing in your cellar."

Father Jean was holding the lantern away from the bed and the two monks, but Pierre looked their way, trying to see who they were.

Father Jean saw this and introduced the brothers to him. "Monsieur LeFou, these two monks are Brother Etienne and Brother Xavier." He left it there, discouraging any more questions about the men.

Presently, Porthos came back with Athos and Aramis in tow. D'Artagnan and Montaigne soon joined them.

"I hear someone's been hiding in the cellar all along," D'Artagnan said to the priest. "And I can see him over there. Do you know anything about him?"

"Only what he told us when he was discovered. Did Georges tell you the story?"

"Yes, but I'm not sure I believe all he said. Do you know anything about his family?"

"No, but I've been here only a few years, and there are several other churches in Rennes. His family could have attended any one of them more recently."

"We need to know the truth about him."

Montaigne said, "I'll ask around town about his family. First, I'll ask him what part of town his family home is in." He went to talk to the young man.

"And we need to know if he has a trade. If he's telling the truth we may be able to help each other," D'Artagnan said.

After Montaigne left, D'Artagnan went to speak to the young man.

"I understand that you are hiding from the men that have come here from Paris."

"Yes. I'm afraid they are looking for me, since my father, who died recently, killed one of King Gaston's supporters. Since they can't kill him, they'll settle for killing me." Pierre looked at the other men standing near the bed. "I see your friend, Brother Etienne, is not well. Are all of you taking him somewhere?"

D'Artagnan didn't answer the question, but asked the young man another one.

"You still live here in Rennes? Do you still have family here?"

Pierre thought a moment, not sure what D'Artagnan was getting at.

"I did. As I said, my father died recently of his wounds. My mother died several years ago, and other family members have either died or moved away. Why are you asking me these questions?

"Do you have a trade, or was your family wealthy?"

"Uh, my family has been wealthy, but not much is left. But as to a trade, I am a calligrapher and scribe. I write letters and documents for people who haven't the skill or education to do it themselves. Why do you ask?"

D'Artagnan thought for a moment, then answered. "I may have a proposition for you that would help us all. I can't tell you what it is right away, though. I must confer with the others."

He called his three friends to the small room they had formerly used.

"I have the beginning of a plan that may rid this city of 'those' men, but we will need the young man's help."

The others looked at each other, then turned to D'Artagnan.

"Do you trust him?" Aramis asked. "But first, tell us the plan."

"Well, he told me he's a calligrapher by trade. This is what I'm thinking."

D'Artagnan described the plan and explained the role that Pierre would play.

"But we have to wait for Montaigne to return."

Chapter Twenty-Two

A few hours later, Montaigne got back, bringing food and information with him.

"I have tracked them to a tavern where they are eating and drinking. I struck up a conversation with them, but it didn't go anywhere. Maybe they weren't drunk enough. I couldn't find out where they're staying."

"If you couldn't find that out, how could any of us?" said Athos. "You are the master spy."

"Well, I listened for a bit before I left. I heard one of them say something about the three musketeers. I don't know what that means."

"I do," exclaimed Porthos. "Months ago, before everything happened and we left on this journey, we met a man in a tavern who was talking about an up-time book by that name. It was apparently written in the future, in the 1800s, by a French author. And it was about us. Porthos," he tapped his chest, "Athos and Aramis." He pointed to them. "And D'Artagnan. It was very popular at the time. The man must have gotten it from a bookseller who had been to Germany or somewhere. Anyway, he had heard of us. One of you called me by name, which he recognized. By then you two were gone. Don't you remember me telling you about it? He accosted me, asking about all the adventures 'we' had in the book. Of course, we had never had those adventures. I had to explain that to him, that we were just three musketeers among many and not that important.

I'm sure I would recognize him again." He turned to Montaigne and asked, "Was one of the men tall and thin, with fair hair and beard?"

"Yes, one of them was. What are you suggesting?" Montaigne asked.

"I'm suggesting that D'Artagnan and I, and you, go back to this tavern. If they're still there, D'Artagnan and I will go in. I will make him recognize me and then deny it. He won't know D'Artagnan, and I'll say that I have distant cousins in Paris but that I've never been there."

Montaigne nodded as Porthos told the story.

"If you can find out where they're staying, and then keep them away, I can go to their rooms to rummage around for information," Montaigne added.

"Try to find a letter from Gaston. We need the seal from it, but bring the letter back with you if you find one. Here's what we plan to do."

D'Artagnan repeated the plan to Montaigne, and then the three of them set off.

∞ ∞ ∞

Five men sat at a large table in a tavern named The Three Cockerels. They had had their dinners and were drinking ale to pass the time before they returned to their rooms.

Two men dressed as laborers entered and found a table nearby, while a third entered behind them and sat near the door.

Porthos and D'Artagnan sat facing the large table. They ordered ale, bread, and cheese, and began to talk loudly.

"Good weather lately," Porthos said. "Easy to find work in good weather, probably anywhere in the city."

Presently, one of the five men took notice of the conversation and looked at the other table.

"That man," he said to his neighbor, "looks very familiar. I'm sure I've met him before. But what would he be doing here in Rennes?"

He went over to talk to the man, since his curiosity was nudging him.

"Hello," he said to Porthos. "You look very familiar. I'm sure I've met you somewhere."

"I don't think so," Porthos replied. "I must look like someone you've met. But sit down with us. Maybe we can figure it out."

The man sat and stared at Porthos for a while, trying to think of where he could have seen him.

"I know! It was in Paris a few months ago. You're one of those musketeers in the book."

"Book? What book would I be in? I can't even read." Porthos spread his arms wide. "And I'm certainly not a musketeer. I'm just a laborer. I find work where I can to get by."

The man's face fell. "It's a book that was written in the future about three musketeers. Their names were... I'll think of them." A minute later he said, "Athos, Porthos and Aramis! That was their names. And you're Porthos. I knew I'd remember."

"My name's Auguste, not Porthos. What kind of a name is that? And how could you read a book from the future?"

"Well, you look like him. I met him in Paris after I'd read that book. I bought it from a bookseller who got it from someone who knew an up-timer. Anyway, I like the book, and I was excited to meet someone who had been written about."

"I do have a distant cousin in Paris. Maybe you saw him. I hear we look a lot alike. You seem like a nice fellow. I don't mind talking to you for a while. Just don't expect me to be that Porthos, or whoever you said."

"All right," the man said. "Would you like to come sit with us?"

"Do you think there's room? Besides, I have my friend, Antoine, here. Your table looks full. Sit with us for a while."

The man sat and introduced himself. "My name is André Boyce."

"So, Monsieur Boyce, are you just passing through or are you visiting?"

"I'm – we're just visiting for a few days, then we'll move on." The man seemed unsure of what to say.

"Oh. Taking a tour of France's best cities? Do you and your friends live in Paris?" Porthos began to try to draw him out.

"I live there, but my friends live in other places . . ." Before he could say more, Porthos broke in.

"Oh! Have you seen King Gaston? Now that he is king, I'm sure the country will be safe from up-time invaders. How exciting to live in such an – exciting – place."

During the exchange, D'Artagnan sat, watching Boyce with a bored look on his face.

"But why would you leave a place like Paris to travel all this way to Rennes?"

Boyce looked at his friends at the other table, but they were all talking among themselves.

"We were sent by the king," he said in a low voice. "I'm sure I can trust you, now that I know you support King Gaston. We are looking for enemies of the Crown."

"Enemies of the Crown? Who would they be? Everyone I know seems glad to have a strong king like Gaston in charge." Porthos looked at D'Artagnan, then back at Boyce. "Maybe we can help you." Porthos was trying to insinuate that they would expect payment for their help.

Porthos seemed excited to be able to help his new friend; so much so that, although he knew better, D'Artagnan was taken aback for a moment.

"Yes, perhaps we can." D'Artagnan added his voice to Porthos'. "But do you think it's wise to discuss matter like this in so public a place?"

Boyce looked around. The tavern was crowded, and although it seemed noisy, people sat so closely together that anyone who listened could overhear what was said at the next table.

"Perhaps we could go to your home," he said to Porthos.

Porthos shook his head. "My home is so small that we would not fit into it. Also, my wife is a shrew. Why do you think I spend my evenings in places like this?"

D'Artagnan said, "I live with my brother and his wife, and their nine children. I sleep in a closet under the stairway."

"What about your room?" Porthos suggested. "Or do you all sleep in the same bed?"

Boyce thought about showing offense, then thought better of it. Auguste was probably just making a joke. "I suppose that would be better than going to the home of either of you."

He went back to the table where his friends were still sitting. "Those two that I've been talking to seem interested in helping us. I want to take them back to our rooms so we can talk privately. Which of you will come with me?"

One of the men spoke up. "Why do you trust them? You just met them. It would be foolish to take them to our rooms." He looked at the other men. "Bring them here so the rest of us can talk to them."

Boyce did so, squeezing two more chairs in with the five that were occupied.

"This is Auguste and that is Antoine," Boyce told his friends, then turned back to Porthos and D'Artagnan. "These men would like to talk to you."

"Of course," Porthos said. "We're glad to meet you, uh…" The other men did not introduce themselves.

Porthos and D'Artagnan were quite amenable to answering the questions even though they didn't answer them completely honestly. When the questioning ended, the others decided that is was safe to take Auguste and Antoine back with them to their rooms.

It happened that they were staying at the same inn, The Black Dragon, that the monks and their guards had stayed in. But, since it had been more than a week since they had left, Porthos thought they wouldn't be recognized by the innkeeper. Just to be safe, they averted their faces when walking to the stairway. It was just a coincidence that both rooms occupied by the king's men were the ones that they had used.

Boyce opened the door to the larger room and ushered the two men into it.

"We can talk in here when the others arrive."

Porthos looked around in awe. "This is surely a nicer room that I have ever seen. Of course, I've never stayed at an inn before. I've never been away from Rennes." D'Artagnan just nodded.

"We have stayed in many inns, and this room is average."

"This is so exciting, to help you on your mission. How do you know where to go next?" As Porthos spoke, D'Artagnan subtly looked around the room, noting where every bag was located.

"The king gave us a list of towns and a map," said Boyce.

"What will you do when you find who you're looking for?"

Boyce thought a moment. "I suppose we'll take the person back to Paris with us."

"So you're looking for only one person?" Porthos said. "Perhaps we can help find him. Who is it?"

Just then the door opened and the other men entered.

"Just a moment," Boyce said, and turned to confer with the others. Then he turned back to Porthos and D'Artagnan, saying, "My friends think it would not be a good idea for you to help us openly. But if you have information about who we're looking for, you could tell us."

"We will, if we know who it is," said Porthos.

After another minute of thought, Boyce said, "It's an important person from Paris who escaped when the former king died."

Both Porthos and D'Artagnan looked wide-eyed, as though they had no idea who the man was talking about.

"He is a cardinal who was close to the former king." Boyce looked impatient that the two strangers seemed to not know who he was talking about. "His name is Cardinal Richelieu."

"Oh," Porthos said, drawing the word out. "We've heard of him. I think." He looked at D'Artagnan for confirmation. "What does he look like?"

Boyce took a sheet of paper out of a pocket, unfolded it and handed it to Porthos. "He looks like this."

Porthos and D'Artagnan looked closely, squinting at the paper. "It's hard to see," Porthos said. "But I don't think I've ever seen him. Have you, Antoine?"

D'Artagnan shook his head. "Doesn't look familiar." *But it is a very good likeness*, he thought.

"But we can look around for you. How about meeting again tomorrow night at the same place?" Porthos told him. "Maybe we'll have spotted him during the day."

Boyce conferred again with his friends, then nodded. Porthos and D'Artagnan took their leave, going back toward the tavern. At the next corner they met Montaigne, who had followed the group but kept his distance.

"They're in the same rooms we had in The Black Dragon," D'Artagnan told him after the three had turned the corner. "We're meeting them tomorrow night at the tavern. It should be safe enough then for you to break in."

The next day was cloudy, but no rain came. Porthos and D'Artagnan went out and walked around town during the afternoon, ostensibly to look for the cardinal. They even asked random people if they had seen a tall, thin older man who they didn't know. A few people said they had seen a man of that description and told them the part of town in which they had seen him.

Later that evening, they went back to the tavern to meet their new friends. As soon as Montaigne saw that all of them were there, he started toward the inn.

Just as he thought, no one recognized him when he arrived. He ordered ale and sat near the stairway. The public room started filling up just as he was served. He finished his drink, then started up the stairs, as though he was going to his room. Once he was outside one of the rooms, he took a small knife out of his pocket and pushed it past the edge of the door. The door opened quietly and Montaigne slipped in. The room had four beds, with a traveling case by each one. He quickly searched each case for a letter from King Gaston. He found nothing.

Then he repeated his actions in the room next door with two beds. That room had a traveling case and saddle bags from all the horses. A search through the case yielded just what he was looking for: a letter from King Gaston to a Boyce Prideux. Montaigne quickly hid the letter in his vest, but before he could slip back out of the room, he heard voices in the hallway.

"It must have been something I ate, I said," said a man. The door knob shook as if someone was trying to turn it, but couldn't because the door was locked.

"No, you're drunk," said another man. "This isn't the room you sleep in; it's that one."

"Oh," the first man said. "Come in here with me. I want to talk to you about something."

"All right. But I want to get something from the other room first."

Montaigne quickly crawled under the bed farther from the door, letting the bed clothes hang down to cover him.

"What do you want from that room? Only Boyce sleeps there," the first man said. "I'll come with you and we can talk there."

"No! I'll get what I want and come right back. You go in and lay down." The second man opened the door and firmly closed it behind himself. Montaigne could see only boots until the other man stooped to rummage in the case, then rose, cursing. "That lying . . . So he didn't get a letter from the king after all." Then he stomped through that door and the door into the other room.

As much as Montaigne wanted to hear what was being said, he felt it was better to leave the second floor. Downstairs, he resumed his table, which had miraculously remained unoccupied, and ordered dinner and another ale.

At The Three Cockerels, Porthos and D'Artagnan joined Boyce and the others at a large table. The other men were eating, so two more meals were ordered.

"Have you found out anything?" Boyce asked them.

"Well, we walked around a lot, and talked to as many people as we could," Porthos answered. "We asked if anyone had seen a tall, thin older man who they didn't know, and several said they had. They pointed several directions where they had seen him, but the direction pointed to most was to the south and east. We walked in that direction, but saw no one by that description. We can look again tomorrow, if you like."

"We'll check that part of town again," Boyce said. "Yes, look more places tomorrow. We'll see you here again tomorrow night."

At that point, one of the men complained of an upset stomach, and left to go back to his room. Another stood and followed him.

After the ones remaining had finished their meals, they all ordered more ale and sat talking and laughing a while longer. Soon enough the three men still there decided to go back to the inn. Porthos and D'Artagnan headed back toward the church, keeping watch that they weren't followed.

Montaigne was waiting for them when they arrived.

"Did you find it?" D'Artagnan asked Montaigne the moment they were together.

"I found one," Montaigne answered. "I haven't opened it yet; I waited for you to get back. Believe me, it wasn't easy to wait, but I thought we should read it together. Also, two of the men returned when I was in the smaller room. One of them came in to look for this letter, but I already had it with me under one of the beds. He was very unhappy that there wasn't a letter to be found and accused Monsieur Boyce of lying to them."

"Hm," was the only thing that D'Artagnan said.

D'Artagnan, Athos, Porthos and Aramis gathered around Montaigne as the missive was unfolded.

After the obligatory from and to, the message was for the men to go to the listed towns and, if they should identify and capture the fugitives, to return them to Paris.

"Now we have what we need," D'Artagnan cried. "Pierre! We need your services."

Pierre immediately appeared, asking, "What do you need for me to do?"

"See this letter? We need you to copy everything on it but the list of towns. Replace the names of these towns with several we will give you. Since the writing is not in Gaston's own hand, you don't have to copy the writing."

"But I can copy the writing, if you want. In fact, that looks like the way I write."

"Excellent! I will give you the replacement names shortly. I need to get some help from Father Jean."

"What direction do you want those men sent? I am familiar with towns to the southeast and southwest of here."

"Even better. But I do need paper and stamp from the priest. Unless you brought those things with you."

"I did. They are my livelihood. I couldn't leave them behind."

"Do you have a blank stamp? The seal on this letter is blank."

"Yes, I have a blank stamp, as well."

"Then please get what you need and bring them here to the table. The sooner we send them away from here, the sooner we can get on our way, too."

Soon the letter was written, sealed, and stamped.

"We will meet the men again tomorrow night," D'Artagnan said. "Montaigne, you can take both letters back to the inn, giving the new one to the innkeeper to deliver and replacing the other where you found it. Just be very careful you are not caught."

"Me? Caught?" Montaigne cried, feigning outrage. "I am never caught because I am never recognized." He then took both letters, making sure he knew which was which, and securing them in his clothing.

"I think we should leave tomorrow night, after Georges and I return from our meeting at the tavern," D'Artagnan told the others. "Those men should be leaving too, but toward the southeast. If we leave during the night, we can be farther along when they leave."

The others agreed with the plan.

Chapter Twenty-Three

The next day, Athos and Aramis went out to gather supplies they would need on their journey. Porthos and D'Artagnan went out again, as they said they would, and Montaigne went out for his own reasons.

At the meeting at The Three Cockerels, Boyce announced that he had received another letter from the king and that his group would be leaving the next morning. They expressed their appreciation to Auguste and Antoine for their help.

"We were excited to help you, but we don't know how much help that was, I'm afraid," said Porthos. "We will continue to look, but we don't know how to contact you if we find him."

"Don't worry about that," Monsieur Boyce told them. "We have received word that he was seen in another location to the southeast."

The two men stood expectantly, their hands held before them. After a moment, Monsieur Boyce realized they were waiting for payment for their help.

He handed each man a few coins for their trouble, and then they said their farewells and left to go their different ways.

At the church, all of their things were packed. The horses had been retrieved from the stable and the cart horse had been hitched to the cart. Brother Etienne had been carried up the stairs, to which he protested that he could have climbed them by himself.

"I thank you for your help with those ruffians, and I will miss your company," Father Jean said when they were ready to leave."

"I talked to LeBeq about the situation, and he said that if they come back, he is to be alerted and will take care of it," Montaigne told the priest.

"We are the ones who are thankful for your hospitality," said Brother Etienne. "I am feeling so much better from your care that all I still hope for is to get my memory back."

"I will pray for your safe arrival at your destination, and for your full recovery," the priest added. "Is there anything else I can do for you?"

"Just tell no one of our plans, or that we were ever here," D'Artagnan said. "Oh, and see that Monsieur LeFou safely returns to his home. The city should be safe for him now."

"I wish to add my thanks to you for helping me," the young man said. "It was my honor to help you send those men off, away from here. I will also keep your secret safe."

Then the travelers got under way.

All the furniture that had been bought in Rennes had been left with Father Jean, since there was no need to take it along. They kept the two lanterns and a supply of candles, just in case.

All the men were rested, some during the day and the others in the evening, before they left. Father Jean had found a map of cities and towns to the north, which was the direction they were going.

"We are going to the north, and I think our first stop is in Betton," D'Artagnan told everyone.

"But you told us we are going to Nantes," protested Brother Etienne. "Isn't that where my family is?"

"Yes, that is where I said we were going, but it was not true. It was only to make sure that the real location was not accidentally revealed," D'Artagnan said. "The direction we are really going is to the north, but I won't say exactly where yet. Don't worry, Brother Etienne, it is a safe place for you.

"As I said, our first stop is Betton. It should be big enough to have a tavern, at least, I think. Possibly an inn." He shrugged. "If there is no inn, we will have to camp. Now, since it is nighttime and most people are abed, I believe we should travel as silently as possible."

It was not possible to travel completely silently, due to the clop of the horses' hoofs and the creak of the wheels of the cart, but there was no more talking until they were completely away from Rennes.

∞ ∞ ∞

The journey to Betton took the rest of the night and most of the day, but the cardinal was able to sleep a bit in the cart. They traveled over soft grass for much of the way, since the roads that existed were very rutted and rough. At one point they stopped for a while to rest themselves and the horses. As they entered the village, they saw a tavern.

"At least we should be able to add to our stores, as well as have a good meal," Porthos said.

D'Artagnan dismounted near the door of the tavern and handed his horse over to Montaigne.

"I'll ask inside if there is a place to stay for the night."

Since there were seven of them, and one required a bed, his hopes weren't high.

"We do have two rooms upstairs for travelers, but they are small. One does have a comfortable bed," the tavern owner said.

"May I see them?" D'Artagnan asked him.

"Of course."

The rooms were small, but the bed was wide enough for both monks to fit, and the other room had enough floor space for the rest.

Brother Etienne was carried to the room with the bed and Xavier accompanied him while the others stowed their belonging in the other room. Then the horses and cart were pulled around to the back in a fenced pasture.

D'Artagnan ordered meals for all of them while the three former musketeers secured a table for the four of them. Montaigne stayed in the room with the monks, waiting for the plates for the three of them.

Brother Etienne seemed very tired, but in good humor. "It's good to be on our way again. Let us pray that the rest of the journey is short."

They drank to that and ate the meals that had just arrived. Shortly the other four arrived and crowded into the small room.

Montaigne announced that he would bed down with the monks, while the other four took the second room.

"Do you think there may be danger," Brother Etienne asked.

"One never knows," was the only reply Montaigne would make.

But the night went undisturbed, and everyone rose rested.

"I know we're nearing our destination, but I can't help but think that some new disaster might befall us," Porthos said.

"We shouldn't borrow trouble," Aramis said to him. "But still…"

"I know," said Porthos. "It could happen."

They took their breakfasts with them, as well as enough food for their lunch and dinner, as they left shortly after daybreak.

Before they left, D'Artagnan had spoken to the tavern owner. "We will be traveling north and east. Can you tell me what we may expect in the way of towns in that direction?"

The man shook his head. "There is not much in the way of civilization that way. A few settlements, some lone farmhouses. Not many estates. I am somewhat familiar with the region, and I can draw you a rough map. But I'm not sure the settlements I mark will be in the right places."

"We appreciate any kind of help. Thank you."

∞ ∞ ∞

"There may be little more than a settlement, so we may need to make camp for the night," D'Artagnan told the others.

"How far will we go today?" Brother Etienne asked. "I'm sure I'll want to get out of the cart and walk a bit before we get there."

"Are you feeling that much better? I'm not sure you should be exerting yourself that much. But we will stop later this morning for a rest."

The road led to a wood not far away which would allow for a brief stop for the travelers.

Several minutes into the wood they found a creek and stopped for the horses to drink and rest. The monks climbed carefully out of the cart, and Brother Etienne was helped slowly toward a small copse.

When he returned and was replaced by Porthos, D'Artagnan asked him, "How are you feeling, Brother Etienne?"

"I feel fairly well. I think my wound has almost completely healed and my knee feels much better. It actually felt good to walk around for a bit."

"I'm very glad to hear that. We are not much more than a week from our final destination, I believe. Perhaps closer. That is, if we have no more interruptions to our journey."

"If that is God's will, and I hope it is. I am very tired of all this traveling, although I don't remember much of it. Can you tell me where it is we are going?"

D'Artagnan looked around. All the others were out of earshot for the moment.

"I promised Cardinal Tremblay that I would tell no one until we are very close."

Brother Etienne looked very disappointed to hear that, and D'Artagnan relented a bit.

"We are going to a place by the ocean. It is a place you will be welcomed by friends, I've been assured."

His expression lightened, as if he remembered the place where they were going.

"I think it is time to be on our way," D'Artagnan told him, and called to the others.

They met no one until near dark, when they came upon a small settlement.

"Well," said Athos. "Not much here."

"It doesn't even look like it has a tavern," added Porthos.

"But it has houses, and with luck, we may find a place to stay the night." D'Artagnan headed toward the nearest house, the rest of the group following him.

A large man came out of the house, brandishing a flint-lock rifle. "We're not looking for trouble here," he said. "Just go on your way."

D'Artagnan stopped and looked around. "We're not offering trouble. We're just looking for a place to stay the night, and we'll be on our way tomorrow."

The man saw the cart and the two monks riding in it. "Are they your prisoners?" He nodded toward it.

"Not at all. We are accompanying the two monks on their way to a monastery. The monk in the cart is injured."

"Well, then, they can come, but not you or your friends."

D'Artagnan motioned for Brother Xavier to drive the cart closer to the house.

By this time people from the other houses had come out to see what was going on. The men gathered around the cart.

"What are your names, brothers?" asked one of them.

Brother Xavier introduced himself, and the cardinal as Brother Etienne. "He has been injured," he repeated.

One man in particular studied the cardinal's face, then he motioned for the first man to follow him a short way away.

"Do you remember a couple of weeks ago when some men came here and asked if we had seen someone? They had a drawing and said it was of Cardinal Richelieu." He pointed to the monk in the cart. "He looks quite a lot like that drawing."

"Those were men loyal to King Gaston," said a third man.

"Yes, and we have always been loyal to Louis. If this is Cardinal Richelieu, then he is running from Gaston and we should give him aid," the first man said. "Sir." He walked back to the cart. "You look much like the drawing we have seen of Cardinal Richelieu. If you are he, and are hiding from King Gaston, you are welcome here."

Brother Etienne looked up at the man in surprise. "My name is Brother Etienne, but I would be grateful if you were to welcome us anyway. We will only stay the night."

"Of course," said the first man, nodding, suspecting that the cardinal had assumed the name as protection. "And your friends are your escorts rather than your captors," he said in a low voice.

"Yes. They are keeping us safe on our journey, just like Monsieur Renard said."

"Is that the name of the man who spoke to us earlier?" At Brother Etienne's nod, he continued. "And what are the names of the others."

The monk pointed to each one, saying his name. "That is Georges Moreau. Next is Gerard LeRoi. Then Emile Gillette and Monsieur Montaigne. They have been very good to me. To us both." Brother Xavier spoke for the cardinal, as the older man had become too tired to continue talking.

"Very well," the first man said. "Then you two may stay the night in my house." After looking at the second man, he said, "And the rest can stay in Monsieur Bernard's barn." He pointed to a large building behind a house. "Pull the cart up beside my house. Your horses may stay in our pasture."

Brother Xavier did as told, helping Brother Etienne out of the cart and into the house.

"My name is Monsieur Severin. This is my wife. Our children are grown and married, so we have a room you can sleep in." The man ushered the monks into his home, then went back to direct the others to where they could sleep.

"You may spend the night in the barn," he pointed in that direction, "and you may put your horses in our pasture. But you should be on your way when the sun rises in the morning. If you have not brought food with you, we will provide it."

"We thank you," D'Artagnan said. "And we will abide by your wishes. We have brought a small amount of food, but it won't last us very long. We can pay for anything you will provide."

Monsieur Severin nodded and went to talk to his friends.

D'Artagnan called the others over and informed them what he had been told. "I think we will be safe here for the night, but one of us should sleep lightly, in case there is some disturbance."

"I saw the monks go into that man's house," Aramis said. "Do you think they will be safe there?"

"I don't know, but it is too late now to change things. We still have our weapons, if anything should go awry."

They turned the horses into the pasture, leaving the cart where it was. Then they took their things into the barn and looked for places to bed down.

Shortly, Monsieur Bernard brought them their meals. It was simple fare, but they appreciated it. D'Artagnan gave their host the equivalent of what they would have paid for the meals in the city.

"My thanks. We are poor farmers, and have to get by with what we grow," Monsieur Severin said. "Now, gentlemen, if you would give me your swords for the night."

At looks of distress and distrust, he said, "I'll give them back to you when you leave. But we don't know you, and we have been attacked before by robbers." He took the swords and bundled them up." Don't worry. We won't use them against you."

When the man had gone, Montaigne said, "At least we still have our pistols. We might as well get some sleep. There's really nothing we can do before we leave tomorrow."

They all did as suggested without much discussion.

The next morning, they collected their swords, their charges, and their horses and departed, thanking the homeowners for their hospitality.

"They were very nice people," Brother Xavier said as the left.

"And generous," added Brother Etienne. "They really don't have much and were willing to share it."

"And hold our swords while we slept," grumbled Porthos.

"Sorry?" said Brother Etienne.

"Nothing."

"There is another settlement around a day's ride from here. I hope it will be big enough to have an inn," D'Artagnan told them.

Their next stop was in Sens-de-Bretagne. It was also small, but there were several shops and another tavern with a few rooms. The trip there was uneventful, except for a shower during the middle of the day. The group was able to take shelter under a large tree. The rest of the day was sunny with enough of a breeze to dry their damp clothing. The cardinal slept most of the way. The trip had been very tiring to him, and he was not healing as well as he claimed.

Although they thought they were safe from the king's men, D'Artagnan and Montaigne kept a close watch for other travelers who might also be looking for them. The few that passed them seemed friendly enough, but they were watched until they were out of sight, and then watched for in case they returned.

Late in the afternoon, after travelling a rough road and taking two rest stops, they came upon another small settlement and found places in a home for Brother Etienne and Brother Xavier. Again the rest of them slept in a barn. This time their weapons were not taken from them.

The next day they rose with the sun and departed, thanking their hosts.

The road was better, and they made good time, only stopping at a stream to water the horses and eat a small meal. Their hosts from the day before had offered them food to take with them and had been paid for it. It wasn't much and they had eaten all of it before they resumed travelling.

Before long, Porthos, who had been riding ahead, spotted a sign post. "Tremblay!" he called to those behind.

"What?" D'Artagnan shouted back. "The cardinal?"

Porthos slowed and turned around to rejoin the group. "No, the town. The village of Tremblay lies ahead. With luck, there'll be an inn."

"With luck," echoed several of the others.

They rode together to the edge of town, where they repeated their actions from earlier days. This time Aramis joined D'Artagnan while the rest waited where they were.

"That looks like a tavern, if not an inn," Aramis pointed out to his friend. Ahead was a two-story building with a sign hanging in front.

"The Red Raven," D'Artagnan read. "Another inn named for an animal. It's no more likely than a blue whale, but if it's really an inn it doesn't matter. Shall we see if they have rooms?"

"Indeed," replied Aramis.

It was an inn and there were two rooms just right for the group of seven.

"Would you like to see them first?" asked the innkeeper, Monsieur Lambert, a short, rotund man of middle age. "And dinner, I assume. I call my wife the best cook in Tremblay."

"If there are beds enough to sleep seven between the two rooms, there is no need to see them first. I'm sure they are clean," suggested D'Artagnan.

"Of course," said the innkeeper.

"And supper sounds delightful, whatever it is, as long as it is hot."

Aramis fetched the others while D'Artagnan stabled the horses and took their belongings up to the rooms.

When all had arrived, Montaigne carried the cardinal upstairs.

"Is the monk ill?" asked Monsieur Dubois. "Should I summon our healer?"

"He is injured, not ill," D'Artagnan explained.

"And you are taking him somewhere to recover?" The innkeeper was trying to get a good view of the monk.

"We are," was all D'Artagnan would say as he entered one of the rooms behind the others and closed the door.

"Well," Porthos said. "It looks just like all the other inns we've stayed in for the last how many weeks."

The cardinal was tucked into one of the two larger beds in that room.

"Where are we now?" he asked.

"We are in a village called Tremblay. We'll stay here for the night, then, if you are feeling well enough and the way is not too rough, we may arrive at our destination in two or three days," D'Artagnan told him.

"Two or three days," he said to himself. "How long have we been traveling? I don't remember all of the journey, of course, but it seems like a long time."

"It seems like that to all of us, as well." D'Artagnan turned to the others. "Who would like to go down to collect our dinners, and who would like to eat down there?"

"Why don't we all, except for the brothers and one other, eat downstairs?" Athos suggested.

Montaigne volunteered to stay in the room while the other four ate in the public room.

"We'll bring your meals up here first," said Aramis. "I'm sure the car . . .Brother Etienne is very hungry, and Brother Xavier, too."

The meals were ordered and three plates were delivered to the room, along with two pitchers of the house wine.

The four friends remaining downstairs took a table in a corner near the fireplace, in which a low fire was laid. There were few others inside, due to the early hour. That gave them a chance to talk without being overheard.

"And you say we should arrive at – wherever we're going – soon?" said Porthos. "I am very ready to be there. When may we know our ultimate destination?"

"Later, but not down here," D'Artagnan told him. "The walls have ears, even though we are sitting in the middle of the room. Ask again when we get back upstairs."

Soon, other patrons trickled in, chatting noisily and ordering wine, ale, and meals. The four men at the table concentrated on eating and listening to the chatter, hoping for fresh information.

Unfortunately, all that the villagers talked about was their lives, their animals, and their crops.

When they finished their meals and returned to the rooms, Porthos asked again where their journey would end.

"Let us go out and check on our horses," D'Artagnan suggested. "You, Emile, and Gerard come with me."

They made their way out to the stable, going in to see that their horses were being taken care of properly. Outside the building, they walked a bit away from it as though going for a stroll.

"North of here we will find ourselves at the north coast of France. According to the cardinal of this village's name, there is an island near the shore which houses a monastery. That is where we are going."

"I may have heard of this place before," said Athos. "Will there be a boat to take us across?"

"There is a causeway which is passable at low tide. We may have to wait to cross if the tide is in."

Porthos spoke up. "Will the monks, and the abbot, welcome us and our patient? What if we must quickly leave again?"

"I was assured that we would be welcome there," D'Artagnan told them.

At that, they joined the others in their rooms for the night.

The next morning they set out, again going north as best they could. There was a road of sorts, and they trusted it to lead them the way they needed to go.

Chapter Twenty-Four

"The breakfast we bought from the innkeeper wasn't much," Porthos complained. "I hope we can find another source for our midday meal."

Athos and Aramis just looked at each other and then at Porthos.

"If you hadn't gobbled your portion so quickly you might have enough for lunch. Don't ask any of us to share," Athos instructed.

D'Artagnan interrupted. "If we come across some place to replenish our stores, we'll stop to do so. I'm sure that what the rest of us have left won't be enough for the rest of our trip."

They rode in silence for a while, and then D'Artagnan rode up beside the cart to see to the cardinal.

He had been asleep, but was starting to wake up as the guard neared.

"Allais, good morning," the cardinal said. "I'm feeling much better today, I think. Perhaps when we stop for a rest I will get out and walk around for a bit."

"I'm glad to hear that, Brother Etienne, but we don't want you to tax yourself. We may have some rough road ahead which could bounce the cart."

"Of course. I will be sure to take care. I don't want my injury made worse."

They traveled on a ways before coming to a small village where they were able to buy food for their lunch, and, possibly, have enough left over for the evening.

"Is there a town ahead which has an inn?" D'Artagnan asked one of the townspeople.

"Well, there's a town to the north, Pontorson, which is large enough to have an inn," he was told.

"Is it along this road to the north?"

"It is. There's not much beyond it, though, if you keep going north."

"No, I think we'll be turning to the east at that point, thank you. But what's farther north than, uh, Pontorson? Isn't it getting close to the coast?"

"It is. There's only an island with a monastery on it that way."

"Oh, then we definitely want to go to the east there. Thank you for your help, my friend." Then D'Artagnan went back to his friends and they went on their way.

The sun was about to set as they passed a group of houses set back from the road, much like the small community where they had stayed a couple of days before.

"I don't want to camp again," said Athos. "Let's see if we can stay the night with those people."

"A good idea, I think," added Porthos. "Even if we have to hand over our weapons for the night."

The group turned around and made their way along a dirt path toward the middle of several houses. As they got closer they could see men coming out with swords, as if to bar the way.

"We come in peace," D'Artagnan called out to them. "We are looking for a place to stay the night and will be leaving at first light." He motioned for the others to hold up their empty hands.

"Dismount and come here," one of the men called out, motioning to a place a few feet from where they were standing. "Unarmed."

D'Artagnan did as he said and told the others to do so, except for the monks.

When they all got to the place indicated, D'Artagnan said, "The two men in the cart are monks, one of them injured. They are not armed."

The man pointed for one of his friends to go to the cart to see.

"Who are you and where are you going?" the spokesman asked.

"We are mercenaries looking for work," D'Artagnan told him. "My name is Allais Reynard. These men are Girard LeRoi, Emile Gillette and Georges Moreau. The monks are Brothers Etienne and Xavier.

The man sent to check on the monks returned, saying, "They say their names are Brother Etienne and Brother Xavier. Brother Etienne is an older man lying in the back of the cart. He's well covered with blankets and such, but I pulled everything back and found no weapons. Brother Xavier, sitting at the front, had none, either."

"Where are you men headed?" the first man repeated.

"We are taking Brother Etienne somewhere to recover from his injury." They were so close to their destination that D'Artagnan didn't want to give any more information than he had to.

The men from the houses got together to discuss what they should do. When the decision was made, the first man called everyone together.

"You may stay the night, but you able-bodied men will sleep in the barn over there. The monks may stay with my family."

"We are grateful, monsieur. That is the same arrangement we had two nights ago and are satisfied with it," D'Artagnan said. "And to show you that we really mean you no harm, we will hand over our weapons until we leave in the morning. And if you can spare a bit of food, we will pay you for it. Our stores are low and we are hungry."

"Of course," the man said. "My name is Marcel Babineau and my friend, here, is Anton Rousseau." The other men had returned to their homes. "Once the monks are settled at my home and you are settled in the barn, I will bring you your meals. Do you have your own plates? We do not have enough for all of you."

"Certainly." D'Artagnan and the others fetched their packs and got out their plates, passing them on to Monsieur Babineau. "Our thanks."

They spent a peaceful night and woke to the first light of day, even though they couldn't see it inside the barn. They collected their belongings and went out to fetch the monks.

Before leaving, D'Artagnan spoke to the homeowner who had hosted the brothers.

"Monsieur Babineau, could you tell us how close we are to the coast?"

"Why, it is not many miles north of here. Where on the coast are you going?"

D'Artagnan decided that, if they were that close, is wouldn't hurt to name their destination.

"We are accompanying the monks to Le Mont-Saint-Michel monastery."

"Then just go north, following this river, until you reach the sea. I have been there, myself, to visit my brother who is a resident monk. There is a causeway that is impassable when the tide is in, though. You may have to wait to cross."

"My . . . our thanks, Monsieur. It has been a long journey, and I'm sure the monks will be glad for it to end, as will the rest of us."

He called the others together to tell them. "Our journey is almost over, my friends. We should arrive later today."

There were cheers from the others, but he cautioned, "We aren't there yet. Save your celebration until we are safely there."

"How do we know which way to go?" asked the cardinal when they were on their way.

"Monsieur Babineau said to go north until we reach Pontorson, then go west until we get to the river Couesnon. Then we will follow it all the way."

The way wasn't far, and they found themselves in the town of Pontorson before noon. After supplying themselves with food and drink, they turned west until they encountered the river they sought.

They set out along the riverbank. It wasn't very wide, and if needed, in places they could ford it. But before too long it widened and they had to move farther from the bank, following a road that went to the north. Eventually the road turned to the east and the party turned with it, but when it showed no sign of going north again, they departed from it and went to find the river again.

"The way will be rougher now," D'Artagnan told the monks, "but we are supposed to follow this course. It will lead us to our destination."

"But why are we going this way?" asked Brother Xavier. "Won't it just lead to the ocean? Are we going to be boarding a ship to another country?"

"Just wait," said D'Artagnan. "You will discover the answers to your questions before the day is out, barring trouble."

Then D'Artagnan moved back to watch behind them, joined shortly by Montaigne.

"I think I know where we're going," Montaigne said to D'Artagnan. "To Le Mont-Saint-Michel."

D'Artagnan nodded. "You know the place?"

"I do. I have been there. Are you certain it is safe?"

"I certainly hope so. I have heard of it, of course, but never been there." D'Artagnan paused. "What if they are not friendly? What if they turn us away? But Cardinal Tremblay chose this place to bring him, so it must be safe."

"No one but you should know, to be most safe. Are you sure no one else knows?"

"Well, I told Brother Etienne where we were going, but didn't name the place. I did ask the man who hosted the monks last night how far it was. He didn't seem suspicious of their identities."

"Never-the-less, we should be watchful."

∞ ∞ ∞

Monsieur Babineau, when the group rode away, was visited by his neighbors, Monsieur Rousseau. "Marcel, I think that monk, the one in the cart called Brother Etienne, may be the Red Cardinal, Richelieu."

"Why do you think that, Anton?" Monsieur Babineau asked. "Have you ever seen him?"

"I have, many years ago. When I was a boy, my family lived much closer to Paris. We once went to visit relatives who lived there. One day we were walking near the palace when he rode by us. I remember well, even though I was young. My cousin ran in front of his horse and the cardinal yelled at him and tried to run him over. Fortunately, we were able to pull my cousin away before he was hurt. We made haste to leave the area and the cardinal rode on. I have always thought of him as a cruel man."

"What a terrible thing to happen!" Monsieur Babineau exclaimed. "But he seemed like a very kind man when they were here. Are you sure it is he?"

"Yes. He did seem kind, but if he is traveling under a pseudonym to hide from the king, his manner would be much different."

Monsieur Babineau thought a moment. "The leader said they were going to Mont-St-Michel. Get our sons. They can ride after them. Tell them to keep their distance, but watch them. I will join them when I can."

"I will come with you," Anton said, and went to find the two boys.

∞ ∞ ∞

Presently, D'Artagnan and his friends found the river.

"Monsieur Babineau said to follow the river, and it will lead us where we're going," said Brother Etienne. "It's good that we have found it."

"The land is rather rough along the bank," Brother Xavier pointed out. "Will we be able to get through it?"

"We will have to go around it, but as long as we go north, I'm sure we will get to where we are going," D'Artagnan assured him.

Before long they did need to leave the riverbank. The woods that grew beside the river stood in their way, and there looked to be no easy way to pull the cart through it. Going east again, they found a rough road that led to the north, around the woods. They made good time on the road, which continued on past the woods, but to the northeast.

"Since the road is going the wrong way, we'll have to travel overland again," D'Artagnan told the others. "It looks smooth enough for the cart."

They left the road and turned back towards the river, going as close to it as they could. Ahead was another wood, but the trees were more widely spaced, and the ground seemed clear of undergrowth and rocks.

"Let's go through, rather than around it," Montaigne suggested. "I don't expect anyone to be following us, but the woods will give us some cover and may slow down pursuers."

"It will slow us down, too," said Porthos.

"But not that much. I've been watching behind us, and I've seen no one," Montaigne said.

"And the day is getting hot," said Athos. "The shade would be welcome."

They entered as close to the river as they could, as the bank sloped sharply and was rocky. The horses had no trouble picking their way between the trees, and the cart didn't bounce and sway as much as it could have. Before long the land dipped and they came to a shallow stream. It fed the river, which had gotten broader as they went north.

"We can stop to water the horses here," D'Artagnan told the rest. "If we're careful and quiet, we won't be seen from the south."

The cart was pulled close to the water, and the monks got out to stretch their legs; the rest of them dismounted, as well.

"I think walking will help me," Brother Etienne said. "Riding in the back of the cart has made my back stiff." He then went off to find a likely tree, helped by Brother Xavier and followed by the others in turn.

After the horses finished drinking and other necessary tasks had been completed, D'Artagnan got into their stores and passed around bits of bread and cheese.

"I know we're getting close and all of you are excited to come to the end of the journey. We must still be vigilant, though. Montaigne has crept to the edge of the wood to watch for others traveling this way. Since we're off the road, there should be no one. If all is well when he returns, we will be on our way."

After a few minutes, Montaigne returned.

"I saw no one, but we should leave now anyway. We'll all feel safer when we are in the monastery."

Across the stream, which they had no trouble fording, the land rose again. In the distance they could see the edge of the wood. They traveled quietly, except for the sounds of the horses' hooves and the cart's wheels. A short way from open ground, D'Artagnan called a halt.

"Would you go forward to watch for others?" he asked Montaigne. "We will watch for your signal that all is clear."

Montaigne did as requested, leaving his horse with the others. He silently made his way from tree to tree, watching for anyone coming around from the side. He was about to signal the others to come ahead, when he heard hoof beats. From behind a large tree, Montaigne saw two young men riding north. He caught a glimpse of a face and recognized the boy as the son of the man who had sheltered the monks the night before. He quickly returned to tell the others.

"I have no way of knowing if they are riding after us or what their intent is," he said.

"We should assume that their intent is not to assist us," D'Artagnan said. "I may be doing them a disservice by saying that, but it is safer to keep our distance. We should stay here for a while. Let's return to the stream where we'll not be seen."

They turned and went back, staying north of the stream and moving closer to the river. The horses were tied to trees next to a patch of grass and the cart was screened by fallen brush. D'Artagnan and Montaigne went back to the edge of the wood, each climbing a tree so they wouldn't be seen.

After half an hour they heard hoof beats again, coming from the south. As the horses passed by them, they recognized Monsieur Babineau, their host from the previous night, and one of his neighbors, Monsieur Rousseau. After they had gone on, D'Artagnan slid from his hiding place and went to the tree Montaigne was in.

"Why do you think they were riding north? Do you think they were following us?" D'Artagnan asked.

"Yes, I do," Montaigne answered. "Why else would they be going so fast? They overestimated our speed, though. I wonder why they didn't come through the woods. If they had, they would surely have seen us." He thought for a moment. "When they do not find us, they will come back, looking more closely. We should be prepared."

Montaigne said he would stay and watch for them to return. D'Artagnan went back and told the others what might happen and to be ready.

"We must find a better place for you to hide," he told Brother Etienne.

"Can you see us here if you stand farther away?" the monk asked. "The brush pile seems to screen us sufficiently."

D'Artagnan mounted his horse and moved back away from them.

"If you both sit or lay flat on the ground, I shouldn't be able to see you. I can see the horse, however." They decided to unhitch the horse and move him farther toward the river, since the ground was lower there. They tied him to another tree, and D'Artagnan went back to look again.

"If we pile a little more brush on, the front of the cart should be hidden," D'Artagnan said. The two-wheeled cart rested on its rear, with the posts the horse was attached to sticking up in the air. "Or we could turn the cart on its side." He called Porthos, Athos and, Aramis to help him turn the cart over. What bags and bundles that had been on the floor of the cart now were on the ground.

Brother Xavier sat down beside the jumble and said, "We might as well go through these bags to see what we have left."

Brother Etienne sat beside him to help, leaning his back against the bed of the cart.

D'Artagnan rode back a way and said, "Now I can't see you at all. Georges, would you stay with them while the rest of us take our places in the trees?"

They took the rest of the horses and tied them with the cart horse. Then they spread out, climbed trees, and waited for the men to return.

They didn't have to wait long. Apparently the fathers had caught up with their sons, and the four of them were retracing their steps.

As they approached the woods, Monsieur Babineau said to the boys, "Did you ride through the woods or around it?"

"Around," the boy answered. "We could see through the trees, and we didn't see anyone."

"Then where are they? We have traveled much faster than they could have, that cart slowing them, and we haven't passed them or caught up.

Besides, the tide is in and they wouldn't be able to cross on the causeway yet," Monsieur Babineau said, frustrated. "Follow me through the woods."

They had spoken loud enough for D'Artagnan and Athos to hear them. They couldn't consult with each other or they'd be overheard. But once the two fathers and their sons had passed, going into the woods, D'Artagnan dropped from his tree, followed by Athos. They slipped silently to the trees Montaigne and Aramis hid in, motioning them to come down.

"The men and boys have come into this wood, searching for us. We must get to the others before they do," D'Artagnan told them. "Follow me."

He went toward the river as quickly and quietly as he could, followed by the rest. The bank was littered with small rocks, but there were no large rocks to obstruct their passage. In minutes, they were with the horses, which made no sound, since they knew their masters.

"Georges!" D'Artagnan called in a muted voice. "Come down here."

Georges slipped down the bank, asking the monks to remain where they were.

D'Artagnan told him of the men searching the woods for them.

"I'm going to move farther along the riverbank to the south, trying to lure them away from you. Leave the cart and its horse and ride as quickly as you can on to the shore. We can retrieve them later. Two of you," he said to the rest, "take a monk up with you. Whoever takes Brother Etienne should place him in front. One of the farmers said that the tide was high, so you may have to hide again when you get there. I will rejoin you when I can."

"Let me go with you. If you are discovered you may need help fighting them off," Porthos urged D'Artagnan.

"I am hurt you think me not up to defeating two farmers and their young sons," D'Artagnan told him. "But if you insist, you may come with me." He turned to the others. "Quickly, now. Go as fast as you safely can. Do not endanger Brother Etienne, but try to get him to safety as soon as possible."

D'Artagnan and Porthos untied their horses and led them along the bank to the stream, where they mounted. Then they looked around to see where their pursuers were.

"Look over there," D'Artagnan whispered to Porthos. The two men and their sons were some way to the east and slightly ahead of them.

"Keep close to the bank and ride south. When we get far enough ahead we can make some noise to attract them."

At the same time, Aramis and Athos took the monks on their horses with them, and they all rode quickly but quietly toward the north.

D'Artagnan and Porthos neared the southern edge of the woods, leaving the men and their sons far enough behind that they could now exit the woods and ride east to distract them. When they reached the eastern edge they started to talk loudly, hoping to attract attention.

"There they are," D'Artagnan told Porthos. "We should talk to them to give the others time to get away." He rode closer and hailed them. "You are the man that our monks stayed with, Monsieur Babineau, aren't you?"

The two groups rode closer to each other.

"I am," the other man said. "You are two of their entourage, I think. Where is the rest of your group?"

"They are resting in the woods a ways back. Brother Etienne was feeling poorly, so we left them there and rode ahead to see what the land we'd be bringing them through looks like," D'Artagnan told him. "But what are you doing here? You didn't say you would be coming this way. You could have shown us the way."

Monsieur Babineau thought a moment, then said, "I did not expect to be coming this way, but circumstances changed and here we are. This is my son, and this is Monsieur Rousseau and his son. You said you left the others behind and came farther? Since we are returning to our homes, we may stop to make sure that all is well with them."

"That would be a kindness, Monsieur. I'm sure they would welcome the opportunity to thank you again for your hospitality," D'Artagnan said. "We will go a little farther to see how much longer it will take us to get to the coast. Farewell."

The two groups separated and went their different ways.

"I hope that the others have gotten far enough that we can cross before these men discover our deception," Porthos said as they hurried to catch up to their friends.

"If not, and they come after us, I'm sure we can protect ourselves and the rest," D'Artagnan replied. "I would like to get there without any bloodshed, though. They are just farmers, not the ones sent to capture us."

"But why would they be coming after us if they weren't sent?"

D'Artagnan sighed. "The cardinal is my master and I try to serve him well, but he has made enemies, and not just of the noble class. One of them could be family of one who felt mistreated by him."

"That could be," said Porthos. "Though I am a Musketeer and work for the king--the late king--there have been times I felt less than love for the cardinal."

They rejoined their companions just as the monastery came into view in the distance. The group stopped and stared in awe for a moment before hurrying on.

The sun was starting to lower to the west, its rays shining on the stone of the large building housing the monastery, making it look as if it belonged in Heaven. As it stood on the top of a small mount, it seemed very grand and tall with many windows and towers. Although they got only a glimpse, each of them was impressed with the majesty of the building.

"We sent the men back to the south to search for you," D'Artagnan told the monks. "But we should keep a lookout in case they see our ruse and come back this way."

"I'll ride behind," Montaigne said, stopping until the rest had ridden ahead a short way. "If I see them, I'll use the signal."

D'Artagnan said, "If he signals us that they are coming, go as fast as you can. The rest of us will delay them however we must."

As they neared the causeway that led to the island, they heard the 'twit-tu-whit' of the signal from Montaigne.

D'Artagnan and Porthos rode back to join Montaigne. They were sitting side-by-side when the men from the settlement approached.

"Where have they gone?" demanded Monsieur Rousseau.

"Of whom do you speak?" asked D'Artagnan calmly.

"The monks, of course! I know that the tall one is Cardinal Richelieu and that King Gaston is looking for him."

D'Artagnan looked down. "Cardinal Richelieu is dead," he said sadly. "The cowardly men of 'King' Gaston murdered him months ago. We are just escorting the two monks here to the monastery."

"Then why did you lie to us about their whereabouts? We would not harm innocent monks."

D'Artagnan smiled. "Because of his close resemblance to the cardinal, I suspected that someone might mistake Brother Etienne for him, although we are so far from Paris I thought it unlikely that anyone from here would have had the chance to see him. But, in case someone from your settlement had ever seen the cardinal, I didn't trust any of you to listen to reason and believe the truth. Now, if you would turn and go back to your homes, you may do so safely. If you still refuse to believe the truth, be advised that the three of us are all very skilled with the sword, and, though we wish not to harm you, we will not let you harm our friends."

The two fathers spoke quietly to their sons. Then Monsieur Babineau said, "We would like proof of what you say. We still believe that monk is Cardinal Richelieu, and wish to speak to him."

"You had that chance last night," Montaigne told him.

"But it was not until this morning that my neighbor, Monsieur Rousseau, came to me with his suspicions."

"Yes," Monsieur Rousseau broke in. "Some years ago I went to Paris with my family and saw him. Because of his treatment of my cousin, I have harbored resentment of him all this time. If this man is not the cardinal, I wish to hear it from him, himself, not be told by mercenaries."

D'Artagnan, Montaigne and Porthos spoke together quietly for a moment.

"All we have to give you is our assurance that the real Cardinal Richelieu is dead and this is, at most, an imposter," D'Artagnan said to them. "There will be no attempt to usurp the crown from this man. He does not want to overthrow the government. He just wants to live out his life with these monks at this monastery. Now please go back home."

The three swordsmen turned their horses and rode back to the north, toward the island with the monastery where their friends had gone.

After the swordsmen had turned and left, the remaining men, younger and older, debated their next action.

"I still believe that was Richelieu. I don't care what that man said," Monsieur Rousseau said. "We must go after him!"

"How can you be sure? You got but a brief glimpse of him yesterday when they arrived." Monsieur Babineau didn't want to put himself and his son in danger, or waste the rest of the day just on the word of his friend.

"I'm sure. If you don't go with us, we'll go alone. We must not let him get to safety." Monsieur Rousseau was vehement about the situation.

Because their community was small and every member was important to the whole, Babineau was loath to risk the Rousseaus' lives for nothing.

"We'll go with you, if you insist on going on a fool's errand. The man stayed in our home. He didn't act or speak like a cardinal of the church. Especially as you said he acted when you saw him before."

Rousseau said again, "I'm sure."

Chapter Twenty-Five

D'Artagnan and the others caught up with the group on the shore, waiting for the tide to ebb.

"As you can see," Brother Xavier told him, "it would be impossible to cross now."

"Indeed," replied D'Artagnan. "We must wait until it is almost gone and then we can cross. I don't want to wait any longer, because, even though I assured those men that he is not Cardinal Richelieu, I'm not sure that they believed me." He turned his horse around to face the way he had come. "If they didn't, we may have to fight them unless we can get across before they catch up to us."

"We may not have to wait long," Montaigne pointed out. "It seems to be ebbing now. As it lowers and reveals more of the causeway, we should follow the edge so that we may cross as quickly as we can."

"Gerard and Emile, you go first, since you have the monks with you. The rest of us will guard the rear."

Just as the two Musketeers and the two monks started toward the edge of the water, Montaigne saw the farmers and their sons hurrying toward them.

"Go!" called Porthos as he turned and galloped after them. Just as he caught up with them, the last of the tide dropped and the causeway was clear.

"Come!" he then called to D'Artagnan and Montaigne. "The way is clear now!"

The remaining two turned, rushing to catch up.

Not far behind, the farmers saw what was happening, and urged their horses on, so that eleven men were rushing across the causeway toward the island which housed the monastery of Saint Michael.

"We must not let them escape us," Monsieur Bellard called to his companions.

They urged their horses faster. As they entered the causeway, the group ahead was at midpoint.

Athos and Aramis reached the island first, a few steps ahead of the rest of their group. They hurried on, since they had to climb the winding road which led to the monastery atop the hill.

The farmers were closing the distance between the two groups as they all dashed up the hill. At the top, at the building's courtyard, they finally caught up.

The commotion of so many horses climbing the hill and clattering onto the paved entryway, as well as the loud voices calling out, got the attention of several of the resident monks.

When the monks saw what was happening at their front door, one of them ran to get the abbot. Fearing an invasion, the abbot brought armed guards with him to the door.

"What is happening here?" Abbe' Marcus asked the riders, who were milling about, shouting at each other.

At the sight of the leader of the monastery, Brother Xavier slid from his place behind Athos and approached the abbot. The cardinal was barely conscious and was unable to walk, even with Brother Xavier's help. Porthos carried him to where the abbot was standing.

Brother Xavier knelt before the abbot, but Brother Etienne remained in Porthos' arms, but with his hand on his friend's shoulder.

The abbot looked from the monks before him to the group of men, still on horseback, milling farther away.

"Sirs! Is there something with which we can help you?"

The rest of the entourage dismounted and knelt not far from the abbot, with Porthos, the cardinal, and Brother Xavier.

Monsieur Babineau spoke up first. "Your Grace, these men are harboring a fugitive who must be returned to King Gaston."

"A fugitive? Who are you, and why have you come here?"

Emboldened, the two farmers and their sons approached the abbot. Monsieur Rousseau pointed an accusing finger at Brother Etienne. "This man is Cardinal Richelieu, and he is hiding from justice."

The abbot looked at the monks and then at the accusers. Then he looked at the rest of the men.

"Come inside, all of you. We will get to the truth, but not out here."

The abbot led the way into the building, leading them to a room with several chairs. He seated himself in a high-backed chair and motioned the others closer.

"Your Grace, might Brother Etienne sit? He was injured and is not fully recovered yet," Brother Xavier asked. At the abbot's nod, Porthos placed the cardinal in a chair, keeping a hand on his shoulder.

"Brother Etienne? These men," he pointed toward the farmers, "say that he is Cardinal Richelieu. Is that true?"

D'Artagnan stepped forward and said, "Your Grace, we have been accompanying this monk to this place to recover from injuries he suffered, but he is not the cardinal that these people are searching for. He does bear a resemblance to Cardinal Richelieu, though, so I can understand why they have mistaken him for the cardinal."

"Ah, I see." The abbot looked at the farmers for a moment. "And you say you are certain he is the real Cardinal Richelieu?"

"We are," exclaimed Monsieur Rousseau.

At that moment a man, who had been hiding inside a doorway hidden by the farmers and the rest of the men, sprang into their midst and stole a sword from the man nearest to him, which happened to be D'Artagnan.

"Traitor!" he yelled as he ran toward the cardinal. "You banished my family and then had them followed and killed. You are an evil man!"

D'Artagnan and the others quickly shielded the cardinal from the man, D'Artagnan borrowed Porthos' sword and beat the man back. Then all but Porthos joined in the fight, they disarmed the man and held him tightly.

"But aren't you the man who came here yesterday seeking safety from thieves," Monsieur Berger?" asked the abbot.

"Yes, but now I see that that traitor is seeking sanctuary, himself, I must capture him for King Gaston."

"I cannot allow any bloodshed in this holy place, and I won't allow you to take this man captive. If you leave peacefully, I will let you go, but you must never return to this island."

The man thought for a moment. If he left now, he could lie in wait for a better time to complete his mission.

"I will go, but I will not deny my accusations of him."

The abbot looked at Brother Etienne, who had regained a bit of strength after the jostling ride across the causeway, for a moment and a look of recognition crossed his face.

A look of recognition also crossed the cardinal's face, as well. "Henri?"

Abbe' Marcus replied with, "Armand?"

"So you are the abbot here," said the cardinal in a breathy voice.

"I never even suspected you might be the famous Cardinal Richelieu. You are from the same region as I."

The cardinal thought for a moment. Memories kept flitting through his mind, memories of his childhood and youth.

"How would I know you if I were really Cardinal Richelieu? You see, after an accident on the way here, I hit my head and lost my memory. I have remembered nothing from my past since that time. Until now." He held his head in his hands.

"Then you're not the cardinal?" asked the abbot.

"No. I am merely Brother Etienne from a chapterhouse near Paris." He turned to D'Artagnan and said, "Monsieur Dubois, please tell the story to these people. I am very tired and I think you are the only one besides me who knows it."

The abbot looked at D'Artagnan and his friends inquiringly. "Well?" he said.

Then D'Artagnan started at the beginning. "As I'm certain you have heard, Cardinal Richelieu and the late King Louis were attacked on their way to visit Queen Anne. The King was killed," D'Artagnan and his friends crossed themselves, "and the cardinal was gravely injured. I was sent to see him, and to remove him from the monastery where he had been taken and take him to someplace safer, here. But before I could accomplish that…well." D'Artagnan hung his head. "But if that happened, I was to find a substitute to play his part, but in secret.

"Forgive me, my friends," D'Artagnan said to the others. "I was admonished by Cardinal Tremblay to keep the secret. As he said, secrets cannot be kept by so many. We two were all that he truly trusted."

Everyone was silent for a moment, thinking about what had been said.

Monsieur Rousseau broke the silence. "You mean he isn't really Cardinal Richelieu? He looks just like the man I remember from when I was a boy."

The abbot said to him, "Memories from so long ago cannot be trusted, my son. You and your friends go in peace."

The man who had tried to attack Brother Etienne, thinking he was the cardinal, left with them.

"Now, let us go to my office where we can talk in private. Explaining your presence will not be hard, nor will that of those other men. It was clearly a matter of mistaken identity."

After they were seated in the abbot's office, he said, "I would like to catch up with you, Brother Etienne. It has been so many years since we have seen each other."

"Pardon me, Abbe', but I must continue my story. It is very important," D'Artagnan said.

"Very well."

"This is not entirely my fault. In fact, I was commanded to keep a secret from everyone, but I can reveal it, now that we have arrived at our destination."

The others in the room seemed to all speak at once, until D'Artagnan silenced them.

"I was commanded by Cardinal Tremblay to take Cardinal Richelieu to a safe place for him to recover from his injury. My deception is somewhat complicated, since he also told me that if the cardinal died before the journey began, to take a, you might say, decoy, in his place."

They all started speaking again, and D'Artagnan silenced them, again.

"You, my friends, believed that this man was really Cardinal Richelieu. And you, Abbe', have been led to believe that this man is really your childhood friend, Armand. You are both correct." After silencing them for the third time, he continued the explanation. "This is the real Cardinal Richelieu." He turned to the Abbot. "I didn't want anyone to know that we had brought the real cardinal here; otherwise, they wouldn't have left believing that that he is only a monk who looks like the cardinal." He turned to the Abbot. "This deception was necessary; I think you'll agree when you have thought about it. We all took false names, except for Brother Xavier, of course. It wasn't necessary for him to do so."

"But you said how would you know me if you were the real cardinal," the abbot said. "How then do you know my name?"

"But we did know each other as children, and you haven't changed so much that I wouldn't recognize you again, even after all these years," the cardinal replied. "My given name is Armand Jean du Plessis."

The abbot gasped. "Of course, my friend!"

The room was silent, for a change, while the old friends embraced each other. Then the Abbot spoke. "I understand your reasoning for keeping secret the identity of the cardinal, and have to agree with it. Now that the truth is known by all of us, I think we can forgive any secrecy. Now, about catching up with you, Your Eminence. It seems as though there is much catching up to do."

"And we have much to talk about. And plenty of time to do so," the cardinal said. "I think it will be a while before I am completely recovered."

"I will be delighted to discuss anything you wish to talk about," said the abbot. "But what of France? We are remote here and don't receive much in the way of news."

"There is much change and distrust in France now. We have been away from Paris for many weeks and many things have happened to us on our way. That can be a story for Brother Etienne, I mean, His Eminence, to tell when his memory is fully restored," D'Artagnan said to the abbot.

"I can help, since I have been with him the entire way," said Brother Xavier. "And I didn't lose my memory."

The abbot looked down at his desk and started rummaging through several papers.

"I received a letter from Cardinal Tremblay a while ago. I had forgotten about it because I didn't yet understand what it meant." He found what he was looking for and exclaimed, "Here it is! The letter says that several men would be arriving at some point and some of them are instructed to follow the request in a separate letter that was included with this one. The names Allais, Gerard, Georges and Emile are mentioned."

D'Artagnan started to chuckle. "Those are the false names my friends and I have been using on our travels. I have been Allais Reynard, but my true name is Charles D'Artagnan. Gerard, Georges and Emile, here are really Athos, Porthos and Aramis of the former king's musketeers. I, myself, was in the Cardinal's Guard and am one of the few still alive. Cardinal Tremblay trusted me to escort the cardinal and Brother Xavier to safety. I requested that my friends accompany us."

"But there is another who you haven't introduced," said the abbot.

"Oh, we know him only as Montaigne. Who knows what his real name is. He worked for the cardinal in matters that were–sensitive."

"That's right," Montaigne said. "The running joke is that no one remembers me for long."

Everyone but the abbot laughed. D'Artagnan explained. "We trust that that will always be true. The kingdom is safer that way."

"But here, take your letter. I suspect that Cardinal Tremblay has given you another assignment now that you've delivered the monks safely." He handed over the letter, which still was sealed.

D'Artagnan opened it while the others looked over his shoulder.

"That's just what it says." He looked at Montaigne. "You're not included, of course, since we met only by chance."

"Of course," Montaigne replied with a look on his face that might have said, "If you believe in coincidences."

"Abbe'," Cardinal Richelieu said. "I have a request of you, if you don't mind."

"Of course, Your Eminence. What is it?"

"Even when I have recovered, I would like to remain here in this monastery for a while."

The Hunt for The Red Cardinal

Brother Xavier spoke up, making the same request. "The cardinal and I have become close, and I would like to stay, as well."

The abbot took only a moment to grant the requests of both.

"Now," the abbot said to the company, "if the requirement made of you in your letter isn't urgent, would you stay with us for a few days? I'm sure the last months you're been traveling has worn on you. You have had to be vigilant the entire time. Please spend some time in our company and rest."

D'Artagnan, the three musketeers and Montaigne eagerly accepted the invitation, agreeing to stay three days before going on their way.

On the third day, they met with the abbot, the cardinal and Brother Xavier to say their farewells.

"It has been an honor for us to be with you on this mission," D'Artagnan said to their fellow travelers. "And to stay here for these few days. Thank you, Abbe', for your hospitality." He turned to the cardinal and the monk again. "I'm glad you will be staying here; it is such a beautiful place, and so serene. If I were a monk, this would be my choice."

The others echoed D'Artagnan's sentiment and, since the tide had ebbed, went on their way.

"Well, we have successfully completed our mission," Athos said. "Cardinal Tremblay's letter said to go south and meet someone. I couldn't read the rest."

"We are going south to meet a Monsieur Bergeron in Nantes. We are to spread more rumors of the cardinal's whereabouts."

"Well, my friends, I am headed back to the east, so I will take my leave. I'm glad we had this time together and that I could help you complete your journey." He waved as his route diverged from theirs.

"Do you think we met by accident or by design," Aramis asked the others.

"It could be either one," replied D'Artagnan. "Montaigne never divulges the reasons for his actions."

The others conceded the truth of the statement, and continued on their new journey to the south.

The End

Dramatis Personae
In order of appearance

On The Matter Of D'Artagnan

Cardinal Richelieu - A cardinal of the church – Prime Minister to King Louis XIII

Monsignor Henri Ryan - One of Cardinal Richelieu's secretaries

Charles D'Artagnan - Lieutenant of the Cardinal's Guard – also known as Charles de Gatz-Casthenese

Charlotte Blackson - Paramour of Charles D'Artagnan – Successful business woman in Paris

André Marro - Former seneschal to the family LeVlanc who knew a name

Manuel Zarubin - Earlier was co-conspiritor in the attempted murder of King Henry IV, King Louis XIII's father – suspected of killing D'Artagnan's father

To End The Evening

Barnabas Marcoli - Young man of Venice

Charles D'Artagnan - Agent of Cardinal Richelieu on a mission in Venice

Aramis - Agent (spy) of Cardinal Richelieu on a mission in Venice – also known as Montaigne

Madam Paulette - A Madam

Two men of the Quinniaro group - Who were defeated

Ramsey Culhane - Kidnapped and freed

All For One

Charles D'Artagnan - An agent of Cardinal Richelieu - also known as Charles de Gatz-Casthenese

Athos - A Musketeer – cousin to Porthos and Aramis – also known as Armund de Sillegue d'Athos d'Autevielle – also known as Athos de la Fère – also known as Gerard Le Roi

Porthos - A Musketeer – cousin to Athos and Aramis – also known as Issac de Porteau – also known as Porthos du Vallon – also known as Georges Moreau

Aramis - A Musketeer – cousin to Athos and Porthos – also known as Henri d' Aramitz – also known as René d'Herblay – also known as Emile Gillette

Montaigne - An agent (spy) of Cardinal Richelieu

Maximilian André Castellans Moreau - Father of a young woman, who thought Aramis had dishonored her

Celine Moreau - Daughter of Maximilian Moreau, who had not been dishonored

Brother Cornelius - A monk who is not what he seems

The Hunt For The Red Cardinal

Luc Boyea - Employee of the house of Louie, Count de Soissons – wants to better himself

André Boyea - Luc's brother – radio operator of the Count

Louis, Count de Soissons - Count of the region including the town of Soissons

Claude de Bourdeille, Comte de Montrésor - Friend of Louis, Count de Soissons

Charlotte Blackson - Divorced business woman of Paris – paramour of Charles D'Artagnan

Charles D'Artagnan - Lieutenant of Cardinal Richelieu's guard – also known as Charles de Gatz-Casthenese

Sophie - Charlotte Blackson's maid

François Leclerc, Cardinal Tremblay - Friend of Cardinal Richelieu – also known as Pere' Joseph

Audrey - One of Cardinal Tremblay's household maids

Allais DuBois - Nom de plume of D'Artagnan

Brother Julius - Monk at the monastery at Clairfontaine

Abbe' Michel - Abbot of the monastery at Clairfontaine

The Hunt for The Red Cardinal

Athos - Musketeer – friend of D'Artagnan – also known as Gerard Le Roi
Brother Jacques - Monk at the monastery at Clairfontaine
Brother Maurice - Monk at the monastery at Clairfontaine
Brother Xavier - A young monk new to the monastery at Clairfontaine
Brother Etienne - Nom de plume of Cardinal Richelieu
François - One of several men who robbed and shot Luc Boyea
Jean DuPont - Cousin of the wife of the innkeeper at Ramboullet
Father Andreas - Priest of the church at Epernon
Roxanne - Father Andreas' housemaid
Marie Antin - Father Andreas' cook, a supporter of King Gaston
Pierre - Town of Epernon messenger
Porthos - Musketeer – friend of D'Artagnan – also known as Georges Moreau
Aramis - Musketeer – Friend of D'Artagnan – also known as Emile Gillette
Gaston - King Louis XIII younger brother and soon-to-be king of France
Terrye Jo Tillman - Uptime radio operator for Gaston
Duke Victor Amadeus - Gaston's brother-in-law
Two men - Friends of Jean DuPont, cousin of the innkeeper's wife at Ramboullet
Pastor Alexandre - Pastor of a church where the travelers stayed
François - Innkeeper of the village and village magistrate
André - Butcher of the village
Jacques - Member of the village keeping lookout
Frederick - Leader of the group that arrived at the village
Abelard, Bruno, Felix, Eustice, and Henri - Members of Frederick's group
Montaigne - Agent of Cardinal Richelieu - friend of D'Artagnan and the others, who is willing to help
Simon Cordonnier - Cobbler of the town of Soissons, who found something
Marie Cordonnier - Simon's wife, who wanted to give it away
Middle-aged man - Who found it, and lost it
Third man - Who found it and lost it, and more
Monsieur Baudin - Who found it and lost it, and found it, and lost it
Monsieur Borde - Baudin's landlord
Pierre Faucher - Who found it and lost it

Annette Faucher - Who took it to the right person
Thomas - Who Pierre thought he took it to
Father Matthias - Who was the right person to take it to
Pascal - Cardinal Tremblay's secretary
Brother Paolo - Monk at the monastery at Clairefontaine
Abbe' Michel - Abbot of the monastery at Clairefontaine
Two old men in Toulouse - Who liked to talk loudly
Henri Lamar - Former cardinal's guard – no friend of D'Artagnan
Jules - A friend of Henri Lamar
Jacques Boucher - Innkeeper of The Black Dragon in Rennes
Physician - Who was called to examine Brother Etienne
François LeBeq - A shady merchant who owes Montaigne a favor
Monsieur Allard - Merchant of second-hand furniture
André Boyce - Leader of the men searching for enemies of the crown
Anatole Boucher - Jacques Boucher's cousin, with whom he doesn't associate
Father Jean - Priest of church that François LeBeq attends, who needs help
Madame LeBeau - Father Jean's cook
Six young men with swords - Who want to rob the church and get their comeuppance
Pierre LeFou - Who was hiding and became useful
Monsieur Severin - Who hosted the monks
Monsieur Bernard - Homeowner who allowed the others to sleep in his barn
Monsieur Lambert - Innkeeper in the town of Tremblay
Marcel Babineau - Villager who hosted the monks in his home and let the others sleep in his barn
Anton Rousseau - Babineau's neighbor, who suspected
Abbe' Marcus - Abbott of the monastery of Le Mont Saint Michel
Monsieur Berger - Threatened Brother Etienne inside the monastery

Printed in Great Britain
by Amazon